Lost and Found in Russia

By

Olga Godim

To Anita
from Olga

Eternal Press
A division of Damnation Books, LLC.
P.O. Box 3931
Santa Rosa, CA 95402-9998
www.eternalpress.biz

Lost and Found in Russia
by Olga Godim

Digital ISBN: 978-1-61572-877-0
Print ISBN: 978-1-61572-878-7

Cover art by: Dawné Dominique
Edited by: Andrea Heacock-Reyes

Copyright 2013 Olga Godim

Printed in the United States of America
Worldwide Electronic & Digital Rights
1st North American, Australian and UK Print Rights

All rights reserved. No part of this book may be reproduced, scanned or distributed in any form, including digital and electronic or mechanical, including photocopying, recording, or by any information storage and retrieval system, without the prior written consent of the Publisher, except for brief quotes for use in reviews.

This book is a work of fiction. Characters, names, places and incidents either are the product of the author's imagination or are used fictitiously, and any resemblance to any actual persons, living or dead, events, or locales is entirely coincidental.

To my muse, Irina.
Without you, this novel wouldn't have existed.

I'd like to thank the women, the mothers and daughters, who inspired me:
My mother, Valentina, for being there for me, always
My daughter, Liza, for crazy ideas about Ksenya
My sister, Sveta, for her songs and for Sonya's words
My aunt, Raya, for her love
My cousin, Julia, for her friendship
My friend, Olga, for her kindness and support

My mentor, Nalo Hopkinson,
for making this novel better.

Doctor Olivia Sampson,
for taking care of me when I needed it.

Also, my profound gratitude to my editor, Andrea Heacock-Reyes, and the team of Eternal Press.

Chapter One
Amanda

Amanda hugged herself tightly, but the goosebumps refused to go away. All day yesterday, her daughter Gloria had been unwell with a cold. This morning, she complained about a headache while coughing and sneezing, distracting Amanda from her students' essays. The stubborn girl shouldn't have gone to work in such a condition, especially under the incessant rain. She should've stayed at home, in bed, and let her assistant deal with their stupid emergency. If Gloria hadn't driven under that ghostly rain, she wouldn't be unconscious right now, hooked to the IV behind Amanda's back.

Amanda stared at the gray, teary lines streaking across the window. The November sky infused everything with its moody lethargy. The white walls of the hospital building opposite the window seemed just a gray background for the gray, weeping trees. The surgeon said that auto accidents happened often in such weather. Gloria played right into the statistics: one more line in the Vancouver statisticians' tables.

Amanda turned. No changes in the bed. Gloria's lovely green eyes were still closed, her face as ashen as the hospital pillow. Even her millions of freckles seemed bleached—a pale brown backdrop for the faded, blue bruises on Gloria's forehead and a large, pink abrasion on her left cheekbone. Only her coppery hair shined like a splash of unwanted color, all sweaty and messy. The disheveled, flaming mass looked alien to the faded, young woman in the hospital bed.

Biting her lip, Amanda hurriedly straightened a corner of the blanket. Then, she rummaged in her purse for a brush. She was useless in the hospital. She couldn't help Gloria. At least she could fix her hair. She moved her chair to the head of the bed and started brushing, carefully untangling Gloria's fuzzy curls and caressing the skin beneath. *Wake up, my daughter*, she pleaded silently. *Please, come back to me. Why don't you wake up?*

The tiny mirror in the brush's handle alternated its reflections. Now, it flashed a coppery lock of Gloria's hair. A minute later, it caught a section of Amanda's neat, dark blonde bob. Once, it even showed one of Amanda's eyes—blue-gray, with short, blonde eyelashes and no mascara. A British eye. Amanda turned the brush to recapture Gloria's gleaming tresses. The amazing color glowed like molten bronze, mesmerizing her. Little curlicues sprang defiantly under Amanda's fingers, escaping the brush.

"Mrs. Barnett?"

Startled, Amanda almost jumped. Her hands stilled in Gloria's hair, and she lifted her eyes. A large, middle-aged nurse hovered at the door to Gloria's small, private room.

"The doctor wants to see you, ma'am."

"Yes, of course." Slowly, so she wouldn't add to her daughter's pain, Amanda withdrew her hands and the brush, dropped the brush in her purse, and hurried after the nurse. Her heart tumbled in her chest with such enthusiasm, she had trouble breathing. Her back ached. She should've gone to her chiropractor, today. Instead, she had to be at the hospital, useless and worthless. She stared at the gray walls, because she couldn't stomach seeing Gloria unconscious. She hadn't even had time to cancel her chiropractor appointment.

Did she remember to turn off the oven? She had a turkey casserole in there. Should she call her neighbor, Mrs. Darney, to check on the turkey? Rubbing her lower back, Amanda entered the office.

"Mrs. Barnett." The young doctor, tall and blonde, came from behind his desk to shake her hand. "I'm Doctor Johansen. I have good news. The X-rays are all clean. Your daughter did have a concussion but a mild one. Only one leg is broken. All the other bones are intact, and the spine is fine. She should be all right as soon as we get her a blood transfusion. She sustained a huge blood loss during the accident, but we're out of her blood type. We've just ordered a supply from the donor bank. As soon as it arrives, we'll load the IV with it."

"She needs blood? Can you take mine?" At last, she would be able to do something for Gloria. Unable to sit still, Amanda jumped up from her chair in front of the doctor's desk.

"I suppose." Doctor Johansen also stood up. "What is your blood type?"

"I don't know. The same as my late husband's. Our daughter should have the same too, right?" She began rolling up the left sleeve of her sweatshirt. "I had a transfusion of his blood once, when I gave birth to Gloria." She lifted her eyes to the doctor's face. "It was in Russia."

"In Russia?" He grinned. "You'll have to tell me about it. Let me just take a sample. It'll only take a few minutes."

"Why? I told you it's the same type."

"Ma'am." He collected a needle from a sealed, plastic pouch and an empty blood test tube from a drawer. "It's a routine requirement to have a sample drawn before any live transfusion. Have you ever had cancer, HIV, or hepatitis?"

"No!" Amanda snapped.

He pricked her finger, collected some blood, and sent it with a nurse to the lab. Then, he settled back at his table. "Tell me about Russia." He steepled his fingers above the desk and leaned on his elbows, his blue eyes sparkling with curiosity.

Amanda relaxed marginally. If the doctor didn't seem nervous or concerned, perhaps she shouldn't panic, either. "Oh, well..." she said, as the memories flooded her mind. She started talking.

She had been a linguist, a newly-minted scholar of Slavic languages and literature, fresh from the university. When a contract had come her way to speed-teach Russian to a group of Toronto journalists who would be working in Russia, she had been overjoyed. Her whirlwind romance with one of her students, the young Irish photographer Donald, had ended in a marriage celebration a week before they left Canada. Together. Amanda was already pregnant.

For months after they arrived in Russia, Donald worked twelve hours a day while Amanda busied herself with her doctorate thesis. Exhilarated by the rare opportunity to dig up the original, Russian sources, she spent countless hours at the Moscow's majestic, colonnaded Leninskaya Library, sometimes forgetting to eat. Of course, she finished earlier than expected. She hadn't been expected to go into labor for another month.

Without Donald to keep her company, she waddled about her hotel room belly first, feeling bloated and lonely. The buds on the Moscow poplars were ready to burst, the snow had almost melted, and the sun sprinkled a strange, viscous desire in the air. A leisurely bus trip to some ancient, Russian towns seemed like the thing to do. It was an opportunity to travel back in time, into the typically Russian mix of grandeur and squalor.

On the day of Gloria's birth, the last day of April, Amanda embarked on a bus trip to Vladimir and Suzdal. According to a photo album she had seen, both towns were architectural pearls of Tsarist Russia. Both boasted multiple old churches, decorated by golden onions of their roofs.

Pity she hadn't seen them. Amanda began feeling unwell on the way to Vladimir. By the time their tour bus arrived at its first destination, her labor was well underway. At first, she didn't say anything, not wanting to spoil the fun for her fellow tourists. The cramps weren't too bad, and she had hoped they would go away. She had some phantom pains before, and she so looked forward to the trip; however, a few minutes before the bus parked near the Golden Gates, Amanda's water had broken. No hope of the pains going away had remained. Instead of the appointed parking lot, the bus's first stop was a maternity ward for Amanda.

"Afterward, they shipped me and the baby back to Moscow. They couldn't wait to get rid of me. You see, I had some complications, and they were terrified to take responsibility," she said, finishing her recital. "Vladimir was a very small town back then. Donald met me at the hospital in Moscow. That was when he gave me his blood." The reminiscence and the rain drumming on the windows lulled her into almost tranquility.

"Fascinating," the doctor murmured. When his phone rang, he picked it up, listened for a moment, and replaced the receiver. The expression in his eyes changed. "That was your test result."

"Why don't you move, then?" She sprang up from her chair. "My daughter needs my blood." She frowned at the doctor, who sat immobile behind his desk.

His sandy eyebrows rose slightly. "Your blood type is 'O' positive, Mrs. Barnett. Very common. Your daughter's blood type is 'O' negative. It's a rare type, and we can only use the same type for her transfusion."

"It's impossible," Amanda said, suddenly alert, as if finally waking up from the gray lassitude of the rain. "Her blood should be the same as her father's. I read it somewhere. My late husband's blood was the same as mine. I told you. My daughter can't have different blood. There is a mix up with your tests. Check, again!"

He narrowed his eyes, nodded once, and stalked out, heading toward Gloria's room. Amanda ran after him, breathing heavily. She was so full of sudden anger, she could barely contain it. The fools would deny her daughter the needed blood because of a botched test! Gloria might die from their error.

"Sloppy work you do here!" Her voice broke into a screech on the last word.

"We'll repeat the test right away," he said. "Please. Calm down, Mrs. Barnett. I'll supervise the test myself." As soon as Gloria's blood filled a test tube, he strode away, leaving Amanda alone with unconscious Gloria.

Calm down, he had said? Was he insane to give such an advice to a mother? Or had he been mocking her? No, she was getting paranoid. She must calm down. Otherwise, she wouldn't be of any use to Gloria. Shaking, Amanda dropped into her abandoned chair. As she smoothed the corner of the pillow with her fingers, she noticed her hands trembling. She pulled the brush with its pretty, mirrored handle from her purse and resumed her coiffure duty. "'O' positive," she whispered. "It's the most common blood type, honey. They'll bring it right away." Spreading the red mane along the pillow, she picked out a twig snagged in Gloria's curls and looked around for a wastebasket. "You'll get better in no time."

The wastebasket stood in a corner. Amanda tossed the twig toward it, missed, and sighed. Couldn't they have put the basket nearer to the bed? Her anger flared anew. Of course they couldn't, if they blundered tests so badly. Granted, there was a crowd in the emergency room, but to mistake a blood type? Inexcusable! Happily, she was here to correct the mishap before anything fatal happened. Someone else had 'O' negative, and that person could go into a coma or worse, if administered a wrong blood type. She read about it somewhere, but she wasn't sure of the details. Her anger popped out as fast as it bloomed, leaving dread and grayness in its wake.

She bent to kiss Gloria's untouched right cheek and almost recoiled. Her daughter's skin was cold. She opened her mouth to scream, noted Gloria's chest rising and falling steadily, and closed her lips with a silent sob. Where was that doctor with the 'O' positive blood?

"Mrs. Barnett."

Amanda looked up. Doctor Johansen didn't have a blood bag in his hands. She frowned.

"Ma'am." He came into the room. "There was no mistake. Your daughter's blood is 'O' negative. They've just called from the bank. It'll be here in thirty minutes."

"Impossible!" Amanda squeaked.

"When did you last check your daughter's blood?"

"I don't remember. She's always been healthy. A cold once in a while, but that's all. How can it be?"

He smiled gently. "You should know."

Amanda's hackles rose. She straightened. "I didn't have another man, if that's what you are implying. I know who my daughter's father was. Both Donald and I had the same blood type. How can my daughter have another?" She clamped down on her rising hysteria.

"Ma'am, I'm not implying anything. She wasn't adopted, was she?"

"No."

"Maybe she was switched at birth, like in a soap opera." His mouth twitched.

Amanda stared at him, her thinking process ensnared by his words. They repeated themselves in her brain like a scratched record: 'switched at birth', 'switched at birth'. The doctor continued talking. Although his words made their way into Amanda's ears, the meaning escaped her. Switched at birth?

"Or the change could've occurred as a result of a trauma, physical or mental. Such things, though rare, are known to happen. I might even write a paper about it." He grinned briefly. "The important thing is we'll soon have the blood. She'll be okay. When she's fine, we can investigate at leisure. Excuse me, ma'am. I have to go. Other patients need my attention. A nurse will come with the blood as soon as it arrives." He left.

Amanda couldn't breathe. She gulped air into her lungs, forced her chest to work, and rubbed her aching back. Switched at birth? Thirty-four years ago in an ancient, Russian town and in an old hospital, it was just barely possible. Two red-headed girls were born on the same day in that decrepit hospital with peeling paint on the walls and one washroom for the entire corridor. Was there any other explanation for a different blood? Amanda shivered.

If Gloria wasn't her biological daughter, who was? Some other red-headed woman still living in Russia, starved and oppressed? Amanda slumped in her chair, petting Gloria's limp hair, playing with the stubborn, coppery spirals. Gloria had always been just like her hair: stubborn, unmanageable, bright like the sun, and sharing her light with everyone. Her beautiful, strong-willed daughter was generous to a fault, picking up the underdogs who needed help and giving from her heart. Without Gloria's support, Amanda wasn't sure she could've dealt with the emptiness left after Donald's death. How was it possible that Gloria wasn't her daughter?

"Mrs. Barnett? Can I turn on the light?"

Amanda focused on the door—a rectangle of light blocked by the massive body of the nurse. Was it already so late?

"I've brought blood for your daughter."

"Yes, of course." Amanda squinted against the glare of the ceiling's fluorescent light. She watched the nurse fuss with the IV, hang the dark bag of blood on a hook, and connect the plastic tubes. Her daughter would finally get the blood.

"'O' negative, right?" she asked to reassure herself.

"Yes, ma'am," the nurse responded. "A night nurse will arrive soon. You should go home and get some sleep."

"I can't leave, now. What if Gloria wakes up?"

"She won't. We've been pumping medications into her. She'll sleep till morning." The big nurse finished with the IV and turned her wide, kind face toward Amanda. The nurse's eyes crinkled at the corners. The name tag on the left breast, huge and sticking out like a mid-sized melon, read "Chelsea".

"Thank you, Chelsea," Amanda said. "I'll wait until the night nurse gets here."

"As you wish, ma'am." Chelsea shrugged, her beefy shoulders hardly moving beneath the green uniform. "Good night." She left.

Amanda turned back to Gloria, entranced by the dark, red drops that traveled along the transparent tubes from the bag to the needle in the pale, freckled hand. The IV maintained a steady rhythm. Like a drum major with his baton, the device led the blood drops of the rare 'O' negative to the young woman's rescue.

Listening to her sleeping daughter's breathing, Amanda smiled at her own metaphor. Even in this extreme situation, her literary training stayed with her. She was mad to doubt herself. Of course, Gloria was her daughter, her blood type notwithstanding. She just had another red-haired daughter somewhere in Russia.

As soon as Gloria was well enough, Amanda would travel to Russia and find her other daughter. They were very well off, she and Gloria. That young woman in Russia might need their help. Perhaps, they could file a family reunion case with the immigration authorities. What would be her other daughter's name? Maybe Tatiana, Olga, or Elena? Maybe Maria? Delighted with her guessing game, Amanda smiled, straightened in her chair, pulled out a notebook and a pen from her purse, and began making plans.

Chapter Two
Sonya

Folding the last of Alexei's shirts, Sonya shoved it into a huge black duffel bag, slightly frayed at the seams. Two years ago, they had come to Canada with six such duffels—brand new and stuffed with clothing like six black pigs. Sonya was stuffed with new hopes as well. She thought Alexei would finally stop drinking, like he'd promised when they left Israel. Now, no hopes remained. She was empty and deflated of hope like a pierced balloon.

The last corduroy jacket went into the duffel, and there was still plenty of space left. Alexei's entire wardrobe—boots, sweaters, and all—fit into half the bag. Glancing around for anything else to pack, she jerkily wiped a tear from her cheek. She wouldn't cry. Crying never solved problems. She had already drained her tear supply. The lousy drunkard would have to choose once and for all. Either he would start working and making money, or he would leave. Today! As soon as he woke up from his thrice-lousy hangover.

Sonya's gaze fell on the window. The rain outside turned into a drizzle, painting gray, teary lines across the glass panes. The rain was weeping for her, lamenting her disintegrating marriage, since she wouldn't. She cursed vilely. Alexei hated it when she cursed in Mat, the Russian sub-language of obscenities. Good. She cursed again, reveling in the forbidden, filthy words and taking delight in her rebellion.

Last night, he couldn't even crawl into bed. He fell down senseless as soon as he stumbled over the threshold. Sonya had to get up, lock the door, and drag him to the sofa. She even removed his stinking shoes, but she drew the line at sharing her bed with the drunken sod. Afterward, unable to sleep, she laid alone in her cold, queen-sized bed, contemplating their future together.

It didn't exist. She couldn't see it. She couldn't go on like this. Not anymore. Even with two jobs, she couldn't make enough money for his unlimited supply of booze and still have something left to pay the rent and buy groceries. She had to think about Ksenya and herself, about her daughter's future. She couldn't support a husband who was drunk twenty hours a day. Even working without weekends or holidays, she couldn't afford an ice cream for her daughter. Remembering the fight with Ksenya in front of a Dairy Queen, Sonya cringed in shame.

She needed an education to get a better job, but education was expensive in Canada. She couldn't save money with Alexei drinking away every cent she made. Sonya's lips thinned. He would have to go. What else would he need? She was furious with him, but she wouldn't kick him out of the house without providing the minimum comforts.

She rummaged in the pockets of his jeans for the apartment keys. Comfort—yes, but not the keys to her life! He didn't stir, just moaned softly. Sonya winced from the sour stench of vodka. The odious man was pickled. He had to get up before Ksenya returned from school. Also, Sonya herself had another work shift later in the afternoon. She didn't have time to wait for the alcohol to wear off and the prince of inebriation to open his eyes.

Fuming, she wrenched the pillow from under his head and pummeled it into submission inside the duffel. Then, she grabbed the blanket off Alexei's big body. He would need a blanket anyway, and this one was already filthy from his muddied jeans.

He mumbled, pawing around without lifting his eyelids. The hammered parasite even grinned in his sleep. Whispering more profanities, Sonya restrained her savage fists. She wouldn't give in to her rage. She was a respectable Jewish woman. Jewish women didn't beat their husbands, even the drunken louts. Breathing heavily, she folded the blanket with slow, deliberate gestures. That was better. Softly, she inserted it inside the duffel. It still had some more space in it.

Springing up, she strode to the bedroom and brought out Alexei's clarinet case. His clarinet was the only thing he cared about. Not Ksenya, nor his wife, but the darn instrument. The warm, polished Karelian birch wood of the case gleamed dully in the gray room. The staccato of rain on the window glass had slackened. The rhythm was steady and lulling like a slow part of a *czardas*.

She had been good at *czardas*. Her shoulders began moving to the beat. Rats! She forced herself into stillness. She wasn't a dancer, anymore. No use pretending. Sonya wanted to wail, to tear at the walls with their mold stains, to break something, but she couldn't afford that. She had to go to work in a few hours. Right now, she had to wake up her good-for-nothing husband and send him out into the November rain before her daughter returned from school. Then, she would have to warm up dinner for Ksenya and prepare some explanations.

Sonya swallowed another curse. As if Ksenya didn't know already. The girl spent as much time as she could with her friends, only coming home to eat and sleep. She couldn't stand her parents fighting, anymore. She begged them to stop, but Alexei wouldn't listen. He would go away and get drunk. Sonya ground her teeth as she recalled their last fight. No more!

She clambered to her feet once again and went into the kitchen. No matter how mad she was with him, she wouldn't send him out hungry. She put four cold chicken drumsticks into a clear plastic bag, added a few slices of bread, and returned to the living room. Alexei continued snoring. She stuffed the food into the duffel. Then, she yanked the duffel's zipper shut. Her fingers trembled.

"Get up!" She shook his long body.

"M-m-m-m."

"Get up, you pissed, rat-arsed cabbage." She shook harder. "Get up, rotten badger."

"What, Sonechka?" He finally opened his eyes, grinning like an idiot.

Sonya's lips curled in disgust. His dreams must've been very pleasant. "Get up!" she yelled, avoiding his eyes. They were large and blue like Ksenya's. Only Ksenya's eyes were not as innocent.

"What for?" He blinked sleepily then grimaced. "Don't scream. My head hurts."

"Good!" Sonya said viciously.

"Sonechka, please."

"Get up!" she squeezed through her teeth. Clenching her fists, she stifled her longing to trounce him. She wouldn't stoop that low. Her mother would never approve. Probably. Besides, he would never fight back. He was that noble. He would drink, instead. Sonya punched the blameless cushion under Alexei's butt.

He groaned. "Don't do that. I really don't feel so well. My head is splitting."

"No shit! You have a hangover, don't you? Do you want some brine?"

Her sarcasm was lost on him. He brightened. "Yes."

"You're pathetic."

"Yes." Now his voice was loaded with remorse.

Sonya shivered. If he didn't get up this minute, she was going to kick him, and her kick would be primed. She had been a dancer, after all. She had steel toes. She might do some real damage. Resisting the urge to kick something, to vent her pain, she straightened and marched toward the window, where the dented bucket she found near a dumpster last year collected the raindrops from the leaking ceiling. The bucket was only half-full. She had time. She would empty it after she dealt with Alexei. She hated him so much now, she could hardly contain her hatred. Or was it unrequited love? She loved him so much in the beginning, but he managed to drown her love in his countless liters of vodka.

"Sonechka, I'm sorry." He rubbed his dark stubble. It was much darker than the blonde hair falling into his eyes.

He needed a haircut, she noted absently.

"I need a shave and a shower, but first I need that brine. Please, Sonechka. Or a small tumbler of vodka." He looked at her like a dog, his gaze full of hopeful devotion. "Did I sleep on the sofa?" He seemed surprised.

"Yeah. You would've slept on the floor, had I not dragged you onto the sofa." Sonya hugged herself tightly, but the tremors wouldn't stop. She felt nauseous. Perhaps she needed to eat. When had she eaten last? She hadn't eaten this morning before work, and she hadn't eaten after she came home. Just a cup of coffee to get her through the rest of the day.

"I had a bit too much, yesterday," he agreed meekly, "but I promise you—"

"No!" Sonya said. "No more promises." She was as tired of her anger as she was of his drunkenness. Better to be indifferent. It took less energy. "No more promises," she repeated more calmly. "Either you start working tomorrow or get out of the house. Today."

"Sonechka, can we talk about it some other time, when I'm more like myself?"

He was always so gentle, so considerate, when he wasn't drunk. Sonya shook her head. "You're never yourself anymore, Alyosha. You've become a Siamese twin with a bottle."

"You're shaking, Sonechka." He climbed to his feet, swayed a little, but determinately pattered toward her. "You're cold." Removing his denim jacket, he wrapped it around her shoulders and smiled in satisfaction. "That's better."

The jacket was warm from the heat of his body. It also had stains of something repulsively yellow and reeked of stale vodka. Although tears stung Sonya's eyes, she stubbornly refused to let them flow. Not in front of him. She shook off the jacket, and it fell to the floor beside the bucket. She stepped away, soundless in her old, bear-fur slippers. In desperation, craving some noise that would reflect the turmoil inside her, she stomped her foot. The soft sound, muffled by the fur, wasn't satisfying at all.

"Alexei Listvin," she said formally, "I can't support the three of us alone, anymore. You have to contribute. I'm completely wiped out. My Visa is exhausted. I work two jobs, trying to make ends meet, and you drink it all away. It was your idea to come here in the first place. I didn't want to leave Israel, but I came with you. I left my parents because of you. I left a career. I was dancing in Israel, and I left my dancing there. I followed you like a good wife, but you just sink into vodka, deeper and deeper every day."

Alexei's eyes flashed. "You were always working in Israel, always away in all those schools and *kibbutzim* where you taught. Ksyushka and I rarely saw you. You were not ours there. You belonged to all those Jews."

"I am a Jew. They're my people."

"They pretended they cared about your folk dancing. In reality, all they cared about was their synagogues and their idiotic *Shabbats* when nothing worked."

"That's nasty." Sonya's pitch rose.

"That's the truth."

"You wanted to immigrate to Israel."

"You didn't have to work so hard in Israel." Alexei's voice climbed in volume, too. "We could've taken a loan and waited until the Canadian visas arrived."

"Then, leave Israel without paying back? No!"

"Many people did so."

"My parents still live there. I had to be honest with the country and with myself."

"You're too honest for your own good, Sofia. We could've applied for welfare here, but no. You had to work. You've put this burden on yourself."

"I pay my debts. We're both young and strong. We can work. I don't want welfare. I can support my family, and so can you."

"Too honest and too proud." Alexei's agitation trickled off. He chuckled sadly.

"You're not proud enough!" Sonya tossed back. "I have to be proud for both of us and work for both of us, because you won't. You said they didn't appreciate your musical genius in Israel. Fine, we moved to Canada. It seems they don't appreciate your genius here as well. You might as well shove your musical ambitions up your ass and work as I do."

She started hyperventilating. She needed to calm herself to finish this. Her eyes fell on his jacket beneath her feet. Excellent! She kicked the garment. The movement transferred to the bucket, and the bucket skidded away. The water inside sloshed madly.

"Rats!" Slowly, Sonya pulled the bucket back in place, aligning it with the dripping raindrops and the gray zigzag of mold that marred the wall beside the window. She didn't want to wipe the wet floor on top of everything else. "I taught dancing in Israel and performed every few months. Here, without fluent English, I'm only good enough to fry burgers and wipe the asses of quadriplegic Canadians. You can do it, too."

"Soon, I'll have a breakthrough, Sonya," he said grimly.

"Now!"

"I can't. I have to be home if they call for an audition. I'm a musician. I can't afford to damage my hands by frying burgers or working in construction." He was patient, explaining his point of view as if she was a silly child.

Sonya bristled. "When they don't call, you drink."

"Sonya—"

"No! No more. I'm fed up with your drinking binges and your promises. I'm tired of you siphoning away my income. I want to take English classes. I want to enroll in the Emily Carr Institute next year. I want to have a career, again. If not in dancing then in the arts. I can. I have talent, but I need that money you're milking away for vodka. No more. Either you start working and earning your keep, or you get the hell out of my life and my house. Today."

"Sonya, I have to practice. When I get a job in an orchestra, you can stop working and enroll full time in any classes you wish. It'll work out. You'll see."

"No. You've been singing the same song for the last two years. I've had enough. If you're not going to work, get out of here and never come back."

"Where should I go? It's raining outside," he said feebly.

Sonya steeled herself. She wouldn't pity him. She was done with pity. "I don't care. Go live with your drinking buddies. Here is your stuff." She rushed to the door and kicked his duffel. Kicking felt good, liberating. If only she could kick him. "Here is $200." She thrust the money into his limp hands. "That's all I can spare. This will be the last money you'll ever get from me. Get out!" She threw the door open.

"My clarinet." He shoved the bills into his pocket.

"It's inside the duffel, and there is some roasted chicken and bread."

"Thanks," Alexei muttered. Shouldering the duffel, he turned to face Sonya. His blue eyes were very sad.

"Will you go work for Nick? Tomorrow morning?" she asked hopelessly. She didn't think he would.

"No, I can't shovel shit. I'm a musician. I need to keep my hands undamaged. I'm sorry, Sonechka." Head high, he turned and stepped over the threshold.

Before he closed the door behind him, Sonya dashed to the window, picked up his jacket, and sprinted back to the door. "Don't forget your jacket." She pushed the dirty bundle into his hands.

He glanced at the jacket then up at Sonya. His blue eyes hardened, but he didn't say a word. He closed the door quietly, and the lock clicked home.

The tiny sound reverberated in Sonya's head. In stunned disbelief, she stared at the closed door. He hadn't argued much. He hadn't fought. He just left. Somewhere inside, she prepared for a long argument. She even prepared to trust him, again. He could've promised to look for a job or go busking tomorrow. Instead, he just left. She clamped her palm to her mouth to stopper the sprouting scream.

"You've driven him out?"

Sonya whirled. "Ksenya? You should be at school. Why are you home?"

Darting to the door, Ksenya threw it open. "Papa! Wait!" Her frantic call echoed in the narrow stairwell, as she pounded down the stairs after Alexei.

"Ksenya! Wait! Put on your coat!" Sonya yelled.

Four stories below, the outside door banged. Alexei couldn't take Ksenya with him. She didn't have a coat on. He would send her back. Sonya listened. He must send her back. Sonya tried to breathe shallowly, so she wouldn't miss Ksenya coming back.

A few minutes later, Ksenya stomped up the stairs and into the apartment, slamming the door with her foot. Panting from her rush up and down four floors, she pointed her thin finger with a short, chewed up nail at Sonya.

"You're a monster!" she said fiercely, her nostrils flaring. Her shoulder-length, sandy hair—the same as her father's—hung limp and damp after her venture into the rain. Her blue eyes radiated loathing. "It's cold and raining. He'll die. You sent him out to die. You're a heartless, frugal Judaist Mug!"

Sonya recoiled. It was the worst thing anyone in Russia could say to a Jew. Alexei never said it, but his daughter just had.

"He could've found a job instead of flaunting his musicianship like a red flag," Sonya snapped. "I was a dancer, too. A soloist. I've given it up for him and for you. For us." She was too tired and strung up to ward her words. "You're my daughter. You're the same Judaist Mug I am, only worse—an ungrateful one."

"I'm not a Jew," Ksenya said contemptuously. "I hate your Jews. I'm a Russian, like my father. You're ready to kill him for a few bucks. I hate you. You scrimp and stint all the time. You wouldn't give me a cent, even if I was dying."

"Watch your tongue! I slave like a donkey, so you would have food on the table. I've spent a crazy amount of money for your flute, because your father deemed a mass-production instrument not good enough for his daughter. I pay for your lessons."

"I don't need your freaking lessons." Ksenya paled, her thin chest pumping up and down. Her small, clenched fists trembled at her sides, as if she wanted to strike Sonya. "You wouldn't even buy me an ice cream. You're greedy. Nobody would believe how greedy you are. I don't need your ice cream, either. I don't need *anything* from you. I'm not your daughter, anymore. As soon as Dad finds a place to stay, I'm moving in with him." She turned her back and proceeded into her room, her bunched up fists still at her sides. She slammed the door in her wake.

"I'm still your mother," Sonya mouthed. Should she run after her daughter? Argue? Explain? Apologize? Slap the silly girl? Tears sprang up, choking her. She smothered a howl that threatened to get out. What was the point? She had lost not only her husband but her daughter as well. Ksenya would never forgive her.

She would never leave, though. Alexei would never have enough money to support her. He couldn't even support himself. Even if he received welfare, he would probably waste it on booze. He would be homeless and probably die of exposure, come winter. Ksenya was right. Sonya had sent him out to die.

She strengthened her resolve. It was his own fault. She didn't pump him with drinks. He did it on his own. Ksenya might hate her mother, but at least now, she would have a chance at a decent future. She would never have that future if Alexei continued to live with them.

Like a surgeon cutting out a tumor, Sonya had done what was necessary. Then, why did she feel so lousy, as if she had just sold her soul for a buck? On some level, she had. She had betrayed them both—Alexei and Ksenya—but she had been fighting for years. Alexei was given more chances than he deserved to stop fooling around with a bottle. He didn't want to. The bottle was easier. Letting Sonya work her tail off while he contemplated his unappreciated musical gift was easier than shoveling shit. Oh, yeah. If she wanted to build a life for her daughter and herself, she didn't have a choice but to push him out. Why did she feel so rotten?

Her heart ached. Unable to see anything behind the film of tears, she grabbed a tissue and blew her nose. Then, she wiped her eyes. Even without the obstruction of tears, her living room didn't appear much better. It contained the same secondhand sofa, the same TV, book shelves full of books and Bohemian crystal dolls, and the same ugly rain bucket. New tears welled up.

Sonya sniffed. If she blocked the bucket from view, concentrating instead on the floor cushions, the room didn't appear too bad. She made the cases for the cushions and the sofa during their first year in Vancouver. The quilted patchwork didn't look like what it was—a selection of cheap fabrics and cut-up old clothes bought in a thrift store. It looked like a galaxy of autumn leaves scattered across a meadow. Sonya smiled through her tears. Crying was unproductive. She should fashion a screen to close off the bucket from the rest of the room and finish the quilted tapestry with a deer to cover the mold stains behind the TV.

She shuffled to her bedroom. Pulling out a black duffel from under the bed, she spread the unfinished tapestry in front of her, caressing a freckled little fawn with her fingers. A green fairy above his nose would look fantastic. Sonya rummaged in her bag of fabric snippets but couldn't find anything green. She pulled out a blue polyester pocket. She could make a blue fairy, with tiny buttons for eyes, but she didn't have any orange fragments for the sun, either. Sighing, she shoved the duffel back under the bed. She didn't have time for sewing, anyway. She had to do her daily warm up.

Despite giving up her dancing career, she still tried to exercise every day between her shifts to keep in shape. Today, dealing with Alexei had interrupted her routine. Sonya shrugged off her sweatshirt, tossed it on the bed, and grabbed a short barre in front of a floor-to-ceiling mirror—the two objects in her apartment that cost more than anything else. She didn't turn on any music. Doing her class music-less would be her punishment for the evil she had wrought, today.

She assumed the first position and sank into a deep *plié*, glancing periodically into the mirror, more as a habit than because she really needed to. She hadn't gained any weight since she stopped dancing professionally, and the lines of her torso and legs were still clear, although there were new wrinkles on the outside of her eyes and on her forehead.

Her hair was the same rich auburn as before—no gray, yet. Her ponytail reached far below her shoulder blades. Pity her hair wasn't as bright as her father's and sister's. Their hair was luminous and fuzzy like coppery wire, while hers streamed down her back in a wave of burnished bronze. She liked their hair better. On the other hand, she didn't have their bright freckles, which was a blessing for a dancer. She smiled into the mirror. Her hazel eyes twinkled beneath the dark lashes.

Then, her smile faded, and her lips curled derisively. She was such a vain creature. Lifting her right leg into a grand *battement*, she stretched her muscles to their utmost. It was so important for a dancer to look pretty that she kept forgetting she wasn't a dancer, not anymore. She didn't have to be pretty. Nobody cared. Not the invalid Jane she tended to, nor the burgers she flipped every morning.

Grabbing the barre with both hands, with her feet in the second position, she leaned back as far as she could, eyes roaming the room upside-down. What was the point of being pretty if her husband was gone and her daughter hated her? To own the truth, Alexei hadn't noticed her for the last couple of years—ever since diving too deep into the bottle. The abhorrent, drunken sponge! She straightened, and the mirror reflected the sudden, impotent fury in her eyes.

Chapter Three
Amanda

"Mom!" Gloria yelled from her room as soon as Amanda opened the door. "They called from the faculty. Something about Chekhov in Norway."

Amanda sighed. "I know. I'm not going to the conference. I'm taking a sabbatical."

Gloria steered her wheelchair into the hall. "Why? You don't have to. I told you I don't need round-the-clock baby-sitting. I'm fine with the chair. You'll get bored out of your wits if you stay home for much longer. I can do anything in the chair. See?" Deftly, she turned her chair around to demonstrate the point.

"I can even dance in it." Gloria's green eyes laughed, as she hummed a dancing tune.

Amanda followed Gloria's waltz on wheels with her eyes. This weird fusion of woman and machinery didn't fit into their elegant hall with its frosted glass doors, etched windows, shining parquet floor, and antique furniture. "You'll scar the floor," she said.

"Ha!" Gloria returned gleefully. "Another month, and they'll remove the cast. I'll be as good as new."

Gloria's bruises had already faded into an ugly yellow, and the swelling on her forehead was gone. Her bright, coppery hair was gathered into a ponytail, leaving a golden nimbus of tiny curls around her face. Smiling fleetingly, Amanda bent to peck a kiss in her daughter's freckled cheek. "Your bossy self again, honey? Impervious wench." Much better than the frightened, irritated creature she had been the first couple of days after the accident, but Amanda didn't say that aloud.

"What's going on outside, Mom? You look cold."

"I'm cold. I'm thoroughly frozen. I think the temperature is into the minuses." Amanda dropped her purse and gloves on a pinewood chest and hung her blue suede parka in the closet. She folded her black scarf neatly, but as she put it on the shelf above the rod, her back twitched. She smoothed her grimace before she turned to face Gloria.

"Take a long bubble bath," Gloria advised. "You look tired, too."

"I shall, later. I've finished the Christmas shopping for you, bought the last gifts on your list." Amanda pointed at the bulging bags she dropped in front of the mirror. It was of the same antique set as the chest, with the matching pinewood frame of carved leaves and birds. "The mall was fiendishly packed."

"Great! Thanks, Mom." Gloria wheeled herself to the mirror. "Malls are always crazy in December." She loaded the bags on her lap and rolled to the living room. "Help me wrap them, will you?"

"Of course." Rubbing her back, Amanda followed the chair. She needed another visit to her chiropractor.

The living room was a mess. Obviously, Gloria had already started the wrapping. The scraps of bright wrapping paper and the cuttings of rainbow ribbons littered the floor. Four coils of ribbons of different colors and a pair of scissors lay on the sofa, where Gloria had just unloaded her bounty of new gifts. Amanda's creamy, plush throw lay collapsed like a crumpled rag on top of the TV. On a coffee table, which Amanda had moved into a corner to allow Gloria's chair room for maneuvering, an impressive heap of wrapped-up gifts piled haphazardly. The wrapping paper glinted in all colors, while Gloria's hand-knitted, silvery-gray mohair shawl peeked from underneath the table. With the empty brand carriers strewn everywhere, the room looked like a landfill.

Undoubtedly, Gloria was herself, again. How her daughter could be such a slob in her personal life and so meticulous in her professional affairs, Amanda couldn't fathom. Sighing, she bent to pick up a fragment of wrapping paper, decorated with a glittering Christmas design. The spangled balls on the paper matched the ornaments swinging from their Christmas tree, set in the alcove in front of a bay window. Wincing from the twinges in her back, Amanda collected the trash into a basket and dragged Gloria's shawl from under the coffee table, folding it smartly and pressing the edges with her fingers.

Gloria didn't notice. Smiling like a happy little girl, she pulled a *Lancôme* cosmetic kit, a gift for her secretary, from a bag, and dropped the bag on the floor. Then, she navigated her chair toward the bookcase, where three different rolls of wrapping paper leaned on the glass doors.

"Evelyn will love it. Thanks, Mom. What paper should I use? Christmas or floral?"

"Floral," Amanda said absently. She had already folded her throw, put it back in its place on the side table, and picked up the empty Lancôme bag from the floor.

"You'll have to drive to the office and give them my gifts before the holiday."

"Fine." Amanda settled into her favorite armchair, an elaborate Italian piece upholstered in cream and pink satin—the only surface Gloria left untouched in her holiday frenzy. She knew her mother loved this chair. Despite all her careless ways, her daughter could be very considerate. How could Amanda wish for another daughter? The other one might be an uneducated, uncaring shrew. Or a cheat. Or a neat freak like herself. Amanda's lips twitched in a faint grin.

"You didn't have to buy such expensive gifts for everyone," she said. "Not for every single carpenter. You spend a fortune every Christmas."

"Don't nag." Gloria shrugged. "Go take a bath. You'll mellow up when you're warm."

It was an ongoing argument. Gloria considered everyone who worked for her construction company as some odd breed of cousins, many times removed. Officially, the company belonged to Amanda, left to her in her uncle's will. An engineer by education, Gloria had managed it for the last seven years, and the company had done much better under her supervision than in the uncle's time.

"These people worked hard to finish that street of houses in Abbotsford before Christmas. They deserve some spoiling. Besides, they're like family." Gloria chuckled. "I will write all the gifts off the taxes as Christmas bonuses." She pointed to the stack of sale receipts on the bookshelf.

"Some family," Amanda grumbled. Stretching her tired back, she groaned.

"Mom?" Gloria perked up, watching Amanda with a slight frown. "Your back is troubling you, again? When did you swim last?"

"Oh, don't scold, honey. I know I have to swim twice a week, but with your accident and this chilly weather..."

"You can't do that." Gloria wheeled closer, concern written on her abruptly grim face. "You have to exercise you back regularly. You know that, or it gets worse fast. Damn, Mom. You're like a baby. You need constant supervision."

"I'll drive to the pool, tomorrow," Amanda said.

"Marvelous, and make an appointment with your massage therapist."

"Okay, okay. I promise. Drop it." Amanda dove into the

Chapters bag for a book on Art Nouveau Gloria had ordered for her designer.

Gloria shook her head in disapproval. "Like a baby," she repeated.

"What paper do you want for this book?" Amanda asked to change the subject.

Gloria pivoted her chair to the bookshelf, selected the wrapping paper with a geometric pattern, and grabbed the book from Amanda's hands. "I wish I could hire another designer. McBride's become intolerable. He wants to be a partner." She put the book on her lap and glared ahead, lips thinning angrily.

"Oh," Amanda said uncertainly. "I thought you liked him."

"I did. I do. He's good." Gloria opened the book and leafed through it, caressing the glossy pages without looking. "Dad was better, though," she murmured. "Why didn't you have another kid, Mom? Father's creative streak might have rubbed off on him. I wouldn't have to subcontract, then. I could've hired a talented sibling and kicked McBride's ass to the moon. Pity I haven't inherited any of father's artistic quirks."

It's because you're not really his daughter, Amanda thought. "Maybe you have a sibling," she blurted. She hadn't been planning to tell Gloria about her Russian schemes yet, not until Gloria recovered completely, but perhaps they should talk now. Perhaps it was time.

"Have you discovered a long-lost son?" Gloria winked at her.

"No. I haven't discovered a long-lost son. I've discovered that you're not really my daughter. I have another daughter somewhere in Russia." Amanda held her breath. What would Gloria's response be to this revelation? Every night, Amanda thought about ways to put it into words, to explain it to her daughter in the most circumspect manner, but she couldn't find any better approach than the blunt truth.

"What is it?" A mischievous dimple appeared in Gloria's right cheek, untouched by the bruises. "A twist from a new book by some obscure Russian writer? Are you fishing for my reaction? Want to translate it into English?"

"No," Amanda whispered. Of all the possible scenarios she envisioned during her nightly speculations, she hadn't thought Gloria would simply discard the news. "The doctor told me your blood type is 'O' negative. Both Donald and I had 'O' positive blood. They probably switched you at birth in that Russian hospital."

Slowly, Gloria's hands stilled, and she lifted her eyes to look at

Amanda. Deep wrinkles cut across her forehead. She opened her mouth, attempted a smile, and closed it. She opened it again and blinked.

"This is a joke?" she asked at last.

Amanda shook her head.

"This is the truth?"

Amanda nodded. Unable to watch emotions flickering across Gloria's face, she surged up and knelt in front of her daughter's chair. "I love you, Gloria," she said hoarsely, caressing her daughter's leg under the worn denim. "You'll always be my daughter, but there is another one somewhere in Russia. She might be starving, unemployed." Amanda's throat closed. It happened every time she thought about her unknown Russian daughter. No matter how often such thoughts visited her lately, she had to fight for air every time.

"She might need my help. Our help. I have to go there and find her. I have to bring your sister home." She smiled weakly. "Maybe she can be your new designer. Maybe she has inherited Donald's creativity. Say something, please." Amanda's gray eyes bored into her daughter's green ones. Would she understand? Forgive?

"So, I have another mother somewhere in Russia?" Gloria said, her lips stretching into a mirthless grin.

"Another mother?" Appalled, Amanda pulled away.

"If you have two daughters, then it follows," Gloria said. "We'll all be one happy family. Two mothers, two daughters, and no man in sight."

"Don't be nasty." Stiffly, Amanda clambered to her feet.

"It's a shock, mom," Gloria murmured. "Allow me some nastiness."

"Right. Forgive me." Amanda bent to hug her daughter.

"Why didn't you say anything before? Why now? Did father know?"

Amanda shook her head, her face rubbing against Gloria's bushy ponytail. She inhaled the familiar lavender scent of Gloria's shampoo and sniffed. "I didn't know myself. I only discovered it at the hospital after your accident. You needed a blood transfusion," she explained helplessly. "The doctor thought I had been unfaithful, but I wasn't. I was pregnant with my husband's baby." Amanda felt tears coming down her cheeks, dampening Gloria's coppery hair. "There was another red-headed girl born on the same day." She licked salt from her lips.

"You told me this tale a thousand times, but I didn't think..."

"Me neither." Amanda sniffed. "I think they switched you by accident." Troubled by a new thought, she frowned. "Maybe it wasn't an accident?"

"Whatever." Gloria's hands tightened around Amanda's shoulders. "You'll always be the number one mother for me," she whispered solemnly into Amanda's ear.

Amanda smiled weakly and straightened. She wiped her tears with the back of one hand.

Gloria's face resumed a serious, even grim expression. "How could you keep this to yourself for so long?"

"It's only been a few days," Amanda said defensively. "You didn't feel well enough. I couldn't risk agitating you prematurely."

"Oh, Mom!" Gloria tossed the half-wrapped book on the coffee table. "Let's order from Peppito. I'm in the mood for some spicy tortillas. I have to think how to proceed from here. First, you should hire a private detective to go to Russia to find that other daughter. Second–"

"Rubbish! I'm going myself," Amanda said.

"No. It's dangerous. The Russians kill wealthy foreigners for their money. They might consider you wealthy."

"I am wealthy," Amanda said. "We are. Besides, I think it would be only fair if we share our wealth with that other woman. My other daughter. I don't even know her name." Shivering, she sank into her chair. Suddenly, she felt surreal. "I must go to Russia."

Gloria wheeled closer. "What about the company, Mom?"

"I'll divide it fifty-fifty in my will. If I ever find her. If not, it will be all yours."

"Fifty-fifty?" Gloria's eyes hardened from living grass to emeralds. "Don't you think it's unfair? The company is my life. I brought it up from almost ruin. I work like a donkey, day and night, to make it successful, and you're going to give half of it to some unknown woman? Just because thirty-four years ago, some stinking, Russian idiot made a mistake?"

"Gloria, honey," Amanda said uncertainly. Her pale, narrow fingers clutched at the tiny pink arabesques that dotted the chair's arm. Gloria's words stung like a whipping. She wanted to flinch, to crawl into a corner and hide. She didn't expect her daughter would suddenly get so greedy. Gloria was never greedy, but she obviously cared for the company much more than she had ever let on. "Maybe forty-sixty," she murmured. "Or even seventy-five percent for you."

"Forget it, Mom. I shouldn't have brought it up. The company is yours to dispose of as you see fit. What do you think my Russian relatives are up to? Maybe they're rich as well." Gloria's gaze turned speculative. "I wonder how many new relatives I have. Maybe a score of brothers or cousins?" She put her large, freckled hand over Amanda's and squeezed faintly. "I'm sorry." Her lips curled, as she lifted Amanda's limp hand for a light kiss. "Don't go, Mom. I'll die from worry. Hire that detective. We can afford it."

"You always wanted a big family," Amanda said quietly. "I never understood that wish before. I never liked crowds. Both Donald and I were only children."

"You're too much inside yourself and your Russian poets. When Dad was alive, you at least had some friends visiting now and again. After his death, you crawled into a shell, and you wouldn't come out. I tried, Mom. You slammed down the lid and wouldn't let me in. Perhaps, you're right. You should go yourself. If nothing else, it should drag you out of that damn isolation. It's eating you alive, and I'm not enough for you. Perhaps that other daughter would be enough."

She would've propelled her chair out of the room, had Amanda not grabbed her hands. "No, Gloria. Don't go. You're enough. I don't need anyone else. You have always been enough for me, the best daughter I could've wished for." She fought Gloria's superior strength with sheer determination. "I just thought that maybe my other daughter needs my help. Please, don't be mad at me, honey. You have to understand. I must do it." Amanda tugged at Gloria's hands until her daughter turned back to face her. "Donald would've understood, had he lived," Amanda mouthed.

Unexpectedly, Gloria chuckled. "Mom, are you trying to manipulate me?"

Amanda sighed deeply. She wouldn't look Gloria in the eyes. She felt her cheeks warming up with a blush. She hadn't blushed for eternity.

Gloria started laughing. "Oh, Mom. I love you. When are you going? Perhaps you have a flock of grandchildren already?"

Amanda's lips formed into a silent 'O'. Suddenly, her blues trickled off. "You think so?"

Gloria shrugged. "You'll stay for Christmas, won't you?"

"Of course I'll be home for Christmas and New Year's, honey. I wouldn't leave you alone, especially in this condition. It's the millennium year. It happens once in a thousand years. I have to be with you. Besides, it might take some time to get a Russian visa. I might only be able to travel there in May or June. I hope."

Gloria picked up the phone book. "Perhaps we should order in some Russian food." She fiddled with her cell phone. Her eyes twinkled. "To celebrate our upcoming Russian connections. From Russia with love! Do you know any good Russian restaurants? Do you want *borsch*?"

Exasperated, Amanda threw up her hands. "Oh, stop clowning, will you? Russian restaurants don't deliver. Order from Peppito, and I'll make a salad."

"I was thinking, Mom. We should record our conversation and offer it to some TV station. I might still. They might create a series from this story. We'll make millions."

Amanda glanced at Gloria. "You know, you might be right, honey. I should write it myself, as a nonfiction book. 'My search for a Russian daughter.' It's so bizarre, it ought to sell well. I'll talk to Suzy from the Writing and Publishing department."

"Record everything," Gloria advised. "Go upstairs and type down our entire conversation right now, before you forget."

"I'm not likely to forget any time soon," Amanda said. "It's still too raw. I have to gain some emotional distance to write it well, and what if I can't find her? Then, there is no story."

Gloria grinned. "Then, in the best traditions of this house, I'll remain the only child."

A new thought occurred to Amanda. "Gloria, if you have a sister and a mother in Russia..." Her tongue stumbled at the concept.

Gloria fought a hysterical fit of laughter. The fit won. She dissolved into giggles. "Then what, oh my mother in Canada? Perhaps I have a couple more mothers—in Uganda, say, or Australia? One mother per continent."

Amanda brought herself under control. "Be serious. They might only speak Russian. Most Russians don't speak other languages. You'll have to learn Russian to communicate with them."

"Fat chance!" Gloria said. "They'll have to learn English."

Amanda headed to the kitchen to start a salad, but one thought persisted in her head, buzzing like a fly. What should she do with the company? Gloria did deserve it.

Chapter Four
Sonya

Sonya covered the platter heaped with apricot *rugelach* with a tea towel. She lowered her nose to the teddy bear printed in the middle of the towel and sniffed appreciatively. The *rugelach* smelled heavenly. Should she allow herself one? Yes! She sneaked a small cookie from under the towel. The flaky crust melted on her tongue, releasing the tangy apricot flavor. Her hand shot out for the second cookie, but she restrained herself. No! No stuffing herself. She didn't want to bloat out like so many former dancers just because she was one, too. Former. She sighed.

She baked the *rugelach* for Ksenya. Sonya tossed a furtive glance toward her daughter. Ksenya was gorging herself on pasta and meatballs as if she was a famine victim. The girl had such a beautiful Russian name: Ksenya. Much better than the name Sonya's parents had wanted her to call the baby: Esther. Anyway, Ksenya didn't look like Esther. She looked like a typical Russian girl, with the shoulder-length, dirty-blonde hair of her dad, his snubby nose, and blue eyes. She was her father's image—soft and fluffy like her name. At least she had been before she turned into a prickly teenager.

Sonya shook her head in exasperation. Ksenya was such a baby. She claimed she hated her mother and the entire Jewish tribe, but she never rejected any food Sonya put on the table. Definitely not *rugelach*. Exasperation morphed into amusement. No kid ever rejected *rugelach*.

Ksenya polished the last meatball off the plate and slid her stool away from the table. "Yummy! Thanks!" she piped, smiling at Sonya. Then, she recalled her purported hostility, and her smile faded. "I need a snack," she said grimly. "I'm staying late with Ashley to study for the test tomorrow. Can I have some of it in a plastic box?"

"Of course." Sonya pulled a large Tupperware container from a cupboard. "Fill it up. Do you want some *rugelach*, Ksyushka?"

"Yes!" Brightening, Ksenya began ladling pasta into the box.

Some snack, Sonya thought. Her lips twitched, but she held her smile to herself. She filled a Ziploc bag with half the cookies from the platter. Everything she cooked disappeared with the speed of light, although Sonya herself didn't eat much. Obviously, Ksenya couldn't eat that much either, or she wouldn't be so skinny. The girl was transparent in sharing everything with her dad, and Sonya didn't mind. No matter where Alexei lived, she fed her husband through Ksenya as a good wife should. *Pathetic*, she thought wryly, as she put the Ziploc and the box into a white Safeway bag—her personal food bank for one pitiful drunk. Was she still hoping that he would change?

"I'm gone!" Ksenya grabbed the bag and skipped out the door.

"*Bon appétit*," Sonya muttered to the closed door. She glanced at the clock—just enough time for a couple of phone calls. Picking up the receiver, she dialed her friend Irina's number.

They had met at the ESL class two years ago: Irina, Nadezda, and Sonya. After the class ended, they still celebrated the New Year's Eves and birthdays together: Irina with her husband and two sons, Sonya with her family, and Nadezda with her husband. This time, it was Sonya's turn to host a party, although Nadezda had already bailed out. She said they were going to Hawaii for the holidays.

"Oh, Sonechka. I can't." Irina's voice oozed sincerity. "We've been invited already. One of my son's friends at school. I talked to his mom at the boys' soccer game, and we just hit it off. They are so rich! They invited us for a New Year's Eve at their house. Another year, maybe?"

"Sure," Sonya said. Her hand holding the receiver started hurting, and she relaxed her grip. "Another year. Of course. How about coming to the Botanical Garden with me? They've already put up their Christmas Lights. Next weekend?"

"Sonechka," Irina said. "I've already seen it with the boys. Last weekend."

"Oh? Sure." Afraid her voice would betray her, Sonya didn't add anything. She knew that the lights display hadn't been on last weekend. Irina was lying.

"We can have a cup of coffee next week, darling. I'll call you, all right?"

"Sure," Sonya said, again. Her temper threatened to get out, forming a tight ball in her throat. She had lost a husband and a daughter. She hadn't thought it would lead to a social vacuum so soon.

"Kiss you. Have to run. Bye-bye." The receiver beeped.

Sonya slammed it down. None of her former friends wanted to meet with her. Some friends! Her mother was right. Nobody wanted a single woman for a friend. When she had been married, even to the drunkard Alexei, everyone felt sorry for her. They had wanted to meet, talk, and hear all the juicy details. Now, everyone avoided her as if she carried a plague. No more juicy details! Vultures, the bunch of them.

Sonya sniffled, suppressing a shudder. Those quasi-friends didn't deserve her, anyway. She left her real friends behind in Saratov, in the Petushko Folk Dance Ensemble, after she had immigrated to Israel. Neither Irina nor Nadezda understood her love of dancing or her fascination with making beauty. She was an artist, while both her fake friends were terribly mundane. So mundane that it grated on her nerves. She never showed it, though. She had been a loyal friend to them both. She supported Nadezda when her husband cheated on her. She helped Irina when her son was sick last year. Then, they both rejected her as soon as Sonya kicked Alexei out. Rats! Confound that alcoholic! Even absent, he still had the power to control her life. On the other hand, good riddance to phony friends.

Snorting mirthlessly, she dragged her feet to the bedroom to dress for her evening shift. In the evenings, she worked as a caregiver for a paralyzed woman named Jane. Such a noble-sounding profession—a caregiver. Yeah, right! An ass-wiper would be more precise.

Realizing where her thoughts were going, Sonya winced, disgusted with herself. Gosh, she was turning into a shrew! Instead of pitying her friendless state, she should reserve her pity for poor Jane, whose fiery spirit struggled to survive in a shriveled, immobile body. What a torture it must be to be unable to move! For a dancer, even a former dancer, there was no worse punishment. She was lucky to have this pliant body still, full of hard muscles.

In her bra and panties, she grabbed the barre and faced the mirror, studying her reflection, admiring the long, pure lines of her hips and thighs. When she still danced, one critic compared her body to a petite, red-headed Barbie.

"Vain creature," she whispered, smiling to herself. Yes, she was definitely lucky, and she looked much more fit than both Irina and Nadezda—her former cows-friends. She stuck her tongue out at her reflection. "Got that? Cows!"

* * * *

"You took your time, missy," Jane grumbled, when Sonya opened the door to the woman's one-bedroom apartment an hour later. "We're going shopping."

"Fine," Sonya said cheerfully. "I see you're ready to go?"

"Yes."

Indeed, Jane was already prepped for a shopping trip. Her remaining white hair was arranged in a neat coiffure, lipstick and rouge applied. A large sapphire and pearls brooch sparkled on the lapel of her formal, dark blue jacket, which looked ridiculous on her withered, misshapen body. She sat in her wheelchair regally, her arthritic, skeletal fingers the only parts of her body still functioning, positioned on the chair control panel. A blue, silk ribbon tied her wrists to the armrests. On Jane's lap, covered with a long woolen skirt, an ancient, turquoise purse rested limply. Beaded embroidery covered the purse. Torn threads stuck out of the beads like disheveled hair.

"I just phoned the Handy DART." Miranda, the young and fat morning caregiver, came in from the kitchen. "Have fun." She stomped out the door.

"That hog doesn't like me," Jane commented acidly.

"You hate her guts, too," Sonya countered. "Do you wish to buy a new purse?"

"My purse was very expensive and chic," Jane said coldly. Her dark eyes glinted with challenge.

Poor Jane didn't have many challenges, Sonya thought sadly. Not ones she could overcome, anyway. Only insurmountable ones. That's why she enjoyed their bickering. It made the disabled woman feel more human, less an appendage to the chair. Miranda never insulted Jane, so Jane hated the young caregiver. On the other hand, Jane loved Sonya, because Sonya offered her a challenge she could win. Unfortunately, sometimes Jane's affection seemed as twisted as her body.

Sonya maneuvered the wheelchair into the lift, pushed the ground floor button, and glared at the offending purse. "It was chic during the Second World War, no doubt," she said.

"You don't posses a fashion sense," Jane spat. "Not an iota. You wear these abhorrent sweatpants everywhere." Her thin lips, outlined by an outrageous, carmine lip gloss, crimped in distaste. She would've resembled a blood-thirsty vampire, but for her pink, toothless gums.

"You misplaced your teeth," Sonya said. "How does that fit

your fashion sense?"

"They chafe my gums."

"Too bad. What do you wish to buy?"

"I need a new lipstick."

"Why? You look like a corpse, anyway."

"Stupid," Jane said in a scratchy voice. "When will you teach me your Mat? I want to swear at you." She had been badgering Sonya to teach her the cussing sub-language of Russians since Sonya started working for her.

"Never. You can swear in English." Grinning, Sonya propelled the wheelchair off the pickup ramp and toward the mall entrance. Despite the dozens of possible operations her electronic chair was capable of, Jane loved to be pushed.

"Cosmetics." Sonya banged on the counter with her hand to attract the attention of a salesgirl with four multicolored ponytails.

"I want to know Mat," Jane whined. Her desiccated hand clutched the control panel of the chair tighter, making the brown age spots stand out on her parchment-like skin. Suddenly, she spun her chair, and a wheel caught Sonya behind the knees.

Sonya grabbed at the counter, but her hand slipped. She teetered and fell on her butt, sweeping the samples of creams and lipsticks from the counter. The salesgirl came running, her ponytails flying after her like four miniature rainbows.

Sonya gasped an obscenity. "Jane! What's gotten into you?"

Jane giggled, pressed the button on her chair arm, and rolled out of the store before Sonya could climb back to her feet. It took a while to explain to the salesgirl what had happened and help put everything back on the counter, except for the two broken samples. Sonya had to pay for them, because Jane and her tousled purse with the credit cards were nowhere in sight.

Cataloguing all the Mat curses she knew, Sonya sprinted in pursuit. If she lost Jane in the mall, she would get into all kinds of trouble with Jane's relatives. She could lose the job. Blasted paralytic!

It took her half an hour to locate Jane, again. She was innocently buying a lipstick from a cart in the middle of the hall, smiling beatifically at the middle-aged, Oriental saleswoman.

"You contrary old crone," Sonya sputtered. "You did that on purpose."

The saleswoman's narrow, dark eyes regarded her with disapproval.

"You're out of luck." Jane cackled, stuffing her new lipstick into her purse.

"You owe me money for the two samples. I broke them because of you."

"You're just clumsy," Jane taunted. "Add the money to my bill. My brother will pay."

"We're going home." Sonya grabbed the chair handles.

"I need new hair clips." Jane whimpered suddenly and loudly. "I'm hungry, too. I want lunch in the Food Fair. I want Chinese."

The passersby stared. Some shook their heads. They probably thought Sonya an unfeeling monster.

"Manipulator!" Sonya hissed. "All right. Let's buy your hair clips." She pushed the chair away from the unwanted attention, running down the hall. She wasn't a monster. She really wasn't. Why were they all staring? Rats! What was happening to her?

"Spiteful harridan!" she muttered. She wasn't sure whether she meant Jane or herself.

"You're upset," Jane said. "Why?"

"None of your business. Shut up." Sonya rolled the chair toward Claire, the accessories shop filled with teenage girls. She looked down at Jane's transparent hair-do, with more bald spots than hair. Why did the old woman want hair clips? Sonya didn't voice her opinion, though. No matter how tempting, Jane didn't deserve the humiliation.

"Buy what you wish." Sonya brought the chair to a halt in front of the counter and danced out before Jane could work up some other mischief.

"You abandoned me," Jane complained several minutes later, piloting her chair like a real pro among the girly currents swirling between the shop displays.

"You managed just fine."

"Why are you so upset?"

Sonya snorted. Jane was too intuitive. "Want to come to the Botanical Garden with me on the weekend? We'll see the Christmas Lights."

"Yes!" Jane said breathlessly. Her old, rheumatic eyes gleamed. "You're inviting me for an outing?"

"Yeah." Sonya smiled. "It's a date. You're good company, rude and impertinent. You cheer me up."

Jane made a small disbelieving sound deep in her throat and closed her eyes. "Take me to the Food Fair, you Russian hussy," she croaked.

"I'm Jewish," Sonya objected, laughing. "Uneducated old crow!

Don't you know the difference?"

"Insolent wench," Jane retorted and smiled.

Suddenly, Sonya wanted to cry.

* * * *

When Sonya returned home later in the evening, Ksenya was watching TV in the living room. An all-boys band was playing something loud and rhythmical. The stage lights flashed, making the TV screen red and oscillating like an ambulance signal. The sound was somewhat similar to the paramedics', too—piercing and apprehensive like a siren. Behind the TV, the fawn tapestry camouflaging the mold spray on the wall reflected the red splashes, as if a lightning storm hit the sunny forest.

Sonya shook her head. She didn't understand pop music. How could Ksenya study classical flute and listen to these tasteless, blasting waves? Sonya opened her mouth to comment, thought better of it, and went to her bedroom without uttering a word. They had too many arguments as it was.

Fully dressed, she plopped down on her bed, stretching her arms wide on top of the bedcover. She stroked the whimsical, creamy silk snowflakes sewn on the blue, striped satin of the quilt. When she was making it, she wanted golden snowflakes but couldn't find cheap, secondhand golden cloth. So, she settled for creamy silk, and the quilt and matching curtains came out festive and elegant, full of ritzy energy.

The telephone rang, and she grabbed the receiver. "Hello?"

"Sonya," her sister Lilia said on the Israeli end of the line.

"Lil'ka? Is anything wrong?"

"Nothing is wrong. I simply wanted to talk to you. Can I talk to my sister?"

Sonya relaxed and lay back down. "I miss you, too," she said. "I've just returned from work." She glanced at the clock. "You're going to work, right? Funny—this time difference."

"Yeah. Let me finish chewing my sandwich. I have half an hour before I must leave. How are you doing?"

Sonya heard her big-boned, freckled little sister chomping loudly on the other end of the line. "I've lost my friends," Sonya said. "As soon as Alexei left, they dropped off."

"Like dead flies," Lilia finished the thought. "Bitches!"

Sonya imagined her sister as she had been the last time they met—at the Ben Gurion Airport before Sonya, Alexei, and Ksenya boarded a plane to Canada. Lilia's mop of coppery hair contrasted with her red and yellow sundress, and she was laughing with the deep, throaty laugh Sonya loved so much. Lilia did everything at full gallop. No middle ground for her younger sis.

"I wish you could visit me, Lil'ka."

Lilia snickered. "Someday. I can't, now. The twins are only three, and Ari is working like a horse."

"I know." Sonya sighed.

"Why don't you come here? You said you have some money stashed for emergencies."

"Yeah, but I want to save it for school. Without the drain of Alexei's vodka, I might be able to double it. By September, I might have enough for the first year."

"You're such a heroine. Why don't you move back here permanently? We'll help in the beginning. You could live with Mom and Dad, save on rent. At least until you're on your feet, again. Without your sloshing Russian beau, they wouldn't mind you and Ksyushka. There're good art schools in Tel Aviv and Jerusalem, and you could teach dancing, again."

"I can't. Ksyushka can't go through a third immigration. First, from Russia to Israel. Then, from Israel to Canada. We can't move again so soon. Besides, she doesn't remember any Hebrew, and neither do I. Another language—no! Also, her father is here. She would never leave him. She hates me as it is."

"Where is she, now?"

"Watching TV in the living room." Sonya chuckled, already feeling better. She liked talking to her sister. "Ksyushka sneaks food to Alexei all the time. I don't mind, but it drains my income. I thought I could save more and faster."

"You're spoiling her."

"Yeah. Goes with being a mom. You should know."

"I do. My hooligans also twist me around their grubby little fingers."

"We'll pull through."

They said their good-byes, and Sonya replaced the receiver on the base. As always, talking to her sister replenished her, gave her an energy boost. Before, when she danced, she danced out all her emotions, good and bad, pounding everything out on stage. Now, she didn't have an outlet for her blues. They stayed inside and festered, unless she painted or sewed. She should start a new project—something for Ksenya.

Sonya wandered into her daughter's den, full of clutter as

usual. What color would look good in here? The room was tiny, containing only a twin bed, a large desk, and a dresser. Sonya blocked Ksenya's jeans and sweatshirts littering the floor from her view. She concentrated on the overall *feng shui*. Perhaps something turquoise or lavender. A marine landscape? Various designs swarmed in her head, as she pattered to the living room.

"Ksyushka, I'd like to make a tapestry for your room. What do you think about a sea scene? With fish and maybe a dolphin?"

"Whatever," Ksenya said listlessly. "Can Dad have dinner with us on New Year's Eve?"

"Sure." Sonya nodded. Would Alexei come after she kicked him out? *I miss him*, she realized with surprise. Could they make up? Be friends? Could he start working? Probably not. She sighed. Anyway, it would be nice to have a holiday dinner together once more. Better than spending New Year's Eve alone with hostile Ksenya. They would probably fight, again. "Tell him he's welcome."

"Thank you, Mom!" Ksenya flew up from her cushion, hugging Sonya tightly. The girl's skinny frame vibrated with excitement. "Thank you! Thank you!"

Sonya returned the hug. Caressing Ksenya's sandy hair, she stared into the night outside the window. "You're welcome, kitten," she whispered. She couldn't speak louder, or she might start weeping.

Ksenya disengaged from Sonya's embrace and launched into an exuberant jig, in rhythm with the screeching TV. "Hooray, Dad is coming!"

"Why don't you run down and check the lottery numbers from yesterday," Sonya said. She always bought lottery tickets, at least one for every lottery drawing. Perhaps, she would be lucky this time.

"Okay," Ksenya agreed quickly. "What would you do, Mom, if you win?"

"What would I do?" Sonya hesitated. "I would enroll in the Emily Carr full time, and I would buy us a nice house." She met her daughter's expectant eyes, blue and shining with hope. Would she take Alexei back? Ksenya wanted that, but Sonya wasn't sure Alexei would agree. "I would help your dad," she said carefully.

"I love you." Ksenya smacked Sonya's cheek. "Yahoo! Let's win!" She hopped to the door, threw on her winter coat, and scampered out.

Sonya gazed after her daughter and fought tears. Her lips trembled. This was the first time Ksenya had said something nice to her since Alexei left. He still held the strings to his daughter's heart. Sonya slid to the floor inside the doorway to Ksenya's room, kicked the door open, and bawled. The door bounced back, hitting her.

She kicked it back, viciously. Tears almost blinded her. She needed to get all the wails out before Ksenya returned. The band on the TV kept up their earsplitting litany, and Sonya screamed, again—a long, loud howl. She was louder than the suckers, she thought in grim satisfaction. She could be their soloist. The red lights kept flashing while she pounded the carpeted floor with her fists, in rhythm with the ambulance tune. Salty drops trickled down her cheeks.

* * * *

VanDusen Botanical Garden was glorious with the Christmas Lights on. For once, the rain had stopped. Pushing Jane's chair around the pond, Sonya contemplated the multicolored lights that coruscated along the shoreline like fireflies. Echoing the melodies, the lights cascaded in a capricious waterfall or chased each other like sparkling fairies over the dark, reflective waters.

Their first Christmas in Vancouver, they had gone to see the lights together: Ksyushka, Alexei, and she. Sonya loved the musical display so much, she danced around the pond in her jeans and parka. Ksyushka squealed with glee. Alexei hummed and clapped loudly, spurring a bursting applause around the pond. This year, when Sonya had suggested an outing, Ksyushka looked at her with disgust.

Jane was exhilarated, though. "Turn left," she commanded.

Obediently, Sonya turned the chair to the left, into an alley. In the darkness, only the silhouettes of the other visitors were visible around the pond. Most of the silhouettes were coupled. Some traveled in larger groups. Sonya's shadow was the only one paired with a wheelchair.

"Talk to me!" Jane's scream was shrill and hiccupping. Her vocal cords were following the rest of her body into inactivity. Poor Jane.

"Once, we went to Hungary on a tour," Sonya started another story. Jane enjoyed listening to Sonya's dancing reminiscences, and Sonya loved telling tales to an appreciative audience. Better to recall her glorious days of solo dancing than wallow in self-pity. "Our ensemble performed in that old castle."

"Will you take me to see the lights next year?" Jane interrupted suddenly. "If I live."

Sonya circled the chair and squatted in front of the tiny, twisted body, bundled up in two coats and a blanket. "I will, Jane," she promised quietly. "Do you want me to dance for you?"

"Now?" Jane whispered.

The music started a new sequence, and the lights sprang up. Straightening, Sonya clapped her gloved hands in rhythm with the musical medley. Her feet found the simple steps, as she spun and stomped her heels after the spiraling lights. She followed the musical tide in a wild improvisation—a mix of her beloved *czardas*, mazurka, and tarantella. Their choreographer at the Petushko would've been horrified if he could see her now, performing such a formless desecration of the sacred art of folk dancing. Sonya didn't care. Her feet, her body, her arms—her entire being was luxuriating in the dance.

When the last note died away, she stilled, breathing heavily and puffing the steaming plumes into the freezing air. The cool, artificial fur of her collar felt nice against her flushed cheek.

"How was it?" she panted.

"Thank you!" Jane screeched. She couldn't clap, so she began keening in her excitement. "Oue-e-e!"

A few shadows behind the chair applauded politely.

"Thank you, everyone," Sonya murmured. Like a proper dancer, she sank into a deep curtsey. She bit her lower lip to keep from keening like Jane. Fortunately, nobody noticed her tears in the darkness.

Chapter Five
Sonya

"Mom! A MAC makeup kit!" Ksenya piped. "Oh, and the bath stuff! Thank you." She sat cross-legged under the plastic Christmas tree, decorated with holiday ornaments Sonya brought from Russia. A small, fuzzy bullfinch spun on its scarlet ribbon beside a sparkling, blue bell. A golden, glass mermaid swung below, reflecting the lights and throwing mischievous sparks to waltz around Ksenya's ponytail.

"What is here?" Ksenya muttered, tearing a red, gleaming packaging. Her tongue peeked out in her eagerness. "A Mimosa necklace? Yahoo!" She jumped to her feet among the colorful snippets of wrapping paper, a pink mascara tube in one hand, a crystal necklace swinging from the other. "Dad, have you seen it? Put it on me." Offering him the necklace, she turned around so he could fasten it at the back of her long, girlish neck.

"What do you have? A sweater. Wow! Cool, with these squiggles. Put it on! Put it on!" She hopped around Alexei, adjusting the new sweater, bringing out the collar of Alexei's denim shirt. The crystals of her necklace glittered merrily.

Smiling faintly, Sonya watched from her chair. Ksyushka was beaming, frisking about her dad, feeding him. Sonya's heart thumped painfully. She wasn't enough for her daughter. She would never be enough. No matter what she did, no matter what gifts she bought, her daughter would always need her father. Sonya swallowed a lump and smiled wider. No point in spoiling Ksenya's fun.

Alexei kissed Ksenya on the temple and lifted his eyes to look at Sonya over their daughter's head. For once, he was sober. "Thanks, Sonechka," he said. "Have you bought anything for yourself?"

"Oops." Ksenya glanced at her mother. "Have you, Mom?"

Sonya pointed to her chest. "This blouse." She bought the peach silk blouse a week ago in a thrift store for three bucks, but they didn't have to know the price. Originally, the blouse was huge, probably a size twenty. After she scaled it down to her size four, made frills for the deep décolletage, and sewed on the black appliqués to cover up the old grease stains that wouldn't wash off, it looked wild and vaguely Gypsy-ish.

Taking a deep breath, she stood up. "You musicians play," she commanded, putting on her stage smile. "Flamenco!" She grabbed her long, black skirt and lifted the flounced edge with two fingers, waving it like a streamer in front of Ksenya's eyes. Sonya's shoulders twitched beneath the peachy, shimmering fabric. One shoulder had slipped off, revealing an expanse of white skin, peppered with pale freckles, unlike her clear face.

"A Gypsy!" her daughter yelled, darting to her bedroom for the flute.

Grinning, Sonya nodded. Her three-layer earrings with a multitude of small, interconnected brass rings chimed approvingly.

Alexei pulled his clarinet out of the bag under his chair. When he straightened, his hands holding the instrument shook. Sonya felt his hungry eyes on her back as she scrambled from her corner to the middle of the room in front of the TV. Every nerve on her bare neck and shoulders quivered under his gaze.

"Let your hair down," he said hoarsely.

Sonya didn't turn. She tugged off the hair clip holding her hair together and let the auburn mass fall. "Where are my castanets?" Hurriedly, she rummaged in a cupboard.

Ksenya skipped out of her room and pulled a trill from her flute. Alexei fell into the counterpoint. An elaborate, silvery melody with a Spanish flavor poured off his instrument.

Hurriedly, Sonya adjusted the castanets, lifted both hands above her head, and let her fingers beat a lustful, gypsy rhythm on the tiny, wooden drums. Slowly lowering her hands and crossing them in front of her breasts with the castanets up, she started the dance—one of her favorites. Alexei followed with the complicated tinkling arabesques; his clarinet's clear notes spiraling around a simple melody of Ksenya's flute. Sonya lost herself in the sensual dance.

Alexei's clarinet wept and wailed mournfully while Ksenya, not entirely understanding her parents' emotions, slowed down. Sonya flowed around the room barefoot, like a real gypsy. Her castanets beat a languid staccato, one finger at a time, melancholy like the clarinet.

Impatient with them both, Ksenya removed the flute from her lips. "Faster!" she demanded and began playing a rapid polka.

"Yes!" Willingly, Sonya adopted the quicker tempo, her feet flashing under the frilly skirt.

The clarinet skipped a note and launched into a new scroll. Its musical tendrils curled rakishly around the straight tune of the flute.

Sonya danced. From the corner of her eye, she saw Alexei and Ksenya together at the table, tossing notes at each other, holding a conversation with their music. They looked happy like a picture on her *Palekh* jewelry box: a Russian knight and a fair maiden. She felt excluded, dancing outside their tightly knitted little family of woodwinds. She was a Jew. She didn't fit on a *Palekh* box. The rough percussions of her castanets didn't harmonize with their sweet, lilting melodies. With a frozen smile, she kept on dancing.

* * * *

After the ABC channel transmitted the midnight New Year's fireworks around the Seattle's Space Needle, Sonya sent Ksenya to bed. "Go sleep in the bedroom," she told Alexei. "You look tired. I'll clean up here, and I'll sleep on the sofa. I have a day off, tomorrow."

"Thank you, Sonechka." He sounded disappointed but ambled to the bedroom without objections. At the door, he turned. "Can I have a shower?"

"Sure," Sonya said. "Take a towel from the dresser." She heard him moving around in the bedroom before the bathroom door clicked and the water started.

Sonya put away the remaining salad and cake and wiped the crumbs off the white tablecloth. Why did she always do all the housework? Other women shared chores with their boyfriends. Why didn't she make Alexei do the dishes?

She sighed. She always felt sorry for him. He had complained about his misinterpreted musical genius since they had met, and she had been so smitten with her Russian troubadour knight, so susceptible to his charms, she had sympathized with him until recently. She still felt sorry for him—a stargazing artist, unable to cope with the hassles of real life and the hardships of immigration. She had always been the strong one in their union, while he was a naïve, cute baby trapped in the gorgeous body of a naïve, cute hulk, with a shock of blonde hair. The little blonde curlicues even covered most of his skin—torso, legs, and all. Soft and exciting to play with. Especially when they were damp after a shower. She played with all of them once upon a time.

Sonya looked longingly toward the bathroom door, her

femininity stirring, aching pleasantly. She had been without a man for so long! She couldn't abide a drunken partner, and today was the first time in ages she had seen Alexei sober and clean. Maybe she should drop everything and slip into the shower to join him or crawl into his bed? He would paw all over her, as always. She grinned, and her hand crept to her breast, cupping one small, round hillock. She tinkered with her peaking nipple through the thin silk of her blouse until the dishrag got in the way.

She dropped her hand. He hadn't invited her after all. She was so far gone, she was ready to service herself, craving Alexei's caress with a longing that twisted her guts. Anyone's caress would be good right now. People pleasured themselves here without shame, she knew, but her parents would be shocked. She shook her shoulders in self-disgust. She was such a slut!

Maybe they could make up after all. Maybe Alexei would start working. He said he had an offer from a small ensemble up the coast. He was going to an audition next week. Of course his hands shook, but he was probably hangover. He still played wonderfully. Sonya hadn't bought any alcohol for this night, not even champagne, and Alexei hadn't asked. Maybe by the audition, he'd be all right. Deliberately slow, Sonya folded the tablecloth and pressed all the edges with her fingers before putting it into the cupboard.

Picking up the torn paper scraps Ksenya left under the tree, Sonya forced her brain into a less luscious venue—her daughter's heritage. Through her father, Ksenya was linked to some minor Russian nobility. Beside them both, blonde and splendid, Sonya often felt like a Jewish drudge—undeserving of their august attention and grateful for the scraps. After all, her Jewish forefathers just owned a tiny shop in a Moldavian village. Only in dance did she feel adequate, but she didn't dance, anymore.

She went around the room, righting her bright, autumn-colored cushions, collecting the ribbons, and adjusting the pillows on the sofa. When she bent to the floor, her rippling mane of auburn hair fell into her face, and she absently flipped it back. Where had she put her hair clip? She couldn't find it. She tied her hair into a ponytail with the thin, red ribbon from one of the gifts and turned on the hot water in the kitchen. Halfway through the dishes, she began humming Tchaikovsky's *Neapolitan Dance* from *Swan Lake*. Had she won her family back?

* * * *

They spent New Year's Day together like a real family. They promenaded in Fraser River Park and then went bowling. The next day, during her break between the burgers and Jane, Sonya went to Safeway for her grocery shopping. After bowling, she had four twenty-dollar bills in her purse—more than enough for her weekly supplies.

"Sixty-two seventy-four," the young cashier said.

Sonya opened her purse, but only one twenty-dollar banknote flashed green in the bills compartment. Where had she put the other twenties? Frantically, she rummaged in the purse. She couldn't have lost sixty dollars!

"Sixty-two seventy-four," the cashier repeated. He looked tired and uncaring.

Sonya stared numbly into her purse. For a moment, her breath caught. She couldn't exhale. She should have three more twenties. Where had they gone? She forced the air out and in.

"Safeway card?" the cashier prodded.

"Yes, right. Sorry," Sonya muttered. Her cheeks flamed. She had never been so mortified in her life. She thrust her Safeway card and her Visa at the cashier. After her latest Visa payment, she should have about $200.00 below the limit. Would it work? She felt light-headed. The cashier swiped the plastic through the machine. Nothing beeped. The payment went through, and Sonya breathed easier.

It was Ksenya. Nobody else could've filched her money. The wretched girl had taken sixty bucks! Sonya's hands trembled as she signed the receipt and loaded her bags. They could've lived on this money for a week, but Ksenya probably gave the money to Alexei to buy booze.

Mutely, helplessly, Sonya cursed. She wanted to cry, to rage, to stomp her feet, but what would be the point? Both father and daughter were thieves and cheats! They had stolen from her. Should she complain to the police? What would that prove? Talk to Ksenya's councilor at school? No, that would be too humiliating. She would just kill them both when she returned home.

No. She couldn't do that, either. Alexei, the coward, had run away in the morning, smiling and leaving Ksenya to face her mother alone. Had he thought she wouldn't notice? He even kissed Sonya's lips goodbye, and she, the foolish woman, melted under his kiss. The filthy swine had robbed her! Again. He had made his daughter steal from her own mother.

She tried to swallow, but her throat locked up. At the memory of his hypocritical kiss, she jerkily wiped her mouth with a sleeve, her entire body shaking. She almost cut her lip with the plastic buckle on her sleeve. Marauders!

"Ksenya!" she yelled as soon as she opened the apartment door. "You took the money!" She couldn't suppress the hysterical notes in her voice. "You thought I wouldn't notice? You pig! How could you steal from your mother?"

Ksenya opened the door to her room, standing proudly on the threshold like a communist heroine caught by the Nazis in an old war movie.

"He didn't have any money!" Ksenya yelled back. "He would be hungry for the next week if I didn't give him those few freaking twenties. You would begrudge him the last piece of bread, wouldn't you? I won't allow it. He's my father."

"The lazy bum can work as I do. He is a parasite and a drunk!"

"You're a heartless bitch," Ksenya spat. "He can't work. Nobody understands his genius. I love him, and I hate you. You kicked him out. Now, you want him to starve to death!" Ksenya slammed the door to her room so hard, the Bohemian crystal dolls on the shelf tinkled in distress.

Sonya stared at the dolls. She bought them when the Ensemble toured Germany. How many years ago? She was still dancing, then. Ksenya was a sweet toddler. Now, the snotty damsel just shut off her mother? Not so fast!

Sonya yanked Ksenya's door open. "You're both rotten!" she raved. "Crooks and swindlers. He's on welfare, for God's sake. He's poisoning your ears, the bloody vampire, to suck me dry of my money. I welcomed him into my house." She sniffed and swallowed her tears. "Nobody even gave me a gift. I spent so much on gifts for both of you."

"You don't deserve our gifts," Ksenya said contemptuously. "You're miserly, selfish, and close-fisted. Get out of my room!"

Sonya started shivering. Before she could break down, she backed out.

Ksenya kicked the door closed. The bar hit home on the other side.

Sonya stood in front of her daughter's locked door. What was happening? How had they deteriorated so quickly? The door started blurring. She couldn't see the crack that snaked from the middle of the door down toward the floor. The entire door was hazy. She blinked fast to shake off the tears.

"He borrowed your freaking money and your freaking ring,

too," Ksenya shouted from her side of the door. "He'll pay you back as soon as he gets the money. With interest!"

"My ring," Sonya mouthed. Shuddering, she dried off the tears. Her hands felt unsteady, not connected right. She shuffled to her room. Her diamond ring, the wedding gift from her parents, was gone from the jewelry box. The *Palekh* pair on the box's black lacquer lid mocked her with their grins. Russian bandits, all of them! She dropped onto her bed and gazed unseeingly around the small room. The tramp had stolen her money, her ring, and her daughter. She had nothing left. Hugging herself, she swayed silently. What could she do?

What about her stash? She surged to her feet. Ksenya wasn't supposed to know about it. Neither was Alexei. She hoped.

Pattering into her walk-in closet, she lifted a pile of towels and pulled out the cardboard packing box from a miniature nightlight. Silently, she counted her emergency cash inside. Nobody had touched it. So far.

Letting out her pent-up breath, she took out two twenty-dollar bills and closed the box, pushing it back beneath the towels. Then, she readjusted the towels to look like nobody had disturbed the pile. With the twenty still in her purse, and the groceries already bought on her Visa, she should manage until the next paycheck. She pulled off her sweat-stained T-shirt with the burger place insignia, dropped it into her laundry basket, picked up a fresh sweater, and stepped out of the closet.

The door squeaked. Startled, Sonya glanced around, but the room was empty. Leaving her sweater on the bed, she tiptoed into the corridor in her jeans and bra. Where was Ksenya? Had she seen the cardboard box? The door to the girl's room was still closed. Sonya pushed on it, but it seemed to be locked.

"Go away. Leave me alone," Ksenya snarled from the other side of the door.

Sonya let go of the handle. Hopefully, Ksenya hadn't seen the cash box. The idea was so distasteful, Sonya almost started crying, again. Sniffing hard, she rubbed the goosebumps on her arms. It was chilly in the apartment. She went back to the bedroom to put on the sweater.

Chapter Six
Amanda

"Gloria, where is your photograph from the elementary school fair?"

Gloria limped into Amanda's bedroom, holding a small photo album. "Here it is—all my school photos. Are you going to take all of them with you?"

"You leg is hurting, again?" Amanda frowned. Maybe she should postpone her trip. Gloria still favored her leg, broken in the fall. It had been almost half a year since the accident. "Shouldn't you go see the doctor?"

"Don't fret, Mom. It's because I've been marching up and down the stairs of that Victorian monstrosity. Five floors and no elevator!" Gloria plopped onto Amanda's bed beside the suitcase. "I'll be fine tomorrow. The physiotherapy is really helpful."

"Couldn't McBride walk up and down the stairs? He knows you had your leg broken."

"Mom, this is the first contract for a hotel renovation we've had in years. I can't risk anything going wrong. I had to see it, myself. Anyway, what can you do? You're leaving. You don't have time to cosset me."

Gloria's volume dropped abruptly, and her tone turned bitter. "You never really have time for me," she mumbled, but Amanda heard every word as if they burned into her mind. The photo album was a dead weight in her hand, but she didn't know where to put it.

"You have unlimited time for that Russian brat of yours," Gloria continued. "A trip around the globe, for God's sake. You have time for your students, you had time for Dad, but never for me." She jumped up from the bed and would've dashed out of the room, but her limping speed was no match for her mother's. Amanda dropped the album and caught her daughter in a tight embrace.

"Gloria, honey. I had no inkling you felt this way," she said urgently. "Do you want me to postpone the trip? I can. I bought the insurance, but I thought you were okay. You said so." She looked into her daughter's eyes, green and glinting. She was afraid of what she could find there, but she had to know. Her pulse hammered. "I love you. You know I do."

Gloria stood rigid for one long moment before returning Amanda's hug. She lowered her lashes, dimming the green glow. The moment passed, and she was her familiar self, again—warm-hearted and smiling faintly at her mother. "Of course, I know. I'm sorry, Mom. Don't mind me. I'm just tired, and my leg hurts, so I whined. I'll be okay. You go and enjoy yourself."

She kissed Amanda's cheek and sat back down on the bed. "I'm happy for you and her, truly I am. I can't wait to meet her. Who is she to me? A quasi-sister, I guess." She chuckled. "Finish you packing, Mom."

Amanda sighed. She knew it wasn't the end, but she didn't want to dig to the bottom. That way lay calamity. She picked the album up from the floor and put it on top of her gray sweatshirt, put her navy-blue jacket over everything, smoothed the wrinkles, and zipped the suitcase shut. "I'm done." She dropped onto the bed beside Gloria.

Did Gloria really feel so resentful, so deprived of her mother's love? Had Amanda been neglecting her? Should she rectify her mistakes? Dedicate her life to Gloria from now on and abandon her quest for a Russian daughter? Would it mend the connection between Gloria and herself, the connection that had been cracking recently? What if it didn't?

"Do you want me to abort the whole scheme? Cancel the tickets?" she asked.

"Definitely not!" Gloria said sharply. "What if she's in trouble? Needs rescuing? You must go, but be careful."

Amanda felt her eyes dampening. She took a deep, calming breath. "Honey, you've been such a huge help. Thank you." She smiled gratefully and fell down, her arms outstretched. One of her hands ended up on a pillow, and the other caressed Gloria's thigh in the tight, olive jeans.

"Ask me if I haven't forgotten anything," she said.

Gloria snickered. "You're such a baby. All right. Your vitamins?"

"Check. In my carry-on." Still supine, Amanda pointed to the door, where her valise, made of the same blue-green tapestry as the suitcase, stood ready.

"Your black crepe dress?"

"What for? I'm not going to an evening party. I'm going to roam the country. I have T-shirts, jeans, sneakers, Capri pants, and my creamy silk suit. They have a holiday on May 9th."

"A couple of days after you arrive. Excellent! It'll cheer you up. What holiday?"

"Victory Day. Over Germany in World War II."

"Ah. Take the dress, anyway. Toilet paper? You said they used newspapers to wipe their asses. You might get a rash."

"Please!" Amanda giggled. "It was before you were born. We just celebrated your thirty-fourth birthday on Sunday. I'm sure even Russians have managed to resolve their toilet paper shortage in thirty-four years."

Gloria laughed so hard, she fell down, too. Her fiery hair spread around her face, covering Amanda's pastel white-and-peach coverlet like a bright, sunny fan. "Oh, Mom. Call me every day."

Amanda grabbed her daughter's hand, squeezing gently. "I will, honey," she promised.

She felt lost for words but resisted the impulse to revisit Gloria's abandonment issues, to worry the painful topic. What would she do if Gloria put an ultimatum in front of her? Which daughter would she choose? The answer was disconcertingly clear: of course, Gloria. Then, why was she even embarking on this absurd trip? If she canceled, she would always feel guilty afterward. She was such a foolish woman. Amanda snorted sadly and settled on neutrality. "Did you check the weather?"

"Yes. They announced rain in Moscow all next week and sunny in Vancouver."

"Just my luck," Amanda grumbled.

* * * *

The flight to Moscow was long and uneventful. Amanda shucked off her shoes as soon as the plane took off. She watched a movie with Nicolas Cage, read, and napped for an hour. Then, she worked on her article about Russian poet Sergey Esenin and his muse and wife, American dancer Isadora Duncan. Then, she napped, again. Intermittently, she ate and drank—a glass of red wine, a glass of white, and a glass of brandy. By the time the plane landed in Sheremetyevo, the Moscow main airport, her entire body felt wrung up, as if she had run a marathon instead of sitting for twelve hours. She hated transatlantic flights. Her feet were so swollen, she had trouble stuffing them back into her shoes.

As soon as she cleared customs, Robert—Donald's old friend and Amanda's former student—rushed toward her with his arms wide open.

"Amanda! You haven't changed." He enveloped her in a bear hug. "Welcome to Russia." His voice softened. "Sorry about Donald." With his rough-hewn face, Robert looked like a Viking. He was a head taller than Amanda and about twice as thick. The airport's bright, overhead lights reflected in his golden-blonde, shaggy hair and beard. There wasn't any gray there.

"Thank you, Bob. It's been some time. I'm over it." Amanda disentangled herself from the Viking's enthusiastic embrace. Looking around curiously, she tottered on her swollen feet after him.

Aside from the signs in Russian and English, the airport looked much the same as many other airports in the world. Maybe it was not as lush as the Vancouver airport, but it was not too bad. Passengers rushed in all directions with their wheeled luggage—past a currency exchange booth, past a newsstand, past a car rental and a coffee kiosk. Only something felt different, scratching at Amanda's strung-up nerves.

Finally, she captured the elusive deviation. The people were different. She could pinpoint foreigners and locals without even hearing them speak. Dressed almost identically, the locals had a distinct facial expression—drawn and unhappy. Their eyes seemed hungry. For food or for kindness, she wasn't sure. Maybe for both. Maybe for blood.

"Bob, I need a rental car." Amanda hurried to catch up with her big friend. "Have you arranged it? Can I drive here with a Canadian license?"

"You'll have a personal driver," Robert said mysteriously. He led the way out of the glass doors of the airport terminal.

Despite Gloria's prediction of rain, the weather outside was sunny and warm. Only a few clouds scattered across the blue sky, like fluffy white cottons. Robert tugged Amanda's suitcase toward a small, dark green car.

A bald, stocky man in an unbuttoned brown tweed jacket stood leaning on the car, his arms crossed over his wide chest. He straightened as they approached. With a magician's flare, he threw open the baggage compartment.

"Good afternoon, Mrs. Barnett," he said, bowing slightly. "I'm Sergey Pechkin." He offered her his hand. As with everything about him, his palm was wide and solid. He accepted Amanda's hand but instead of a handshake, he bent over it and brushed his lips across Amanda's knuckles in an old-fashioned kiss. "Welcome to Moscow," he said with a faint curve of his lips. His quick gaze traveled along her trim figure, clad in pink jeans, a black sweater, and a purple blazer. His gray eyes gleamed in appreciation.

"Thank you, Mister Pechkin." Amanda pulled her hand free. "Thanks for signing my visa." Suddenly, she felt shy. Why was she shy? The man was a tad older than her daughter, in his mid-forties at the most. She should be feeling like an old matron, like a patronizing professor with a young, ignorant student. Instead, she felt small, protected, and feminine—a long-forgotten feeling. Sergey's solid width seemed somehow flattering. For the first time since Donald's death, she sensed a man's interest in her, and she suddenly wanted to return the favor.

Silly old hen. She berated herself mutely. He was just playing host to a rich, Canadian broad; however, his kiss and smile said otherwise, hinting at an intimate invitation.

"Call me Amanda," she blurted, ducking into the front passenger seat of the car to hide her embarrassment. Let the men deal with her luggage.

"You call me Sergey," Sergey said as he settled at the wheel. Robert folded his large frame into the back seat. "I have a self-interest in helping you, ma'am." Sergey turned the key in the ignition. "I'm a journalist. My magazine wants the exclusive rights to your story in Russia. I'm going to cover it, so I'll accompany you on your search for your daughter. My Lada is at your disposal." Keeping one hand on the wheel, he encompassed the car's modest, brown interior with an expansive gesture. "I hope you don't mind?" Two golden teeth flashed in his mouth when he grinned.

"Of course not. I'll be glad to have your company. Sergey?"

"Yes?"

"You have a wonderful command of English, but I'd like to speak only Russian while I'm here." She switched to Russian. "I hope you don't mind."

"I was hoping to refresh my English," he said, petulant like a young boy.

"I'll invite you to Vancouver next year," Amanda promised impulsively. The car bumped on an invisible rut, and she winced.

"Could you tell me more about your mission? Your family?" Sergey asked.

"Later."

The car finally reached Moscow, and Amanda stuck her nose to the window. She remembered the city as stately and proud, and the memories of the Moscow Metro still infused her with nostalgia. Now, the city terrified her.

The entire street blocks resembled open markets—noisy and untidy. The counters under dirty awnings were piled with clothes, shoes, and some other objects Amanda couldn't see clearly, since the car moved too fast. Scraps of wrapping papers and some unidentifiable, greenish fragments littered the sidewalks. Pale-faced Muscovites mulled about the makeshift stalls, blocking the passage and spilling into the roadside. Dark-haired, swarthy individuals in fur hats or checkered caps—obviously not Russians—strolled around arrogantly, as if they owned the district. Maybe they did. The markets, one after another, dotted the main highway from the airport to the Kremlin. What conspired in the back streets, Amanda wondered?

"What are they all selling?" she asked, as another of the crude markets whisked by. A smell of rotten cabbage wafted past the open window of the car. Wrinkling her nose, she rolled up the window.

"Everything." Sergey's wide-set, gray eyes darkened.

Amanda detected a smudge of bitterness in his polite, velvety baritone.

"The entire country seems to forget how to make things. Everybody is only buying and selling. My wife works at a bakery kiosk near a Metro station." His pursed mouth jerked derisively. "She sells cakes and tortes. Earns good money, too."

Amanda bit her lip. The guy was married, after all. Of course, if he were single, it would've been too good to be true.

Sensing her unease, Robert barged in. "You'll start for Vladimir next week, after the long weekend. We've planned an entertainment program for you this week. On May 9th, we'll all go to the Poklonnaya Gora. They've built a large museum complex there to commemorate the Russians' victory over Hitler. They're going to have a huge celebration. I also bought tickets to the Bolshoi Ballet. You'll love it."

"Thanks, Bob," Amanda murmured. "I hope you'll give me a day or two to recover my bearings. I'm kind of fuzzy."

"Of course. Sorry. Tomorrow, we'll only take you to the Kremlin and to the Alexandrov Garden. You have to see the Neglinka River in the open. It was hidden in the pipes when you last visited, and it's decorated with a fountain and with Russian fairytale statues. We'll show you the monument to Peter the Great, as well. There is a controversy about it. Some hate it, but I think it's marvelous."

"Okay," Amanda said faintly, overwhelmed by Robert's list. "I wish to do some shopping, too. I need Russian souvenirs."

"You'd better buy them in Vladimir," Sergey intruded. "The souvenir industry is flourishing there."

Again, Amanda detected traces of bitterness in his tone. Ignoring his remark, she half-turned to Robert, who was sprawled behind them. "Where is my hotel?"

"You're staying with me and my wife," he boomed.

* * * *

Robert's wife Rebecca was big, tall, and, fair—a fit partner for her Viking husband. After dinner, Rebecca sent Amanda straight to bed via a hot shower. "Leave the poor woman alone," she ordered, when her husband suggested a night out.

"It's early, yet," Amanda protested. She swallowed a yawn and tried to keep her eyes open. "Only seven in the afternoon. I have to adjust to the local time. Just give me some coffee, please."

"It's early morning in Vancouver. You'll adjust gradually. How long did you sleep on the plane?"

"A couple of hours."

"To bed with you!" Rebecca's voice brooked no arguments.

Meekly, Amanda obeyed. She fell asleep instantly.

When she woke up, it was still dark. Her bedside digital clock showed 3:20. Climbing out of bed, she tiptoed barefoot across the small guest room. Outside, below her sixth-story window, a couple of electric street lights illuminated a small park, surrounded by tall, brick buildings. Robert told her that the entire complex was occupied by foreign journalists and minor diplomatic staff.

Amanda gazed down at the trees that stood with their branches still naked. A faint smell of bulging buds, ready to burst open, drifted to her nose through the small, open window leaf. In Vancouver, the rhododendrons were already in full bloom, but the Moscow spring was slow and late. It was also raining. Gloria's forecast had been correct after all.

Somewhere in this country, still in the last grips of winter despite the May calendar, Amanda's other daughter waited to be found. Sighing, Amanda turned on a reading lamp affixed over her bed. She wasn't sleepy, anymore; might as well finish that article about the effect Isadora Duncan's dancing had on Sergey Esenin's poems of the last period of his life.

* * * *

"Rebecca, why are the windows armored?" Puzzled, Amanda glared at the colored photographs of cheeses and sausages decorating the metal plates behind the huge, glass windows of a grocery store. Located on the first floor of a beautiful, eight-story building built in the 1950's, the store had a sufficient selection of breads, pastas, meats, and dairy products, although not as wide as she was used to at home. Only the produce section was dismal. The smelly onions, disheveled cabbages, dirty carrots, and potatoes were so unappetizing, Amanda hurried past the counters. What was there to protect with armored metal?

"Thieves would break in otherwise," Rebecca said. "The rest of the country is not as fortunate as Moscow."

Amanda nodded. "Okay. This is fortunate. I understand. Where do you buy produce? I'd like some fresh strawberries."

Unexpectedly, Rebecca burst into laughter. "You've forgotten where you're. They tell an old joke here about a Russian man and an American. 'When can you buy first strawberries?' the Russian asks. 'At nine in the morning, when a store opens,' replies the American. 'What about you?' The Russian says, 'In June.'"

"You're kidding!" Amanda said.

"No. There is fresh lettuce and radishes at a public market. Green onion, too. I'll pick them up myself, later. We'll have a Russian spring salad. You're in Russia, Amanda."

"I see. I'm in Russia," Amanda repeated.

Later that day, Rebecca took her sightseeing. Robert was busy, so they went without him. Amanda dutifully admired the recently restored old churches around the Red Square. Although the churches were too gaudy for her taste, when Rebecca brought her to the shore of the Moskva River, she gasped in all sincerity. The huge, new monument to Peter the Great rose in the middle of the dark gray river.

"It's lovely and so majestic! So Russian," she said.

Rebecca snorted. "Some disagree. The sculptor is Georgian, you know. Zurab Tsereteli."

Amanda leaned on the parapet, holding her black umbrella tightly and marveling at the beautiful statue. The famous Russian tsar stood proudly on the bow of his ship that sailed along the Moskva River. He stared ahead into the future—a cruel visionary, propelling his resisting kingdom into the new age with ruthless determination.

"I'm absolutely in love with it," Amanda said. She didn't want to leave, until Rebecca pulled her forcibly away toward the Kremlin and the Alexandrov Garden.

In the garden along the Neglinka River, cute little statues out of the Russian fairytales scampered merrily all the way to the big fountain with its horses. The rain that had been falling steadily since the night of Amanda's arrival finally caused all the tight buds of the trees to break open. Bright green, spring foliage shimmered like an emerald web in front of the old, dark green spruce trees beneath the red brick, Kremlin wall.

"Are you hungry?" Rebecca asked, huddling under her umbrella. "There is a subterranean mall under the Manege Building. We can grab a bite."

"Yes, let's get out of this rain," Amanda agreed.

"You're from Vancouver. You must be impervious to rain." Eagerly, Rebecca hastened her steps, rushing past the crowd of tourists along the Neglinka River to the pedestrian underpass to the mall.

Amanda followed without haste, inhaling the sweet spring scent of water and leaves, unexpectedly enjoying her solitary vacation. The last time she had gone anywhere as a tourist, she was with Donald. They had gone to Spain, together. She thought she would never relish any new sights without him, but she did. She had her Russian daughter to thank for it.

Her eyes opened wide, as if she had just woken up from an enchanted slumber. Everyone had their umbrellas open, and she halted, transfixed by the view. All those multihued umbrellas seemed to screen Neglinka from the rest of the garden. In Vancouver, most people—Amanda among them—preferred black umbrellas. Here, an unbroken ribbon of colorful umbrellas looked like a rainbow that had stepped down to Earth, to pay tribute to Neglinka—a tiny brook inside the gigantic megalopolis.

Neglinka gurgled quietly under the rain, indifferent to the homage. The newly minted leaves soughed above the water like a green whisper. Awkwardly holding her umbrella with her shoulder, Amanda took a few snapshots with her camera. This would be a great illustration for her "daughter" book.

"Amanda, hurry up!"

Amanda caught up with Rebecca. "Rebecca, look. It's so beautiful." She slowly folded her own black umbrella, shaking off the water.

"You're a romantic," Rebecca said with a chuckle.

They ducked into the mall. The familiar names jumped at Amanda: Gap, Guess, Mantique. "It's all the same." She grimaced in disappointment. "I didn't need to fly around the globe to see these shops. I could've driven downtown. Takes fifteen minutes."

"I told you." Rebecca pulled Amanda toward the Food Fair. "I'm famished. I hate the rain."

"Oh, look!" Amanda halted suddenly, excited again. "This is Russia. I want a picture for my book. Nobody would believe it otherwise." She thrust her camera into Rebecca's hands and darted across a steady stream of people. In the middle of the shining mall, between the familiar Guess label and a European fur store, the marble ceiling was leaking. Water dripped steadily into a bucket some considerate soul had placed under the leaking spot.

The bucket had probably been used a few years earlier, during the construction of the mall. It was splattered with paint, dented, and rusty. Maybe it had even been used during the Russian Revolution. Amanda's eyes sparkled with glee. The bucket looked as old as the Kremlin, and it was full to the brim, spilling out dirty water. A rainbow puddle was spreading around it on the marble floor, forcing people to circumvent the ancient implement in growing semi-circles.

Amanda posed behind the bucket, in the middle of the puddle. "Take a picture, Rebecca," she crowed. "Hurry, before someone takes it away."

"A dreamer, too," Rebecca muttered, clicking the camera.

A saleswoman stood leaning in the Guess doorway. Dressed in an elegant, red business suit, her feet wearing expensive, black high-heels, she regarded Amanda and Rebecca, both in their old, wet jeans and sneakers, with haughty displeasure.

Chapter Seven
Amanda

Victory Day, May 9th, dawned sunny. Still in bed, Amanda stretched lazily. Today, they would go to the victory celebration on the Poklonnaya Gora—the hill in the middle of Moscow, where the Muscovites built a museum complex to commemorate their Victory over Hitler. Tomorrow, Sergey would drive her to Vladimir. Very soon, she would meet her daughter for the first time. What would she say to her?

Amanda glanced at the clock: 6:45. Nobody was up, yet. The jet lag was still affecting her sleeping. She pulled out her notebook and started drafting a possible introductory speech to her daughter. What was her name? She still didn't know. She would use an 'X' for now.

"Hello, dear X. You know, I'm your mother. They switched you and my daughter during birth." No, that sounded ridiculous. Amanda crossed off the text and started again. "Hello, X. I'm Amanda Barnett. I live in Canada. Recently, I've discovered that my daughter is not really my daughter. I think you're my real daughter, because..."

Amanda grimaced in exasperation. This was even worse.

Ripping off the ruined page, she crumpled it into a tight ball and tossed the ball into the wastebasket in the corner. The paper ball didn't make it, dropping short of the basket. Amanda stared at the clean sheet. What was she going to say? Maybe she should abort her mission, at least for a little while? Maybe she should call Gloria, instead? She didn't have to think about what to say to Gloria. Grinning at the absurdity of the notion, she grabbed the phone.

Gloria answered on the second ring. "Mom! You haven't called for three days!"

"I'm fine, honey. Sorry. Too many impressions. How are you? You know, Russian women dress so much better than we do."

Gloria laughed. "I love you, Mom."

* * * *

"I'm sorry I was busy all morning. We'll reach Vladimir before dusk, anyway. I promise," Sergey said a couple days later. His green Lada sped east, taking them closer to Amanda's Russian daughter with every passing kilometer.

Unfortunately, Amanda still didn't know what to say when they would finally meet. Maybe, the young woman wouldn't believe her? Maybe she was happy with her life and wouldn't want to accept her new, Canadian relations. Before arriving in Moscow, Amanda hadn't wanted to think about her first conversation with her new daughter. She trusted her instincts to guide her. Now, she cursed herself for a fool.

There should be some serious psychological research already done on the subject of long-lost children, switched at birth. She couldn't use a soap opera as a guideline. She had six months to get ready. Why hadn't she conducted any scientific investigation? She was a professor. Why was she plunging into this—the most important meeting of her life—unprepared like a fifth grader?

"Amanda? Something is bothering you?"

Amanda squinted against the sun that beat into her eyes. The green meadows rushed by the window. She lowered the sunshade of the car as far down as it would go and put on her sunglasses.

"I don't know what to say to my daughter," she said feebly. "Anything I come up with sounds lame. The situation is only good for a silly TV series. It doesn't translate well into real life."

Sergey snorted. "It'll come," he said. "Think about something else."

"About what?" Amanda turned to look at him. His solid figure and the glistening crown of his bald pate abruptly filled her with new confidence. In profile, he wasn't beautiful, not even handsome. His nose resembled a duck's beak—flat and wide.

He smiled fleetingly before returning his attention to the road, but his elusive grin made her heart skip a beat. The quick caress of his eyes more than made up for the ugly nose.

Amanda swallowed, her imagination plummeting from the high concepts of motherhood down toward her stomach. She squeaked out the first words that popped into her mind.

"Tell me about your family."

His face hardened, and his eyes turned to steel. "I'd better not. I don't like the topic."

"Okay," Amanda said quickly. "Sorry. I didn't mean to offend you."

"You didn't," he said. His flitting grin came back and went, again. "Have you thought about the bribes you'll need to get the information? Do you have cash, in American currency?"

"The bribes? American currency? No. I have some Canadian money. Forty dollars or so. I have credit cards."

Sergey's shoulders shook with silent laughter.

"What's so funny?" Amanda bristled. "The Canadian dollar is just as good. It's been steady for years." *Unlike the Russian ruble*, she thought spitefully but didn't voice such uncharitable thoughts. Let him laugh. She wouldn't descend to his level. The Russian boor!

"Amanda." Sergey finally brought his hilarity under control, although his lips still twitched and his wide nostrils flared. "You need information from some thirty-odd-year-old records. It means the clerks will have to search a few drawers, leaf through old ledgers, perhaps go to another room, or even to the archives in another building. The rules about such searches are ambiguous at best, and most clerks don't know them. It would be a private endeavor for the majority of them."

"Surely, there are service fees? Why do you call them bribes?"

This time, Sergey laughed so hard, he had to stop the car. Still chuckling, he half turned to face Amanda.

She pouted, waiting for his explanation in stony silence.

"There might be a service fee, but it's usually low, and the clerks wouldn't get it, anyway. The money goes to the government, or whatever ruling body owns the office. You have to give the people an incentive to do their jobs."

"In Canada, people go to jail for such a felony," Amanda said acidly. "They are paid salaries to do their jobs."

"In Russia, people can't live on their salaries," Sergey said grimly. "In many cases, it's below the poverty level. They need bribes to survive."

Amanda deflated.

"Consider those bribes service fees," Sergey advised, as he restarted the car. "We'll stop at the Currency Exchange in Vladimir. They'll take your credit cards."

"Then, why American money?"

"Because nobody here knows what a Canadian dollar looks like or what it's worth. They wouldn't be sure whether it's money or colored paper. Trust me, Amanda. Get American. Nothing to do with your patriotism, believe me. Just common sense."

"How much do I need?" Suddenly, she was afraid she wasn't

rich enough to pull it off. A deep bribe could be anywhere from tens to hundreds of thousands of dollars, and if she had to bribe five or six clerks, she could be out by a six-figure sum in no time. Gloria would be mad. Maybe she should abort permanently? She hadn't thought it could be so expensive.

"Fifty dollars is enough for one person. For a hundred, a clerk would roll over backwards for you."

Amanda winced. She discerned the same bitterness in his words as she had espied earlier, the first day they met. Now, she understood it. The man was a patriot, and he was ashamed for his country and his people, reduced to such disgrace by poverty. She opened her mouth, closed it again, and stayed silent for some time. How much would he get for this assignment, for driving and baby-sitting her twenty-four-seven, she wondered?

"Tell me about your research on Russian literature," Sergey said at last.

Glad to indulge in her favorite topic, Amanda obliged. "I study the roles of women in Russian literature. Women writers, women poets, women muses, and women protagonists. Do you know that Karolina Pavlova was a contemporary of Pushkin, one of the best Russian poets of that time, and nobody knows about her now?" She talked, and Sergey nodded thoughtfully, without taking his eyes off the road.

"I'll drive from here," Amanda offered later. They were trudging toward the car after a snack at a roadside café. To Amanda's chagrin, the café didn't have anything decent, except for the traditional Russian pancakes. Even those were not too tasty.

"It's a standard, not automatic," Sergey said.

"I can drive a standard."

"A woman of many talents." Keeping a straight face, Sergey sprawled across the passenger seat, winked, and closed his eyes.

"Poser," Amanda muttered. She pulled out of the parking lot. By the time she reached the highway, she was navigating the unfamiliar roads with Sergey's old, frayed-along-the-edges road map. He was fast asleep, snoring like an elephant. No, rather like an untamed boar.

At least the man had one real fault, Amanda mused as she steered the car past a tourist bus. She had already passed three other buses carrying different foreign flags. Obviously, like at the time of Gloria's birth, Vladimir remained a strong tourist attraction for the foreigners.

To block off Sergey's loud, quavering oinks, Amanda turned

on the car's CD-player. The only familiar name was Vladimir Vysotsky. She knew and disliked the Russian bard and his rude songs. Vysotsky's poetry was too unrefined, almost vulgar, but somehow, he fit this little car and the crazy country behind the car window. Fine! Filled with perverse satisfaction, she let the singer fill the car with his hoarse, screaming poems. Although Vysotsky yelled his painful songs at top decibels, Sergey didn't stir. Amanda drove on.

Around five in the afternoon, they entered the city of Vladimir. By that time, the rain had started again, painting slanting, gray lines on the window glass. Amanda parked the car at the sidewalk and turned to her passenger.

As soon as the car stopped moving, his eyelids fluttered open. "Arrived?" His voice sounded slurred and coarse after a couple of hours of snoring. He stretched and growled like a dog, his hands touching the ceiling. He glanced at Amanda.

"Sorry I dropped off like that." The powerful muscles of his chest quivered under his thin, blue-and-white jersey shirt.

"You snore," she accused. She tried to keep her gaze firmly on his face, but her eyes seemed to have a different agenda, straying lower of their own accord, to the sprinkling of dark hair in the V of his unbuttoned shirt collar.

"I know. Some irregularity in my nose. What time is it?" He jerked up his sleeve to look at his watch. "It's five already." He yawned. "Move over, Amanda. I'll drive to the Currency Exchange." He opened the door and raced around the front fender toward the driver's door.

Amanda scooted to the passenger's seat.

Sergey dove in and shook his wide shoulders. "The rain is freezing."

At the Currency Exchange, Amanda got $1,000 in American bills of fifties. She also bought ten blank, white envelopes the Exchange office conveniently sold. Under Sergey's indulgent gaze, she stuffed two bills per envelope and stored all ten envelopes in the inside, zipped-up pocket of her purse. She had never carried so much cash, and she felt nervous.

"Let's go to the hotel," Sergey said. "The hospital office is closed. We'll go there tomorrow, first thing in the morning." The silky softness returned to his voice, and the ordinary words sounded like a caress, making Amanda shiver.

If he booked one room, she decided she would kick him out. She was paying too much attention to his voice and the width of his shoulders as it was, and the arrogant Russian didn't even notice. She savored the thought until they arrived at the hotel. Sergey picked up two keys at the reception counter.

"How much?" Amanda pulled out her Visa.

"The magazine pays all expenses. Your story should be sensational." He grinned and dropped Amanda's key into her palm. "My room is across the hall. Go freshen up a bit. We'll meet at the restaurant downstairs." Swinging his key on his finger, he crossed the hall to his room, half-turned, flashed a wide, golden-toothed grin to Amanda, and disappeared behind his door.

You're crazy, woman, Amanda thought as she dropped down on the bed in her room. The room was small and contained only a queen-size bed, two side tables, a chair, and a narrow desk. Not a Five Stars hotel, and not even a four. Just a modest hostelry catering to an average tourist. An average *foreign* tourist, she amended. The reception's desk clerk spoke fluent English. Would a room look different in a hotel that only housed Russians?

She looked around with new eyes. The headboard, the tables, and the desk were all wood—not plywood or plastic—polished and varnished to the dark brown of walnut. Perhaps it *was* walnut. The bedcover and chair cushions were of expensive, light-yellow brocade with green pine boughs interlacing in an elegant, slightly convex design. The built-in closet's door and, next to it, the door to the bathroom were both made of the same wood. With her finger, Amanda traced the tiny, carved arabesques of the frame surrounding a full-length mirror in the closet's door panel. The mirror reflected her thin finger and the pale-pink nail polish.

She turned on the bathroom lights. No bath. Just a shower stall, screened off from the rest of the tiny bathroom by panes of etched glass. The patterned tiles covered the walls from floor to ceiling—tiny, chocolate houses and trees on a creamy background. The sink was beige, as was the toilet. She sniffed at the off-white, fluffy towels. They smelled of lemon verbena. Maybe it was a five-star hotel after all. That magazine wanted her story so badly, they spared no expenses.

She gazed at her reflection in the bathroom mirror. Her dusty-blonde hair didn't show any gray yet, and her skin was relatively smooth, but her gray eyes were firmly bracketed by the chicken legs of wrinkles. She didn't look her age, but she didn't look young and vibrant, either. Sergey was a virile man, not much older than Gloria. He couldn't be interested in her. He was just doing his job, worming his way under her skin to get as much of her story as he could. The rotten charmer! He had almost fooled her, and she was ready for him to enthrall her, thinking with her vagina instead of her head. Like a horny teenager.

Amanda squirmed. No, not a teenager. A horny, aging woman, grabbing for her last chance with a younger man. What a pathetic scenario! Perhaps she should write it all in her book. Publishers and readers would love some dirty laundry. They called it sincerity. She grinned and turned on the shower.

An hour later, she was clean and rested. She put on her best makeup, styled her hair, and marched downstairs to the bar. Her hips swayed above the high heels of her pumps. Bless Gloria for having insisted that Amanda packed her black, sequined dress. She hadn't forgotten how to flirt, yet. The Russian bear would get a dose of his own medicine. She would knock him off his feet and have fun doing it! Licking her lips, Amanda sailed into the bar to do battle.

* * * *

The next morning, she was sorry she had. She did remember how to flirt, but her metabolism had forgotten how to drink. Her head rattled from the smallest noise, and Sergey, the Russian swain, didn't seem to be affected at all by all those vodka martinis they had consumed, yesterday. He looked as cool and sappy as a pine cone as he opened the car door with a smart bow. Amanda sniffed. His aftershave even smelled of pine needles.

"Hangover, Amanda?"

Amanda lifted her nose into the air and instantly regretted it. The sun, even filtered by a thin layer of clouds, struck her sensitive eyes. *Maybe he was a spy*, she thought sullenly, rummaging blindly in her purse for her sunglasses. Maybe he conspired with the waiter and drank only water. Amanda donned her sunglasses and settled into the car. Yeah, right! Maybe, she was an idiot. It was much more possible. Sergey turned the key in the ignition, and she winced from the clatter. Yes, she was definitely a fool.

"This is the maternity ward," Sergey said a few minutes later. He stopped the car and nodded at an old brick building.

"What is that?" Amanda pointed at the curly, wire fence surrounding a long, gray barrack across the street. "Looks like a prison."

"It is," Sergey said.

Amanda blinked. "A prison next to a maternity ward?" She

didn't remember ever being in this place. "Do they have another maternity ward? I'm not sure it was here."

"This is number one, the biggest. Let's check here first." Sergey climbed out of the car.

Amanda followed him into the hospital. Why wasn't her memory stirring? She only remembered that the snow hadn't yet melted that day, April 30th, thirty-four years ago. It had still been lying in shady corners in packed, black heaps, despite the bright sun. She remembered her surprise when someone told her it was snow and her exhilaration at seeing another red-haired baby. It had been her daughter, and she hadn't recognized her.

She didn't remember the other mother—just a vague silhouette, short and plump. No name, no face. Nothing. She remembered how they had laughed together. They compared their red-haired baby girls and complained about the scarcity of doctors and nurses. Amanda remembered that, too. It had been a long weekend. May 1st, a state holiday in Russia.

Suddenly, she felt dizzy. Soon! She would meet her daughter soon for the first time. Her heart pummeled rapidly in her chest, and she had to gulp air through the tightening in her lungs. What would she say? She shook her head to dispel the dizziness and rushed after Sergey.

The medical personnel in their white gowns passed to and fro along the hall. Young men and old parents sat in the waiting room, talking quietly. A nurse in a white gown pushed a gurney with a moaning woman into a cross-corridor. Strangely, no words reached Amanda's brain and no faces registered. They remained gray outlines, like that woman who had been the mother of her daughter for the last thirty-four years. Sucked into her surreal memory, Amanda grabbed the wall to keep upright.

"Amanda?" Sergey halted and turned back to her. "Do you want to sit down? You're very pale. I can do it without you."

"No, thanks." Sergey's hand on her elbow steadied her, flinging her back into reality. Breathing deeply, she smiled, ashamed of her display of feelings. "I'm fine. Yesterday's drinking binge, no doubt."

Sergey grunted noncommittally and turned into the reception area. Before Amanda said anything, he introduced himself as a journalist from Moscow and asked for the records for the last forty years. "I'm doing a research on the red-headed babies in Russia," he concluded brazenly.

Amanda recognized his smile, sweet and suave—his working

face. She kept her tongue still and breathed through her nose.

The receptionist, a middle-aged, overweight, and swarthy woman with a dull and puffy face, melted. "Of course. Go to that corridor and turn right. The records room is in the basement."

"Thank you so much!" Sergey's smile flashed, again. "Can I mention your name in my article?"

That clinched it. Amanda bit her lip to maintain a serious façade and not dissolve into mad giggles.

"Tamara Poleschuk," the receptionist said in a breathy voice.

Before any other scene of this farce developed, Amanda pulled Sergey into the indicated corridor. "You're despicable," she hissed, fighting laughter.

He grinned unrepentantly. "If I told her it was for a foreigner, we would be fighting with red herrings and filling out forms until Doomsday. It's much faster this way, and no fuss. That's why I'm here."

"You didn't have to flirt so outrageously," Amanda spit out before she could process the words. When she did, she felt herself turning crimson. She was grateful for the dim light in the stairway. It concealed her embarrassment. Somewhat.

"Jealous, Amanda?"

Amanda wouldn't reply or look at him. With her spine ramrod-straight, she strode into the records room. She had made a fool of herself. She didn't have to compound her stupidity by a verbal acknowledgement.

The records room was long, filled with old, wooden bookcases stuffed with white cardboard boxes. Paint peeled from the walls, and a crack ran across the ceiling, stained by some dark encroachments. Apparently, this hospital hadn't yet transferred its records into a computer.

The woman at the front desk was about Amanda's age, with a ponytail of gray, lusterless hair and a pale face, lined with wrinkles. Amanda staggered from the hopelessness filling the woman's eyes—gray, like Amanda's.

"Amanda, that's your show," Sergey whispered in English.

Amanda cleared her throat and told her story.

"You gave birth here?" The woman's tired eyes began to sparkle.

"I think it was here," Amanda said. "I'm not certain. It was in Vladimir. Could we look at the records from that day, please?"

The record clerk frowned, and her wrinkles deepened. "I'm not sure I can allow a foreigner to look at the records. There are some forms you should fill out. Perhaps I should call my supervisor."

Her bony hand stretched toward the telephone, hovered uncertainly, and dropped back onto the desk while her eyes devoured Amanda.

"Perhaps there's a service fee for speeding it up?" Amanda hurried on. "I hope this will cover it. We don't have much time to go through the official channels." She pulled out one of the envelopes with a hundred American dollars and put it on the desk.

The woman snatched the envelope, glanced inside, and smiled with obvious relief. "Yes, of course. What year was it?" She stood up.

Amanda told her the date. The woman disappeared between the shelves of her domain. She came back to the table carrying a white box in both hands.

"Let's see," she said, opening the box. "April 30th."

Amanda held her breath.

The woman's long, emaciated fingers leafed through the folders in the box. Finally, she pulled one out.

"Amanda Barnett, Canada, a girl," she said, her short nail without nail polish moving across the handwritten form. The ink had already faded to a light blue, and the lined paper had turned brittle and creamy.

"Yes, that's me," Amanda mouthed. "So, it *was* here."

The woman continued reading. "There were five other girls born on the same day. I'll write down the names and addresses for you." She pulled out a fresh sheet of paper and settled at her desk. "Of course, I don't know which one was a red-head. The records don't say."

"Of course," Amanda whispered.

Afraid her burning gaze would slow the woman's pen, Amanda looked around. The closest wooden bookcase was so old that the finish rubbed off in many places. The naked, gray wood looked like patches of lichen on the formerly bright yellow varnish.

"Here it is." The woman offered Amanda a list of five names.

1. Irina Alpashkina
2. Nina Savchenko
3. Tatiana Vetrova
4. Dina Goldberg
5. Elena Panashvili

Every name had an attached address. Amanda felt nauseous. One of those names was the mother of her daughter. *I'm losing it*, she thought suddenly. She was the mother, not that faceless woman. Or was she?

Chapter Eight
Sonya

"Ksenya!" Sonya called from the door. "Slattern! You could've cleaned up."

Nobody answered. Of course, the girl wasn't home. As usual, she returned after school, gobbled up her lunch, and skipped out, leaving a pile of dirty dishes and a jumble of cutlery scattered around the tiny kitchen. The kitchen looked like a horde of hungry rats had swept through it. With practiced eyes, Sonya assessed the numbers of forks and crumbs. Well, maybe not a horde, but certainly more than one rat. Ksenya fed someone, probably Alexei. He stole her money, her daughter, and her food. He never even said thank you.

"Glutton, drunkard, and a thief," Sonya murmured without rancor. She was too tired to be angry. Besides, was it really stealing if his daughter offered him food? No matter who had paid for it? Sighing, Sonya tossed her purse onto a narrow dresser and untied her sneakers.

For Alexei, this was a matter of survival. If he didn't eat what his daughter provided, he would starve. Alcoholism was an illness, and Alexei needed treatment, but he didn't want it. He wanted to play music, to be a genius. Idiot! Criminal! He was pulling Ksenya into his abyss with him. Sonya couldn't imagine what she could do to stop their mutual slide into nowhere.

At least she understood Ksenya. For the girl, stealing from her mother was as much a part of her teenage rebellion as being sloppy. Ksenya was pushing her mother, testing waters, and being noble in the process. She was saving her father. Sonya cursed in disgust. Blight Alexei for driving this wedge between her and her daughter. One of these days, Ksenya would push her mother too far.

Not today, though. Let her feed her drunkard dad one more day. Let her be his savior—on Sonya's expense. Gosh, she was so close-fisted! Ksenya was right about that.

Sonya grabbed an apple from a wooden platter on the table and put a kettle on the stove for tea. She should eat more, herself.

She was losing weight, but she didn't have the energy. Nibbling on the apple, she gathered dirty plates, cups, and spoons. In a couple of hours, she would have to leave for her shift with Jane. Then, Ksenya would come home...and litter, again. Sonya would clean up again, because it was easier and faster to scour the place herself than to argue with the girl.

Sonya picked up a smelly pair of socks from the sofa, tossed them into the laundry basket, and turned on the warm water. Biting into the apple and holding it with her teeth, she wet a dishrag and twisted it savagely to squeeze out the water. She wiped the greasy counter clean before putting the remaining half an apple down.

"Why won't she clean up after herself?" she muttered to the sink, diving into her dish washing routine. She chomped on the apple viciously. She didn't really need an answer. She just vented her frustration. Her kitchen sink understood, or pretended to. It listened to Sonya's grievances in calm silence, like a therapist, wisely refraining from ever giving advice or remarking that Sonya's real problem was Alexei's drinking and not Ksenya's habits.

After finishing the dishes, Sonya wiped the fridge and attacked the dry, slightly scorched yellow blobs on the stove top. "She is punishing me, isn't she?" She scrubbed harder. "For having kicked her precious daddy out?" The liquid soap bubbled, but the yellow stuff resisted her exertions at first. What had the girl cooked? Sonya sniffed at the biggest blob. It smelled cheap and fishy. She winced. Sometimes, just pouring out her troubles into the sink along with dirty, soapy water helped. Today, it didn't, but the stove was finally clean.

Sonya pulled a bowl with defrosted chicken from the fridge and began cutting it into small pieces for a *satsivi*—one of Ksenya's favorite dishes. Like the sink, the cutting board was Sonya's friend, although not a therapist. It was a dancing instructor, inspiring Sonya to shut up and move. Alas, not in a dance, but any movement was better than the immobility of despair.

* * * *

"Hi, Jane." Nodding goodbye to departing Miranda, Sonya waltzed into Jane's room.

Jane sat in front of a window, in a deep armchair upholstered in the expensive blue and beige damask. Outside the window, young maple trees swayed with a slight breeze. A bright blue acrylic blanket with a picture of a white unicorn covered the short, screwed-up appendages that passed for Jane's legs. Her greasy hair was gathered into a short, ratty pigtail.

"I'm dying," Jane said, her voice scratching at Sonya's nerves.

Sonya winced. "You have been dying for the last fifty years," she retorted.

"Soon," Jane promised ominously.

"Well, you're not dead, yet. So, let's bathe you and wash your hair."

"Turn my chair," Jane commanded.

Sonya obeyed, turning the chair to face the room.

"My brother took me to the hospital this morning. They did a bunch of tests." Jane's voice sounded broken, moving up and down the scale and hiccupping, mauling the words. Sonya had to strain to understand the longer phrases. "I don't want to die. Stupid, huh?" Jane's face crumpled. Coarse, stumbling chirps escaped her lips. There were no tears. Her tear ducts were dry.

Sonya stared, her heart aching for Jane. Compared to Jane's tragic life, Sonya's problems were so insignificant. She had problems with money, but who didn't? Every second household harbored a dysfunctional family, too. Nothing unusual in that. Jane was rich, but all her money wasn't enough to make her healthy and able. At least Sonya's problems were statistically average. The realization struck her. She represented statistics. She should stop whining.

"Jane," Sonya said quietly. "I'll wash your hair, and then I'll..." What? What could she do to cheer up the poor woman and make her forget her troubles for a short while? "Do you want me to dance for you?"

Jane stopped her dry crying. "Yes!" Her eyes narrowed. "Strip dance?"

"Strip dance?"

"I hate your sweats."

"Okay," Sonya said a little uncertainly. "I can tell you my problems, too. Maybe they'll make you feel better."

"You have problems?"

Sonya burst into laughter. "Yes, you self-pitying little pretzel. Did you think only you have problems?"

They fell into their usual game of insults, and Jane perked up. "Pilgarlic!"

"Flotch!"

"Infantile gump!"

"Bald slackumtrance!"

By now, Sonya knew more insults in English than she had ever known in Russian. Jane owned a dictionary of insults from Shakespearean times and demanded they both studied it and used their knowledge. The more outrageous, the better. *Life-supporting insults*, Sonya thought sadly as she undressed Jane and washed her contorted, wizened limbs and her gray wisps of remaining hair. Afterward, she deposited Jane, clean and dressed in fresh clothing, onto a sofa in the spacious living room.

"So, you want to see a strip dance?"

"And hear your problems!" Jane demanded happily, like a little girl anticipating a bedtime story.

Why not, Sonya thought. Jane enjoyed a good gossip, and what gossip was better than Sonya's disjointed affairs with Alexei and Ksenya?

"All right," she said. "I need music."

She pulled a few CDs at random from Jane's impressive rack and examined the titles. She needed something slow and sensual. Perhaps an Indian sitar? Ravi Shankar? Perfect! Sonya inserted the CD into an expensive music center and pushed the "Play" button, while she went to pull the thick, golden brocade draperies over the windows. "We need twilight."

The sitar tinkled mysteriously behind her back. She turned on the two matching Tiffany lamps standing on both sides of the sofa. The lamps flooded the room with soft, colored light. "Show time," she murmured, stopping in the middle of the room and pivoting to face Jane, who watched breathlessly.

Slowly, Sonya began rotating her hips, warming up the muscles, dancing in place, nailing Jane with an intense gaze. Inserting her thumbs into the waistband of her sweats, she slid the gray sportswear down, baring her caving midriff. Then lower still, revealing her dark blue panties. They were simple, comfortable cotton—not lace or anything sexual—but Jane whimpered.

Electrified by her audience's reaction, Sonya straightened, holding the sweats in place just above her knees with her leg muscles. Her upper body oscillated. She lifted her hands over her head, plunging all ten fingers into her hair. The hair clip holding her bun blocked the way. With a languid gesture, she threw the clip toward Jane.

Jane squeaked.

Sonya's breasts stuck out as she bent her spine backwards,

almost facing the ceiling, gyrating and writhing in her starvation for music and dance. Dimly, she felt her sweats sliding lower, dropping to the floor. She heard Jane moaning, but she blocked out everything, as she always did when she danced. She surrendered to the lustrous allure of the exotic sitar strings.

She lifted her right leg high, almost to her face, pulled off the sock, and tossed it away. The thick carpet of the floor tickled her bare toes. She repeated the movement with her left leg, but this one went above her head. She had to strain to reach it. After the second sock flew away, she wriggled her toes in the air before slowly lowering her foot to the floor. She didn't hear Jane's twittering, anymore.

When she tore off her sweatshirt and began twirling around her fallen clothing, clad only in her bra and panties, Jane screamed.

Sonya woke up from her dancing trance. Ravi Shankar kept on playing, but she stopped moving, breathing deeply.

"Jane?" She pattered closer to the sofa. Her body, hot from the dance, began to chill.

"Why did you stop dancing?" Jane screeched. She sounded angry. "Dance!" Hurt gurgled in her voice, but she was unable to let it out. She couldn't even cry properly.

Sonya felt so much pity for the older woman, she could've cried for her. "I'm getting older," she said, swallowing hard and making her voice smooth and firm. "I can't dance, forever. I should find another way to earn money."

"Stupid!" Jane carped. "Dance, now!"

"I want to be a designer. I want to enroll in the Emily Carr."

"Tell me your problems!"

Sonya snorted. "Okay." Picking up her clothing from the floor, she dressed hurriedly. She didn't turn off the music or open the draperies. Instead, she sat down beside Jane on the sofa, leaning on the back of it. "Okay," she repeated faintly. "Where do I start?" She shivered from the sweat that congealed all over her body. "I usually have a shower after dancing."

"Then, have a shower. You can wash your hair, too. Is it sweaty?"

"Yes. Thank you, Jane. I'll be fast." Sonya darted for the bathroom.

"Come back naked," Jane yelled after her. "I want to see all of you. Don't dress up."

Sonya stopped at the door and whirled. "You want to see me naked? You're a pervert."

"Please," Jane whispered. Her lips parted, her small eyes glazed over, and her pasty skin flushed. Her obvious sexual arousal looked frightening inside the inept, expiring body.

Sonya came back, kneeling in front of the sofa. "You'd like it, would you?" Compassion gripped her throat so tightly, she couldn't speak above a rustle. Revulsion twisted her guts. She clamped her lips together and inhaled deeply.

Jane's colorless eyes focused on Sonya. "So beautiful!" she hissed.

Sonya swallowed and went to the bathroom. Of course, Jane's psyche was twisted like her body. It would've been a miracle if it weren't. Poor Jane. Turning on the shower, Sonya climbed in. She stood under the jets of hot water until she was numb. She didn't use any of Jane's shampoo or soap, just letting the water wash off her frustration and pity, for Jane and for herself. Then, she wrapped a fresh towel around her middle, used a smaller one to dry her hair, and came out, running barefoot over the thick carpet.

"You came!" Jane's little, wrinkled face lit up.

"Yeah," Sonya muttered, unsure why she did. "Your death wish coming true." She dropped the bigger towel and dried her hair in front of Jane, allowing the woman to devour her with her eyes. She was used to such leers from men and knew how to defuse their ardor. She didn't know how to deal with Jane's acute pleasure. She wanted to cry.

"Have you ever seen a ballet, Jane?"

"No," Jane said faintly. "My brother doesn't like me watching beautiful people. He thinks I would be...envious."

"Cheeses! Of course, you are. You would be an imbecile if you didn't feel envious. Where is your hairdryer?"

"In the cabinet beside the bathroom," Jane said.

Like everything in Jane's house, the hairdryer was expensive, with a built-in brush. The device buzzed and vibrated in Sonya's hands like a living thing, surrounding her with the warm blow-kisses, inviting lassitude, and warming her naked body. Impatiently, she tugged at the wet knots in her thick, auburn tresses.

"My ex loved brushing my hair," Sonya said with a self-deprecating grin. She still missed him. He had always been so tender, untangling the snarls in her hair with great patience. He had always made brushing a caress. Sonya jerked harder, grimacing while blotting the memory with pain.

"I'd love to brush your hair," Jane said.

"You must be a lesbian."

Jane giggled. "Why did you push out your ex?"

"He is a drunk." She had made the decision to live without him. She wouldn't go maudlin over the stupid moments of hair-brushing. "I should cut this blasted mane short!" she spat vehemently. "Shear off the entire fleece, like a sheep."

"Don't. Wait until I die."

"Jane, you're a manipulating bitch. I'm getting dressed."

Jane smiled but didn't say anything until Sonya, fully dressed, dropped onto the sofa beside her.

"What about your daughter?" Jane asked

Sonya shrugged. "She resents me for kicking out her father, and she steals my money for him."

"Poor Sonya," Jane said. "My life is much simpler."

"Just what I need. Pity from you. Do you want to watch TV or read?"

Jane disregarded Sonya's suggestions. "Do you love him still?"

Sonya snorted. "Probably. A crazy woman that I am. He stands between me and Ksenya, even when he isn't there, like the evil wizard in Swan Lake."

"Tell me about Swan Lake."

"Fine." Sonya snuggled more comfortably on the sofa. "Do you want more light?"

"No. I like the dark."

Sonya began telling Jane the *libretto* of *Swan Lake*. She ended up singing every theme—Odette, Odile, and the sorcerer. She even danced a little, performing some kind of a synopsis ballet. Humming the sorcerer's ominous tune, she realized that it didn't fit Alexei. Her ex was soft and weak, inviting pity, like Jane. To some extent, he was disabled, too. Mutilated by vodka. Despite his big, sexy body, he was like a sick, oversized puppy.

"Of course, Ksenya loves him," Sonya murmured, settling back into her place beside Jane.

"Have you ever danced Odette?" Jane demanded.

"No, I was a folk dancer. I didn't make it to a ballet theatre. Too much snarling and biting. Besides, my legs are kind of short for classical ballet."

"Bullshit! You have to strip dance," Jane pronounced, deadly serious. "It ought to pay more than caring for me."

"You want to get rid of me?"

"I want you happy," Jane breathed. "Will you visit me when

you dance, again?"

"Right." Immersed in her inner revelations, Sonya didn't listen. "He tells Ksenya that he loves her, and she falls for it. It's an illusion, empty words, but they work like a fertilizer for her. She is blooming, Jane. Why?" Sonya herself had stopped believing in Alexei's love declarations long ago, but Ksenya still believed. Which one of them was a fool?

"She likes to be noble. Being noble is intoxicating. She is empowered by caring for him," Jane said.

"Huh?" Sonya lifted her eyes. "Why wouldn't she care for me, then?"

"You're strong. You don't need her care."

"I do!" Sonya watched the lamp on Jane's side of the sofa. Tall and elegant, with the unusual design of storks and reeds, it was probably antique. The lamp on her side was more mundane—just pieces of stained glass fused together in an abstract pattern. "I want a Tiffany lamp for my home," she murmured absently. "When I'm rich, I'll buy one." Her thoughts returned to her family. "I think Ksenya wants to believe his fantasies. He surely believes them, himself. He should've been a writer instead of a musician. Should I tell her I love her, too? A hundred times a day, like he does? She would ridicule me." The reeds on the shade of the Tiffany lamp seemed to bend slightly, as if before a wind. They held Sonya in a thrall, pulling her eyes away from Jane.

"Yes. Tell her," Jane said.

"I don't have time. I work a lot." Sonya was getting angry, but she still wouldn't look at Jane. "You don't understand."

"I understand. Take up strip dancing," Jane repeated. "It'll free you. It'll make you happy, loved. Everyone wants to know she's loved." She sounded wistful. "I've never seen a strip dance before today."

"Neither have I. Only in movies." Finally, Sonya glanced at Jane. "I love my daughter," she said. "I would die for her. Doesn't she know? Is his smooth tongue more important than my work?"

"Yes," Jane said. "What happens during a strip dance?" Her eyes blazed.

"You're so degraded, Jane." Sonya shook her head. "What happens? I suppose women undress slowly with music, as I just did for you. Men ogle them. Then, men pay money."

Maybe she *should* try strip dancing. Maybe Jane was right?

Chapter Nine
Sonya

When Sonya returned home late at night, Ksenya was already sleeping. Softly, Sonya closed the door to her daughter's room.

"I love you, Ksyushka," she whispered. Of course, her daughter couldn't hear, but it didn't matter. She would follow Jane's advice, anyway. Jane was right. She should repeat the words in the morning. Without turning on the lights, Sonya pattered to her bedroom and dove into her solitary bed. Definitely, she would repeat the words. Ksenya needed to know. "I love you, little vixen," Sonya murmured to her pillow just before falling asleep.

She dreamed of the old times. She still danced, then. Ksenya had been a preschooler. Alexei played his clarinet in the ensemble's orchestra. They were so happy in that dream.

The telephone's shrill rings woke Sonya up. She could hardly keep her eyes open as she peered at the dim, green digits of the alarm clock: 3:20 in the morning? Rats! She was having such a nice dream! Who could that be?

"Hello?" She yawned.

"Sonya?" Her sister's voice was thin, reedy.

Sonya's heart tumbled painfully. Her yawning mouth snapped shut. A call from Israel at this hour could only mean trouble. She didn't want to hear it.

"Lil'ka? It's the middle of the night here."

"I know," Lilia said. "Father died last night."

Sonya jerked fully awake. Died? He hadn't been ill. Why had he died?

"Sonechka, are you there?" the receiver prodded.

"How did he die?"

"He fell asleep with a book and didn't wake up. A saint's death, some say."

"Sonechka." Sonya's mother Dina's husky voice replaced Lilia's dignified murmur on the other end of the line.

"He wasn't a saint!" Dina screeched. "He was an old fool! I told him not to carry that contraption home, but he wouldn't listen. It was too heavy for him, and too hot. He wouldn't drink enough water, and he wasn't young, anymore. Fool, fool, old idiot!" She whimpered, and the telephone went mute, the connection broken.

In stupefaction, Sonya stared at the receiver for a while before slowly replacing it on the station. Then, she hastily dialed her mother's number but got only a busy signal. She abandoned the useless phone and snuggled back under the warmth of her blanket. She would try to call back later.

"Couldn't they have waited until morning to tell me?" she mumbled. "There is no rush, now. A few hours wouldn't change anything."

She pulled the blanket tighter over herself, but she couldn't sleep, anymore. She couldn't cry, either. She should be able to, but she couldn't. *Why*, she wondered? *Why can't I cry*? Her mind whirred with unwanted thoughts. Why had her father died? He wasn't so old. He had been an engineer in Russia, always inventing something, always tinkering, and always bringing gadgets home. She would never see him, again. What a strange word—never.

She tried to imagine him as he had been at the airport, before they left Israel—strong, supportive, with the wrinkles of laughter around his eyes, and an expression of concern on his face. Instead, her mind played a trick on her, picturing him with a book in his bed. Dead. Cold. She shivered under the blanket and tried to block the image, but it refused to go.

She stared at her digital alarm clock, watching the minutes slip away in green. Thirty-seven, thirty-eight, thirty-nine, forty. Only twenty minutes since the call, but they seemed like forever.

She hadn't seen her father for a couple of years, since moving to Canada, but there had always been hope. Now, that hope was gone. Ksenya would never again see her grandpa. They would never again caterwaul the insipid Russian ballads together, never laugh together. Sonya felt tears gathering in her eyes. At last.

Still naked, she shot up from the bed and rushed to her closet. Tomorrow morning, she would have to fly to Israel for the funeral. How much did a ticket cost? A thousand? Fifteen hundred? She didn't remember. Should she take Ksenya with her? Could she afford two tickets? Probably not. She might have to borrow off her Visa even for one ticket. Pity. She just started to pay off her debt. Wincing, she lifted the pile of towels, pulled out the checkered box for the miniature nightlight, opened it, and stared in confusion.

The money was gone. The box was empty.

Where was the money? She should have had $1,100.00 in there, in twenties and fifties. Had she dropped them? Puzzled, she glanced at the floor, while the empty box dangled from her fingers. No bills littered the floor.

Ksenya!

Suddenly, Sonya couldn't breathe. Somehow, the girl had learned about her stash. She had given it all to Alexei, no doubt. Sonya couldn't fly to the funeral, couldn't see her father one last time, couldn't hug her mother in her grief, couldn't even cry together with Lil'ka. She couldn't afford to borrow $1,100 or more off her Visa. She was already almost to the limit.

Taking a deep breath, she dropped her bare buttocks down onto the cold carpet of the closet, covered her mouth with both hands, and wailed. She cried until she was too cold. Her naked skin ached from the chill, and her eyes stung from the salty tears, but she kept on shuddering and keening until she was blue and covered with goosebumps. Then, she stood up and shuffled to the bathroom. She shook so hard, she only managed to turn on the light on the second try. Her fingers felt too frozen and numb to obey her. Her mind felt muffled in cotton. Every thought was a struggle. She stood in front of the bathtub for a long time before she remembered to turn on the hot water for a bath. Her daughter robbed her of the chance to say the last goodbye to her father.

By the time she came out of the bath—warm, pink, and wrinkled like a dry mushroom—it was six. Tying on the belt of her fuzzy and white terry bathrobe, Sonya put the kettle on to make tea. No point in waking up Ksenya too early. The money was already gone. Sonya settled at the kitchen table with her tea and watched the rainy sky outside turn from the dark gray of the night into the not-so-dark gray of the morning.

"Mom? Good morning." Ksenya, in her pajamas with faded ducks, shambled to the bathroom. A few minutes later, she emerged with her nose puckered. "What did you do? Had a bath at night? It's all steamy." Her hair still mussed up from sleep, she looked dainty and cute, like a doll. Sonya's own little doll-thief.

"Your grandfather died last night," Sonya said. Despite a huge cup of hot tea, her voice was still hoarse from crying. She didn't move from her stool. "Grandma called."

"Died?" Ksenya stopped halfway to her room. "Really died?" Her voice squeaked.

"Yeah, really." Sonya stood up and came closer. She couldn't loom over her daughter, since they were the same height, but Ksenya flinched. Obviously, she saw something unpleasant in her mother's face.

"I can't even fly to the funeral," Sonya continued. She tried to stir up some emotions, but everything was dead inside her, as gone as her father. "You took all the money."

"Oh, fuck," Ksenya whispered, looking at the floor. "I'm sorry, Mom." She actually sounded contrite. "I didn't know Grandpa would die. Dad was sick. They would've evicted him from the room for not paying. He'll pay you back."

"When? When my father is cold and worm-eaten in his grave?" Her voice sounded lifeless even to her own ears.

"Listen, Mom. I told you I'm sorry." Ksenya raised her eyes. Her cheek still had indentations from her pillow. She looked soft and warm, like a baby. She looked loving. Tears sparkled in her blue eyes, and her lips trembled. "I'll miss him," she whispered. "I loved Grandpa." She lifted her hands for a hug. "Mom!" She stepped closer.

Something that had been dead inside Sonya suddenly exploded. The sharp shards burned all over her body: in her heart, her eyes, her mouth. She hated the pillow indentations on Ksenya's cheek with a sudden, flaring passion. "You loved him? Thief!" She slapped Ksenya's pink cheek. "Rotten liar! Hypocrite!" She slapped another cheek.

Ksenya stood immobile, trembling. Her hands clenched at her sides. Her eyes seemed huge, following her mother's every move. Both the girl's cheeks reddened from Sonya's blows. Sonya's right hand stung. She looked at it in surprise and dropped it into the soft pocket of her bathrobe. Then, she turned back to her empty tea mug. "Liar," she said again, softer this time.

Her heart hurt worse than her hand. If she stayed in the kitchen, she would dissolve into a bloody mush. Her eyes were dry, and so was her throat. Unable to cry anymore, like Jane, she marched to her bedroom and slammed the door. She had another hour before she must go to work. Stretching out on the bed in her robe, she threw the blanket over her head and tried to think of nothing. She had never slapped Ksenya before. Never even spanked the girl. What would happen, now? Her interest was detached, clinical. She didn't really care.

Maybe, she should call in sick, today? She couldn't possibly work as if nothing happened. No, she couldn't afford to lose the money.

She left for work without seeing Ksenya. Surprisingly, the routine of the grill actually calmed her down. Indifferent to the chaos of her thoughts, the burgers sizzled furiously. The eatery buzzed all day with students and office workers. Sonya just existed there, not really aware and moving like a living automaton. Open a package. Toss the frozen burgers on the grill. Wait. Flop. Wait. Fill a bin and start again. A perfect job for an upset immigrant—neither thinking nor talking required.

Perhaps, her fight with Ksenya wasn't so bad after all. Perhaps, in the evening they should have a wake for her father—just the two of them. Mother and daughter.

On the way home, she made a detour to a Polish deli and bought pastrami and a package of indecently expensive chocolate truffles. Tonight, they would celebrate her father's life. She couldn't fly to Israel, but she could grieve for him here.

From the Skytrain window, Sonya watched Vancouver shrouded in a veil of rain and plotted her evening with her daughter. She should apologize to Ksenya. Yes, that's it. She would try to explain everything, with all the bills and numbers out in the open. She would follow Jane's advice and tell Ksenya how much she loved her. Ksenya was smart. She would understand, wouldn't she? Then, they would kiss and make up. Just before Sonya slapped her, Ksenya wanted a hug. Sonya just couldn't deliver it at the time. She winced while remembering. She was such a dismal mother. Maybe they should have therapy, together. Yeah, and pay for it together, too...as soon as they won a lottery. She sighed.

She knew something was wrong even before she opened the door. Usually, Ksenya wasn't home at this time, and the house was quiet. Now, Sonya could hear voices, three of them. Had the girl brought friends?

She was still deciding whether it was good or bad when she opened the door and saw two strange adults sitting at her kitchen table. A silver-haired man looked like a wrestler, ridiculous in a suit and tie. A middle-aged Chinese woman wore a business suit all in black. Between them, Ksenya looked like a wronged little girl, innocent and rebellious. She was talking animatedly. At the sound of the door, all three looked up. Ksenya clamped her lips shut.

"Mrs. Lis-ti-vin?" the woman said uncertainly. Like many Asians, she couldn't pronounce Sonya's last name.

Sonya frowned. She tried to capture Ksenya's gaze, but the girl wouldn't look at her. What was up?

"I'm Sofia Listvin, Ksenya's mother," she said.

"We're from the Social Services," the man boomed. "I'm Ken Palmer. This is my partner, Mia Chan." He pointed at the woman.

Mia Chan nodded.

Sonya's gaze switched between the three at her table. She put her purse and grocery bag on the dresser, took off her coat, and came to the table. "Social Services?"

"Your daughter complained about child abuse," Mia Chan said sternly. "She called and told us you'd beaten her." Despite wearing black, she looked like a Chinese ice queen. Even her narrow, black eyes radiated glacial cold. "Is this true?"

Both Mia Chan and Ken Palmer watched Sonya. Ksenya didn't look up.

"I'd beaten her?" Sonya said softly. She wanted to apologize, but Ksenya decided she wanted a war. Sonya's lips thinned. The sly girl had called up the cavalry. Fine! Let the foolish little brat have it the way she wanted. Sonya stepped closer, leaned on the table, and faced her daughter. The only three stools in their kitchen had all been taken by Ksenya and the Social Services representatives, so she stood in front of the table.

"Yes, of course." Sonya didn't look at any of the Social Services. Instead, she stared at Ksenya, who kept her eyes firmly on the table. "I beat her all the time. Do you see the bruises? I torture her." From the corner of her eye, she saw Mia Chan jotting notes in her note pad.

"You shouldn't be sarcastic, Mrs. Listvin," Ken Palmer said. "You might end up arrested and charged with child abuse."

"Child abuse?" Sonya snorted bitterly. "She stole $1,000 from me, and I slapped her. My father died last night in Israel. My mom called, and I can't even fly to the funeral, because I don't have the money. My daughter stole the money and gave it all to her alcoholic father. Did she tell you that? I work two shifts every day, and he drinks his welfare and my money away. Yes, I slapped her. I should've reported her to the police, instead. So, arrest me."

She motioned with her chin toward her bag of Polish delicatessens. "I bought chocolate truffles and pastrami. I wanted us to make up and have a feast together—a wake for my dad. You can eat it all alone, Ksenya. Have a feast by yourself to remember your grandfather." Her lips trembled, but she gritted her teeth, raised her eyes from the top of Ksenya's head, and gazed into the gray, rainy afternoon outside the window. Her rain bucket near the window was almost full, she noted absently.

"Ksenya?" Ken Palmer said.

"If I get arrested, you would take her from this house and put her into foster care, right?" Sonya asked. She wasn't sure she would object. Getting arrested might be more restful. "I might get mad at her, again. I might attempt another beating if she steals, again. Would you take her?"

"No!" Finally, Ksenya lifted her eyes. She looked terrified. "Mom! No!"

"She can't steal from a foster family, correct? Neither food nor money. She would be arrested then too, right?" Sonya felt as if she rode a roller coaster. A moment ago, her throat hurt from the suppressed misery. Now, she was suddenly so angry, she couldn't think coherently. Her hands clutched the edge of the table. She turned toward Mia Chan. "Would she be arrested if she stole $1,000 from a foster family?"

"Probably, if it's not the first offense," Mia Chan murmured. She didn't look at Sonya, staring instead into her notebook. She didn't write in it, anymore.

"Then, her father wouldn't get any more money," Sonya mused. She grinned vengefully. "Not from me, nor from her. Take her away!"

"No!" Ksenya howled like a wounded creature. "Mom, please. Don't let them take me away."

"I beat you all the time!"

"No! I lied! Tell them I lied." Ksenya scrambled from behind the table. "Mom?" She grabbed Sonya's sweatshirt with both hands. "I lied. I swear I lied. Don't let them take me away. Say that it is not true." She was trembling and shaking Sonya.

"Has she really stolen from you, Mrs. Listvin?" Ken Palmer asked. "Do you want to file a report?"

Sonya sighed. "We had a fight in the morning," she said quietly. Like her bitterness, her anger disappeared. She just felt tired. "No, I don't want to file a report. I bought truffles to make up, but she called you."

"Mom, I'm sorry," Ksenya pleaded, still holding Sonya's shirt in both fists. "For Grandpa, and for everything." She was weeping openly, bawling, and sniffing. "Dad would've been on the streets without this money. He needed it, Mom. I'll look for a job, myself. I promise. I can do burgers, too. Maybe, they'll take me at your place? Mom? They won't take me away? Please! Don't let them. I'll pay you back."

"Oh, Ksen'ka," Sonya murmured. "We're both so stupid." She hugged her daughter and sank to the floor, taking Ksenya with her. They clinched tightly, crying together. When Sonya finally lifted her head, sniffing long and hard, and jerkily wiping the tears and snot from her face with a sleeve, both Social Services had already vanished.

"They...are...gone," she reported, sobbing convulsively.

Prostrate, with her head on Sonya's lap, Ksenya shuddered, her cheeks damp. "Mom, I love you, but I love him, too. He'll die if I don't help. What should I do, Mom?" Her thin shoulders shook.

Sonya's jeans felt damp from Ksenya's tears. Silently, Sonya petted the girl's sandy hair, threading her shaking fingers through the soft, dirty-blonde locks. Maybe, Ksenya was right. Maybe, she should take care of her father. Maybe, this was love? Why at Sonya's expense? Sonya's throat was clogged, although she couldn't cry, anymore. She didn't know what to answer her daughter.

Chapter Ten
Amanda

"It was easier than I thought," Amanda said.

They sat together in the car. Sergey looked up the addresses on his map, marking each one with a red cross. Three red crosses already adorned the map of Vladimir. His red marker spiraled over the geometrical lines and angles of the city streets, like an eagle seeking another landing spot. Sighted. Pointed. Landed.

Amanda fidgeted. What took him so long? He could read Russian better than she could. Forcing herself to sit still, she smoothed a wrinkle on her jeans with a finger. The wrinkle instantly folded back. Angry, Amanda applied her entire palm to her thigh and pressed slightly to keep the wrinkle from reappearing. This time, the wrinkle submitted.

Lifting his head, Sergey glanced at her, his bushy brows climbing up. "Four of them lived in town. Irina Alpashkina lived in Vasilyevo," he said. "It's a village to the south. They have a monastery there."

"I'm not interested in sightseeing, today," Amanda snapped. "Let's go."

Sergey's face was inscrutable. He started the car. "First stop—Tatiana Vetrova. It's the closest to the hospital."

Amanda nodded. "Sorry," she said grudgingly, vexed with herself. This search was turning her into a grouch.

"It's all right. I understand. It's not every day you meet your long-lost daughter."

Amanda didn't answer. The phrase sounded suspiciously sentimental. Although Sergey's expression was absolutely serious, the entire enterprise seemed more and more likely to dissolve into a bad sitcom. Unfortunately, it was her life, and if she hated anything more than being ridiculous, she couldn't remember at the moment. She stared out the window while Sergey navigated the narrow streets. As soon as he stopped the car on the river bank, her heart hiccupped.

Now? Nauseous with apprehension, she opened the car door and scrambled out.

An old, two-story building painted yellow stood on the opposite side of the street, between an old, wooden church and a small park. A café on the first floor, called *"Ogonki"*—"Small Lights" in translation—was filled with Hungarian tourists. A bus with the little red, white, and green Hungarian flag was parked outside.

After they crossed the empty, narrow street, Amanda and Sergey circled the building and stepped into a backyard, from where a staircase led to the second floor. The backyard wasn't paved. In the shallow, black puddles from the yesterday's rain, rotting cabbage leaves floated on top of the rainbow oil stains. A few dense bushes screened the backyard from the alley and the park beyond. From the back door of the café, the smells of fried potatoes, stale bread, and spoiled milk drifted into the staircase, mixing with the joyous scent of young leaves.

Amanda tiptoed around the puddles, trying not to muddy her white running shoes. With light oozing only from the open door downstairs, she saw just enough not to trip on the wooden steps. In front of her, Sergey seemed like a wide, black shadow moving steadily up the gray stairway. They stopped at the top landing. Neither door on both sides of the stairs had a number. The door to the right was obviously metal, glinting faintly.

"I should've brought a flashlight," Sergey muttered. He blindly searched for a buzzer around the wooden door to the left. His palm made light knock-knocks, the sound differing depending on what he hit—the wood of the door or the tiles of the wall. Then, the knocks stopped. He had found the buzzer.

"Damn, it doesn't work." He knocked on the door, again. This time with his fist. Nobody answered.

Amanda located a buzzer in the middle of the metal door. She pressed it. This buzzer did work. It tinkled melodiously, like a small, silver bell.

"Who?" a gruff voice asked from behind the closed door.

"I'm looking for Tatiana Vetrova," Amanda said in Russian, straining her vocal cords to carry through to the other side of the door. "Does she live here?"

"She is downstairs, working in the café," the voice said before coughing wetly, wheezing as if it belonged to a very old woman.

"Thank you," Amanda said uncertainly. "What about her daughter?"

The voice said something she didn't catch, and the volume dropped, as the person on the other side shuffled away from the door.

"Wait. Do you need help? Should I call a doctor?"

"Amanda," Sergey whispered, tugging at her sleeve. "Let's go. You've frightened her."

"Why?" Amanda followed Sergey out. "She is unwell. I wanted to help."

"I can't explain. It's too complicated. Believe me, she is afraid. You saw the metal door."

"Yes." Amanda said quietly. She thought about her own house in Vancouver. Beautiful, large, and expensive, it was located in one of the best areas of the city. It didn't have a metal door, and its locks wouldn't stop a determined burglar. The entrance door was part etched glass and part wood, and neither Gloria nor Amanda had ever been afraid to open it, although they did have a burglar alarm installed.

She should bring her daughter home as soon as possible. In Vancouver, they would open the door together and stand on the threshold, watching the chestnut trees along the street rustle their leaves in a breeze off the bay. They would have a picnic on the front lawn and invite all the neighbors for a "welcome home" party. In Vancouver, her Russian daughter would never be afraid, again.

Amanda scurried after Sergey, who strode purposefully around the house toward the entrance to the café. Soon. She would see her daughter soon. Maybe the woman that worked in the café, Tatiana Vetrova, was the mother of Amanda's daughter. Amanda should invite them both, she decided on the spot. Maybe, Tatiana Vetrova was Gloria's mother. Amanda shivered at the thought. She would never give up Gloria, but maybe she would have to share. She frowned at the idea. Maybe this Tatiana person wouldn't want a Canadian daughter as strong and self-assured as Gloria. Gloria wouldn't work at such a seedy eatery. Amanda's lips curved. Gloria would turn it into a posh restaurant. She was such an elitist. Amanda slipped into the café behind Sergey's wide back.

A woman about her age, with thin, flaxen hair tucked beneath a red headband with white polka dots, was sitting in a corner behind a check register, reading a paperback. Two younger women, both wearing similar headbands over their straw-colored hair, waited the tables. All the tablecloths were also red with white polka dots, as were the identical aprons of the waitresses. People occupied every table. A buzz of Hungarian speech floated between the tables.

The younger waitress darted into the kitchen, returning in a moment with a full tray and a brilliant smile. The older waitress looked serious, even grim. Her eyes sank into her pale cheeks. She unloaded her tray, nodded grimly to her customers, and headed back to the kitchen. Sergey started after her.

Amanda made a beeline for the cashier. “Hi, I’m looking for Tatiana Vetrova.”

The woman lifted her eyes from the book—a detective novel, judging by a shooting gun on the cover. “That’s me.” She looked uneasy.

Stumbling at every preposition, Amanda told her story.

Tatiana’s eyes became huge as she listened. By the time Amanda was done, both waitresses and Sergey surrounded the cash register. Several tourists raised their heads from their respective soups and cutlets, trying to understand the hushed conversation.

“You’re that Canadian,” Tatiana said at last. “I remember you, but these are my daughters.” She pointed at both waitresses. “Sveta was born on April thirtieth that year, but she’s never been a redhead. They’re my own daughters.”

The older of the two waitresses nodded. “Never,” she confirmed wistfully. “I wish.”

Tatiana spared her an irritated glance and turned back to Amanda. “I’m sorry.”

“Of course. Sorry to bother you.” Amanda smiled weakly and backed toward the door.

“Do you want lunch? On the house,” Tatiana said suddenly. “*Rassolnik* is the best, today. I can’t see you leaving my café so upset. You’ll find her. Sit down. Eat. Vera!”

“Sure, Mom.” The younger waitress skipped toward the kitchen, again. “That’s so-o-o romantic!” she sang. “Dad, just listen!” The swinging kitchen door closed, cutting off the rest of her announcement.

Some of the tourists who got enough of the story to understand the proceedings were explaining it to the rest, and all eyes turned toward Amanda. Smiling self-consciously, Amanda followed the older waitress Sveta to a small, gray Formica table in the far corner—the only one without the red tablecloth and no chairs. There were a couple of stools tucked underneath.

“So, your daughter was born on the same day as I,” Sveta said quietly. “Lucky her.” She didn’t smile. Moving like a zombie, she wiped the table surface and pulled out the stools. “Sit down, please.”

"Sveta, what's a *rassolnik*?" Amanda asked.

The young woman glanced at her in astonishment. Then, a slow grin spread across her narrow features, as if it had to fight for control over her face. "You speak Russian so well, I forget you're not from here. It's a soup with pickles and barley," she said. "My dad cooks a really good *rassolnik*. The best in Vladimir." Still grinning, she went to her other clients.

* * * *

"I never tried *rassolnik* before. I liked it," Amanda said to Sergey some time later, as their car headed to the next address on the list. "I'm glad it's not pancakes. I'm tired of pancakes." She stuffed a notebook page with a recipe and the mailing address of Tatiana Vetrova into her purse. As soon as she returned home, she would surprise Gloria with *rassolnik*. She should invite the entire Vetrov family for a visit. Amanda liked the names of the young women: Sveta and Vera. What was her other daughter's name? Would she like *rassolnik*?

"That cook of theirs is excellent," Sergey agreed. "Family business." He wanted to say something else but checked himself. "Have you tried other Russian foods in Vancouver?"

"Some," Amanda said absently, gazing out the window. "We have a couple of Russian restaurants, but they're different. Everything tastes different. I miss fruits and veggies. Nothing is available, neither in stores nor at restaurants. I want strawberries." Even to her own ears, she sounded petulant. Again. "I'm sorry, Sergey. It just burst out. I guess I'm more upset than I realize."

"It's May." Sergey snorted, his hands resting lightly on the wheel. "Strawberries will appear soon. We have four other names, Amanda. Don't despair. One of them ought to be her."

Amanda nodded broodingly.

Their next address was a typical, Russian wooden hut. There were plenty of them sprinkled around Vladimir. The gangly young girl who opened the door was not more than fifteen, with a yellow ponytail. A thick ring of black mascara surrounded one of her light, gray eyes. Another eye was still mascara-less, fringed by the short, blonde lashes. One of her hands held the squeaking door open while another clutched a pink tube of mascara.

"Panashvili? They lived here before us," she said through a mouthful of gum. "They moved out a few years ago. I think they moved to Georgia." Chewing vigorously, she pointed the circular brush of her mascara outside, as if Georgia was across the street. "None of them had red hair. They were all black-haired. They were Georgian." Indifferent, she shrugged her thin shoulders and shut the door.

"Two down, three to go," Amanda said. "By Murphy's Law, my daughter will be the last one."

"Then, perhaps we should reverse the order." Sergey grinned.

"Whatever order we use. Don't try to outwit fate. Who is next?"

"Nina Savchenko." Sergey turned the car into a narrow street, planted with linden trees. "Should be somewhere here. House number fifteen." After driving for some time, he stopped the car and glanced at Amanda with guilty eyes. "It's not here."

Amanda stared. There were houses numbered five and seven. Then, across a narrow lane, a small park bordered a school stadium. Next stood a three-story school, painted white. Kids of all ages streamed out of its doors in every direction, creating a ruckus. A few adults trickled in. A mongrel dog ran across the stadium, barking in excitement. In a sand enclosure among the park bushes, two toddlers played. Their mothers sat on a bench nearby. Young leaves whispered among themselves above the people's heads.

"Tomorrow morning, we'll go to the district passport bureau and find out where the people from the house number fifteen moved to," Sergey said. "Don't mope, Amanda. We have two more addresses to cover."

"Maybe fifteen is on the other side of the school," Amanda murmured.

Sergey obliged, driving carefully and slowly to allow the children to cross the street. On the other side of the school, the numbers picked up, starting from nineteen. The opposite side of the street with the even numbers continued uninterrupted from two to twenty-eight.

"Let's go see if perhaps Dina Goldberg is the one you seek." Sergey accelerated again, turning into the main street to drive to the opposite end of town.

"She is a Jew," Amanda said.

"Jewish people often have red hair. You don't like Jews?"

"No, it's not that." Amanda gazed out the window. "It would mean my Gloria is a Jew by blood." She brightened. "She is very smart. She always said she might've been a Jew. It's funny, you know? It's been an inside joke in our family." A smile crept over her face, reaching her eyes. "I have to buy souvenirs for Gloria. I'd like to see Suzdal, too. Tomorrow, whatever happens today, let's take a break and do some sightseeing and shopping."

"What if we find your daughter, today?"

"Then, I'll buy souvenirs for both of them. I should do it, anyway. She wouldn't buy herself any Russian souvenirs if she lives here, right?"

"Probably," Sergey said. "Haven't you brought anything for her from Canada?"

"No," Amanda said. "I hope she'll come back home with me. I bought a house for her. Gloria is renovating it right now." Noticing Sergey's incredulous gaze, she added defensively, "It's not far from my own house. Of course, it's much smaller, but it's a very nice neighborhood."

"No doubt," Sergey said without inflection. "Let's find her first."

This address existed. It was off the tourist path, in an old, dirty pink apartment building featuring five stories, three entrances, and peeling paint everywhere. Where the paint had faded completely, the original red bricks of the walls looked like bleeding wounds on the filthy body of the house.

The staircase was in a worse condition than at Tatiana Vetrova's house. The heavy, repulsive stink of old urine hovered over the landings. Feces caked in the corners. Although the doorway didn't have a door, the lonely, rusty door hinges still stuck out. Tiny windows on every landing were so grimy, they let through very little light.

"Do they ever wash these staircases?" Amanda asked, angry at the terrible squalor people lived in.

"Who?" Sergey shot back. "The staircase doesn't belong to anyone, and there is no money to hire a common janitor."

Amanda winced. That poverty issue, again. The staircase and the elevator in Robert's house in Moscow were in much better condition, but it was a house where foreign journalists lived. They probably had hired a common janitor. They definitely had more money than most locals. Silently, she trudged after Sergey to the third floor.

The young man who opened the door didn't look like a Jew.

"What?" He didn't sound friendly, either. He looked like an inebriated, belligerent brigand, with his unshaven, bloated face and bloodshot eyes. He also reeked like a keg of cheap beer.

Amanda glanced back. Sergey's encouraging balk loomed behind her shoulder. Inhaling deeply, she asked about Dina Goldberg.

"No Goldbergs here," the man said. "No other Jewish rabble, neither." His lips twisted into a scornful grimace. He burped, turned sharply, presented his disdainful back in a ripped, blue sweatshirt, and slammed the door. The beer-cabbage stink that expelled from his mouth lingered on the landing.

Amanda held her breath. "Bad ventilation," she murmured, tiptoeing down the stairs after Sergey and trying not to step in someone's poo.

"A nice Russian specimen," Sergey commented, his voice cold, syllables clipped sharply. "The Goldbergs have obviously moved. Good for them. We'll find out at the passport bureau, tomorrow." He caught Amanda's elbow and steered her toward the car. "Do you still wish to drive to Vasilyevo?"

"Yes, please," Amanda said.

The drive to Vasilyevo took almost two hours. Sergey made a wrong turn and ended up on a narrow country road. Riddled with ruts and puddles, it brought them to a gravel pit.

"Dead end," he muttered, laboring to turn the car around. He said something else under his breath.

"You're swearing, Sergey?" Amanda tried and failed to maintain a serious façade. Her lips quivered. "I thought you a perfect gentleman."

He glanced at her with an expression of a teenage boy caught smoking pot, rebellious and embarrassed at the same time.

"What?" Amanda said. "I know all the Mat words. I read a research paper. Very educational. I've just never heard them."

"Sorry. You shouldn't have. I was mad at myself," he mumbled. Abruptly, he perked up. "There is a research on Mat?"

"Yes." Amanda grinned openly. "Several. They say the Russians have very peculiar prohibitions on voicing those words. Intelligent people don't say them in front of the opposite sex, and they don't write them down, although both sexes use them profusely, especially at times of emotional upheavals. When I gave birth to Gloria, everyone spoke those words at the Maternity Ward except me. I didn't know them, then. Some women used them so inventively. They tried to teach me—a very interesting experience."

His cheeks and ears pinkened. "Be quiet, woman. Tell me where to go." Sergey threw the map in her direction.

"Why such a strange attitude toward a few words?" Amanda persisted.

Sergey bit his bottom lip and drove on silently.

Hiding a grin, Amanda opened the map. As soon as she

returned to Moscow, she would refresh her memory of Mat from Robert. Or better still, from Rebecca. Maybe she would even ask her Russian daughter. She should know how to use all those funny words that had so many rules attached. Snickering mischievously, Amanda traced the road they were following with her finger.

"As soon as you reach the intersection, turn left," she instructed.

It was after eight in the evening when they finally found Vasilyevo—Irina Alpashkina's village. Light shone behind the curtains in many windows along one muddy, unpaved street. Laughter and music drifted from beyond the line of one-story wooden houses. Without street lights, Amanda couldn't distinguish the colors of the houses in the growing darkness, but the sounds of a celebration pulled them toward the village green.

They left the car and followed a narrow path between the two fences toward three long, wooden tables laden with bread platters and casseroles. People packed tightly on the benches around the tables. A few oil lamps and candles sparkled off the bottles and glasses. An old man with a weather-beaten face, lined with deep wrinkles, was playing an old concertina. Women crowded him on both sides, laughing tipsily. A few youngsters danced, with lots of enthusiasm but no real skills as they stomped around on the grass. The girls swirled their handkerchiefs and squealed while the boys squatted, hopped, and hooted. In the dusk, Amanda could discern no details of clothes or faces, but the smell of strong liquor hung in the air, making her wince.

"Sing, Pasha," someone yelled.

The man with the concertina opened the bellows wide and closed them again sharply. He chuckled, and his fingers flew over the buttons of the instrument. Starting a different tune, he sang in a hoarse voice of a drunkard. His song was bawdy and clever, an adventure of one of the Mat words—the dick. Frilled with the entire Russian vocabulary, it drove to Turkey on a shuttle trip, danced "*Cazachok*" in the middle of the Red Square, got drunk in Germany, traveled on an American submarine, and participated in many other fascinating around-the-globe escapades.

Enraptured and motionless, Amanda listened, trying not to miss a word. The singer relished his narration, cackling with glee, stringing effortlessly verse upon verse; his fantasy and rhyming abilities seemingly inexhaustible. His audience laughed so hard, some fell off the benches.

He was obviously improvising. After a while, a large, gray-haired woman picked up the story, and it immediately lost its jocular flavor. Amanda looked around for Sergey. As usual, he hovered behind her back, smiling faintly—her Russian knight-protector.

"Let's go back to the car. I must write it down," she whispered, frantically tugging him out of the circle of drunken revelers. "It was authentic, Sergey!" The scholar in her was breathless with excitement. "It was fantastic! A proper, Russian folk song. I love it."

"I recorded it," Sergey mouthed into her ear, patting his trousers' pocket. "I'm a journalist, remember. If you behave, I might let you listen, again."

"Marvelous!" Impulsively, Amanda grabbed his jacket, pulled his face down, and kissed him.

"Yeah," Sergey murmured as he squeezed her arms with both hands, deadly serious. "That's what I meant."

He kissed her back, and she let him, enjoying his male scent and his prickly whiskers. It'd been so long since she had been kissed. Finally, he pulled away. Amanda licked her tingling lips, trying to restore her inner balance. She glanced around, but in the night, alleviated only by the starlight and the half-wheel of the moon, nobody paid attention to them. The winsome ditty had deteriorated into a rude, swearing match with everyone partaking in it and trying to out-scream each other. The harmonist still played but didn't sing, anymore.

"Sweet," Sergey said. "Let's ask about your girl and get the hell out of here."

Amanda tumbled back to Earth. What was she doing? She was kissing a man half her age and married into the bargain, and her daughter might be watching. She was so pathetic! She couldn't look Sergey in the eyes. He had already moved ahead of her, mingling with the crowd and asking questions. His satiny baritone effortlessly overcame the musical obscenities. Amanda pulled herself together and stumbled after him. Thankfully, nobody could see her flaming cheeks in the darkness.

She only captured the end of Sergey's latest inquiry. "...Irina Alpashkina?"

The man Sergey addressed had an untidy, dark beard, threaded with silver and dotted with bread crumbs. "Yes, the bitch was my wife. Died, poor soul." He hiccupped. A fat woman at his side wrapped herself around him, breathing something into his ear. He shook her off.

"Do you have a daughter?" Sergey prompted. "We heard she had red hair."

The man guffawed and emitted a long diatribe of Mat words, interspaced with adjectives and pronouns.

Amanda tried to interpret the meaning, but it stubbornly escaped her, except being exceptionally rude and uncomplimentary to women.

"If my daughter was a redhead, I would've taken a belt to her mother's behind," the man said, still chuckling. "I did, anyway. They are all bitches, the females. Need a few lessons once in a while. Nad'ka, my daughter, is a bitch, too. Not a redhead, no, but pretty all the same. All them pretty bitches are sly. She is living in the North with her buddy." He noticed Amanda for the first time and snorted. "Your bitch is sly, too." His roving eyes were stripping Amanda.

She shivered, feeling as if his gaze was a hoarse brush, scratching her skin and painting her with slime.

"Sleek bitch." The man snickered appreciatively before launching into his second Mat-infested speech.

Amanda clutched at Sergey's arm with both hands, holding him with all her might. His muscles bunched under her fingers, and she heard his breath quickening. "Don't start a fuss," she hissed. "Please, Sergey. Let's go."

He whirled, grabbed her shoulder, and dragged her away toward the main street.

The man's laughter drifted behind them like a malicious, shadowy tail. "Feed your old slut better."

"Moron," Amanda muttered in English.

Sergey didn't talk. He opened the car door for her, shoved her in, got in himself, started the car, and drove away with slow, deliberate gestures. His eyes were stony, and his mouth pursed shut. If the steering wheel had been made of glass, Amanda thought it would've shattered the moment Sergey's blunt, powerful fingers closed around it. Good thing the wheel had been fashioned of a sturdier material.

Chapter Eleven
Sonya

"Mom. Maybe, Grandma can come here?" Ksenya asked. They sat together at the kitchen table, replete after devouring all the pastrami with fries and half a box of truffles.

"Maybe," Sonya agreed, sipping her tea. "She shouldn't mope all alone in her house, and Lil'ka is busy with the twins."

"They are so cute in the photos," Ksenya said wistfully. "With Grandpa."

"Yeah." Sonya contemplated taking another truffle. She probably shouldn't. It would be best if her mom came to Vancouver. At the very least, it would distract her from grief.

"She expects me to fly to the funeral," Sonya mumbled absently. "What should I tell her?"

"I said I'm sorry!" Ksenya flared.

Sonya's eyes shot to her daughter's flushed face. She didn't want another confrontation. "I know, kitten." She sighed. "I accepted your apology. I can't tell my mom that you stole the money. How else can I explain that I'm not coming for my father's funeral? Lil'ka knows about my stash. She knows I should have the money. God, Ksyushka. What a mess! What can I do?" She didn't expect an answer. She took another truffle, instead.

Ksenya also put another one in her mouth, munching thoughtfully. She sucked on her Sprite. "Could you pay with your Visa?"

"It's almost to the limit. I can hardly pay the minimum dues. No." Sonya played with her mug, twirling it around.

"Tell her, then," Ksenya said sullenly. Her hand hovered over the bag of truffles and retreated without taking another chocolate.

"I'll tell her that I can't leave my jobs. They might fire me if I do." Sonya grimaced. "They really might, at the burger place, anyway."

Ksenya stared at the table without answering. Her thin finger doodled on the gray, plastic surface.

Sonya glanced at the wall clock. "It's late enough to call Israel." She stood up and headed for the phone near the sofa. "I can't postpone it for much longer."

"Tell Grandma I love her," Ksenya murmured.

Sonya dialed. Dina answered on the second ring.

"Mama." Sonya rushed her explanation. "I can't come for the funeral. They would fire me if I leave, now. Will you manage? Lil'ka will help, right? Come to us after the funeral. I miss you so much, and Ksyushka misses you. You haven't seen her for so long. You were going to come in the summer, anyway."

"Together," Dina whispered. Tears pulsated in her voice. "We were going to come together, me and your dad. I don't know, Sonechka."

"Come, Mama. I love you.

"I love you too, Sweetling." Dina's voice was hoarse, as if she was crying but stopped to answer the phone.

"Have you been crying? Oh, Mama. I wish I could come."

"I wish it, too," Dina whispered.

"Call me if you decide."

Dina sniffed haltingly before the telephone in Sonya's hand went silent. She replaced the receiver and turned. Ksenya was watching her, her eyes huge behind the tears.

"She wants you to come?"

"That train is gone, Ksenya. I can't. I don't think she is coming here, either." Sonya started cleaning up after their feast. Ksenya didn't budge from her stool, following Sonya's quick moves with her eyes. *She is so lazy*, Sonya thought. Resentment welled up inside her. She opened her mouth to deliver a scathing comment, when Ksenya stirred.

"Mom! You're cleaning like you're dancing," she said dreamily. "I like watching you when you do chores. It's almost like when you danced, and I watched from the wings. Sometimes, when you vacuum, I peek from inside my room and pretend it's the theater. I just open the door a tiny bit and watch. Do you remember you had that Moldavian dance with a broom?"

Sonya clamped her mouth shut, turned from the fridge to face her daughter, and sank into a deep, graceful curtsey. Her hands performed an elaborate curtsy wave, a bag of truffles still clutched in her fingers. "You can applaud," she declared regally. If she didn't hide behind a stage smile, she would've started crying.

"Yahoo!" Ksenya squealed, clapping madly.

That night, Sonya couldn't fall asleep. She wanted to see her mother, but on the other hand, she didn't. Dina had always been much more strict and demanding than her husband. Sonya longed to see her father, to put her head on his shoulder and unburden herself of all her troubles, as she had as a child. That luxury would be denied her, now...forever. Her dad, Gregory Goldberg, had been the best man she had ever met. An engineer and a prankster, a loving father and a tolerant husband. Why did he have to die so young? He had only been sixty-two, and they would never know why. The Israeli law forbade the autopsy, unless the circumstances were suspicious. Would they consider dying in bed with a book suspicious? Probably not.

She turned on her nightlight, the same one that had once upon a time resided in the box she now used as her safe box. Not so safe, apparently. A tiny grimace twisted her lips. Pulling photo albums from a drawer under her mirror, she settled cross-legged on her bed and draped the blanket around her shoulders like a mantle. If she couldn't see her father alive anymore, she could at least see his photos.

Here he was with both of his daughters: Lilia and Sonya. They sat together in a boat on a pond near their *dacha*. Sonya was twelve at the time. Dina had taken this photo a few minutes before Gregory announced a crocodile attack and capsized the boat, dunking both his girls and himself in the shallow pond. Sonya grinned as she remembered.

In the other photo, he stood with Sonya after her graduation performance of a Spanish dance. She was still in costume with her castanets. Gregory beamed at his daughter. Now, Sonya stared at her father and her younger self. She hadn't been married, then.

"Mom?" Ksenya poked her tousled head inside Sonya's door. "I can't sleep. What are you doing?"

"Looking at the photographs. Want to join me?" Sonya patted a place beside her and opened up her blanket.

Ksenya darted from the door, snuggling under the blanket. She leafed rapidly through the album. "Where is your wedding photo with Dad and Grandpa? My favorite. Here it is." A smile lit her face. "You're like a princess here, and Dad is like a prince."

Sonya sighed. "I like it, too," she said.

* * * *

A couple of weeks later, Dina called. "Sonechka, I've bought a ticket," she said grimly. "I'm coming for three months. I'll be in Vancouver on Monday."

Flummoxed by the sudden reverse of events, Sonya gulped. "Mama, why? What's made you change your mind?"

"You don't want me to come?" Dina sounded unsure. "You said—"

"Of *course* I want you to come. There is a reason, right? Anything wrong?"

"I'll tell you when I come. Nothing is wrong, exactly. I just need your help."

"Can't Lil'ka help? It would be less expensive."

"No. Besides, she went to Eilat for two weeks and left the kids with Ari's mom. He's gotten a free hotel as a bonus from work. They couldn't choose the time, and Lilia was exhausted. They both needed rest."

I don't need rest? Sonya thought bitterly. She was ashamed of her own spite, but she couldn't help it. She tried to keep it out of her voice. "Of course come, Mama. We'll be glad to see you."

After she put down the receiver, she fretted. What was it that Lilia couldn't help their mom with? She tried to call Lilia, but her sister obviously hadn't taken her cell phone with her. Sonya only got the answering machine.

* * * *

At the airport, Dina looked tired from the long flight but as plump as ever. Her brown eyes were dull. She wore her old, brown coat and the terrible, silk monstrosity of a scarf she was so attached to. Faded yellow with printed, lilac cats, it was ugly and as old as Sonya. It had been Dina's wedding present from Gregory. Her father's taste in clothing had always been dismal.

Sonya hugged her mother. "Welcome to Vancouver, Mama," she murmured. She touched the scarf, but it didn't disintegrate as she half-hoped it would. It was Chinese, she recalled. So many years ago, the Chinese manufactured really good stuff, lasting for centuries. *I will buy her a new scarf as soon as I can*, she thought during their ride home. Despite being her father's gift, it was still ugly. She would take Dina shopping and make it into a rebirth ceremony. They would throw this yellow abomination away. In all probability, the new scarf would be Chinese, too.

At home, Dina settled at the kitchen table for her announcement. "Sofia," she said. "I need you to refuse your father's inheritance."

Sonya blinked. "I don't have any inheritance, do I? The only thing you and Dad owned jointly was your little flat in Petah Tikva. It's still yours. No?"

Ksenya curled up in a corner of the sofa, listening intently. "You have an inheritance, Mom?" she chimed.

"There is a problem." Dina tossed a sour glance in the girl's direction. "Your father didn't leave a will. By the Israeli law, the flat will be divided equally amongst his heirs—Lilia, you, and me."

"Mama, I don't need that flat. I'll sign your papers."

Dina shook her head sadly. "It's not that simple in Israel."

A surprised, little laugh escaped Sonya's lips. "Nothing is simple in Israel."

Dina ignored her daughter's jab. "I need a court order," she said. "The civilian court is expensive. I've decided to go to the Judaic court in our synagogue. It's much cheaper."

"Right," Sonya said. "You need a specific paper? We'll go to a notary public—"

"I have the documents issued by the court," Dina interrupted. "To be accepted in the Judaic court, your signature on it must be authenticated by a rabbi."

Sonya switched her flabbergasted gaze between Dina and Ksenya.

The girl's eyes danced, as she burrowed deeper into the sofa. "A rabbi?" she mouthed.

Dina was very serious. Sonya should've been serious too, but amusement bubbled inside her. Suppressing her indecent hilarity, she bent across the table and squeezed her mother's pale, plump hands.

"Don't fret, Mama. There are a few synagogues in Vancouver. I'll call one of them tomorrow and make an appointment with a rabbi. We'll get your papers signed by the end of the week."

* * * *

Three weeks later, the papers remained unsigned. Sonya needed to talk to her sister about it. She picked up the phone but put it back down. First, she had to see her mom and Ksenya off. They were going shopping. Jumping up from the bed, Sonya pattered to the door.

Dina was already dressed, but Ksenya couldn't decide which scarf she was going to wear. Her grandmother knitted three different new ones for her.

"Take the striped one," Sonya advised. "It'll look best with your jacket."

"Okay." Ksenya wrapped the long, bright red and cream scarf

around her thin neck once, then twice. The red *pompons* on both ends still hung below the hem of her hip-long, blue jacket. She glanced at Sonya. No matter how much they disagreed about everything else, in the matters of clothing, Ksenya still trusted Sonya's taste.

Sonya put up both thumbs. "You look terrific, kitten," she said.

"Right." Eager to be off, Ksenya turned to her grandmother. "Let's go."

"Sonya, don't forget to call the synagogue," Dina said. She sailed out the door after Ksenya.

"I won't forget," Sonya muttered. She sighed and returned to her bedroom. It was amazing how well Dina and Ksenya got along. Today, Dina was taking the girl to a mall for a shopping spree. They both were excited. They had talked about it all morning.

Grinning, Sonya picked up the phone and called her sister. "Lil'ka, how was Eilat?"

"Tremendous! The twins have forgotten me, the ungrateful brats. How is Mama holding on?"

"I think she's dealing with her grief. She's almost fine, aside from the fact that we still can't sign those papers. She thinks I'm not trying hard enough."

"Tell me. There is an anecdote there somewhere, right?"

Sonya growled in frustration. "Right. Now, they left me to tackle it alone."

"Where're they get off to?"

"Shopping. Mama said she had some money stashed specifically for Ksenya. My little sucker is walking on clouds. Every day, a new rag. Can you imagine?"

Lilia was silent for a while. "Aha," she murmured finally. "Mom is bribing her. Wise. So, what's going on with your signature? I didn't have any problem with mine. I just went to a synagogue. Took about an hour."

"I don't know." Sonya held the receiver with her shoulder while she made the bed. "Maybe we have different rules. I called two synagogues, but it was the same. First, a receptionist said that the rabbi would call me back. They never did. Then, a week later, I called again. She said the rabbi was busy for the foreseeable future, and I should call another synagogue."

"Strange. What are you going to do?"

"I'm going to the third synagogue, today. I'm not calling, anymore. I'll talk to a rabbi myself." She marched into the living room.

"Gearing up for a fight?" Lilia snickered.

"I hate fighting. I always hated competitions." Sonya picked up her rain bucket. It was full, again. She poured it into the toilet and returned it to its place beside the crack in the wall.

"Tell me about it! If you weren't such a chicken, you might've danced at the Bolshoi instead of your obscure ensemble."

"Don't." Sonya said grimly. "I loved the Petushko. Any advice regarding the synagogue?"

"Nah. Keep me informed, sis." There was some muffled, Hebrew comment, probably to Lilia's baby-sitter, before Lilia's voice came back. "So, how is Mama, really?"

"She is angry at me, but I think it's good for her. Between my troubles, Ksenya, and those synagogues with their busy rabbis, she's kind of forgotten about Dad. At least, he has slipped to the back of her mind. I think." Sonya opened the freezer, trying to decide what would be good for dinner—chicken or salmon. Deciding on the salmon, she pulled the long, pink package out of the freezer.

"She was crying every day here."

"She doesn't cry," Sonya said. "She doesn't have the time. She cooks and cleans. She even scrubbed my bathtub last Thursday."

"You made her scrub your bathtub?"

"Idiot," Sonya said and chuckled affectionately.

"I love you, Son'ka," Lilia said. "I wish I could help."

"We'll pull through. Have I told you? I talked to Jane before Mama came. Jane almost talked me into trying strip dancing."

"What?" Lilia gasped. "Are you crazy?"

"That was Mama's reaction, too. You're both so old-fashioned."

"You want to try strip dancing? Really?"

"No. Not really. I'm not sure. I was contemplating it for a while but decided I'm too old-fashioned as well. I was ashamed even to mention it to Ksenya. Jane was very disappointed in me."

"Good," Lilia said. "I don't like that quadriplegic of yours. She is a bad influence."

"She is fully emancipated." Sonya snickered. "Bye-bye, sis. Kiss the twins on the cheeks."

"Yikes. They drool."

Sonya snorted. "Then, kiss their butts."

Lilia's throaty laugh still reverberated in the receiver when Sonya finally ended the call. Somehow, her sister always managed to lift her spirit, even half the world away. Sonya put on her coat and went out. She had just enough time to visit a synagogue before her shift with Jane.

On the bus ride to the synagogue, she contemplated her course of actions. She had never been to a synagogue before. Neither she nor her parents were religious. Besides, Alexei was Russian. While she had been with him, she had never had any inclination. Maybe she should have. Maybe that's why the rabbis wouldn't help her? Because she didn't belong. Maybe she should start going to a synagogue every Friday night, or at least on Jewish holidays. It was a place of worship for her ancestors, after all.

She went up the stairs, passed under the greetings carved over the entrance in both Hebrew and English, and entered the silver, double doors of the synagogue decorated with Stars of David.

Nobody was inside the small antechamber. A window of blue and white stained glass allowed soft, diffused light in, illuminating a stack of neatly folded, blue and white *tallits* in a glass cabinet at the door to the empty prayer hall.

Cautiously, Sonya opened another door and stepped into a deserted corridor. Her lips moved as she read the Hebrew notes dotting the white, plaster walls. She still remembered the Hebrew letters, although she couldn't translate the words. She had forgotten their meanings.

On the second floor, an aged secretary directed her to the rabbi's office with the dark, wooden furniture and bare, white walls. The combination created an atmosphere of age and sober contemplation, although the building didn't look that old. An old, bearded rabbi sat writing at his cluttered desk. He stood up when Sonya entered. A question glinted in his shrewd eyes behind the wire-rimmed glasses.

"Hello, sir," she said quietly.

"*Shalom*, *Geveret*. How can I help?" He didn't come out from behind his desk or offer his hand.

Maybe, it wasn't traditional, Sonya wondered. His appearance, however, was very traditional—the black *kippa*, the gray sideburns, and the prescribed, white tassels dangling out of his pants' pockets. He would fit in very well in Israel, but he looked out of place in the middle of Vancouver. Sonya shook the cobwebs out of her head and launched into her mother's story.

"I'm so sorry for your loss, ma'am." He did come out from behind his desk at that moment. He patted Sonya on the shoulder. "Of course, I'll do all I can to help your mother—a Jewish widow from Israel. It's a *mitzvah*. Tomorrow, I'm leaving town for an orthodox conference in San Francisco. When I come back, I'll give you a call."

"Thank you," Sonya said. "Are you coming back soon?"

"In a few days. I'm not sure."

"Thanks. Here is my card." She put her card on the old man's desk.

"You're welcome, dear." Now, he shook her hand and even opened the door for her.

That went well, she mused as she trotted down the stairs. She could be assertive after all. She should've visited a synagogue before. Perhaps, she should start coming to this synagogue, at least on holidays. When would be the next Jewish holiday? She scanned the corridor with the Hebrew notes on the walls but could see nothing resembling a calendar. The rabbi would know, though. She would ask him when they met, again.

"This guy will call," she said later that night, as she updated Dina on her progress.

"Hmmm," Dina returned noncommittally.

"Yes, he will, Mama. You'll see. He was like in those tales they told us at the *ulpan,* with long whiskers and all."

Dina snorted. "Sofia, would you grow up," she said, her voice laced with disapproval. "This is not a ballet *libretto*." She shooed Sonya out of the kitchen and started washing the dishes while Sonya and Ksenya snuggled together on the sofa.

Ksenya giggled. "Long whiskers, Mom?" She exchanged an understanding glance with Dina.

Sonya felt a tug of envy. Ksenya would side with anyone against her. With her father. With her grandma. To suppress her unreasonable jealousy, she switched the subject. "I told you I put an advertisement in the 'Russian Vancouver' about doing clothes alterations. I got a call, today. A woman wants me to hem her skirt. She'll bring it in on Saturday."

"How much will you charge?" Dina asked as she rubbed the stove top.

"Mama, you don't have to do that." Sonya felt guilty, although she didn't want to stand up and go clean the stove. Her nest under the old, black and brown checkered throw was too cozy. Ksenya nuzzled warmly against her side, fussing with Sonya's hair. If not for the twinges of guilt, Sonya would've been in bliss.

"You just rest," Dina said firmly. "You worked all day. So, how much?"

"Fifteen." Sonya purred from sheer pleasure, as Ksenya dragged her fingers through Sonya's hair

"You should charge twice more," Ksenya instructed, massaging Sonya's scalp.

"No." Sonya's eyelids drooped. "That's a common price. Ksyushka, if you don't stop, I'll fall asleep right here."

Ksenya's soft lips touched Sonya's neck.

Sonya sighed. *I need so little to be happy these days*, she thought lazily.

Chapter Twelve
Amanda

"Horrible!" Amanda said skeptically. She was looking at her naked self in the mirror of her hotel room. Last night, they returned to the hotel after midnight. She had been terribly fatigued, almost unable to move. She dropped into bed without taking a shower.

This morning, after taking a long, hot shower, she examined herself, still pink from the hot water and squeaky clean. She was sixty. Her breasts were hanging, and there was this hated belt of fat around her waist, although judging by her jeans, she had lost some weight. The emotional merry-go-round she was on since she started her search was at least good for something.

She ruffled her short, damp haircut. Recently, her hair had started thinning both north and south, but on the whole, she didn't look half-bad. Better than many women in Russia. They dressed better, though. She grinned at her reflection and dragged a palm along one cheek. Her skin was still smooth. She had been swimming regularly for at least fifteen years. She ate healthy food, and she flossed after meals. Opening her lips, she admired the two even rows of white biters. Although most of her teeth had fillings, they were all intact, except for the wisdom ones. Even her back didn't trouble her here, despite the interruption in her swimming routine.

Maybe she should have a liposuction on the hips? She poked a finger at the fatty padding at her side. Maybe she should try her luck with Sergey. If they had some fun during this trip, nobody would know. Would she belittle her search for her daughter by such impure thoughts or impure actions? On the other hand, her daughter was conceived as a result of such thoughts...and actions. Between Donald and herself.

She grinned, but her grin faded quickly. She still missed Donald. She missed his hands on her body, his smiles, and his kisses. Was she stupid to entertain such thoughts again at sixty?

She squinted into the mirror, trying to imagine Donald's cheekbones—delicate, like an Irish maiden—his shorn auburn curls, and his soft hazel eyes. Instead, Sergey's wide features, bald head, and ugly duck's nose shimmered in the steamy mirror. Steamy? Gosh! She had forgotten to turn off the shower. She was really getting old. She darted back into the bathroom.

An hour later, she was ready for anything, especially a hearty breakfast. She descended the stairs in her pale pink, denim jeans and jacket. She was so famished, she could devour even the inescapable Russian pancakes. They were not too bad, after all, and she had lost weight despite gobbling them up every day. She would order the pancakes with honey and sour cream. No! She would order the most expensive variety—with caviar. Let the magazine pay if they wanted her story.

At the bottom of the stairs, Sergey was waiting for her. "Good morning, Amanda. You look delectable. I'm sorry about yesterday."

"Don't be," Amanda said. "I'll write about the bona fide Russian experience in my book. The insults of that man were a small price to pay for the privilege of listening to that amazing song. They were both real, Sergey." She smiled disarmingly. "I want pancakes with caviar."

Sergey sighed. "Your wish is my command." He didn't sound happy.

The passport bureau was in a nondescript, one-story wooden building painted gray. It was probably some other color long ago, but under the gray and overcast sky, the bureau seemed gray and overcast, too. Amanda counted eight people sitting in the long corridor. The corridor, like the faded outside walls, was gray.

"Who is the last?" Sergey asked.

A young woman in a painfully green overcoat lifted her hand, as if at school. Sergey nodded and settled onto the opposite bench. Amanda dropped down beside him.

"You think it'll take a long time?"

"Hopefully, not more than a couple of hours," he said without enthusiasm.

"What kind of an office is it? What do they do here?"

"They keep records."

"They are not computerized?"

Sergey grimaced. "Not yet. Not everywhere." He lifted his melancholy eyes, and they suddenly sparkled. He bent to her ear. "You look so pink and sweet in this gray office, like a candy. I'm salivating."

"Happy to be of service." Amanda inclined her head regally and pushed him away. "You've chosen a strange location for a compliment." She wasn't sure his comparison to a candy was a flattering one, especially at sixty. A sixty-year-old candy didn't sound enticing. "Talk to me, Sergey. Tell me about this office. I've heard some sinister rumors."

Sergey shrugged. "Nothing sinister. In Russia, everybody registers at the address where they live. So, if you're looking for someone, you can find him or her in this office."

"Don't you have telephone books? We have everyone listed in the White Pages. Of course, if they move between editions, the telephone and the address might be outdated until the next book comes out."

"How often the new editions are published?"

"In Vancouver, once a year. I don't know about the other cities."

"Everyone is in the book?"

"If they want to be. Some people don't like to be bothered, especially celebrities, so they have unlisted phone numbers."

"The government still knows?"

Amanda shrugged. "Why would the government want to know my address? I'm not a criminal." She thought about it. "Actually, lots of people do know—the credit cards, the utility companies, and the banks. We're all registered in so many places."

"We're all registered in the passport bureaus," Sergey said gloomily.

"So, if you move, you just inform one place—a passport bureau. Do they distribute information to all the utilities, like electricity, cable, and phone companies? It might be a more efficient system than ours."

Sergey snorted. "I don't think they distribute anything. Actually, in many cases, we have to have a permit to move. Especially to Moscow or St. Petersburg."

"Permit from whom?"

"From a passport bureau."

"Why?"

"Our system," Sergey said reluctantly, "kind of ties a person to his living space."

Amanda wrinkled her nose, not comprehending. "You live in Moscow, right? Let's say your family wants to relocate to St. Petersburg. Let's say you don't own anything. You just rent an apartment. Can't you move and rent in another city?" She looked at him expectantly.

"It's not that simple. I tried to explain it to Robert, but he doesn't understand, either. He's been living in Russia, on and off, for the last five years. Let's talk about something else, Amanda."

He was ashamed again, but this time, Amanda couldn't fathom the source of his shame. Robert always said Russians were enigmatic. Maybe she would never understand completely. She changed the subject. "Do I need one of my bribe envelopes here? It's a government office, right?"

"Most definitely, you'll need one of your envelopes here. Maybe two."

Amanda nodded and unzipped her purse. She took out two of the envelopes from their designated pocket and dropped them into the main compartment, for easy reach.

"Don't tell them you are a Canadian," Sergey whispered into her ear.

She glanced at him, understanding dawning. "More forms to fill?"

"You learn fast." He smiled.

By noon, they finally entered the office. The clerk, a middle-aged woman dressed in a cheap, brown business suit, had her hair pulled back into a tight, mouse-gray chignon.

Amanda produced the list of names the hospital had provided and repeated her story, pointing at the addresses of Dina Goldberg and Nina Savchenko. Following Sergey's script, she omitted her Canadian citizenship.

The woman's eyes began to sparkle. "Your daughter was switched at birth. That's terrible. Do you wish to punish those responsible?" She glanced at Sergey, measuring him. "You're the father?"

He smirked.

"No," Amanda said in irritation. "He is not the father. He is a friend. I don't want to punish anyone. I think someone made a mistake. It was a long weekend, and most medical personnel..." she sighed. "They were celebrating. I just want to find my daughter."

"Well." The clerk stood up, went to an *étagère* near the window, and returned with a sheaf of paper forms held together by a green, plastic clip. "You have to fill them all out and mail them in. The address is here." Her stubby nail with the bright, carmine nail polish pointed at the bottom of the first page. "You'll receive the results by mail next month." She offered the sheets to Amanda.

Tossing a furtive glance at Sergey, Amanda dove into her purse for one envelope. She left the second one in. "There is probably a fee for the service. Would this cover it?"

The woman hesitated briefly before accepting the envelope. She glanced inside, her fingers separating the two fifties. When she lifted her face, her eyes glinted in happy calculations. "If you want it done in a hurry, there is a double price."

Amanda pulled out the second envelope. "Tomorrow?"

"I can't." The woman said apologetically. "Come on Monday. The archives are in another building. I'll go there myself tomorrow, but you'll still have to fill out the forms. Bring them back by three, before we close. You don't have to wait in line, again. Just pop in and drop the forms on my desk." She gazed longingly at the envelope in Amanda's hands.

"You're very kind." Amanda put the second envelope on the desk and picked up the forms. "I'll come back as soon as the forms are ready."

Outside the office door, she turned to Sergey. "Monday?" she whispered.

"It's a cosmic speed, Amanda. She can't do it any faster."

"I suppose. Of course, you were right—two envelopes." She looked right and left along the narrow corridor. "Do they have a table where I can sit down?" She could only see benches filled with people along the gray walls.

"Come to the car. You can write inside."

Amanda nodded. "I will never know," she mused as she followed Sergey toward the car, "why one envelope is enough at the hospital, but two are required here?" She stopped in front of the car, waiting for Sergey to unlock the doors.

"Because the hospital clerk hardly ever gets such requests, but here, it's a common occurrence. So, you have to pay double to speed up the process."

Amanda settled inside, using a thick photo album she bought that morning as a writing pad. "I feel ignorant, like a second-grader," she complained. "They really should have a fee schedule. It would be so much easier if everyone knew the price. Why call it a bribe if it's a necessity?"

Sergey snorted derisively. "Then, we'll all have signs hanging around our necks."

"Why not?" Amanda said absently, filling out the forms. "Wear them like identity cards. You know, like at a conference. Laminated."

Sergey guffawed. "You're a treasure, Amanda. What will you do after you finish with the forms?"

"I'll go shopping. Alone. Tomorrow, you'll drive me to Suzdal.

Deal? What will you do, today?"

Sergey grinned. "Write your story." He bent until his mouth touched her ear. "And wait for you."

Her neck tickled from his imperfectly shaved jaw. His grin was contagious. It jumped from Sergey's lips right into Amanda's ear and traveled all the way to her eyes. "Maybe," she said aloud. *Almost definitely*, whispered her inner voice. Her throat felt dry, and her heart somersaulted in anticipation. Suddenly, she felt young, again.

* * * *

When she came back to the hotel from her shopping expedition, she spread her purchases on the bed to admire them all at once. Between the green pine boughs, tastefully woven into the light yellow brocade of the bedspread, two huge and gaudy Russian dolls winked at each other, as if sharing a joke. Each one had a dozen smaller dolls inside. Beside them, an entire Russian fairytale, complete with a prince shooting at Kaschey and a princess on a white steed, decorated a large, *Palekh* jewelry box. Gloria would love it.

Amanda picked up a set of *Khokhloma* bowls and caressed the smooth, cool surfaces with her fingers. The floral design sparkled gold as she turned the black and gold vessels under the soft light of the overhead chandelier. Cute little swatches of red berries added piquancy to the overwhelmingly sweet pattern.

Why did Russian souvenirs look like exquisite art while Canadian souvenirs often resembled cheap trinkets? Maybe because Russians made them themselves, with centuries of tradition behind them, while most of Canadian souvenirs were made in China? Maybe because Russian culture was so much older than Canadian? Russians had already made *Khokhloma* in the 17th century, when only Salish people and wild beasts walked the Pacific coast of Canada.

Her gaze fell on the three Pavlovo-Posad shawls, unfurled over her pillow like a huge, colorful fan. She picked up the one she selected for herself—the magnificent, white and pink confection called Diadem. Wrapping it around her shoulders, she crossed the room to the mirror.

The pink, stylized flowers poured over the thin, white wool in an elaborate bolero. The rose-tinted filigree of the fringe bumped against her jeans. With a simple black dress, it would look terrific.

She tilted her head, whirling in front of the mirror, and humming. She lifted one shoulder and the other in a semblance of a dance. Over her pink denim, it looked good, too.

She scampered back to the other two shawls on the bed. The tag on the green one she had bought for Gloria bore the name Bracelet. The other—a blue shawl with a romantic, *soubriquet* Bouquet—was reserved for her other daughter. The one whose name she still didn't know. Would the unknown young woman like the blue shawl?

Amanda's smile faded as she picked up the tag on her shawl. She hadn't noticed it at first, but all the names were in English. The shawl makers seemed to target foreign tourists. Although the craftsmanship was gorgeous, the garments cost only $35 apiece. It was a negligible price for the tourists who could afford the airfare but a huge amount for the Russians. How could the people making these beautiful things live in such squalor? How many rubles would thirty-five dollars exchange for?

She stopped her calculations before the resulting price soured her mood. Why had Russia been so poor for so long? She frowned. The land was fertile, the people talented. Alas, she had never been good with political issues.

Shaking her head, Amanda pushed the unexpected sadness away. She arranged the green and blue shawls on the pillow, made the folds level, and smoothed out small wrinkles in the soft wool. Adjusting the pink shawl around her shoulders, she tossed one last look in the mirror and headed for the exit. Sergey was waiting, and she needed his smart hands, tantalizing tongue, and scratchy whiskers. She shouldn't make him wait much longer. Beaming like a girl, she sailed out the door.

* * * *

The next morning, she still felt like glowing, although many of her muscles ached slightly. She was unused to the vigorous workout with a forty-year-old man. The old churches of Suzdal, recently restored and gilded, were just what she needed to complete her sense of well-being.

"That was exquisite!" Amanda settled into Sergey's Lada, her head reeling with the impressions from the majestic Cathedral of the Nativity of the Mother of God. The blue onion domes with their golden stars and crosses competed for tourists' interests against the fantastic, stone carvings on the white walls. Cameras flashed around the dignified, white edifice. "They don't know what is inside," Amanda muttered, nodding at the crowd. "They wouldn't have wasted their time outside if they did."

"What did you like best?" Sergey was in no rush to start the car. "Did you like the Golden Doors?"

He hadn't accompanied Amanda on her inside tour, and she was grateful. Despite the mob of German tourists, without him at her side, she felt almost private, standing in front of the marvelous iconostasis, imagining a woman's life in seventeenth century Russia. What had that long-dead woman prayed for? Amanda had prayed a little herself, for both her daughters and for the success of her expedition. Although she wasn't religious, the unearthly beauty of the frescos made her feel as if her soul soared.

"The Golden Doors were marvelous," she murmured. "Oh, and the frescoes..." Her throat felt tight.

"You're crying," Sergey accused softly.

"Rubbish." Amanda wiped off the unaccustomed tears. "It's such a spiritual experience! Strange. I'm not really into spiritual." She smiled self-consciously, ashamed of her leaking state. "Vladimir's Assumption Cathedral was also very interesting, but the sheer number of churches here in Suzdal is overwhelming... and the quality! It's a very small town."

Sergey turned the key in the ignition. "Now, I'll take you to my favorite place in Suzdal, to the Museum of Wooden Architecture. They brought wooden churches and houses there from all over the region. It's an entire village made of wood."

The paved parking lot of the museum, with its cars and tourist buses, looked incongruous beside the wooden palisade. They didn't belong together. A group of Japanese students trotting through the gates also felt alien to the place.

"How charming!" Amanda said as she and Sergey strolled among the wooden huts. "Such workmanship!" She caressed a dark, wooden wall polished smooth by the passage of years. When her palm encountered a wide *nalichnik*—a carved, wooden window apron—she traced the elaborate design with her fingers. Unlike the grand cathedral, this little museum looked cute and homey. She wouldn't mind living in it for a while. Such a cabin would be great for her summer retreat on Cultus Lake. Only she would have modern plumbing installed inside. She grinned at her own whimsy.

"Better not touch," Sergey murmured. "It's very old."

"Right. Sorry." Amanda snatched her hand away and hurried

after him toward the central square of the village, which was the hub of the tourist activity.

"Wait!" She stopped in front of the Church of the Transfiguration. Its three onion domes and layered roof, covered with aspen planks, had become silvery gray over the years, adding a translucent quality to the warm brown of the main building.

"How beautiful!" she breathed. "How have these things survived for several centuries?"

"Many didn't," Sergey said.

"How old is this church?"

"This one? More than two hundred years."

"What is that?" Amanda pointed to a small, wooden roof surrounded by the Japanese.

"A walking well. You must walk to turn the crank."

"Walk?" Amanda pushed her head between two jeans-clad, Japanese shoulders. "Wow!" she said, eyeing the strange ladder on the ground. "Such an unusual design." Smiling faintly, she stepped away and turned slowly in a circle, surveying the tiny village. The young greenery, the smells of wood and Earth waking up from the long Russian winter, filled her with an unexpected sense of completion. Without planning to, she dropped into a poetry mode.

"It calls for Esenin," she declared. Flashing a grin at Sergey, she launched into one of her favorite Esenin's poems, relishing the poet's ties with his land. Another poem followed, and then a third one, and still they weren't enough. Poetry poured out of her. Spring and the Russian land—they had been born together. A few steps away, Sergey stood unmoving, his face inscrutable, eyes glistening.

"This," Amanda breathed, encompassing the entire village with a wide sweep of her arm, "belonged to the Russian poets." She switched from Esenin to Fyodor Tyutchev, and from him to Afanasy Fet, almost singing their inspired words of spring and rebirth. The rhymes coming out of her mouth sounded like sacred hymns, and Sergey's gray eyes brightened in response.

"This belongs to my daughter!" She beamed triumphantly at the small crowd gathered around her. People started clapping. She had never before recited her beloved Russian poetry to listeners who could appreciate it. Feeling like a rock star, she bowed and waved to her small audience, as if she had just performed for a stadium of thousands instead of a dozen bored Russian tourists.

Shaking his head, Sergey pulled her back toward the parking

lot. "You are such a romantic, Amanda," he said. "What if your daughter was raised by a Jewish family, the Goldbergs?"

"Possible, but somehow I don't think so. Gloria must be Russian. She is so generous, so giving. She would fit here."

"What I do know," Sergey said, "is that you must've been Russian yourself in your previous incarnation." He added almost inaudibly, "Ladushka." His intense gaze pierced Amanda.

She pursed her lips and looked away, toward the wooden village. A blush warmed her cheeks. Any reply to Sergey's whisper would be inadequate. In ancient Russia, men bestowed the names Lada and Ladushka on their beloved women. Of course, it was the name of Sergey's car as well, but she didn't think he had meant the car just now. Like so many times since entering Russia, she got a dry, scratchy lump in her throat.

Sergey's knuckles brushed against her jaw, his feather-light touch penetrating to her toes. "Ladushka," he repeated quietly, "we'll find your daughter on Monday."

Embarrassed, Amanda dove into the car. "I like Slavic poetry. It rhymes well," she mumbled.

* * * *

On Monday, they got through the line at the passport bureau by two in the afternoon.

The familiar clerk greeted them without much enthusiasm. "I'm sorry I don't have better news for you. First—Nina Savchenko. Her husband was a military officer. The entire block where the school is now was reserved for the military. They all left the city two years after your daughter was born. I don't know where they went. The Army personnel don't inform us. Perhaps you could write to the Army headquarters in Moscow?" She didn't sound too hopeful.

"What about Dina Goldberg?" Amanda prompted.

"She wasn't registered at that address." The clerk shrugged apologetically. "The people who were registered were Elizaveta and Abram Kogan. Perhaps they were her parents. There was a Dina Kogan registered there a few years before that time, but then she moved away, to be with her husband Goldberg, I suppose. Jews always marry among themselves. She might've come back to her mom only to give birth."

Amanda's heart plummeted. "So, where are Dina's parents, now?" she asked hopelessly.

"Abram died in 1988. Elizaveta moved out, but we don't know where. Probably to live with her daughter. I looked. I promise you, I looked. I raised documents for many years. There is no Dina Goldberg in Vladimir, never was. I think the Goldbergs live somewhere else." She pushed a sheet of paper with the results of her search toward Amanda. "I'm sorry," she repeated. "Perhaps they moved to Israel. Many Jews do."

"You tried," Amanda said gloomily. "Thank you very much." Taking the useless paper, she turned around and shuffled out of the office. She was facing a dead end.

Chapter Thirteen
Sonya

Enough was enough! Sonya planted herself firmly in front of the telephone. She would call the rabbi's office, now. He promised to call, but he hadn't. More than a week had already passed. "I'm calling the rabbi's office!" she announced.

Dina lifted her head from contemplating her cards. She didn't say anything, but her soulful glance was laden with accusations.

"Don't interrupt, Mom. I'm winning," Ksenya tossed over her shoulder.

Dina's attention returned to the cards. "No, you're not." She threw a card on the table. "Beat that!"

"Ha!" Ksenya said.

Sonya tuned them out, shook her head, and dialed. She never liked card games.

"Synagogue," said a low contralto on the other end of the line. "Can I help you?"

"Hello. My name is Sofia Listvin," Sonya said. "I talked to Rabbi Bloomberg a week ago. He promised to call me as soon as he came home from San Francisco. Has he returned, yet?"

"Ummm," the contralto said doubtfully. "Yes, but he's at home, today."

"Could you give me his home number?"

"No, I'm sorry. It's against our policy to give out home numbers. I can pass on your message."

"Thank you." Sonya disconnected. By now, that was a familiar refrain. They all promised to pass on her message, but nobody had called back. She stared at the telephone. It was simple, black and cheap. The cheapest she could find. She was getting tired of being cheap. In the background, her daughter and mother argued about the cards, but Sonya didn't care. They were in the audience. She was on stage. She would dance. If the secretary didn't want to help, she would get that traveling rabbi without his secretary's help.

She pulled out the White Pages from the shelf under the phone. There was only one Bloomberg, on 29th Avenue, who lived close to the synagogue. "Gotcha!" she muttered triumphantly as she dialed the number.

"Hello," said a thin, female voice.

"Hello," Sonya said. "I'd like to talk to Rabbi Bloomberg."

"My husband's just left for his dental appointment. He should be at the synagogue later today. Can I take a message?"

Sonya repeated her story about her dead father, her mother, and her inheritance.

"I'm sorry for your loss," the wife said. She sounded kind and compassionate. She also sounded quite old. "Try to call the synagogue in an hour."

"Thanks," Sonya said. She gave the rabbi's dentist two hours before she picked up the phone, again. It was her day off from working with Jane, so she had all the time in the world, and it was only three in the afternoon.

"The rabbi is in a meeting," the secretary said. "Can I take a message? He'll call you tomorrow."

Sonya tossed down the receiver. She would call tomorrow herself. She would get that elusive rabbi! She jumped up and headed to her bedroom. She didn't think that either Ksenya or Dina noticed. They were too busy with the cards. Tomorrow morning, they were going to Victoria together.

"I'm going to practice," Sonya announced. Nobody answered.

In her bedroom, she turned on Mozart, threw her sweatshirt on the bed, and grabbed the barre. Her quick glance in the mirror revealed a thin woman with lilac stains beneath her hazel eyes, auburn hair arranged in a severe bun, and nostrils inflated with anger. Mozart's frisky strings suited neither her dark mood nor her exhausted appearance. She inhaled deeply and started her class. Maybe, it would cheer her up.

* * * *

"Mom, the ferry was so cool!" Ksenya announced as soon as she skipped inside the door. "Did you know it had six decks? It's huge!" She darted to her bedroom.

Dina followed Ksenya into the apartment much more slowly. "Four flights of stairs are too high for me to climb," she panted. "Hello, Sonechka. How have you been without us?" She sank onto the sofa. "You need a place with an elevator."

"Hi, Mama." Sonya pecked Dina on the cheek. "Rest. Dinner will be ready in half an hour. So, how did you like Victoria?" She turned back to the sink to finish peeling potatoes.

"Interesting. They have a wonderful museum. Pity you couldn't have come with us."

"I told you I couldn't leave for four days." Sonya tossed a quick glance toward Ksenya's room, but the door stayed firmly closed. "How did you two get along?"

"She is a sweet girl when she wants to be." Dina grinned. She had almost recovered her breathing by now. "We were fine. What are you making?"

"A stew," Sonya said.

"Any progress with that rabbi?"

Sonya grimaced. "Oh, yeah. I called right after you two left for your trip. His wife said he was visiting his brother in Calgary. She was expecting him back by Wednesday."

"Did you call on Wednesday?"

"Yes, Mama. I did." Sonya's knife tapped furiously against the cutting board. If she could have chopped up that itinerant rabbi, together with the potatoes, she probably would have. She was getting flustered all over, again. "He was attending a *bar mitzvah*," she said acidly. "His secretary said he would be in the office on Friday morning. Today."

"And?" Dina perked up.

Sonya stopped her exertions to look at her mother. "This morning, his wife said I should call back after the *Shabbat*."

With a deep sigh, Dina sank back into the cushions. Her lips moved, although she didn't curse aloud.

She never did, Sonya thought in irritation. Her mother was a very proper woman, but some situations called for cussing. It let out steam. To avoid Dina's affront, Sonya refrained from cursing herself, with some difficulty. Biting her lip, she slammed her knife on the marble counter. It made a satisfyingly loud clink.

"I tried, Mama. I really did," she snarled.

"Of course," Dina responded. "Calm down."

"Why? I'm fed up with our nation! Your cumbersome Jews have been kicking me back and forth like a Jewish football. Why are our people so sly? What is the reason for these games? If this shifty rabbi doesn't want to meet me, why wouldn't he come out and say so, for God's sake?"

"We Jews make the worst anti-Semites," Dina murmured disapprovingly.

"Yeah," Sonya muttered. "Good for us." She picked up a spoon with a long handle to stir the stew. It simmered sluggishly. "They said it's a free service, but I'd pay, gladly. We both would. It would only take a few minutes. Why is everyone so loath to lift a finger?" She felt her ladle stumble on the bottom of the pot. Something was stuck in there. She applied some pressure, but whatever was stuck to the bottom refused to cooperate. "Rats!" Sonya snapped. "Move!" She pushed harder. The stew bubbled vigorously, and the ladle was finally free. She sighed in satisfaction. A stew was much easier to beat into submission than a rabbi.

Thoughtful, Dina watched Sonya's struggle with the recalcitrant stew. "Lilia didn't pay anything," she said. "It was in Israel, though. Maybe here it's different. Your Canadian rabbis are sure slippery."

"It's not our Canadian rabbis! It's your freaking Jews." Sonya leaned on the counter, glaring at her mother. After several moments, she chuckled weakly. "My freaking Jews," she amended.

Dina laughed, too. She stood up and ambled around the counter to hug Sonya's thin shoulders.

"Oh, Mama. I love you." Sonya kissed Dina's wrinkled cheek. "Careful, my hands are dirty."

"Sonechka," Dina said. "Tomorrow, I'll go with you to another synagogue, and we'll make it happen, together."

"Mama, you don't speak English. You can't make anything happen here. Besides, tomorrow is *Shabbat*."

"You'll speak. I'll provide the fighting spirit. We'll go on Sunday, then."

"All right," Sonya said darkly.

* * * *

"Sonechka, I'm sorry I'm pushing you into this," Dina said during the bus ride to the synagogue. "I'm flying back home in a month. I need those papers signed."

"I know, Mama. You're right. I'll be strong," Sonya promised. "I won't give up." She repeated the words to herself like a mantra all the way to the rabbi's office. *Don't give up!*

This synagogue was small and old, with no decorations. The young rabbi, bright-eyed and pink-cheeked, hastily stood up from his seat behind the cluttered desk. He didn't even have a beard, yet. Only dark down clouded his round, blushing face. His innocence and naivety shined through the thick lenses of his glasses.

Sonya felt something stir inside her; something she thought had shriveled after so many months of disuse. Alexei hadn't noticed her in the last two years, ever since he dunked too deep into the bottle. Stunned by the boy-rabbi's solemnity and sheer beauty, she stared. He was so big, towering over both Sonya and her mother! He was the first male specimen she wouldn't mind touching her since Alexei. She definitely wanted to stretch her hand and caress his blushing cheek. Was the downy stubble on his face as soft as it looked?

"*Shalom*." The boy nodded gravely. "What can I do for you?"

Suddenly, Sonya knew that he posited a real question, not a salesperson's formula. This youngster obviously wanted to serve his people. Darn, he was so beautiful!

Dina's elbow dug into Sonya's side. "Talk!" her mother whispered fiercely in Russian.

"Right." Sonya jerked and flushed guiltily. Had her mother noticed her crazy arousal? Throwing a quick glance in Dina's direction, Sonya explained their predicament.

The young rabbi pondered her request for a few minutes. "I'll have to set up an appointment for you, ma'am," he said finally. "Probably next week. Leave your phone number, and I'll call you as soon as I arrange everything."

Impossible! He was the same as the others? He wanted to kick her away? No! Sonya pursed her mouth tightly. The gorgeous youngster would be sooo disappointed. She had the new mantra—no quitting. "Sir," she said tersely. "Maybe, we shouldn't postpone it."

"Don't allow him to send us away. Do it, now," Dina whispered in Russian. Apparently, she had guessed the gist of the conversation. She thrust the oversized envelope containing all her documents into the rabbi's hands and plopped into the chair in front of his desk. "I'm not leaving here until he does it, or I die of old age, whichever comes first," she declared.

He grabbed the envelope, more as an automatic reaction than anything else, and recoiled from Dina's assault.

"Could you do it now, please," Sonya translated. "It won't take much time, right?"

"I can't." His peachy cheeks darkened. "I need two more rabbis for the procedure to be legally binding. As soon as I arrange for them to come here, I'll give you a call. Please!" Pushing the envelope back into Sonya's hands, he adjusted his glasses with a thick finger. His huge, brown eyes begged her to understand and forgive. The fine hairs on his hands gleamed in a beam of the spring sunlight from a window.

"Of course." Sonya blushed. She didn't mistake the boy after all. He was a good one. "This is my phone number, sir." She dropped her card on the desk and pulled Dina from her chair. "Let's go, Mama. I'll explain later. He'll contact us."

"Thank you," he called after them.

Outside the closed door of the office, Dina dug in her heels. "What did he say?"

Sonya translated.

"Two more rabbis?" Dina's brows shot up. "No wonder nobody wanted to do it. Too much bother. Lilia didn't say anything about two rabbis."

"It's probably easier to find two additional rabbis in Israel," Sonya muttered. "He'll call."

Dina's expression turned skeptical. Obviously, she didn't believe it.

* * * *

The boy proved her wrong. He called three days later, inviting them to come to the synagogue the following Monday.

"Aha! I told you he'd call." Sonya performed a short, spirited jig, using the scissors she was holding as castanets. She had just finished hemming pants for an old man—her third client in a week. Her alteration business was really taking off, and she was feeling powerful. Maybe she could leave the burger place soon. Snatching the pants off her coffee table, she waved them like a mantle in a toreador dance, humming a Spanish tune from *Don Quixote*.

"Fine, fine." Dina flinched. "Put the scissors away. So, we've encountered one decent Jewish boy in Vancouver? So what?" With one plump fist, she punched the dough she was kneading for a pie. "I wish you could find yourself a nice, Jewish man."

Ksenya sat cross-legged on the sofa, watching them both with an indulgent smile. At her grandmother's comment, the smile vanished. "She can't, Grandma," she announced menacingly, solemn like a judge. "She's still legally married to my father."

Dina winced.

* * * *

The rabbi's small office seemed even smaller and more cluttered with the two additional rabbis, obviously pensioners. The oldsters' identical black *kippas*, white beards, and whiskers made them look like twins. They were both very old, shaking from age, although they beamed benevolently at their young host, Sonya, and Dina.

Sonya fidgeted, uneasy under the old men's faded, rheumy eyes. The youngster conducted the ceremony with the flare of a straight-A student.

"Are you sure you wish to give up your inheritance in favor of your mother?" he asked.

"Yes, I'm sure." Across his desk, Sonya reached for the paper, but he held it firmly.

One of the older men raised his trembling hand, covered with pale spots. He was probably a redhead in his youth, like Sonya's father, although his freckles had grayed out together with his hair and beard. "You cannot refuse your inheritance in favor of your mother without your mother giving you something in return," he announced in a quivering tenor.

Both Dina and Sonya gaped. "What?"

His wobbling finger pointed at Dina's scarf, the same yellow terror belonging on a scarecrow she had arrived with. "Give her your scarf, *Geveret*," he ordered.

Sonya's eyes glinted in sudden exhilaration. She would destroy the scarf as soon as she could. "Yes. Give me the scarf, Mama," she said quickly.

The freckled oldster glowered.

Dina untied the scarf and pushed it into Sonya's hands. "Of course."

Sonya shoved the scarf into her pocket.

All three rabbis nodded in satisfaction, and the youngster at last released the paper into Sonya's hands. She signed it. Dina signed it. The three rabbis signed it.

"Done!" Sonya murmured, as they hurried to the bus stop. "We did it, Mama!" She felt such relief, she was giddy. The sun beamed on them, and the wind picked up. Cold and damp, it stirred the puddles from last night's rain.

As they passed a garbage bin, she glanced furtively at her mother, saw that Dina was busy buttoning her coat, and threw the bunched up scarf into the bin. It snagged on an invisible obstacle. She pushed harder, her hands shaking, and heard the old silk tear as the scarf fluttered down into the bin. One yellow, silk thread flapped in the breeze, caught on the edge. She rushed to catch up with her mother.

"Let's go to a mall and buy you a present to celebrate," Sonya sang in triumph.

"Don't be silly. You shouldn't waste your money on me," Dina replied absently. "I'll bake a cake." She stretched her hand toward Sonya without looking. "Give me the scarf, Sonechka."

"No," Sonya said. "I threw it away. That was my part of father's inheritance. You gave it to me yourself in exchange for the house. By Jewish law, it was mine to do with as I please. All three rabbis witnessed it."

Dina's jaw dropped as she stopped abruptly. "You're not serious!" She lifted her scandalized gaze. "Sonya, give me the scarf! It's chilly."

"No! It's in there." Sonya pointed at the garbage bin and laughed. "Let's go buy you a new one."

"You've thrown it away? It was your father's gift."

"It was ugly, Mama." Sonya kissed Dina's pale cheek. "Come with me, please. Let's shop together at least once. You went shopping with Ksenya. Let me buy you another scarf. Please." She knew she was pleading, but she couldn't help it. Abruptly, it was the most important thing right now, and her lips quivered. She turned to face her mother.

"Oh, honey," Dina whispered. "Of course. You'll buy me a scarf, and I'll buy you a new coat. Deal?"

Sonya opened her mouth to say "No".

"Ksyushka told me about the money," Dina said. "We had a long chat on the ferry." She steered Sonya toward the bus stop. "Let's go to a mall and have a nice dinner, together. We have to talk."

"Okay." Meekly, Sonya followed Dina to the bus stop.

* * * *

"Sonechka, I have some money saved. A few thousand dollars," Dina said, when they settled into a window booth in a White Spot restaurant. "Your dad received it from Germany, as a settlement for his family's evacuation during the war. I want to give it to you."

Sonya watched the clouds outside move against the sun. "Mama, no. I can't."

"Sonya, listen to me."

"No." Sonya's eyes followed the clouds' aggression. The sky was rapidly getting darker.

"Sonechka—"

"Mama, I made the decision to marry Alexei. You were always

against it." Sonya still wouldn't look at her mother.

"He was already drinking," Dina said quietly. "The Russian pig has ruined your life."

"No, he didn't. I loved him, and I was happy. It was only here, that he wouldn't stop drinking." Sonya fell silent, waiting while the waitress deposited their salads on the table. As soon as the waitress glided away, she continued. "I think I still love him," she said softly. "I dream about him. When I kicked him out, I hoped he would do something. Stop drinking, maybe. Ksyushka loves him so much."

"Yes, she does." Dina plunged into her salad with unnecessary force. "More than he deserves," she mumbled with her mouth full of lettuce.

Sonya stirred her cucumbers with a fork. Then, she put one slice in her mouth. The tangy dressing tasted bitter. "I'm a slut," she said. "I dream of Alexei at night, but in the daytime, I'm ready to jump into bed with anyone. That boy-rabbi, for example." Her lips crimped.

"I wouldn't mind jumping into bed with him, too," Dina said.

Sonya woke up from her trance of self-disgust. "No!" She looked her mother in the eyes and grinned suddenly.

Dina nodded. "He was just so sexy." Two pink spots appeared on her pasty cheeks. She kept on attacking the variegated foliage on her plate. "My life with your father wasn't always easy," she murmured to her salad.

Sonya shook her head and put another cucumber into her mouth. This one didn't taste so bitter. In fact, it was savory. She crunched on her cucumber, enjoying the sharp seasoning.

"Can you reconcile with Alexei?"

Stubbornly, Sonya shook her head. "Not unless he stops drinking. Not likely."

"How about that man you hemmed the pants for?"

"Mama, he's almost *your* age!"

"He asked me if you were single. He's a widower."

Sonya stopped chewing. She swallowed slowly. "I suppose," she said. "He owns his place. He said he's a department manager with some accounting company."

"He can support you while you study."

"Mom, you're like that serpent in heaven, tempting me with a golden apple. It's so mercenary. Besides, I don't really like the guy. He wears his pants too short."

"You don't know him, and you're hardly in heaven at the

moment. You can live with short pants. At least he's a Jew."

"True." Sonya put the last cucumber slice in her mouth. This one was bitter, again. Probably one bitter cucumber spoiled the entire salad. "Maybe," she said. On the other side of the windowpane, the rain started, again. Had she remembered to empty her rain bucket in the morning? Her eyes fell on the large bundle at her side—her new leather jacket. Dina paid $500.00 for it. Maybe Sonya should start dating that man. What was his name? Yuri, she recalled vaguely. He was bald and overweight, but he seemed nice. Moreover, he was loaded. She sighed. If he asked, she would give him a chance and see where they would end up.

Chapter Fourteen
Amanda

Amanda pushed away her empty plate and leaned on the back of her plush chair. She was replete with the delicious, fried sturgeon. "This was lovely!" she said with a faint smile.

"I knew it would lift your spirit." Sergey caught her hand and raised it to his lips.

"Yes, but what do I do, now?" Amanda pulled her hand away. "The sturgeon hasn't solved my problem. We have to go back to Moscow. Would the Army headquarters tell me where to find Nina Savchenko?"

Sergey repossessed Amanda's hand. "We can try. Before we pack up and hare off to Moscow, there is one more thing we could do here." He tossed money on the table and pulled Amanda off her comfortable seat. "Let's go, darling."

"Where?" She hurried after him.

Grinning mysteriously, he got into the car and opened Amanda's door. "Get in, Ladushka."

Sighing, Amanda scrambled into the Lada. She was getting used to Sergey's fond sobriquets and his comforting presence. Last night, they had spent together, again. She dreaded the upcoming separation. She had only known Sergey for a few days, but it felt as if she was granted a second chance in life.

Her first life with Donald had been good, although like any family, they had their ups and downs. After he died, she felt bereft, drifting aimlessly. Sergey revived her. With him, it felt like a honeymoon again, but she was old enough to realize that honeymoons didn't last.

She held her door open, her eyes examining Sergey's solid frame in the next seat. His hands rested on the steering wheel, wide and reliable. His gray eyes twinkled with warmth. Where Donald had been a torch—hot, quick, and volatile while lighting the way and burning everyone, including himself—Sergey was a stout, Russian oven, keeping heat forever, trustworthy, and rooted into the ancient land of Russia. Maybe meeting him was Amanda's real purpose for coming here? Maybe, her daughter was just a pretense? She would feel so cold when his warmth inevitably withdrew from her side.

"What can we try?" she asked and slammed the door shut. She was getting to be so maudlin, she was disgusted with herself. She shoved the safety belt's buckle into its lock with needless force. It didn't want to go in, or her hands shook. She wasn't sure which. She shoved it again and again, getting impatient. The buckle stubbornly resisted her fumbling.

Sergey watched her struggle for a few seconds. Then, he chuckled, leaned toward her, held her trembling hands with one large palm, and quietly secured the belt with the other hand. Before he straightened, he planted a light kiss on Amanda's cheek.

"We're going to be detectives," he said. "It's late afternoon, already. People are coming home from work. We're going back to the house where Dina Goldberg nee Kogan lived. If we go from door to door, someone might remember her. Her parents lived there for years. Perhaps, we can learn something. Perhaps, someone remembers the Kogans' granddaughter. They might recall whether she was a redhead or not. Perhaps, the girl visited her grandparents on vacations. At least, we might learn whether we should chase the Savchenkos."

"That would mean Gloria is a Jew." Amanda's spirit sank even lower. She kind of hoped that wouldn't be true. Her cheeks heated up. She had always considered herself open-minded. She respected Jewish people. They were the smartest bunch and very much family-oriented. There were many scholars among them. She had several Jewish friends, but she was a Canadian with British ancestry. The sudden discovery that her daughter might be a Jew by blood would need some time to settle in. Would Gloria accept it?

Sergey snorted without mirth. "Take heart, Amanda. She might not be. Then, we'll pursue the Army line." He started the car.

Abruptly, Amanda hated her name. Ladushka was so much better, even if she didn't deserve it. Sergey was right. She wasn't his warm, loving Ladushka. She was a cold-hearted, British prude, Amanda. Unable to find words to redeem herself, she lifted her nose and cloaked herself in a mantle of silence.

The house stood perpendicular to the street, one of seven similar houses along the block. People young and old walked down the street in both directions. Children held their mothers' hands, chatting loudly. Two young men talking sports passed Amanda and Sergey.

Rioting greenery in the inner yards and around the houses camouflaged the decaying fences and wooden benches that hadn't been painted in forever. Empty doorways, stripped of doors, still gaped at Amanda like empty eye sockets.

"There is so much greenery," she said, trudging miserably in Sergey's wake. "The soil must be very good. I wonder why there are no flowers."

Sergey glanced back over his shoulder. "You speak such good Russian, Amanda. You recite our poetry better than some Russian actors. Sometimes, I forget you're not Russian."

"Did I say something stupid? Again? About flowers, right? I'm sorry. It was just a mindless inquiry. I miss our flowers. Vancouver is blooming in May."

He stopped abruptly, whirling to face her. "I'm sorry," he said. His eyes warmed up. "Tell me about flowers in Vancouver."

"I miss them," Amanda repeated. She basked in his gaze, craving his touch. Why wouldn't he touch her? Was he repelled by her anti-Semitism? She wasn't anti-Semitic. She truly wasn't. She winced.

"The whole city is in bloom in spring," she hurried her explanation. "We have a Rhododendron Alley in the VanDusen Botanical Garden. It's like a multicolored carpet hanging between the trees. A kilometer-long carpet on both sides of the alley, and there's this flower bower in the Queen Elisabeth Park. We have rhododendrons and azaleas in almost every garden. In my garden, too—white and peach...and tulips...and begonias. I love begonias. Also roses, but they aren't blooming, yet." She knew she was babbling but she couldn't stop. She was pathetic!

"I wish I could see all this," he said wistfully.

"Come for a visit," she breathed.

His lips twitched. "Let's find your daughter first."

He would never visit her, Amanda thought forlornly.

"I'll take the first door." Sergey pointed toward the dark hole in the pinkish wall. An old man stomped out at that precise moment, glared at Sergey's outstretched hand, and issued a long and inventive oath in Mat.

Sergey barked an appropriate response in the same language, glanced at Amanda, and winced. "Sorry," he mumbled.

Amanda snickered. "I'll take the second door." She marched further along the dirty, pink wall and ducked into the second doorless opening—the one where Dina Goldberg's parents had lived a long time ago, on the third floor. Careful not to step into any suspicious piles, she climbed to the top floor and started from the right-hand apartment.

"Kogans? On the third floor? I don't know," said a young, fat woman in a dark, sleeveless dress. She slammed the door in Amanda's face.

An old geezer in the door frame of the opposite apartment cackled, hunching like a comma. "I've only lived here for two years. Don't remember any Kogans."

Sighing, Amanda went down to the fourth floor but had no luck there, either. She didn't buzz again into the Kogans' former flat. One meeting with its rude occupant the other day had been quite enough. She tried the second door on the landing, but after some shuffling behind the steel door, nobody opened it.

"I just want to ask a question," Amanda informed the closed door. "Open, please?" She rapped on the door with her palm.

The door stayed firmly closed.

On the second floor, an ancient lady dressed all in black said she remembered the Kogans and their daughter Dinochka. "I didn't see them much. I don't go out often. Rheumatism is a beast," she grated, leaning on her cane. She didn't know whether Dinochka's daughter was a redhead, and she thought Dinochka had a son.

Amanda almost swore in Mat. Only the thought that she might shock the old woman held her lips shut.

On the first floor, both doors were protected by metal grills. A girl child with a blonde ponytail and a huge, blue bow opened one door. "Come later, when my mom is home," she said. "You can talk to Grandpa now, but he doesn't hear well." She pointed to her grandpa, who stood behind her, looking belligerent. A huge beer barrel of a man, his torso and beefy arms were naked and covered with a dense forest of gray hair.

"Thank you, dear," Amanda mouthed, beating a hasty retreat.

Nobody answered in the other flat on the landing. Amanda came out, squinting into the late-afternoon sunshine. She hated being a detective. Studying Slavic literature was much more fun. A gust of wind blew from the river, and she shivered in her thin, tweed jacket. Despite the bright sunshine, the air was getting chilly.

Sergey was nowhere in sight. Maybe, he was having a better luck. A few steps away, behind a screen of tall shrubs, children played in a sand box. A young woman, burdened by a multitude of white plastic bags in both hands, scuttled past Amanda. An orange cat frisked around the woman's feet and dashed into the house.

Amanda headed toward the next doorway, doorless like the others. A bench stood near the entrance—the only one in the neighborhood that had mysteriously survived with all four legs intact. Two old women occupied it, chatting animatedly. One of them had on a large, dark brown coat. The other had a huge, gray shawl wrapped around her shoulders. The shawl was fuzzy and very thick. It was nothing like the ornate, thin shawls Amanda bought a few days ago. It seemed so cozy, she suddenly wanted to huddle under it. After plodding up and down five flights of stairs, her feet needed to rest.

"Could I sit with you for a few minutes?" she asked the woman with the shawl.

"Of course," the woman said. She seemed surprised. "You're not from here, are you?"

"No." Gingerly, Amanda sat on the edge of the bench. Would it hold her weight in addition to the other two women? The bench stood steadfast.

"A tourist? Got lost, have you?"

"Not really," Amanda said. "I'm looking for someone. They lived here before. Maybe you know—the Kogans?" She pointed vaguely in the direction of the middle entrance.

"Of course," the woman in the shawl said. "I went to school with Dina, their daughter."

Amanda turned to her in surprise. The woman didn't look her contemporary. She looked about twenty years older, pale and wrinkled. Also, she was missing a few teeth.

"Do you know where Dina lives, now?" Amanda held her breath.

"I think she lives in Moscow with her husband. After her dad died, her mom moved there with her."

"Thank you. Do you know if Dina's daughter was a redhead?" Amanda felt like a hound on a scent, straining in her eagerness.

The woman looked at Amanda with suspicious eyes. "Why do you ask these questions? Are you from the police? Is Dina in trouble?"

"No! No! Her daughter is a redhead, isn't she? Have you seen her?" An involuntary grin stretched her lips.

"Well, yes," the woman said reluctantly. Her friendly attitude dwindled into coldness, and her gruff voice dropped even lower. "Both Dina's girls are redheads, and so is her husband. Why?"

Amanda smiled widely. “Thank you so much! You know, I’m from Canada.” She launched into her story one more time. Somewhere in the middle of it, Sergey joined them, listening to her narrative with his habitual, wry grin.

“Oh, my God!” the woman in the shawl whispered. “You’re searching for your daughter!”

Her friend shook her head, her small eyes full of wonder and envy. “Such a fantastic story,” she said. “Like on TV.”

“Yes!” Amanda almost screamed. “Oh, I’m so grateful.” She laughed while her eyes leaked. She wiped off the tears, although a smile lingered. “Do you know the names of Dina’s daughters?” Her lips trembled.

“I think the older girl is Sofia,” the woman said thoughtfully. “The one born here. The younger one is Lilia.” She smiled, too. “You’ll find her.”

“Sofia,” Amanda said dreamily. “Moscow. Thank you so much!” Unable to keep her bubbling emotions in check, Amanda hugged the woman, surprising herself. She had never hugged a stranger before. She began crying, sobbing into the warm, fuzzy shawl while clutching it with both hands. “Thank you, thank you, thank you,” she muttered.

“Oh dear,” the woman said faintly. She patted Amanda’s shoulder and sighed deeply. “You’ll find her. I believe Sonya studied at the Moscow Ballet School. She is a dancer.”

Amanda pulled away. “I’m sorry.” She wiped her wet cheeks with both hands. “Thank you.” She sniffed.

“I wish you all the best in your search,” the woman said solemnly.

“Thank you,” Amanda repeated. She stood up. “My daughter is a ballerina,” she informed Sergey, almost singing the last word.

“So I’ve heard,” he responded curtly, bowing to both women. “Thank you, ladies.” Then, he pulled a notebook from his pocket and addressed the woman in the shawl. “I’m a journalist, writing Amanda’s story. My name is Sergey Pechkin. Could I tell my readers your name? You did help her tremendously.”

“Tremendously!” Amanda echoed, beaming at all of them. She stepped closer to Sergey.

The woman in the shawl sighed again, her eyes shining wetly. “Of course. Lyubov Kasatkina.”

Her friend in the coat giggled.

Amanda pivoted back toward the women. “Thanks, Lyuba,” she said. “I love these Russian names. They are so soft, like this shawl." She put her hand on the woman's shoulder. "So soft," she repeated, her fingers burrowing into the shawl, threading through the gray, downy stuff while her tongue caressed the unfamiliar name variations. "Lyubov, Lyuba, Lyubochka. Sofia, Sonya, Sonechka." She couldn't stop smiling.

Lyubov laughed. "You like my shawl? I have another one like this. My sister knits them. They are better than those Orenburg lacy shawls you can buy in souvenir stores. Thicker and warmer, but nothing fancy." She stood up. "I'll bring it for you."

"You sell them?" Amanda perked up. "How much?" She opened her purse.

"It's a gift," the woman said sternly and disappeared into the house.

"Did you know Dina Kogan, too?" Sergey asked her friend.

"Yeah." A leer split the woman's broad face. "I've lived here since the house was built. Went to the same school. Nice girl, Dina. Never mind she was a Jew."

Amanda shrank away. Had she herself sounded just as spiteful?

* * * *

Sergey drove to the hotel in silence. Amanda sat next to him, smoothing the folded square of the shawl on her knees. It was still fuzzy and warm, but it didn't give her as much joy, anymore.

"Anti-Semitism happens in Russia," he said after a while.

"I guess it happens everywhere," she replied gloomily. She added, "Sonechka Goldberg." She smiled. "I know her name, now.

"She might not be a Goldberg, anymore. You realize that, don't you?" Sergey said.

"Why?" Amanda switched her surprised gaze from the shawl to him.

"She might be married. She is what, thirty-five?"

"I hate you. I must've been mad to start this insane search." Amanda hit the shawl with her fist. The fist sank into the gray fluff. Her knees didn't even feel the blow beneath the mass of down, and her fingers unclenched by themselves, playing with the feathery, woolen strands. "Sonechka," she murmured, again. Uncannily, the name was calming her down. "She is thirty-four, like Gloria." Abruptly, she lifted her eyes at Sergey. "I might be a grandmother."

His hooting laughter reverberated within the confines of the Lada.

Chapter Fifteen
Sonya

Sonya had met Yuri once before, for coffee and a movie, soon after her mother left for Israel. Today was their second date, and Yuri invited her to his place after dinner. He had been talking about food all the way from the restaurant, driving his new Chevrolet with one hand and helping himself to express his point with the other. His tenor sounded sour.

"The *entrecôte* was a little tough, but the salad was good and juicy, right? Large portions, too." Yuri patted his belly as he opened the door to his apartment to usher Sonya in. "How was your fish?"

"Crispy," Sony said with faked enthusiasm. "Especially the tail."

Yuri didn't get her sarcasm. Oblivious, he barged on with his critical overview. "On the other hand, they can't prepare desserts, and they charge too much. I didn't like the mousse. Did you like your pie, Sonechka?"

"No," Sonya said. She never liked talking about food. Food talk bored her. Last time, Yuri talked about movies. "Your apartment is very clean," she said to change the subject.

"Yes," he agreed happily. "I have a good housekeeper. I pay her fifteen bucks an hour to come and clean every Friday. She cooks, too. Makes great beef enchiladas." He dragged his finger along the shiny surface of a drawer in his foyer. "See? No dust."

"I see," Sonya murmured. She needed to dust her place, too. She forced her attention back to Yuri. So, he liked good food and made enough money to pay a housekeeper. Unable to decide whether that was good or bad, she studied her surroundings.

The dark, wooden table and chairs with carved backs looked polished and expensive, like one would find in a furniture store. The dark green, leather sofa and loveseat seemed pristine, as if nobody ever sat on them. Everything screamed "money!" but there was no ritzy feeling here like in Jane's house. No prints on the walls, no Tiffany lamps, no classy Art Nouveau ceramics, no houseplants. Here, the money was mundane and boring. To come alive, this house craved a woman. It needed a pinch of eccentricity. Sonya rubbed the silky surface of the sofa with her finger, pressing a little. The green leather bounced back like a living thing. Perhaps, this place had been secretly coveting her artsy touch?

She dropped down, sinking into the deep cushions. She might like it here. "Wow!" she said. "Is it new?"

"I don't spend much time in the living room." He came closer, looming over her. He regarded her with hungry eyes. "Would you, ahem, like to see the bedroom?"

Sonya grinned. "Definitely." Was he shy? She stood up. Even in her heels, she had to stretch her arm to pat his slightly hanging jowl. A bit fat for her taste, but beggars can't be choosers. She crossed the floor to the music unit.

Mewling, he followed her like an overstuffed puppet, hulking over her—his petite puppeteer. He was probably twice her weight if not more, and she relished the feeling of control over this big man.

"Nice CD collection," she said, although she didn't know most of the names. Not a surprise, really. She only knew classical music and folk tunes. She never had time for rock bands, Russian or otherwise. She never liked them, either. He obviously did, and she wanted to boost his ego a little.

"Do you want some music?" he asked eagerly.

"No, just looking. Maybe later." She started toward the kitchen.

He caught up with her, enveloping her in a hug from behind. "I want you so much," he mumbled in her ear.

Snickering, Sonya extricated herself from his awkward, suffocating embrace. "All in good time, Yuri. Show me your kitchen."

"After." His tenor took on whining qualities. "Let's do it, now." He pulled at her arm.

She allowed him to drag her all the way to the bedroom and the king-sized bed. This room showed signs of being lived in. A large TV was here. A pile of newspapers on a bedside table. A dark blue bathrobe hung on a hook inside the door. He wore a bathrobe? It must be size twenty. She opened her mouth to ask, noticed a few male cosmetic bottles on the tall dresser, and stayed prudently quiet.

Yuri dropped onto the striped yellow and turquoise bedcover and began undressing frantically. "Hurry up, Sonechka," he panted, pulling off his socks. His fat fingers shook as he tore at the buttons of his shirt. "I can't wait much longer."

He wasn't going to undress her. Alexei had always undressed

her. He played with every item of her clothing and the skin beneath. He kissed and licked all of her before he ever got to the important parts. She always paid him back kiss for kiss, tickle for tickle, admiring his lean, muscular body and his musical fingers. She didn't admire Yuri's meaty chunks. Why did she expect foreplay from this behemoth? She must be a half-wit.

No comparisons, she told herself sternly. Snorting under her nose, she pulled off her thin, chocolate brown tunic with gold, sequined appliqués. She bought it many years ago, when their ensemble toured Czechoslovakia. She had a huge success there as a soloist, especially in the Russian and flamenco dances. The country didn't exist anymore, but the luxurious tunic still looked great. Alexei adored it, but it was lost on Yuri. What a pity.

Rats! She was comparing them, again!

Yuri opened up the blanket and plopped onto the navy sheet with a loud "Whoosh!" His naked body was thick and soft, the fat deposits swaying like jelly, white on dark linen. "Come!" He stretched his plump arms toward her, breathing heavily. A behemoth in heat. Sonya chewed on her lower lip to keep from laughing aloud. Although they didn't turn on the light, the evening was still young, and even with the draperies closed, she could see his pleading, hopeful eyes and his standing dick. It was smaller than Alexei's.

"Right!" Stop comparing, she ordered herself. Then, she smiled brightly and dove into the bed.

Yuri rummaged in the bedside table. "Condom, condom," he muttered. As soon as he sheathed his mid-sized equipment, he latched on Sonya's mouth, pawing at her body with his soft hands, searching blindly until he found the appropriate opening. Then, he guided himself in and started pumping like crazy.

"Harrumph, harrumph," he wheezed.

The rest happened so fast, Sonya couldn't believe it. It was nice while it lasted, despite the small dick, but it didn't last nearly long enough. In the end, Yuri screamed like an enraged bull and dropped down, squishing her into the mattress with his beefy bulk.

"So good," he puffed. "Oh, you're so sweet, Sonechka. So sweet."

Sonya squeaked under him. "I can't breathe, Yuri. You're too big."

He rolled off her and gave her an awkward pat on the thigh. "Too fast? I'll be slower next time. You did enjoy it, didn't you?"

"Of course," Sonya lied. "You're so powerful."

He licked his fat lips. "You're like a chocolate mousse, my sweet! Better than in any restaurant." He groaned, as his big finger left a squiggly trail over her breast.

Sonya kissed his short neck, while her belly ached, dissatisfied and betrayed by Yuri's quickie. *There won't be a next time*, she vowed to herself. She wanted a man, but not this one. She wanted another one. The one who could drive her delirious with his caresses and quench her lust. The one who drank too much and didn't want her, anymore. She felt like crying. No matter how much money Yuri had, and no matter how kind he was, he wasn't for her.

"I have to go," she whispered. Scrambling out of bed, she pulled on her beige slacks.

With woebegone eyes, Yuri watched her fastening her bra. "Can't you stay the night?"

"No. I'm sorry, Yuri." She bent down to give him another small kiss. His cheek was very soft, velvety. Almost like Ksenya's. *Some praise for a grown man*, Sonya thought sadly, turning away from the bed. She could have never mistaken Alexei's stubbly cheek for Ksenya's. Another foolish comparison.

"Ksenya is waiting for me," she said.

"You're spoiling her. You told me she was disrespectful, and you just let it go. You're too lenient, Sonechka. You should be stricter."

Adjusting her brown tunic, Sonya turned to face him. "You don't have your own kids, Yuri. You don't know. It's not so simple. Wait until you have children."

"Okay," he said hastily. "I'll give you a call. Tomorrow?"

"I'll call you," Sonya said. "Don't get up. Your lock is automatic?"

"Yes." He blew her an air kiss. "I'll miss you. I'm missing you, already."

Sonya faked a smile and darted out, into the elevator. What a poor, fumbling fellow. Her mother would've called him a klutz, and she would've been right. He would have to wait for her call for a long time. He was such a disappointment! She ran out the door of Yuri's building and turned left, toward the bus stop.

As she strode past the rented houses, she inhaled the combined aroma of spring flowers, fresh earth, cooking, and auto exhaust. She felt sorry for Yuri. He was a fine man, a bit on the fat side but hardworking and sober, and he seemed genuinely attracted to her. Too bad she didn't share his attraction. She had just started dating him, because she wanted sex. Sonya winced. It didn't sound good, using Yuri like that.

The row of tall rhododendrons she walked past stretched along the neighboring house. The refined beauty of their white and pink clusters seemed ethereal and unearthly, almost too much for the simple, dark green background of their leaves. In the fragrant twilight, the bushes seemed to flaunt their porcelain-like majesty. They hugged the wall like a floral curtain, hiding the first-floor windows. Sonya was alone on the street—alone with the fairytale rhododendrons.

Two years since they moved here, and the rhododendrons still stole her breath away. She crossed the lawn to touch the waxy petals. In the growing darkness, the blossoms resembled theatrical props. They were too huge and gorgeous to be real. She sniffed. No smell, just like the props. She sighed in disappointment.

Across the street, a gigantic bush of yellow rhododendrons reached to the second floor, curving around a flower bed stuffed with blue and crimson pansies. Salmon begonias, hanging from the second floor balcony, crowned the entire bouquet. Sonya grinned at the gaudy splendor. She still smiled as she opened the door to her apartment.

"Hi. It's marvelous outside," she murmured.

Ksenya was standing in front of the hall mirror, applying a thick layer of black mascara to her eyelashes. Pink blush that matched the color of the mascara tube covered her cheeks. She wore cut-off jeans, and her little breasts almost fell out of the deep cleavage of her carmine T-shirt. Only a few, lacy strips held them in place. Compared to the magnificent rhododendrons, the girl looked vulgar and cheap.

"Ah," Sonya said uncertainly.

Ksenya whirled toward the open door. "What?" Her voice was loaded with defiance.

Sonya schooled her expression into neutrality. "Nice shirt."

"Grandma bought it."

"You bought it yourself with Grandma's money," Sonya corrected. She shook her head and started for her room. Why was Ksenya dressing like that? The whole getup was tasteless—the exaggerated makeup and the shirt. "You should have more style," she muttered. "You look like a hooker." She was sorry she had said it the moment the words escaped her mouth.

Ksenya stiffened. "What?" she asked belligerently.

Sonya smiled sheepishly to soften the sting. "Listen, I didn't mean to—"

"Look who is talking," Ksenya blurted out at the same time. "You're still married to my dad, but you're sleeping with that disgusting, fat man. How much does he pay you?"

"Don't talk to me like that!" Sonya snapped and then grimaced. She didn't want to fight. Besides, Ksenya was right. Yuri did pay for her dinner at the restaurant. How did the girl know they had just slept together? Was she guessing? Should Sonya be ashamed? She didn't feel ashamed. She felt tired and unfulfilled. Her emptiness ached.

"I just follow your example," Ksenya said contemptuously.

"What example? Why don't you follow my example in everything?" Sonya tossed her bag on the dresser. The keys jingled inside, mocking her and stirring her anger, cold and bitter. She flung the door shut and took satisfaction in its loud bang, the only satisfaction she had allowed herself all day. No! She wouldn't fight with Ksenya, today. She had already decided not to see Yuri, again. She unzipped her blazer with a slow, deliberate movement of her wrist.

"I cook, clean, and do laundry." She kept her voice even. No fighting! "I pay the bills. Why don't you follow my example in that?"

"Because you didn't teach me," Ksenya shot back. "When I was young, you were always busy working. You didn't have time for me. You *still* don't."

"You're kidding me. Why don't you stay home, and I'll teach you how to cook dinner. I have the time, now."

"I don't. It's too late," Ksenya said with conviction. "I'm almost fifteen."

Sonya opened her mouth, but no words came. Too late? Even her anger deflated from surprise. She glanced outside, and it was fully dark. The evening had set in. "You're right, it's late," she said, pretending she misunderstood. "Where are you going?"

"I'm meeting with Ashley." Ksenya grabbed her backpack.

"You were much nicer when Grandma was here."

"Grandma loves me," Ksenya said and skipped out the door.

The door slammed shut. Sonya stared at it. Was Ksenya right? Did she ignore the girl when she was younger? It wasn't too late to rectify now, was it? Gosh, she was such a dismal mother. Ignorant, too. Where was Ksenya going this late in the evening? Meeting with Ashley? Should she call Ashley? No, she shouldn't. If Ksenya learned Sonya was checking on her, she would make another scene. Maybe she really was meeting Ashley. They were friends.

Sighing, Sonya stepped out of her black pumps and pattered

to the window barefoot. The rain bucket was full. She picked it up and went to the washroom to empty it. Then, she changed into her house sweats and headed to the kitchen.

It wasn't too late to teach Ksenya how to cook. The girl just didn't want to learn. She was lazy and immature. Beat that, Sonya hurled silently at her absent daughter. Still brooding, she put a deep pan on the stove, poured in some oil and water, and tossed in pork to stir fry. While the pork simmered, she cleaned the veggies. Her knife danced on the cutting board as she hummed a Red Army march. The march fit in with her knife-wielding activity. She was halfway through the carrots when the telephone rang.

"Sonya?" Lilia's voice filled her ear.

"Hey, sis. How is Mama?" Sonya held her cordless phone with one shoulder while she sliced the carrots.

"Almost recovered from her jet lag," Lilia reported. "She sleeps until six in the morning."

"Good. How was the Judaic court? No problems with the papers I signed?"

"No, it was just a formality. The flat is hers. I can't believe they put you through so much trouble there for a mere signature."

"Plus two additional rabbis. Don't you forget that." Sonya surveyed the pile of sliced carrots and picked up two fat celery sticks. Ksenya loved celery.

"I wouldn't dream of it." Lilia snickered. "How is your relationship going with that man?"

"Yuri?" Sonya shrugged and almost dropped the phone from her shoulder. "No how. We've met a few times, but it didn't work out."

"Had sex, yet?"

"Would you stop your dirt digging?" Sonya said in exasperation. "Yes. It wasn't as good as…" she trailed off. "Yuri was too fast. He huffed and puffed and made noises like a hippo in heat, but it went nowhere. Lurid enough for you?"

Lilia laughed. "Still pining for your drunken hubby?" she asked when she could talk.

"None of your sisterly business!" Sonya snarled. She wiped one of her wet hands with a paper towel, grabbed the phone, and jammed the "Off" button with too much force. "Yes, still pining for him. The fool that I am," she muttered to the dead phone. She poured all the vegetables into the pan and started stirring. The phone rang, again.

"What?" she barked into it.

"We ordered a tombstone for Dad," Lilia said. "A simple one."

"Yeah." Sonya dropped onto the sofa. "Sorry I hung up on you. I'm touchy these days. It's just...I don't know what I want. One day, I ache for Alexei. Another, I hate him. I live in limbo, as if waiting for something to happen. I want to dance, but I know I'm getting too old for it. I thought I wanted Yuri. I like his compliments, but I don't like him. I'm such a wimp. I want a fairy godmother to come and relieve me of all my troubles, to tell me what to do. I would obey." She chuckled sadly. "I think I need a therapist, but I don't have the money to pay one."

"I'm here for you," Lilia said. "I can't help, but I can listen. That's all the therapists do. They listen."

"I know. I think I've started to make peace with Ksenya," Sonya said. "Since Mama left, we've both been trying. We're kind of rebuilding bridges, but we slip all the time, both she and I. Wish me luck, Lil'ka."

"I do, with all my heart," Lilia said. "I'm just glad my boys are still young."

"Enjoy it while you can. They'll grow up," Sonya predicted gloomily.

Chapter Sixteen
Amanda

"Mom! Where have you been? You haven't called for a week. I was worried sick!"

Grasping the white phone receiver, Amanda smiled at her reflection in the mirror. "Gloria, don't scold. I love you, too," she said. "I miss you so much. I'm sorry I didn't call. We went to Suzdal, and I recited Russian poetry there, in front of a wooden church. People clapped." She traced the ornate carving of the mirror frame with her finger.

"You lead a busy life. Have you found her?"

"I found her!" Amanda sang. "Her name is Sofia. She is Jewish and a ballerina. We're going back to Moscow tomorrow morning. I'll tell you all the details when I get back. I'm definitely writing this book. So many juicy details!"

"She is Jewish?" Gloria repeated slowly.

"Her mom's name is Dina Goldberg."

"You mean my mom's name is Dina Goldberg, and I'm a Jew?"

"Gloria." Amanda said sternly. "You're *my* daughter. Don't you ever forget that!"

"Mom, this is all such a muddle." Gloria's strained chuckle came through the phone line. "Have you two met, already?"

"No. At least I know the name, now. We'll meet, soon. How are the renovations on her house going?"

"You haven't even met her, and you already worry about the house. Have you worried about a house for me before I was born?"

"Ummm, Gloria," Amanda said uncertainly. Her reflection in the mirror stopped smiling. She hadn't found Sofia, yet. Was she losing Gloria, already?

"Kidding," Gloria said hastily. "You know, Mom. I'm not sure I'm kidding. It doesn't sit too well with me. You're so enthusiastic about her. I shouldn't be jealous, I know. It's not rational, but I am. I never had any competition for you before, never understood siblings' jealousy until now. A funny feeling. Maybe I should buy a house for my mother too, and renovate it. For symmetry."

Amanda's breath caught. "A house for your mother?" she

mouthed, appalled.

"Don't pay attention to my grumbling," Gloria said. "I've been thinking. I can't wait to meet your daughter, really I can't. I wonder how she looks, besides red hair. I don't even know what the connection between us is. She must be my sister-in-bafflement."

"Naughty!" Amanda forced a laugh.

Gloria laughed too, and her laughter sounded unnatural. "By the way, Happy Mother's Day, my dear mother-in-Vladimir."

"Thank you, honey." Amanda felt grateful for the change of topics. "I forgot. They don't celebrate Mother's Day here." She turned away from the mirror. She didn't like the desperation in the eyes of her reflection.

"Make your own celebration," Gloria advised.

"I will. I have to hurry. We're driving back to Moscow in a couple of hours, and I'm not packed, yet."

"Do you have much to pack?"

"I bought some stuff," Amanda said. "Souvenirs. You're going to love them. They're so Russian."

"As if I don't have enough Russian stuff by now," Gloria said quietly. "I have a Russian Jewish mother, for God's sake. When you talk to her, give her my congratulations. I can't wait to meet her."

"You have a Canadian mother. I'm your mother," Amanda retorted. She was getting riled by Gloria's constant nagging, but she stifled her irritation. Gloria's concerns were understandable. "You have no competition, honey. I promise," she said softly. "Nobody can replace you. Sofia is just a new...adventure. A discovery. Please, don't be mad at me. I'm having such a good time. Sergey is a sweet companion."

Oops! She winced. It wasn't often that her mouth ran away from her like that. If she was still facing the mirror, she would probably see her cheeks turning red. She hadn't been planning on confessing to Gloria, but she was too upset to mince words, and she couldn't retrieve her revealing utterance.

"Really? Have you found yourself a boyfriend at last?" Amanda heard Gloria inhale sharply. "Of course! Mother!" A gurgle of laughter came through the line. This one was sincere, gleeful even. "Shame on you. In a foreign country!"

"Don't be so judgmental. Everybody has one these days." Amanda shrugged. "Even Suzy from Writing and Publishing, although she looks like..." Terrified at her lack of manners, Amanda clamped a hand to her mouth before she compared her colleague to a domestic beast. She had always abhorred gossiping. What was happening to her?

Gloria laughed again, joyously. "Mom, please. I'm joking. I'm happy for you. Do you have his picture? Can you e-mail it to me?"

"No," Amanda said. "I'm going to hang up."

"I love you, Mom." Gloria giggled. "How old is he?"

Amanda put the receiver on the station with utmost care, trying not to make a sound. She suspected Gloria laughed uproariously at her prudish reaction. Impertinent girl, Gloria! She was making fun of her mother. Amanda's lips curved. So what? She was having fun herself.

Her smile faded. Gloria seemed to forget about her jealousy, already. Or maybe she didn't wish to further sadden her mother, but Amanda remembered. They had just passed a dangerous bump together, she and Gloria. Had they reached an understanding? She didn't think so. How many more bumps still loomed ahead? Siblings' jealousy was powerful. She had read about it. Heard about it. She had simply never experienced it firsthand. Would Sofia be jealous, too? For whose affection?

Amanda shook her head. She was already losing her way in the jumbling labyrinth of relationships she herself had created. No more upsetting thoughts! She would pack, instead. All would be well with Gloria. She was bright and kind. She would accept her new sister. Eventually. Would Amanda accept a new mother for Gloria? Would Sofia accept Amanda?

Resolutely, Amanda stood up. No more torturing herself with the questions she couldn't answer. She would wait and see, hoping for the best. She pulled her suitcase from the closet, but the pile of gifts on her bed looked daunting. She couldn't fit it all into the suitcase. It was full of clothes on the way here. She would have to load everything into Sergey's car in their shopping bags and lug those bags into Rebecca's home. She would probably need another piece of luggage just for the gifts, when she flew home. To her daughter. With her daughter. She sighed.

* * * *

"You know, Sergey," she said several hours later, watching his firm hands on the wheel. The Lada was speeding out of Vladimir, leaving behind the ancient city and Amanda's brief love affair. She felt simultaneously sad and rejuvenated. "This last weekend was Mother's Day in Canada."

"Oh, really? Is it a state holiday?"

"No, we don't have any time off because of it, but every kid knows. Last year, Gloria took me to Victoria on Mother's Day. She gave me a huge basket of roses."

"We usually celebrate Mother's Day on March 8th, International Women's Day."

"How do you celebrate it?"

"We present our women-coworkers or women in our families with flowers. The tradition is a small bunch of mimosas."

"Mimosas? Ewww!"

"You don't like mimosas? I think they're cute—fuzzy and yellow like tiny chickens. My daughter adores them."

This was the first time he had ever mentioned his daughter. Amanda pretended not to notice. His previous rebuke at her question about his family often replayed in her mind. She wished she had asked Rebecca before embarking on this trip. She would definitely rectify her ignorance when they got back to Moscow.

"The operative word is chicken," she said primly. "I really, really prefer roses."

"I'll keep that in mind." Sergey said. "Next time I see you, I'll bring roses." There was a smile in his voice, although not a muscle quivered in his serious face. "Or is it only for mothers and daughters?"

"No. Roses are good, anytime," Amanda said firmly.

In Moscow, Sergey delivered her to the door of Robert and Rebecca's apartment building. He didn't press the buzzer. Instead, he pushed Amanda's back to the gray, stone wall near the entrance and caged her with his hands on both sides of her.

"I'd better find out about Sofia Goldberg through my channels," he said. His face was so close, Amanda's nose almost touched his scratchy whiskers. "The Moscow Ballet Academy is a serious institution. I'll deal with them through the magazine." His eyes glittered dangerously. "Goodbye, Ladushka."

Amanda stuck her tongue out, licking his cheek.

He growled deep in his throat, glanced around quickly, saw nobody, and planted a firm kiss on Amanda's lips. "Branded as mine," he breathed into her half-open lips before releasing her and pressing the buzzer.

Without his body touching her, she felt so bereft, she wanted to wail.

"Who's there?" Rebecca's bass came through the intercom.

"I'll call as soon as I have news," Sergey mouthed and jogged back to his car.

"Me," Amanda squeaked into the intercom. "Home from Vladimir." Her eyes followed Sergey into his Lada. It was so monumentally stupid to tumble like this for a man so much younger, but she couldn't help it. When he was around, her heart was dancing, soaring like a *virtuoso* in a ballet. She already missed him. Desolate, she gazed at the back bumper of his departing car.

"Amanda!" Rebecca exclaimed. From her big breast, it sounded like a bellows. The door tinkled quietly, informing the visitors that someone inside was welcoming her guest.

Amanda adjusted her jacket, picked up her suitcase and the multitude of shopping bags, and started toward the elevator. A mirror in a brass frame inside the old-fashioned elevator reflected her puffed up lips and shining eyes.

"You didn't call!" Rebecca pounced as soon as Amanda stepped into the apartment. "What? Tell me. Did you find her?" She tossed Amanda's suitcase into the guest room and towed Amanda toward the kitchen. "You hungry? Want some tea?"

"Tea is great," Amanda agreed. While she munched the tiny sandwiches Rebecca piled onto a plate in front of her, she told the big woman everything. She even bragged a little about the off-hours in Sergey's room, but only a little. Even talking about him made her smile.

Rebecca shook her head. "You old tart," she said with admiration. "I'm so happy for you, but guard your heart, dear. There is no future in that corner. You must realize that."

"It's kind of late," Amanda said glumly. "Tell me about his family. He didn't want to talk about it."

"You asked?"

"I asked."

"He's married, but he doesn't live with his wife. I don't know the details."

"What about his daughter?"

"She is about ten. She lives with her mother and has some kind of kidney problems. She needs dialysis every several days. He'll never leave her."

"Ah. The one who loves mimosas," Amanda murmured.

Rebecca stared at her. "I'm sorry for you, honey," she said after a while.

The next morning, Amanda settled down in front of her laptop. What should she put into her book? She had accumulated lots of notes, but she had to organize them, and she still wasn't sure whether to include her torrid affair with Sergey or not. It would be good for the sales, but would it damage her career? Not likely? What about *his* career? Maybe married journalists in Russia, even if they were separated from their wives, were not supposed to have extra-marital flings? She could use a different name for him, she supposed. Would he write about their affair in his own series of articles? No. The affair was irrelevant to the search for her daughter. Better to keep it out. She would make a separate file and write about it as a love journal, an addendum to the main story.

A couple of hours later, she glanced at the clock. Only 10:50. When would Sergey call? Amanda poured herself a cup of coffee and typed a couple more pages, but it didn't go well. The text was dry, like a shopping list. Maybe she should do something else.

She opened a new file and began writing about Sergey and the development of their relationship. That one went much better, with lots of adjectives and some Russian poetry thrown in. When she glanced at the clock again, it showed 2:30. Her coffee cup was empty, and she had only reached their trip to Vasilyevo and the Mat song. She licked her lips and typed some more. If Gloria ever read this file, she would probably stop respecting her mother, altogether.

Grinning like a demented woman, Amanda glanced at the clock, again. It was 3:10. Why hadn't Sergey called? She needed to hear his voice. She definitely needed a break. She saved the file and opened the CNN news on the Internet. It wasn't very uplifting, with all the problems in every nook of the globe. The Middle East boiled, as always. She clicked the window shut and went to the TV in the living room. Turning it on, she flipped through the channels.

One showed a Russian children's movie. Amanda didn't like it. It was old and sugary sweet, about an ugly dog and communist propaganda. Another channel showed Russian news, which was even worse than CNN. On the third channel, an action film was at full gallop—the hero shooting, swearing constantly, and doing stunts. She was still watching it, when Rebecca returned home.

"Amanda, what are you doing?"

"Watching TV." Amanda switched the channel, again. Devilish luck—a soap opera! The heroine bleated about her long-lost son while her partner tried to steal her checkbook.

Muttering Mat words, Amanda savagely terminated the TV and ambled to the kitchen after Rebecca. "There is nothing to watch," she complained.

Rebecca laughed. Is there ever anything to watch? In Canada?

"No, but I thought..." Amanda glanced at the clock. It showed 5:15. Where was Sergey? How much time would a call to the Moscow Ballet Academy take? Not more than fifteen minutes, surely.

Rebecca began setting the table for dinner, but Amanda couldn't bring herself to help. Everything around her felt like a set from a soap opera, utterly unreal—the scratched kitchen cabinets, Rebecca, the bubbling red pot of meatballs. She went to the window and watched three preschooler boys playing in the inner yard. They shot from their sticks with the same intensity and mastery as the hero of the action flick on TV.

"Look at them. The future action idiots of Russia," Amanda said bitterly. Then, she grimaced at her own snobbery. Sergey wouldn't approve. She would disappoint him, again. She heard Rebecca *tsking* behind her back, but she didn't care.

The greenery below was so dense, it entirely obscured some areas. From her window on the sixth floor, Amanda couldn't see anyone baby-sitting the boys. Probably their grandmothers, she mused, listening to the faint, feminine laughter carried above the foliage. Was she a grandmother, too?

She ground her teeth. Maybe Sergey got bored of her, already. She knew she had never been an exciting partner. Donald had often complained that she was too cool and reserved. Had she been cool with Sergey? She didn't think so. Remembering a few of their escapades in bed, she felt her cheeks heating up. She hadn't been reserved at all. More like wanton and shameless. Did it matter? She probably wouldn't see him, again.

"I'm going to the Ballet Academy tomorrow morning," she said without turning.

"Amanda, give the man a chance," Robert mumbled.

She whirled. "Hi, Rob." She hadn't heard him come in. For such a big man, he was surely quiet. He was already at the table, stuffing his mouth with meatballs and talking around them, gazing at her reproachfully. "Sergey said he would do it. He always does what he promises."

"He's had the entire day!" Amanda settled at the table, pushing her steamed veggies around the plate. Nothing tasted good, not since last night. Resolutely, she forked a load into her mouth. Was she becoming creepy in her pining? She swallowed and took another mouthful. She wasn't a teenager, crazy with hormonal overload. She was sixty, for heaven's sake. She couldn't lose her appetite over a Russian male twenty years her junior. She refused to. Categorically! She had her pride. She grabbed a couple of fresh radish heads from a crystal bowl in the middle of the table and crunched energetically.

"He'll call, Amanda," Rebecca said.

"I just want to learn where my daughter is," Amanda said.

"Yeah." Rebecca also attacked a radish.

Robert frowned. "Ladies, what's going on? You're frightening me. Some female secrets?"

"Shut up!" both Amanda and Rebecca said simultaneously.

* * * *

The next morning, Amanda decided not to write but to transfer photos from her digital camera to the hard drive of her laptop. Gloria wanted to see Sergey's photo. Should she send it to her? She hadn't realized how many pictures she had taken—over 100. The transfer was almost over when Rebecca poked her head inside the guest room.

With a vague grin, she offered Amanda a black, wireless phone. "A male voice. For you."

"Tease!" Amanda snatched the receiver. "Hello."

"That's me, Ladushka," Sergey said. "I have news. I'm coming over in an hour, and I'm bringing you roses."

"I'll be waiting," Amanda breathed. Pressing the "Off" button, she bit her lip. Was she waiting to hear about her daughter, or was she just waiting to see Sergey? Maybe they could rent a room in a local hotel and spend another night, together? Her pulse quickened. Rebecca had been right. She was a tart. Her lips quivered. Had Sergey been thinking about her, too?

An hour later, he offered Amanda three long-stemmed, red roses before settling into an armchair beside Rebecca's coffee table. Amanda found a cut crystal vase in Rebecca's cupboard, put the roses in water, and dropped into the armchair opposite Sergey. She pointedly ignored Rebecca's knowing smirk. Rebecca put a tea tray on the coffee table between Sergey and Amanda and perched primly on a tall bar stool in front of her kitchen island.

Absently, Amanda glanced at the bottom of one of Rebecca's thin mugs, painted with a slew of wild flowers. "Roy Kirkham. Made in England," read the label. Rebecca had probably brought her tea service with her from home. The delicate mugs looked classy beside the gorgeous roses.

"I love roses," Amanda murmured. "Thank you, Sergey." She started serving tea.

"Perhaps something stronger than tea," Sergey suggested hopefully.

"Talk!" Rebecca ordered. "The poor woman has been going crazy without a word from you." She nodded at Amanda.

"Rebecca!" Amanda blurted.

"All right. Bad news first," Sergey said. "There's no Dina Goldberg listed in the Moscow address directory."

"Died?" Amanda put the teapot back on the tray, but she didn't risk lifting her cup. Her hands shook. "She wasn't old, not much older than me."

"Not necessarily," Sergey said. "Perhaps moved or remarried. No Sofia Goldberg either, but..." He lifted his thick finger in the air, waving emphatically. "I called the Moscow Ballet Academy. They did have Sofia Goldberg as a student. She graduated sixteen years ago from the Folk Dance division and was hired by the Petushko Folk Dance Ensemble."

"Where?" Amanda mouthed. She leaned forward, forgetting about her tea, absorbing Sergey's words. His gaze lapped at her like a warm sea wave, and she shivered. Her answering smile almost split her face.

"Oh, cut the crap, Pechkin," Rebecca growled. "I'll go shopping later and leave you two amorous idiots alone for a couple of hours. Just finish your briefing first."

Amanda turned crimson.

Sergey didn't even raise a brow, although his mouth twitched. "Yes, ma'am," he said. "The ensemble's hometown is Saratov. I called them. The dancers are on a tour of China right now. Sofia Goldberg worked for them as a lead dancer until six years ago. Then, she quit. The secretary couldn't tell me where she is, but as soon as the troupe returns home in the fall, I'll contact them. I'm sure some friends of hers know where she is."

"In the autumn?" Amanda's spirit fell.

"The Academy also provided me with the Moscow address Sofia lived at when she was a student. Of course, it was sixteen years ago, but we can go there and check, today. In a couple of hours, when people return from work." Sergey tossed a sly little glance in Rebecca's direction.

"Oh, Sergey, I love you," Amanda whispered.

"All right. I'll leave you two lovebirds, together." Rebecca stood up. "Amanda, be home by nine." She marched toward her bedroom to change.

"I have a curfew," Amanda sang, her voice husky. "Like a teenager." She laughed silently.

"Rebecca has a wicked sense of humor," Sergey muttered. He didn't move from his armchair until the door lock clicked in the corridor. Then, he jumped up, pulled Amanda from her seat with both hands, and enveloped her in a crushing embrace.

Amanda's lips melted under the onslaught of his. He moved his head lower, toward her neck and shoulders. Everywhere he kissed, she sizzled.

"Your mommy has left," he said, his soft lips still touching her. They tickled Amanda's skin as they moved. "Come on, Ladushka. Show me your bedroom."

Breathing erratically, Amanda whimpered and complied.

* * * *

A few hours later, Sergey's Lada headed toward Sofia's former address. "It was so easy," Sergey said. "As soon as I mentioned the name of my magazine, the secretary spilled the beans, most willingly. Of course, it helped that I knew the girl's name. That was the real stopper when we started."

"Aha," Amanda said, distracted by the multi-story houses that rushed by the car window, block after block. Moscow was so huge, and her stay here so short. A few more days, and she would be leaving. If they didn't find Sofia today, she might never find her daughter.

"Amanda, Ladushka," Sergey said quietly, echoing her thoughts. "Don't despair. If we don't find her today, I'll contact the Ensemble when they return home from their tour."

"Thanks, Sergey." She refused to look at him. "Is today our last time, together?"

"Probably," he said. "Anyway, I'll see you to the airport."

"I hope your daughter gets better," Amanda said. "Rebecca told me about her."

He nodded silently, his hands gripping the wheel tighter.

The white house, Sofia's former residence, had nine stories, built like the letter L, with five doors in the long wing and three in the short. A grocery store on the first floor faced the street. Amanda and Sergey took entrance number three and stepped into the elevator. The bulb inside was so weak, it hardly gave off any light. Just enough to see the buttons with the floor numbers all chewed out.

Sergey sighed. "Vandals," he said quietly, his finger counting the ugly, plastic holes. "I think this is seven." He pushed. The elevator shuddered and moved up.

"You were right," Amanda said when they came out. "This is the seventh floor." The number seven was inserted in the wall above the elevator door—a huge, black digit, made up of small, square tiles. All four apartment doors on the floor were reinforced by steel.

A young woman who opened Sofia's former door wore a pink silk negligee. One white knee flashed in the lace of the split hem, trimmed by a multitude of tiny, silk rosettes. Her hair fell down her shoulders in a strawberry-blonde waterfall. Posing languidly, she lifted her hand to lean on the door frame.

"What can I do for you, sir?" she asked Sergey. She ignored Amanda.

Amanda's heart contracted painfully. This whore couldn't be her daughter.

"We are looking for the Goldbergs, Dina or Sofia," Sergey said with a leer. "Are you Sofia?"

"Na-ah," the woman purred. "I live here alone. I'm Alena, but I can be Sofia for you, if you want me to." She smiled invitingly.

"Another time, Darling," Sergey said. "How long since you moved in, Alena?"

She thought for a few seconds. "About six years," she said.

"Thank you." Sergey inclined his head and backed away toward the elevator door.

"I'm glad she's not Sofia," Amanda said after the elevator started its descent. She felt light-headed in her relief. She didn't think she could accept a strumpet as a daughter.

"Her?" Sergey snorted contemptuously. "In my experience, Jewish women don't go that road. Besides, she's a blonde, not a redhead."

"Bottle blonde," Amanda corrected. "What will we do, now? Play detectives, again? There are eight entrances and nine stories in the house; four apartments on every landing. We'll be at it until September, just in time for the ensemble to come back to Saratov."

"Let's ask around," he said. "Perhaps some old gossips remember either Dina or Sofia."

"Okay," she agreed unenthusiastically.

Unfortunately, none of the elderly women sitting on benches in the inner yard remembered any Jewish woman.

"Let's go," Amanda said at last. "We're wasting time." She was already almost reconciled with her failure. Maybe, it was for the best. She had one great daughter with Gloria. She didn't need another. Her soap opera season had finally ended. Maybe, the next episode would start in September. Maybe not. She sighed, but her sigh morphed into a smile. It was time for her real-time series finale, with a big, sexy bang.

"I'm sorry, Ladushka," Sergey said, striding beside her across the yard toward the street.

"You'll ask at the Ensemble when they come back," Amanda said. "Meanwhile, I invite you for our last dinner, together. Pick a restaurant. This one is on me, not your magazine."

"Good idea," Sergey murmured.

They passed a wooden table, where three gray-haired oldsters engaged in a loud battle of dominoes. They passed a children's playground, where several kids cavorted in a sand box. At the back door of the grocery store, an old man in a sleeveless, white undershirt, dirty and ripped, smoked silently and followed their progress with jaundiced little eyes.

"Looking for something?" he asked when they leveled up with him.

Sergey stopped so suddenly, Amanda almost bumped into him. "Looking for someone," Sergey said. "Good afternoon. Perhaps you knew them. They lived here some time ago." He offered the man his hand. "I'm Sergey Pechkin, a journalist."

The man glanced at Sergey's hand and then transferred his gaze to his own big hand, almost black with grime. Wiping the palm twice on his dark trousers, sagging at the knees, he grabbed Sergey's hand in a tight grip. Under Amanda's eyes, they engaged in a squeezing match. When they finally disconnected, Amanda detected vague, satisfied smirks on both male faces. She kept her mouth tightly zipped.

"I know everyone who lived here for the last two decades. I've been working as a loader and butcher at this store since it opened. Who are you searching for?"

Amanda let Sergey do the talking.

'Well," the man said, unimpressed by Amanda's quest to locate her daughter. "If there was something in it for me, I might be induced to remember."

Sergey looked at Amanda.

"The envelope?" she asked.

Sergey nodded.

Amanda fished out one of her $100..00 envelopes, offering it to the butcher.

He glanced inside and grinned in satisfaction. "Oh, yeah," he said. "I remember the Jews. The old man was a redhead, like an orange balding one, though. They always bought the most expensive meat from me while they lived here. They moved to Israel." He paused. "About six years back."

"What about their daughter?" Amanda broke in.

"I recall they had two daughters. Both red-haired like their daddy. I think they all moved together. Wait, maybe not. One was a dancer or something." The man stuffed Amanda's envelope into a pocket of his filthy trousers. "I really don't know, but I think there was a talk about that dancer girl staying. Her husband didn't want to move to Israel or something."

He shook his head. "Fool. Anywhere would be better than here. I would've moved if I were a Jew." Spiting out the still smoking stub of his cigarette, he pressed it into the asphalt with the sole of his boot, twisting energetically. "Smart people, Jews. Running like rats from a sinking ship. Maybe I should look for some long-lost, Jewish grand-auntie or something. Many people do." He sniggered. "Maybe I was a Jewish bastard. I have to get back to work." Cackling and emitting long strings of Mat invectives, he stomped inside the store.

"Fiend!" Amanda spat. "Anti-Semite! Extortionist!" She loosed a Mat diatribe of her own. She was getting rather fluent in it.

"Amanda! Please, don't." Sergey winced. "I can't stand you swearing like a stevedore. Let's have that dinner you promised me. We'll drink champagne and dance until morning." Putting a calming hand on Amanda's behind, he steered her toward the car.

"Right," Amanda said. "We'll celebrate my upcoming reunion with my daughter and to hell with my curfew. I'm flying to Israel." She turned to Sergey. "Stay with me all night. Show me your Moscow. Can you?"

"I would've given you all of Russia if I could," he whispered. "To hell with your curfew, Ladushka. Yes, I can. Come to my flat after the restaurant."

"Sure." Amanda narrowed her eyes. "Maybe *instead* of a restaurant?" She showed him the tip of her tongue. All her muscles shivered in anticipation, and her belly clenched.

"Thrifty woman! Feed your man first, or he'll get cranky."

"Russians!" Amanda breathed. "No style."

Chapter Seventeen
Sonya

Sonya's white socks thumped softly on the thick, brown carpet of Jane's home. Rika Zarai's Hava Nagila was a short but intense piece, and one of Sonya's favorites. She had often danced it in Israel, always to the wild appreciation of her audience. Jane didn't disappoint. Unable to clap, she keened, and her small eyes glinted in agitation.

"More," she panted coarsely, when Sonya finished the dance. "Please, more."

"Don't scream so much, Jane. You'll damage your throat." Breathing deeply to restore her wind, Sonya curtsied, her mouth stretching into a satisfied smirk. After two years of not performing, she was obviously out of shape, but she wasn't too bad. Happiness frolicked inside her like a hummingbird, fluttering its brilliant wings and filling her with sparkling helium. She felt like floating in the air, weightless. Perhaps, she could get back to dancing. Perhaps, her time wasn't up just yet. Some ballerinas danced until fifty. *Although, they never danced on such a thick carpet*, she thought wryly. Neither had she until now.

"Dance," Jane pleaded. "I'll be quiet."

"Okay." Sonya couldn't believe her own excitement. She thought she had reconciled with her danceless existence. Obviously, she had not. She pattered to the music center to change the CD, but what she yearned to do was to fly. Away! To some glittering stage with its blinding lights and adulating public. Only her duties to Jane and Ksenya kept her grounded. Should she let go? Spread her wings and fly? Could she dare?

"I brought more music," she said. "*Cazachok*!" She pressed the "Play" button. This Russian folk song was always a winner. Her white leotard and a flowered, sleeveless tunic with a white sash fit the dance perfectly.

Grabbing a chair, she planted it firmly in the middle of the room. Her hazel eyes sparkled in triumph. "Mister Chair!" She curtsied to the piece of furniture as if it was a partner. In a sense, it was—a partner and a prop. Dancing around it, she played with the seat and the back. She lifted her toes on the seat in coquettish *battements*, bowed and skipped around, improvising impishly. Always before, she danced *Cazachok* with a partner, but a chair was almost as good.

Jane giggled and hummed quietly but kept her promise. She didn't yell, anymore.

Sonya finished the dance and knelt beside Jane. "What do you think?"

"You have to dance!" Jane screeched. "You're so beautiful when you dance." Her voice dropped to a whisper. "Do it. For me. Promise."

Sonya felt tears coming. "I'll try," she promised solemnly. "If I get a show, you'll be my first guest of honor." She straightened. "I'll have to give up the burgers, then. I need time to practice."

"I can be your sponsor," Jane said gravely.

"Thank you, Jane. You're giving my life back to me." Sonya bent to kiss Jane's wilted, gray cheek.

"You're stinking like a wet dog," Jane said, contrary again. She wrinkled her nose. "Yikes! Smelly!"

"Of course I am, you withered, old mummy." Sonya laughed. "I'm drenched in sweat. I need a shower." She stepped toward the door. "You have a rare behind-the-scene experience. Only the privileged can smell the dancer's sweat." She snickered. "I'll be quick, okay?"

"Live for me," Jane breathed, almost inaudible behind Sonya's back.

Sonya shivered but didn't turn. She couldn't. Hastily, she turned on the shower to block off Jane's words, but they lingered in her mind. The warm water couldn't wash away Jane's pain along with her own sweat.

* * * *

When she returned home, she opened the door to the gargling of running water. She peeked into the kitchen. Ksenya was washing dishes, dancing in front of the sink, eyes half-closed, dark blonde hair swishing. Some rhythmic beats leaked out of her headphones. Sonya frowned. She would have to redo half the dishes, after Ksenya completed her close-eyed chore. On the other hand, this was the first time Ksenya ever washed dishes without a prompt. The girl had obviously wanted to impress her. Sonya retrieved her head back into the hall. She should express her gratitude loudly but not yet. She'd let Ksenya finish the washing first.

Quietly, Sonya shucked off her sneakers and sank onto the sofa, lifting her feet onto a floor cushion. After an afternoon of dancing, carrying Jane from place to place, and listening to her spiteful nagging, Sonya was glad of some peace. Jane had obviously wanted to punish her for her dancing. Such a contrary creature—Jane. One moment, she offered a sponsorship and the next, tormented Sonya with incessant complaints.

Shaking her head, Sonya studied her feet on a cushion with critical eyes. Jane was right. She ought to go back to dancing. She still wanted to make fabric art, but she could do both. If only she made more money. Gosh, even as tired as she was, she still craved dancing! Her feet moved in some crazy, polka steps to Ksenya's disjointed rhythm from the headphones. Nobody in this darned city could dance folk better than her. After all, she trained at the best ballet school on Earth—the Moscow Ballet Academy. When should she start? Next month, maybe? First, she had to quit the burgers and find herself a rehearsal place.

Her gaze fell on the bright cushion, again. She should make the costumes for her dancing. The more outrageous, the better. Something with colored feathers. She always wanted to wear feathers. Sonya's hands itched to grab a sketchbook and draw the new design. It shimmered in her mind—swirls of pink feathers on a brown background. Elegant and flashy simultaneously. Marvelous. She closed her eyes and fell into a daydream. Feathers danced with her there.

"Mom?" Ksenya put her head around the partition that separated the living room from the kitchen. Her headphones circled her neck like a dog collar. "I didn't hear you come in."

"Ah?" Sonya came awake. "A couple minutes ago. I didn't want to interrupt your...music."

"Tenderloin Boys," Ksenya said loftily.

"Ah," Sonya said, again. She nodded, as if the name of the band meant anything to her. "Nice name. Come, give me a hug." She beckoned with her finger, smiling faintly. "Thank you, kitten, for doing the dishes."

"It's okay." Ksenya beamed as she bent to hug Sonya. Her lips touched Sonya's cheek. "You tired?"

"Yes. I danced for Jane, today. I'm thinking...maybe I can start dancing, again. I'm not too old, am I?"

"It's great! Do it!"

Sonya sniffed, suddenly uneasy, her elation fleeing. She shifted on the sofa to face her daughter. Was it a tobacco smell she sensed? "You smoked?" Her voice went up an octave.

Ksenya flinched, and her smile erased. "No!" Hastily, she stepped back.

Sonya jumped up, kicking the golden cushion away. "You smoked!" She poked a finger at Ksenya's chest in a black T-shirt. "You stupid wench. You mustn't smoke. You won't be able to play flute if you smoke. Don't you know that? You'll ruin your lungs and your lips. Idiot! A flutist shouldn't smoke."

"What do you care?" Ksenya shot back. "If I don't play flute, you won't have to pay for the lessons. Cheaper for you. More money for your dancing." She glared.

"How dare you?"

"You don't care, anyway. You always carp that everything is expensive. You only care about your freaking money."

"I'm trying to save money!" Sonya couldn't control her voice, anymore. It came out as a hysterical scream. Her hands cramped into fists at her sides. "For both of us. So I can dance, again! So we can go to Penticton during your vacation, as we talked." Why did she always have to explain herself?

"So, save. Don't pay for my lessons!" Ksenya yelled back. "I don't want your freaking vacation. I want an iPod."

"Cretin!"

"Miser!"

Sonya dug out her last resort. Maybe it would snatch the girl's attention. "Your dad will be unhappy with you, if you stop the lessons."

"Don't touch my dad!" Ksenya paled. "You only talk about him when you need to. You kicked him out. Now, you're threatening me with him? You're a manipulator. He loves me." She marched to the door, grabbed her jean jacket and black baseball cap, and jerked the door open. "I'm going to his place." She slammed the door behind her.

"Wait!" Sonya rushed to the door but stopped herself. Let Ksenya spend the night at her dad's. No harm in that. They both had to cool off. The girl would be back tomorrow, for dinner if nothing else. Such scenes had happened before. Sonya's thoughts circled back to the beginning of the quarrel. What a wretched, dimwitted notion to start smoking so young!

Ksenya hadn't even turned off the water. Sonya turned off the water and returned to the sofa. What could she do to stop Ksenya's smoking? Was it too late, already? Should she explain how bad smoking was? Ksenya already knew that. The teachers talked about smoking at school, but lots of Ksenya's classmates smoked nonetheless. Sonya dropped back onto the soft cushions. Their pattern of autumn leaves was still warm and inviting. Why did she suddenly feel so cold?

She rubbed her arms. The smell lingered in her memory, familiar but unrecognizable. What kind of cheap cigarettes smelled so strangely? Not like tobacco at all. What crap had the silly girl put in her mouth? Maybe she told the truth, and it was some funny candy? Sonya cringed. Had she misjudged Ksenya? Rats! She had just ruined everything. How had the situation deteriorated so rapidly from them both smiling to the bout of insults?

Should she apologize to her daughter...again? Probably. Gosh, she was so tired from constantly fighting with Ksenya and feeling guilty afterward. Why did she always believe the worst of her daughter? Because it had been true often enough. Did Alexei know about Ksenya's smoking?

Sonya glanced outside into the night and covered her face with her hands. Her entire body felt like dry pulp, after squeezing all the juice out. She hadn't realized how exhausted she was until now. She stretched out flat on the sofa, on the red and yellow maple leaves. She didn't want to move until the fall, when the land would be covered with a similar carpet of leaves. Only they would be alive, rustling, and smelling faintly of rot and rain. What was it she smelled on Ksenya?

She didn't wish to go to Alexei's place, tonight. She didn't wish to move, and it took at least forty minutes on a bus to get to his basement. Tomorrow, she had another morning shift. Let Ksenya sleep at Alexei's, tonight. They would reconcile tomorrow.

Lying very still, Sonya listened to her own breathing. Maybe it was tobacco after all. It definitely wasn't anything edible. What was it? Where had she encountered such a reek before? Who had it? The smell spun in her subconscious, seeking a match.

Suddenly, she bolted upright. She found her match! The one and only time she visited Alexei's dirty, little nook, his roommate had the same stink. "Pot," Alexei had explained to her. He puffed at it too, once in a while, he had said. Ksenya was smoking marijuana? Oh, gosh!

Sonya stared at the closed door. How bad was it? Did Alexei know? Did he care? Had he given it to her? More than once? Sonya shivered. No! Whatever he was, he wouldn't introduce his daughter to drugs, not even if he smoked them himself. He wouldn't push it on Ksenya, either. Especially if he was drunk. His sense of smell was skewed by the booze.

Oh, gosh! Oh, gosh! Oh, gosh!

Sonya's eyes jumped from object to object, never focusing long enough for recognition. Was it all her fault? Had she driven Ksenya into drugs? What else did Ksenya use? Did she do injections? Heroin? Cocaine? Sonya hadn't seen her daughter naked for a long time. Having become overly shy recently, Ksenya didn't undress in front of her mother, anymore.

The terrifying thoughts gripped Sonya in their cold clutches. Unable to keep still, she started pacing. What could she do? How could she help her daughter? Could she find the source of Ksenya's drugs? Could she kill the bastard? Her gaze traveled from the door to the tapestry with its freckled fawn, to the window, to the rain bucket. *Three-quarters full*, she noted absently.

Where did Ksenya get the money to pay for drugs? Terror twisted Sonya's stomach. Since Dina left, the girl hadn't taken any money from home. Where from, then? Sonya felt sick, as her eyes continued their mindless trip around the room. Did Ksenya steal the money? From whom? Had she been shoplifting? Sonya's gaze landed on the phone near the sofa. If Alexei had a phone, Sonya would've called him, but the detestable drunkard didn't own a phone. Too expensive for his sloshing belly. Who else could she call? Who could help?

Nobody.

Maybe she should have a glass of vodka instead of this senseless pacing? Or lie down? No point in walking herself to madness. Judging by Alexei's example, it was easy to drown her shame and guilt in vodka. Pity, she didn't have any alcohol in the house. She stopped buying it long ago, and the liquor store was already closed. She should stock some brandy in her room. She loved brandy. Dropping flat on her back, she stared blindly at the ceiling while the tremors ran along her body. Her hands clutched at the silken golden leaves of the cushion.

Fight, fight, fight! Fight for your daughter! She listened to the silent scream inside her head. "Fight? How?" she whispered. Her mind was blank. She was tired of fighting. Finally, she fell asleep on the sofa.

* * * *

"You're pulling my hair, foolish woman!" Jane chirped the next day. "It hurts, Bumble-head!"

"Sorry, Jane," Sonya said. "I'll be more careful." She untangled Jane's thin, gray strands. Sonya's fingers moved on automatic, while she pondered Ksenya's problem. What to do?

"You forgot the ribbon!" Jane's shrill voice reminded her.

"Sorry. I'm not myself, today." Sonya picked up the ribbon to redo the braid.

"I'm never myself," Jane muttered bitterly.

"I understand," Sonya murmured. She felt as paralyzed as Jane when it came to Ksenya.

"No, you don't," Jane said. "You can walk. What is your problem?"

"My daughter is my problem." Sonya's hands stilled in the gray hair. "Yes, I can walk. I can even dance, jump like a lunatic, or stand on my head. It won't make any difference. She won't listen to me. She's smoking weed."

"Pah! Big deal! She can walk, too. Dance and jump. Be grateful."

Slowly, Sonya circled Jane's chair to face the woman's shrewd, little eyes. "I'm sorry, Jane," she whispered. Her throat felt so tight, she couldn't speak aloud. "You're right. I should be grateful."

"You're really not yourself, today," Jane said. "You never insulted me."

Sonya only thought for a few seconds. "Filthy manipulator!" she said, letting lose an obscene line of Mat words. She didn't feel much better. Maybe a tiny bit.

"That's right." Jane beamed. Then, she frowned. "What was that? Russian Mat?"

"Yes."

"What did you say? Teach me."

Sonya shook her head.

All the way home, she rehearsed what she would say to her daughter. Perhaps, she should introduce Ksenya to Jane. Jane was wise, her courage and tenacity endless. She stripped all problems to the bare bones. She couldn't afford to dwell on the irrelevant. Ksenya might learn something from Jane.

When Sonya returned home, the apartment was empty. All her speculations had been for naught. Ksenya hadn't been home. The wench had the temerity not to come back! Surveying her lightless kitchen from the doorway, Sonya pursed her lips and grabbed her bag's shoulder strap tighter. This time, she wouldn't let go. She would drag her daughter back home, even tie her to a bed if she must. She wouldn't allow the girl to become an addict. She would fight for Ksenya, even against the girl's will. She had learned something from Jane as well.

Furious, she slammed the door shut, whirled, and stomped down the stairs. She should be grateful that Ksenya could walk? Dance and jump? Ha! Maybe it would've been better if Ksenya couldn't. At least then the stupid girl would not have been able to get into trouble behind her mother's back. She would be home, safe and sound. Like Jane...

Plague on you, Sofia, she thought in sudden terror. What are you thinking, imbecile woman? You can't wish your daughter disabled. Though, the sly thought persisted. Maybe just a tiny bit, easier to control.

Sonya's feet carried her to the bus stop, while her mind spun around itself, trying to solve the unsolvable. Gosh, she was such a terrible mother! If her old and wise grandma, long gone now, had ever heard such thoughts, she would've said, "Bite your tongue." What should Sonya bite if she didn't say it aloud? Knock her head on a brick wall to get some sense into it? She snorted unhappily.

The bus driver gave her a curious look, but she ignored him. She plopped onto a seat at the back of the bus and kept on fuming. Blight on the Listvins, both father and daughter, for bringing her to this madness. They could've called. Even though the accursed drunkard Alexei didn't own a phone, it didn't mean he couldn't have called from a public phone or from Ksenya's cell.

The bus was getting fuller, but the seats on both sides of Sonya incongruously remained empty. Sonya glanced at the people standing in front of her, holding onto the overhead bar, eyeing her with unease. They didn't like the stormy expression on her face? Fine! She didn't need anyone sitting nearby.

Her brain circled back, closing the circuit. Ksenya knew her mother would be worried. The deceiving, little bitch didn't call, because she wanted to punish Sonya. Right! Both Listvins would be very disappointed. They would get what they deserved. Sonya would wring their miserable necks, she was that angry. They had never seen her enraged. Good! She would spring a surprise on them. She would change her name back to Goldberg. Yes, that was it! She smiled.

A burly man standing right in front of her inched away. He was afraid of her? What a novel idea! Nobody had ever been afraid of her before. Her smile widened. She had never been that mad, either. It felt good, cleansing. She didn't want to be a Listvin any longer. There were too many Listvins, already. More than enough for one Vancouver. Both father and daughter didn't care about her feelings. She didn't wish to share their name, either.

The alley leading to Alexei's den was dark. While Sonya was on the bus, the rain started drizzling sluggishly. She wound herself so tightly, she didn't bother to open her umbrella. She might as well get wet. She hadn't checked her rain bucket, either. Let it overflow. She didn't care about anything, anymore. She wanted out of her detested, leaking apartment, out of this detested, joyless life. She wouldn't be a slave to the Listvins any longer. She would be free. Hooray! Let Ksenya live with her father if she wanted to. Sonya couldn't care less.

Alexei's basement front door wasn't locked. *There was nothing to steal inside*, she thought contemptuously as she yanked the door open.

"Alexei!" she yelled, marching to his room at the end of the dark corridor. A roommate's head stuck out of the washroom, his disheveled, greasy hair forming a slovenly outline in the darkness.

"What?" Sonya yelled.

The head disappeared.

Sonya yanked open the door to Alexei's room. "You could've called!"

"Why?" he asked. He was sitting at his chipped table on an equally old stool—the only seat in his tiny closet of a room. His dark blonde, stubbly beard made him look like a pirate down on his luck. A plate of boiled potatoes and a full bottle of vodka in front of him reinforced the image. A mattress with his blanket, his duffel, and his clarinet case were the only other items in the room, besides a squad of empty bottles and cans in the corner. When Ksenya visited, she slept on the mattress, and he slept on the floor. The girl wasn't there, now.

"Where is Ksenya?"

"Haven't seen her for a while." He eyed Sonya sullenly.

"She went to see you last night. Hasn't been home since."

He surged up, his hands striking the table. The stool tumbled. "She wasn't here last night." He crossed the room in two large steps.

Still standing at the open doorway, Sonya lifted her head to stare at him, as he towered over her. "Where is she, then?" she squeaked, plummeting down from the heights of her righteous fury. Dizzy, she had to grab something not to fall down. The closest thing to grab was Alexei's bare arm. She grabbed at it, sinking her nails into his flesh. Where was Ksenya?

"Sit down." Guiding her to the table, he righted the stool and pushed her down. "Tell me what happened." He rubbed his forearm, where Sonya's nails left four small, deep marks.

Sonya inhaled deeply to dispel her dizziness. Her hands clutched at the table edge. Nauseous from the smell of alcohol, she pushed the bottle away. "We fought last night. She left." She cleared her throat, clogged with fear. Where was Ksenya? Breathing fast, Sonya tried to remember what was important in yesterday's row, but nothing else came to mind. They exchanged a few angry words, and Ksenya left, as usual.

"Maybe, she ran away," Sonya said, studying the bottle of vodka. It had a white and blue label. It looked cheap. It would've been great if Ksenya had run away. It would definitely beat the alternative. Sonya gripped the table edge tighter. If she didn't hold on for dear life, she might fall down and disappear. Like Ksenya.

Alexei went to his knees in front of her. "Sofia." His voice was steely. "Take hold. What happened, yesterday?"

Paralyzed by terror, Sonya opened her mouth, closed it, and shuddered. She stared at him, unable to squeeze out a single word.

"Damn, woman! Snap out of it!" He slapped her cheek hard.

Her head swayed from the stinging blow. Sonya shivered once, hard, and her hand flew to her cheek. She licked her dry lips. As abruptly as it settled, her dizziness lifted. She exhaled slowly. "We fought, and she left," she repeated, still holding a palm to her tingling cheek. She finally remembered another important thing. "Gosh, Alyesha. I smelled marijuana on her, but I didn't recognize it until after she left. I thought it was regular cigarette smoke, so I confronted her. It was just a normal fight."

"A normal fight." Chuckling unhappily, he climbed to his feet.

Sonya stood up, too. "You're not the one to judge me!" she snapped.

"I'm not judging you." He picked up the bag she dropped at the door and pushed it into her hands. "Let's go to your place and use the phone."

"Right." Following him out, Sonya ran to catch up with his longer strides. "What if she uses other drugs, too? The ones I couldn't smell?"

He didn't answer. When she caught up with him, his face was grim.

Chapter Eighteen
Amanda

"No down, no feather," Sergey said in Russian. He squeezed Amanda's hands and bent his head to kiss every finger.

Amanda didn't move, gazing at the top of Sergey's polished, hairless scalp that reflected the airport lights. She knew the expression. It was the Russian equivalent of "Break a leg" and required the routine answer, "To the devil", but she couldn't say it. "Thank you," she whispered instead.

He lifted his head. "You're supposed to say—"

"I know. 'Thank you' is better. For everything."

"Let me know how your search progresses in Israel."

She nodded.

He touched her hair lightly. "Ladushka," he mouthed. "Go." He pushed her away.

She was the last of the passengers in the lobby. A young, black-haired guard in the uniform of the Israeli airline El-Al glared at them from the gate. She nodded again and hurried toward the exit. She didn't dare look back.

Why wasn't she twenty years younger? Why wasn't he anything but Russian? Life was so unfair. If she could, she would probably spend the rest of her life with Sergey. Even move to Russia. Unfortunately, the offer hadn't come. Sergey's main concern was his daughter, not Amanda.

She settled into her aisle seat and resolutely opened her laptop. She would shake off the blues and work. Moping never solved problems. Furthermore, there was no solution to her ridiculous, hopeless attraction to Sergey. It didn't have a happy ending, and they both knew it. She still had her diary of their whirlwind affair and her photos. Maybe she should write a romance novel?

She chuckled unhappily. No publisher would ever accept a romance with a sixty-year-old heroine and a hero twenty years younger. Maybe a grotesque or satire, she speculated gloomily, but definitely not a romance. This chapter of her life had already closed as hermetically as the airplane. There was no way back. She must move forward and keep positive. She had more than four hours until they landed in Tel Aviv. She would use the time to organize her notes. Clicking on the yellow icon on her screen, she dove into the pile of memory snippets. Sergey featured in the majority of them.

After she worked for a while on their Suzdal trip, Amanda opened the file with the text of the Mat song. Memories cascaded over her, sweet and poignant. She reveled in the bawdy freshness of the words. Reading this song would always remind her of Sergey.

A strange, guttural moan to her left alerted her, and she turned her head. Her neighbor, a young Slavic-looking man with sandy hair, was reading her file. His eyes glittered madly. His thick lips moved without a sound.

"I'm a researcher," Amanda said loftily and hit the "X" button. The file winked closed. "From Canada."

"Great stuff!" The man cackled. "Did you make it up yourself?"

Amanda didn't answer. She regarded her neighbor with a cold glare, reserved for the most obtuse of her students. When he averted his eyes, still grinning, she opened the Suzdal story, again. In Suzdal, Sergey called her Ladushka for the first time. Fortunately, she wrote this file in English. She hoped her impertinent, young neighbor couldn't read English.

She bit her lip and forcibly dismissed the painful memories. *A travel book*, she reminded herself sternly. She was writing a travel book, in search of her daughter. She had never written a book before, only professional papers. What was important and what was not?

Should she keep out her chats with Rebecca? Were her shopping trips relevant? Would it be too political to include her contemplations on the poverty in Russia? Did she need the descriptions of all the souvenirs she bought? Maybe she'd better record everything and let a publisher decide. Should she include the Mat song? In translation? Her lips twitched while her fingers danced over the keyboard.

* * * *

Tel Aviv was hot. As soon as Amanda stepped outside through the sliding glass doors of the airport building, she felt as if she stepped into a cooking oven. She was being cooked. Under the brutal, white sun, she would burn into a cinder if she wasn't careful. She spotted a taxi and hurriedly dove into the air-conditioned cab. She inhaled the cool air gratefully. Let the driver in his *kippa* and a black beard deal with her bags. How could he wear a beard in such a climate? Vancouver was so much better, despite the constant rain.

The car sped along a wide street, past the shops and shoppers, past the off-white, beige, and brown buildings—old and new, tall and squat. Amanda stuck her nose to the closed window. She had never been to the Middle East before.

"Have you been to Israel before?" the driver asked in Russian, echoing her thoughts. "Visiting relatives?"

"You can say so." Amanda replied in the same tongue, grinning absently. "You don't look Russian."

"I'm *sabra*," he said proudly. "I was born here, but my parents are from the Ukraine. It helps business to know Russian."

"Do you speak English?"

"Of course. Do you?"

Amanda laughed. "I'm Canadian. I speak Russian, because I teach Russian language and literature. I'm from Vancouver."

"What are you doing here?"

"I'm...visiting my daughter." It was true, almost. "Is my hotel far from the airport?" She had given him the name of her hotel earlier.

"It's on the sea shore. Modern. You'll love it."

They entered the old city, and the driver swore suddenly. The words were in Hebrew, but Amanda couldn't mistake his tirade for anything but a vicious oath. She turned to glance through the opposite window. At the nearest intersection, the charred remains of a house gaped like a wound. A team of city workers in gray uniforms were cleaning away the debris.

"There was a fire?" She pointed back, as the car whirred past the sad corner.

"A terror act," he said. His eyes in the rearview mirror glinted with loathing. "Another damn suicide bomber. Killed and maimed a bunch of dancing kids last night. There was a *discothèque* in there." He mouthed another oath before adding a bit calmer, "I forgot where the address was. Otherwise, I'd never have driven a passenger past this place. Sorry, lady."

Amanda felt cold. Her daughter lived somewhere here. Maybe her granddaughter as well. Maybe her granddaughter had been dancing at that club last night. What if she had been hurt? Then, Amanda would be late. *Please, let it not be true*, she pleaded with whatever high power was listening. She would forget about

Sergey. She would never succumb to carnal pleasures, again. She would persevere in her search until she found her daughter and her grandchildren and took them away from this terrible place, from the suicidal bombers, and the blown-up *discothèques*.

Before now, she never paid much attention to the Middle East. The conflict in Israel had never affected her life. Once, a few years ago, she had gone shopping on Robson Street and seen a group of Palestinian protesters on the steps of the Vancouver Art Gallery. They had been screaming some propaganda, but she had crossed the street to avoid them. Most people had.

She couldn't avoid the memory of that burned disco club. She would probably remember it until the day she died. It wasn't a distant news report. It was a ruined building a few blocks away from her hotel. She could come there, again. She could touch the blackened walls. In Vancouver, those protesters didn't blow up anything. Here, they blew up dancing kids. Suddenly, Amanda wanted to puke. She swallowed convulsively.

The driver, quiet since the ruined *discothèque*, turned a corner, and the car glided toward the modern, high-rise hotel. The Mediterranean Sea splashed 100 yards away, beyond the promenade adorned by fancy street lights and an ornamental fence. Beneath the fence, the tide susurrated faintly, leaving scattered dollops of foam on the yellow sand.

White, dominant sun shone from above, sweeping its hypnotic, all-mighty rays along the empty beach and the scarcely populated promenade. A few steps away, under a striped red and green awning, a small eatery provided a few drowsy patrons with some local fare.

Instead of getting hungry, Amanda felt nauseous. She climbed out of the car into the roasting heat of the street. No wonder they had siestas in this climate. It was hard to move. Apathy settled inside her. She just wanted to lie down and bake like a loaf of bread. Suddenly, she felt ancient.

"Go on, Canadian," the driver said, motioning to the sliding glass doors of the hotel. "I'll bring your bags inside. Your skin is too fair. You'll burn."

Hastily, Amanda obeyed.

* * * *

As soon as she finished showering, she called Gloria. She needed to hear her daughter's voice, to reassure herself that Gloria was safe. What time was it in Vancouver?

"Mom?" Gloria's sleepy voice came through the receiver. "It's after midnight." She yawned audibly. "How was your flight?"

"Sorry if I woke you up, honey. The flight was uneventful. It's devilishly hot here. The street is like an oven. The hotel is air-conditioned, though. Are you all right?"

"I'm fine. Mom, what's wrong?" Gloria's voice sharpened.

"Oh, Gloria. I saw a blown-up *discothèque*. We drove past it. The taxi driver said it happened yesterday. There were kids dancing there. Now, it's a blackened ruin."

"Shit," Gloria said. "I read about it. Perhaps I should come?"

"No! I'll just find her, and we'll fly back together. I don't want my daughter, any of my daughters, to spend one minute more than necessary here. It's dangerous." Hearing hysteria throbbing in her voice, Amanda lowered her tone. "What if my grandchildren were there?" she whispered.

"Oh, Mom. Calm down. Nothing bad will happen to them. If you even have them. The stats are all against it. They say more people die in Israel from car accidents than from terrorists."

"How encouraging." Amanda chuckled weakly. "I suppose you're right. My stupid imagination." She changed the topic. "Rebecca said one can find anyone in Israel. It's all computerized. There's a special office here to find people."

"What office?"

"I don't know." Amanda leaned against her chair's back. Talking to Gloria was therapeutic, although lately, every conversation was fraught with tension. The dynamics of their relationship was changing, but her love didn't diminish. She hoped Gloria understood.

"I miss you, honey," Amanda said. "I'll ask at the reception's desk."

"Mom. When you see Dina, please ask her if I can come for a visit. I'd like to meet my mother. I even started taking Russian lessons."

"I'm your mother!" Amanda exploded. Her heart started thumping, again.

"Mom, it works both ways. If Sofia is your daughter, then Dina is my mother."

"You're both my daughters," Amanda said stubbornly.

"Then, you're both my mothers!" Gloria began laughing. "It's like a royal minuet. One step ahead, two steps to the side, spin, and switch places. Such a complicated dance. I'm not sure even you know the rules."

Amanda sighed. "I'll ask her."

"Thanks. Maybe I should take Hebrew for beginners, too," Gloria mused.

Amanda's sudden fear was cutting. For a moment, she felt like she swallowed a spoonful of broken glass. It hurt. She hated the idea of Gloria investigating the Jewish connection. Thinking about losing her daughter to the unknown Dina was hard, but she understood the necessity. Thinking about losing Gloria to the Jews was unbearable and unnecessary. She breathed deeply and forced her irritation down. "You don't need Hebrew. English is good enough."

"Mom. If I'm a Jew, I should know something about my nation. The history. The religion."

"You're not a Jew," Amanda snapped. Was it the price she would have to pay for finding her blood daughter? She didn't want to pay such a price. It was too steep. Should she backpedal? Abort her search altogether? Did it make her an anti-Semite? She wasn't one. She should purge the abominable attitude from her thoughts. Could she purge it from her guts? She wasn't sure, but she would try. If both her daughters wanted to be Jews, she would accept it, even embrace it. As long as they were both alive and well. Unhurt by terrorists. Safe with her in Canada. Maybe Sofia wouldn't even want to be a Jew if she didn't have to. Amanda winced at her own hypocrisy.

"Look, Gloria—" she said quietly. She needed to explain.

"Mom. I love you, but I must know who I am."

Maybe she didn't need to explain after all. "I love you, too. Honey, you're my daughter. Well, Dina's daughter too, but...the rest is just peelings."

"I know." There was a faint smile in Gloria's voice. "Be careful, Mom. Don't allow any Palestinian terrorists to put a bomb under your ass. I'd miss you, Mrs. Barnett."

"I'll be careful, Miss Barnett," Amanda promised.

After talking to Gloria, she felt revived. Everything would be well. She should go outside and explore the city. She donned her green Capri pants, flat white sandals, and a white T-shirt. She applied sunblock to her face, neck, and arms before heading downstairs.

The receptionist—a young and beautiful woman with incredibly smooth, peachy skin—lifted her huge, dark eyes to smile at Amanda. "Can I help you?" She wore the hotel's buff uniform with the dignity of a queen, and an elaborate beret, knitted from red silken threads, covered her hair. Her name tag read "Ranit". Her English was perfect.

"Yes. Thank you, Ranit. I'm looking for a friend. I know she lives in Israel, but I don't know where," Amanda said.

"You should go to Misrad Apnim, our Ministry of Interior," Ranit said. "If the woman you're looking for is registered in Israel, you'll find her. It's too late today, and tomorrow is *Shavuot*—the offices are closed. Then, it's *Shabbat*. You'll have to wait until Day One."

"Four days!" Amanda wailed.

"I'm sorry, ma'am." Ranit shrugged apologetically. "You can take some tourist trips. There are the brochures in English." She pointed to a stand in the corner, stuffed with colorful pamphlets. "They operate year around. There might be some trips available in the next few days. You can call from your room."

Amanda nodded politely. "Can I go for a walk? I saw that burned *discothèque*. It was terrible. Is it safe to walk around?"

Ranit's dark, liquid eyes turned into glittering coals. "It's safe for our guests," she said crisply. "They never blow up foreign tourists."

"Thanks," Amanda mumbled. She felt cold. Did she offend the girl by her remark? She hadn't meant to, but she wasn't sure what to say to make it better. She retreated, instead. What had caused Ranit's sudden hostility? Unable to fathom the answer, she bought a map of downtown Tel Aviv at a corner kiosk and stepped boldly outside, into the hot, shimmering air.

All the shops were open. She turned away from the rustling sea and window-shopped for a while, turning at random, until she came to the open market. "Carmel Market," said her map. She eyed the noisy street with some misgivings. It looked like an exotic Eastern market in an old movie. Maybe it was. The first booth on the right sold cheap shorts and T-shirts. The one on the left side of the aisle offered purses and bags. A couple of stalls deeper, she saw some pastry rolls and suddenly felt her mouth watering. She was ravenous. Was it safe to buy food at this market? She decided she would risk it. She hadn't eaten since five in the morning.

She wandered the market for a couple of hours, listening to the yells of the sellers and the bargaining of the buyers. Pajamas and toys, cheap jewelry and shoes of dubious manufacturers, mirrors, and pots—the market offered a mind-boggling selection. When she approached a stall selling hats piled higher than she was tall, the bored owner, middle-aged and clean-shaven, latched onto her. He tried Hebrew first, saw that she only smiled faintly, and switched to crooked English.

"Lady needs hat, yes?" he asked. "Try!" Jumping from behind his stall, he placed a large, straw hat on Amanda's head. "Beautiful, *yaffa*, yes." He approved his handiwork, grinning and nodding.

Amanda glanced at herself in the mirror hanging on one of the wooden poles that supported the awning above the market. She looked so ridiculous in the huge hat that she laughed. "No, not this one." She gave the hat back. "Thank you."

"Green one then, yes?" He disappeared behind the mount of headgear on his table, returning in a moment with an olive-green, canvas panama decorated with beads.

To reward him for his exertion, Amanda put it on, glanced in the mirror, and giggled. She looked ludicrous. Enjoying the game, she tried a few more hats and finally settled on a small, white straw confection with a coquettishly curved brim and a few bright, silky butterflies sewn around the white ribbon. Proudly wearing her new hat, she paid the happy salesman and continued her excursion through the crush of people.

Nobody seemed to be upset about the blown-up *discothèque*, or even mention it. Nobody was looking around, checking for lurking terrorists. Didn't these people know? Or were they so inured to the danger, they didn't notice it, anymore?

To Amanda's surprise, the Russian language flew between the tarpaulin walls, almost as dense as Hebrew. She bought some sweets and devoured them, chasing the pastry down with a water bottle. Then, she bought a couple of peaches and a huge tomato, all so appetizing that she couldn't resist. Washing them from the same bottle, she munched happily as she roamed between the stalls.

Behind the produce market, an artisan market attracted her even more. Amanda loved the atmosphere of a fairground that always hung around such installations. As if in a museum, she sidled from table to table, examining glass ornaments, silk scarves, and colorful china, enjoying herself and the wares.

"What is that?" She came to a stop in front of a table covered with little, brown statuettes. They looked like netsuke, but the material was way off—neither old wood, nor stone, nor ivory. Picking up a small figurine of an antelope with her baby, Amanda fingered smooth brownish texture.

"It's a netsuke—a mold from the Hermitage collection," a short, plump man on the other side of the table said in English with a strong Russian accent.

Amanda switched to Russian. "Do they have a good collection of netsuke in the Hermitage?"

"Oh, you're a Russian, too," the man said with relief, also reverting to Russian. He rubbed his small hands together in an unconscious, rapid gesture. "The best in Russia. I worked there before we moved to Israel."

"I'm not Russian." Amanda smiled. "I'm Canadian. I teach Slavic languages and literature at the university. I just flew here from Moscow."

"You're not Jewish?"

"No."

"A tourist?"

"Kind of. Not really. I'm looking for someone." Amanda noticed the man's raised eyebrows and shrugged, feeling the need to explain. "I knew her many years ago. When I went to Russia, I searched for her, but she moved to Israel a few years back."

"Then, you have to go to the Ministry of Interior. They have everyone in their database."

"Thanks. The hotel clerk already told me, but she said tomorrow is a holiday, and then it's Saturday, and I have to wait until Monday." Amanda couldn't quite keep the resentment out of her voice. She had traveled so far, and now these silly holidays interfered.

He chuckled. "Yes, that's right. Not until Monday, though. Here, a week starts on Sunday—Day One."

"Right, that's what she said." Amanda put the antelope back on the table and picked up another netsuke of an old, stooped woman. The tiny details were amazing. "Thank you. Are you a scholar? Do you make these things yourself?"

"They are just molds, cheap copies." Grinning self-deprecatingly, he pulled a crumpled handkerchief out of his pocket and wiped his round, pink face and his sweating neck. "I'm an art historian. I worked at the Hermitage before we immigrated, but there is not much demand here for such a profession. I brought the molds with me, so I make and sell these." He stuffed his handkerchief back into his pocket and pointed at his table, populated by the netsuke-like trinkets.

"Good business?"

"Not bad. Weekends are better, though. The market is quiet, now."

"It's quiet?" Amanda's eyes widened as she glanced quickly back toward the hubbub of the main produce lane.

"It can be much louder. We're closing soon, so the people are leaving, both sellers and buyers. *Shavuot*."

"Do you celebrate it?"

He hesitated before replying. "Not really. I don't even wear a *kippa*." He pointed at his head, covered with a thick, tangled mass of brown curls. "I'm secular. Are you alone here?"

"Yes." Putting down an old woman, Amanda picked up a dainty, ornamental elephant, all curlicues and spirals. It was so cute, her lips twitched.

"Good, isn't it? The original is from the eighteenth century," the man said helpfully.

Amanda nodded, fingering the tiny elephant. It seemed to smirk at her, as if it knew it belonged. "I'll buy it. How much?" She pulled out her wallet. "Can you recommend what I should see here? I have three days to kill until Sunday. I've never been to Israel before."

He told her the price, which was very reasonable, and counted change back from her twenty-dollar bill. "I'll tell you what," he said. "I'm a widower. I live with my daughter and her husband, and I wouldn't mind getting away for the holidays. How about I give you a tour of Israel in the next three days?" He looked hopeful. "I'll be your local guide. That's if you have nothing better to do. I'm Michael."

His shy smile was charming. Why not? Of course he was a head shorter than her, and his nose was almost as big and round as the rest of him, but his face was kind, and his brown eyes twinkled with humor. Also, she really had nothing better to do.

"All right," she said. "I'm Amanda. We have a date tonight, Misha." Calling him by the Russian diminutive of Michael, she offered him her hand. In spite of herself, she liked the little man. He was about her age, and wrinkles lined his forehead, but he was bursting with enthusiasm. He accepted Amanda's handshake and surprised her with his dry, sure grip.

"Great. Let's go to Old Jaffa, tonight." He grinned in triumph.

"Is it a restaurant?"

"You don't know?"

"No. I didn't have time to buy a tourist guide. My trip here was...unexpected."

He laughed. "Gorgeous! Jaffa is a historical, little village at the edge of Tel Aviv. It's very charming, like a theatrical background.

There are a few good restaurants and galleries there, although many are closed, tonight. You'll love it. There is that Russian seafood restaurant. M-m-m!" He sighed blissfully.

Amanda snickered. "Okay. Can you pick me up at seven?" She gave him her room number and the name of her hotel.

He clapped his hands and winked. "Superb! Amanda, there is a mystery surrounding you. An unexpected trip to Israel is unusual. I'm going to play a guessing game with you, can I?"

Amanda couldn't help herself. She laughed. "Yes, you can. You'll never guess."

"We'll see," Michael said. He lifted his chubby hands in the air in front of Amanda and waved like a stage magician. "I'm gue-e-essing," he drawled in a deep, guttural voice, stretching the vowels. His round, brown eyes became narrow slits. "Tell me all your de-e-ep, da-a-ark secrets!" Then, he opened his eyes wide. "Has it worked?"

"No." A smile tugged at the corners of Amanda's mouth. "It might yet. Keep trying."

That evening, Michael took Amanda to Jaffa. The next day, they went to Tzfat, the city of artists and cabbalists. The day after, Michael drove his little old Peugeot to Haifa, showing Amanda the Bahai temple and the funny funicular up the mountain, made up like a train. The train wagon's floors were terraced, like stairs.

Amanda loved their trips and their amusing conversations. Michael knew a great deal about art, history, and the architecture of Israel. He knew all the best restaurants everywhere, too. On the third day, after he exhausted all his powers of deduction and introduced all the possible scenarios that could've brought Amanda to Israel unexpectedly, he cried defeat.

"Would you tell me what brought you to Israel?" he asked, as they drove back to Tel Aviv from Jerusalem.

It was the evening of their third day together. Amanda sat quietly, gazing into the growing twilight outside the car window. Jerusalem had been an emotional explosion—a shock to all her senses. She needed time to recover from it.

"Jerusalem is a holy city," she said at last. "Maybe that's why I came here. To visit her?"

"It is holy," Michael agreed, "but you didn't know it before."

"No. I had another reason." She smiled flittingly. "I'm looking for my daughter." She knew Michael well enough by now to realize he wouldn't mock her, so she told him the truth.

"I would never have guessed," was his reply. He glanced at her quickly and drove for a long time in silence. "What will you do when you find her?" he asked, as they approached the outskirts of Tel Aviv.

"Take her away from here."

"She's been raised a Jew. She might not want to leave."

"Misha, it's dangerous out here. I saw that blown up *discothèque*." Until today, by an unspoken mutual agreement, they hadn't talked about anything personal. Now, Amanda couldn't stay quiet. "I can't stand thinking that my grandchild might've been there. I don't even know if I have one, but such thoughts are killing me. Wouldn't you want your children far away from such a place?"

"I'm a Jew," he said. Amanda almost felt him shedding his outer shell of an entertaining, old intellectual, baring the steel core inside his chubby, soft exterior. His face changed expressions, became hard. He didn't look at her, his eyes trained on the road. "Both my grandsons are serving in the Israeli army, now. I wouldn't have chosen it any other way, despite the danger. It's our country. If we don't fight for her, nobody will."

"I'm sorry," Amanda whispered. "Israel is not my country, and I don't want my daughter or my grandchildren to fight for her. I want them safe in Vancouver."

"Nowhere is safe these days," he said grimly.

"True," Amanda breathed.

The car stopped in front of her hotel. Michael climbed out, rolling around toward the passenger side of the car on his short, stubby legs. For such a small man, he could move amazingly fast. He opened Amanda's door and helped her out.

"I hope I didn't offend you, Amanda," he said softly, holding her hand.

"No, and I hope I didn't offend you." Amanda pulled her hand away. "I've had a marvelous weekend thanks to you." She smiled. She really liked the little man and was unwilling to end the friendship they developed over the last three days. "Care for a cup of coffee in the hotel bar?" she asked.

"No. I have to get home." Still, he lingered.

Amanda pulled her business card out of her purse. "Misha. If you or your daughter or your grandsons ever visit Canada, come to Vancouver and stay with me. I have a big house in the best neighborhood. Lots of space, and there is only me and my daughter, Gloria."

"Thanks, Amanda. I might yet." He took the card. "There

might be an addition to your household, soon. Your new daughter might have a dozen children." He winked.

Amanda grinned. "Good. I have to tell you something else."

"What?" He perked up.

"Come have a coffee with me, and I'll tell you."

"All right. I'll just lock the car." He dove into the car for the key. When he pulled out, he faced her. He didn't smile. "My wife died from cancer twelve years ago. Since then, I haven't spent such a great time with a woman. Not once, until you. You make me feel alive, again. Not flirty or something, but alive. Kicking. Thanks, Amanda."

"Oh, Misha!" Unable to answer his unspoken question, Amanda whirled and led the way inside the hotel.

"My daughter Gloria is the one who had been switched," she said after they got their coffees and sat down at a small table in the darkened restaurant. "I talked to her on the phone, yesterday. She was raised a Canadian and a Protestant, like me, but she's a Jew by blood. She told me the same thing you did. She wants to fight. She wants to make Israel safe."

Behind his coffee cup, Michael listened intently, nodding occasionally. His shrewd, brown eyes pierced Amanda.

She went on. "She wants to come here. I'm terrified, Misha. What if instead of acquiring another daughter and taking her home, I'll actually lose the only daughter I know to Israel? Gloria is so hot about it. She is a very passionate person. She even went to a synagogue to listen to a Friday service."

"What did she think about it?"

"She got bored." Amanda's lips crimped in a sad grin. "A small conciliation."

"I don't go to a synagogue," Michael said. "I'm agnostic."

Chapter Nineteen
Sonya

Alexei emptied the rain bucket, kicked it back into place under the crack, and joined Sonya on the sofa.

She put down the receiver. "The police don't know, either," she said in a small voice. She had already called Ksenya's cell phone. Her daughter didn't answer. She called all the hospitals in the Greater Vancouver area, but nobody knew anything about a fourteen-year-old girl with dirty-blonde, shoulder-length hair.

Sonya felt adrift, floating in the sea of fear. What happened to Ksenya? Where was she? Had she run away? Had she broken her legs? Was she lying alone in the darkness under the rain somewhere? Did someone kidnap her? Someone sinister? This line of thought was too painful to follow to its logical conclusion. Sonya shunned away from it. No. It only happened in thriller movies. Real girls from poor, immigrant families didn't get abducted. Ksenya had probably run away. Then, she would be brought back by the police.

"The police will find her, right?" she asked.

"Call her friends." Alexei was sitting beside her, his large, long-fingered musician hands hung loosely between his knees. His unkempt, overgrown hair fell into his face. He stared at the floor.

Sonya touched his coarse, tangled beard. He never had a beard before.

He recoiled then glanced up quickly, his eyes hard, looking inward.

"It's midnight." She snatched her hand away. "Sorry. They're all asleep."

"Call!" he ordered hoarsely, motioning to the phone.

Obediently, Sonya picked up the phone again and dialed Ashley's number.

"Hello?" croaked a sleepy, bewildered male voice on the other end.

"Hi. I'm sorry to call so late," Sonya rushed, before the man threw down the receiver. "Your daughter Ashley is a friend of my daughter Ksenya. Ksenya is missing. She hasn't been home since last night. Could I talk to Ashley? Please. Maybe she knows something."

"Ummm. Wait," the voice said.

Sonya waited, breathing evenly and trying to slow down her galloping heart.

Finally, the silent phone revived. "Hello," Ashley said cautiously.

"Ashley, it's Sonya. Ksenya's mom." Sonya explained everything one more time. With every repetition, Ksenya's absence was becoming increasingly real, filling out every cubic centimeter of the apartment like an ugly, life-sucking cancer. Sonya felt sick, suffocated.

"I don't know," Ashley said. "I haven't seen her for a couple of days." She hesitated.

"What? Tell me anything, please."

"She might be with Felix," Ashley said reluctantly. "She made me promise not to tell you, but maybe...I should."

"Who is Felix?"

"Her boyfriend."

"She has a boyfriend? Where does he live?"

Alexei growled beside Sonya. She glanced at him. His fists were bunched, knuckles white with tension, although his pose on the sofa hadn't changed.

"I don't know where he lives," Ashley said. "He has a place somewhere on Main."

"He goes to school with you?"

"No, ma'am," Ashley whispered. "He's older, a grown up." Her voice had become almost inaudible. "He's...a druggie and a pusher," she blurted and hung up.

"A drug pusher?" Sonya echoed, stupefied. "Felix?" She put down the receiver, risking a quick peek at Alexei, again.

He was watching her, eyes narrowed, sharp cheekbones rolling beneath his beard. He's lost weight, she noticed absently.

"Lives on Main," she piped.

Alexei stood up. "I'll find him."

"Now?" Sonya jumped up and ran after him down the stairs.

"Someone on Hastings will know where he lives."

"Do you think she might be with him?" Even that disgusting possibility was preferable to the horrifying scenarios of Ksenya kidnapped for organs or dead on a remote roadside. That one kept popping into Sonya's mind, no matter how hard she shook her head to discard it.

Let Ksenya be with that druggie, Sonya pleaded silently, afraid to hope. Let her be alive! Anything else they could fix. They could get back together with Alexei, if that was what it took. She would work for both of them. She was strong. Just let her daughter be alive. She was sprinting ahead without thinking, when Alexei pulled at her arm.

"The bus stop," he said. "Don't cry, Sonya. We'll find her."

Sonya lifted her head to look sheepishly at the bus stop sign, striped white and blue. She would've mindlessly run past it, if Alexei hadn't stopped her. She must take hold of herself. "I'm not crying." She blinked a few times until his face came into sharp focus. Sniffing, she wiped the moisture from her face with her sleeves. Her sleeves were too wet from the rain, not much use at all. Her arms shook. "It's the rain," she clarified.

Maybe she should get out her umbrella? Before she completed the thought, her mind jumped to a new speculation. "What if that guy has AIDS?" she mouthed, looking across the dark street. A few cars sped past, but mostly the street was empty. Who wanted to be out on such a dismal, rainy night? "What if Ksenya...?" She couldn't finish the sentence, couldn't give voice to the horror.

She clenched her fists to stop the shaking. She had to be strong for Ksenya. No hysterics! Not now. She inhaled and exhaled a few times to regulate her breathing the way they taught at the dancing academy. It didn't work. She couldn't slow her racing heart. A blender of fear whirred in her stomach, making her nauseous.

"You're going to beat me up?" Alexei asked suddenly. "Right. Do it. I deserve it." His tone was low, laden with self-hatred.

Swallowing hard, Sonya looked down at her fists. They were in fighting position in front of her, shaking like a Parkinson boxer. Who was she going to fight? Felix? AIDS? She lowered her arms to her sides. Maybe if they were down, close to her body, the tremors would stop. She pressed the fists into her hips.

"The buses probably quit for the night. We need a taxi." She forced one of her fists to open, pointing half a block ahead, to the glowing red and green neon sign. "They have a public phone at Seven-Eleven." Her pointing finger shook, too. She stopped trying to immobilize it. As long as she kept her head, her shaking hands didn't matter. Only Ksenya mattered.

"The buses run till one in the morning. We'll find her," Alexei repeated softly.

* * * *

Hastings Street around the intersection of Main never slept. Too many homeless. Too many druggies. Sonya never got off the bus at this stop. She hated the place. Ksenya hated it, too. How could she stay with her druggie Felix in this neighborhood?

Sonya followed Alexei from one prone form to another, as he questioned the creatures. Most of them were men but some were women. Even Sonya's shaking stopped in the face of so much misery. The faces of these people were so dull, so scrunched up by hunger and drugs, they seemed alien to the human race.

Contrary to her expectations, they were not hostile. They seemed lethargic. Even the snarled obscenities they hurtled at Alexei instead of answers didn't seem very offensive. They just talked this way. Maybe, these people were indeed aliens, poisoned by the drugs? No humans could live in these conditions.

Alexei prodded one blanketed heap with his boot. "I'm looking for Felix. A young one."

"Fuck you." The man's voice was slurred. "Felix? Don't know. Maybe Paul knows." Without opening his eyes, he pointed toward the majestic steps of Carnegie Library.

Alexei mounted the steps. "You Paul?"

Paul wasn't asleep. His face, weathered and wrinkled, was marked by old and new sores. Some of them were scabbed over, others oozed. His denim jacket was so dirty it shined under a street lamp. A filthy blanket covered his legs.

"Felix," Paul whined. "The junkie?"

Sonya averted her gaze. She couldn't look at Paul. Ksenya couldn't have aligned herself with the inhabitants of this place. It would be intolerable. Better not to see. Maybe it hadn't happened, yet? She would do anything not to let it happen.

"Yes. Where can I find him?" Alexei demanded, standing over the man. The rain sluiced heavily on all of them.

Paul coughed. Or maybe that was his version of laughter. Sonya wasn't sure. Unable to look at the old addict, she stared at the library doors, instead. Alexei growled beside her.

"Alyosha, offer him money," Sonya whispered in Russian, her gaze glued to the intricate handles of the doors.

"How much do you have with you?" he asked in the same tongue.

"About a hundred."

Alexei turned back to the man. "Hey, Paul. Dog's shit. How about twenty bucks?"

Paul cackled. "Sixty?" he croaked hopefully. Sonya ventured a glance at his grinning face. His front top teeth were missing. The remaining bottom teeth seemed brown. She shuddered in revulsion and turned away again, rummaging in her bag for the money.

"Forty," Alexei said firmly.

Paul grabbed the two green twenties. "Ming Grocery," he rasped, pointing with the bills in his fist. He started coughing, again. "Top floor." He hacked harder. Around them, several heads lifted, the eye whites flickering in the darkness, paying attention to Paul's grimy fist with the money, gazes following the banknotes like compass arrows.

Alexei steered Sonya away, marching rapidly, almost dragging her with him. After a few turns, he stopped in front of a four-story, stone building. A street lamp beside the entrance was dark. Shadows swayed in the rain, but nobody was sleeping on this street. Probably because there was no awning above the boarded-up store, no protection from the rain. One window was broken in, gaping like a black hole. The sign saying "Ming Grocery" was still attached above the door, upside down and hardly visible. When Alexei opened the door, the stench of stale urine hit Sonya in the face. She almost gagged from the relentless odor.

"Stay here," Alexei said sternly.

She didn't listen, pattering up the stairs after him, shaking the rainwater from her soaked hair, and trying not to inhale too deeply. In front of her, his boots made dull, thumping sounds in the dark staircase. Sonya stumbled and grabbed the rail. Who else had touched it before her? Maybe it had been Paul? Her fingers jerked on the wooden bar. She felt the multiple layers of dirt through her skin, but she didn't let go. Maybe Ksenya touched it last? Sonya grabbed tighter. Her fingers were wet, anyway. She might as well wash the wretched rail.

On the top floor, two doors were black on black, almost invisible. "Which one?" she asked in a breathy voice.

"Sniff," Alexei said.

Sonya sniffed at the right-hand door. Suddenly, she felt stupid. Although the reek of urine was weaker here than downstairs, it might still interfere with her sense of smell. Or maybe she had just gotten used to it. She felt nothing.

Grimacing, she stepped toward the other door, brushing past Alexei. It was there, the unmistakable smell of weed. Very slight. She dropped to her knees in front of the door, bent, and sniffed beneath it. Abruptly, she loathed herself. Even more, she loathed the man behind the door. He reduced her to kneeling at his door. He had taken away her daughter.

"I hate this guy," she said. "I'll kill him. Here." She sniffed again and sneezed twice before climbing to her feet.

"Take a number," Alexei grunted and knocked on the door. When nobody answered, he started kicking.

Sonya turned her back to the door and began hitting it with the soles of her sneakers. "Open the door!" she yelled. "Open!"

"What?" A young man cracked the door open. Above his head, a weak light illuminated his bleary eyes, sleek sandy hair, and a wispy goatee of a teenager. A few lone hairs wobbled off his sunken cheeks. A long tear snaked down the right side of his white, sleeveless shirt. A thin chain held the door from opening completely. "Shut up, you bitch." He smirked at Sonya and yawned.

"Ksenya!" Alexei bellowed. "Where's my daughter, punk?"

"Daddy?" Ksenya squeaked from inside the apartment.

The youth's eyes widened. Before he could slam the door shut, Alexei's hand streaked in, grabbed the boy's hair, and pulled his face out, squishing it between the door and the frame. "Open the door," Alexei squeezed through his teeth.

The boy's lips quivered. "No."

Alexei's fist connected with the boy's nose, drawing blood. "Open the door," he repeated menacingly.

The boy made some mournful, little sounds. Blood dribbled from his smashed nose.

Alexei lifted his fist, again.

"No! I'm opening." Felix's eyes watered, tears intermixing with blood. After several seconds of fumbling, the chain fell away. Alexei's fist connected again, this time with the boy's midsection, sending him flying into the room. Sonya rushed past them both, past the kitchen, and into the one-room apartment. Along one wall, a battalion of flowerpots held some greenery. At the window, a mattress lay on the floor. Ksenya sat on it, holding a sheet to her neck. A floor lamp in a corner illuminated a huge, flat screen TV below and Ksenya's pale face with a large, bloated bruise spreading over her left cheek. The left eye was puffy. Dried blood marred the left corner of her mouth. Both her eyes were wide open.

"Mom!" she peeped faintly.

"Oh, baby." Sonya dropped to her knees in front of the mattress. "Are you all right?"

"Aha," Ksenya mouthed, her terrified eyes fixed behind Sonya's back.

Sonya's ears popped open to the sounds of breaking pottery, Alexei's vicious swearing, and the boy's mewled protests. She turned. In all the time she had been married to Alexei, she had never seen him so enraged. He had always been polite and soft-spoken, always ready to smile. Now, he was hitting the helpless boy with such savagery that she shivered. He pounded at the bloody face in front of him, kicked with his hard boots, wrenching the boy's skinny body around like a broken doll, shouting obscene Russian curses in the guttural, frenzied barks, and disregarding the sickening sounds of broken bones. Even if Felix had been fighting back before, he didn't fight, anymore. All the pots had already been broken. Spilled earth and potsherds mixed on the floor with blood and starry marijuana leaves, ground into mash by Alexei's boots.

"Alexei, stop!" Sonya screamed.

He didn't hear her. Lost in his wrath, he landed blow after blow with bitter efficiency.

"Stop! You're killing him."

"Yes!" he roared and kicked again, emitting a new stream of invectives. His face contorted with a blend of agony, fury, and triumph.

Sonya grabbed at his arm. "Stop, you idiot!" she screeched, hitting him on the arm, tugging with all her might.

He didn't notice her feeble attempts. "Dirty worm!" He kicked again and again. "Shit eater!"

"Stop! Look at Ksenya!"

Alexei stopped before he landed the last blow, his foot aiming for another kick. Breathing heavily, he glanced at Ksenya and slowly lowered his foot to the floor. He didn't look at Sonya.

"Don't, please," Sonya whispered. "He's not worth it."

The boy thrashed in a corner, among the broken pots and smashed weeds, whimpering. One of his arms was twisted at an odd angle. Another covered his bloody face.

"Ksenya, get dressed!" Alexei's voice cracked like a whip.

The girl flinched, scurrying away from him to the farthest corner of the mattress, trembling and clutching at her sheet.

"Don't be afraid of me, daughter," Alexei said roughly and turned away from the mattress, watching his victim with a dark, brooding expression. His chest pumped up and down. His eyes glittered. Fists opened and closed spasmodically. His knuckles were bloody.

Sonya found Ksenya's jeans and T-shirt on a chair behind the

TV. "Get dressed," she said quietly, tossing the clothes to the mattress. "Can you?"

"Yes," Ksenya whispered back. Keeping an eye on her father, she hurriedly got dressed.

"Ready?" Alexei asked without turning.

"Yes," the girl breathed.

"Sonya, get her out of here."

"No, Alyosha. Don't." Sonya stepped in front of him, between him and the cowering, sniveling youngster.

As if sensing someone coming to his defense, the boy flailed, groaning pitifully.

"Please, don't. Come with us." Sonya put her palm on Alexei's billowing chest, feeling his frantic heartbeats under her fingers. "Please."

Shaking, Ksenya plastered herself in the open doorway, as far away from the carnage as she could, eyes wary.

"Please, Alexei." Sonya watched the wrathful need for vengeance melting off his face, replaced by bottomless fatigue. The lines around his mouth deepened.

"Yeah," he muttered. "You scum!" He addressed the boy he had just beaten to a pulp. "Never come near my daughter, again."

Felix twittered.

Alexei turned toward the exit. "Right. Let's go." He strode to the door but stopped in front of Ksenya.

She was watching his every move with the eyes of a trapped rabbit.

"I love you, daughter," he said quietly and stepped out.

"Come." Sonya snatched Ksenya's jacket from a hall tree near the door. Taking Ksenya's hand, she dragged the listless girl out of the apartment and down the stairs. With the ruckus they had created, she thought all the doors would be open, but none were, although there was light beneath a couple of them. Obviously, in this building, such racket was common. Outside, the rain still fell.

Alexei led the way. Sonya followed, firmly holding onto Ksenya's hand. The girl stumbled after her, suspiciously docile, like a zombie. In the maze of little streets, Sonya wasn't sure where they were, but Alexei knew.

"Give me a quarter," he said at last, when they reached a public phone. He dialed. "You need a taxi."

He waited until a yellow cab rolled to a halt in front of them.

"Take her home, Sonechka," he said tiredly.

"Come with us, Alyosha." Sonya's voice quivered, laced with

exhaustion and the residue of her fright.

Alexei snorted mirthlessly and walked away, disappearing around a corner. He didn't turn. Shivering under the cold rain, Sonya stared after him.

Ksenya climbed inside the taxi. "Mom," she called. "Let's go home."

Chapter Twenty
Amanda

Misrad Apnim was as ordinary as any government agency Amanda had ever seen. Modern, glassed-off offices, a narrow waiting area stuffed with uncomfortable chairs, and a red number dispenser at the door. She slept late last night, so she came into the Ministry at around eleven. The digital display above the office door blinked number fourteen, just as she walked in.

Pulling a paper slip with the number thirty-seven from the dispenser, Amanda settled into a corner chair, beside a small coffee table loaded with glossy magazines in Hebrew and English. The girl in the next chair, dressed in a khaki Army uniform, glanced at Amanda briefly and turned away. The old couple on the other side of the table talked animatedly in Russian mixed with Yiddish. The woman hissed unhappily at her partner. The man in a *kippa* defended himself in a whisper, gesticulating wildly. His cane stood forgotten at his knee.

Amanda tuned everyone out. Maybe it was a blessing she had to wait in this line. Since leaving Vancouver, she hadn't had much solitary time to sit down and take stock. Her life had been a romp ever since her plane landed in Moscow.

First Sergey, then Michael. Was she becoming a whore? No, she hadn't taken their money. She had just taken her pleasure. She shivered from the memory. Until Moscow, she had only had one man in her life: Donald. In the last two weeks, she had already had two. Would she ever stop?

Gloria told her repeatedly that she had been hiding in a box after Donald's death. As always, her headstrong daughter had been right. Now, Amanda finally climbed out. Not climbed, really. Nothing so sedate. When Sergey opened the lid of her box in Moscow, Amanda had erupted out of it like champagne.

She grinned faintly at her analogy. Right! She supposed she was still frothing, although it felt different with two such different men. With Sergey, all her senses had been in constant tumult, teetering on overdrive. With Michael, it felt cozy in comparison. Not as much a turbulent explosion but rather a nice massage therapy.

She never wanted the therapy session to end.

She thought she wouldn't be able to get over Sergey, but she had hardly thought of him since landing in Israel. Why? She hadn't liked Michael very much at first, but he had grown on her in the few days they spent together. What was happening to her? She gobbled up those men's affection like a victim of a years-long famine. Had she been sensually starved with Donald? She hadn't felt starved at the time.

Amanda pulled a *Khokhloma* pen she had bought in Vladimir out of her purse. It was so bright and Russian, it didn't fit inside this faceless, Israeli office. Fingering the pen, she studied the polished red and gold floral design on the black background. Sergey and Michael were opposites, like red and gold. They both fit inside her, like the patterns of the pen did. What had attracted her to the two such different men?

Amanda opened her notebook. She was a researcher. She would make two lists and compare them. Excited at the upcoming scientific project, she licked her lips and grinned wickedly. Dividing the page in half, she wrote "Sergey" at the top of the left side and "Misha" at the top of the right. Several minutes later, the left column featured "tall", "strong", "bald", "clever", "aggressive lover", "passionate", "considerate", "Russian". The right column sported "short", "fat", "lots of brown curls", "intelligent", "highly educated", "funny", "tender lover", "Jewish". Fiddling with the pen, Amanda stared at her lists. The only thing that united both men was their strong sense of national identity.

Amanda lifted her eyes to look around. The number display over the office door flashed twenty-six. The girl in the uniform had already disappeared. The couple on the other side of the table had stopped fighting. They were doing a crossword puzzle.

Amanda returned to her contemplation, doodling clover leaves on top of her lists. Why was their national sense so alluring. Maybe because she didn't possess one herself? Despite being a second generation Canadian, she thought of herself as a surrogate British. Her mother and father had, too. Donald had been Irish, no doubt about that. When had they first established Canadian citizenship? It was 1947, she recalled. When she had been born, she was still a British subject.

So, that was it? Being a Canadian was just too easy. No one threatened to wipe the Canadian nation from the face of the Earth. No one tried to invade Canada for at least a couple of centuries. Gloria was a Canadian, though. Much more so than her mother.

Oh, yeah! Amanda grinned in private amusement. Gloria was exploring her Jewish connections right now. Her Russian connections, too. Amanda's grin faded. She glanced at her lists, covered with clover leaves, and clicked the pen closed.

Fingering the pen, she stared at the placards in Hebrew on the office wall. Gloria was drifting away from her, away from being a Canadian and a Christian, away from Amanda. The closer Amanda was getting to Sofia, the further away Gloria seemed, and nothing Amanda had said appeared to make a difference. Every time they talked on the phone, they argued. About what? Some small stuff, inconsequential. Was Amanda losing her daughter for good? Could she fix the situation? They never showed this problem in sitcoms. She winced. She couldn't use a stupid TV series as a manual of her life.

What if she lost Gloria and didn't find Sofia. Even if she found her physically, would Sofia accept Amanda as her mother? Canada as her home? What if she was an Israeli patriot, like Michael? Would she accept that she wasn't a Jew by blood? Would it make a difference? Would she move to Canada?

Suddenly, an obscenity sprang to Amanda's lips. She swallowed it. She couldn't swear in an Israeli government office, although she wanted to. She never considered any possible legal hurdles, but the immigration authorities might not grant Sofia a permanent status. What should Amanda do, then? She was such a fool. She should've thought about these complications before. Should she call Gloria and ask her to find out all the legal aspects of the case? Would Gloria be incensed, again?

Maybe Amanda could sponsor Sofia into Canada? Could she adopt Sofia? Was it ever done with adults? Could it be done when Dina was still alive? What about Gloria? Would Dina demand to adopt Gloria? Would the immigration authorities take away Gloria's citizenship? The whole situation might turn into a legal nightmare.

Amanda felt her heart rate intensifying. She shook her head, fed up with her churning apprehension. No, she wouldn't panic beforehand. She would be calm. For the sake of both her daughters, she would be reasonable. Gloria often laughed at her for her overactive imagination. She wouldn't fall victim to it. First, she would find Sofia. Then, she would talk to Sofia and Gloria. Only after that, Amanda would panic.

She chortled at her perverse logic, dropped the pen into her purse, and tossed a quick glance at the electronic panel above the door. Thirty-five. One more, and it was her turn.

In the end, it proved easier than she had feared. She didn't have to justify her case or anything, just pay a small fee. Since she didn't know Sofia's last name, which might've changed after the girl's marriage, she gave Dina Goldberg's name and approximate age to a tall, thin female clerk in a small cubicle. Of course, the clerk spoke fluent English. She filled out a couple of forms, typed in the information, and after a short search, the computer spat out three addresses. By mid-afternoon, Amanda was back in her air-conditioned rental Honda in the underground parking.

She stared at the Ministry printout with the names. One Dina Goldberg, seventy-four years old, lived in Eilat. The second one was fifty-nine and lived in one of the northern *kibbutzim*. The third one was sixty-three and lived in Petah Tikva. Hopefully, one of them was the one Amanda sought, but which one?

Not Eilat, Amanda decided. Dina wasn't so much older than Amanda. It could be either of the other two. Amanda consulted the atlas of Israel, spread on the passenger seat. She would start with Petah Tikva. It was closer to Tel Aviv. She could drive there, today. If this Dina wasn't the right one, she would drive to the *kibbutz,* tomorrow.

Should she phone first? No! What could she say? If she started asking about the birth date of Dina's daughter on the phone, the woman might get too scared. If Amanda asked whether or not Dina's daughter was a red head, Dina might simply throw down the receiver. No, no, no! She must conduct this conversation in person.

Amanda swallowed her non-existent saliva. She was getting so close to her goal, she felt light-headed, floating. An insane question tinkled in her head: What if none of the three was her Dina? What would she do, then? Maybe, it would be for the best. No complications with Gloria, status-quo preserved. She started laughing, but the laughter petered out soon, turning into a muted, solitary sob. *Ground, woman*, she told herself sternly. *Get to the end of the road first, and then throw hysterics, if necessary.*

She started the car and, by habit, rolled down the window as soon as she left the parking garage. A big mistake. It was too hot outside, almost unbearably hot. Hastily, she pushed the button to roll the glass back up. Michael said it was *khamsin,* today—a hot wind off the desert. Yeah, right. They probably had this *khamsin* here every single day. How could people live in such a climate? Gratefully, Amanda inhaled the cool air inside the car and frowned from the headache throbbing in her skull.

Maybe she should postpone this meeting until she felt better. She didn't have any painkillers with her. She didn't often have headaches. Why now, of all days? She grimaced. Should she grab a bite to eat on the way, so she wouldn't feel so nauseous? Or was she just nervous?

She licked her lips again, but her mouth was dry. She wasn't hungry, and she didn't want to leave the cool interior of the car for the baking atmosphere outside. The air beyond the car window shimmered from the heat. Amanda steadied her hands on the wheel and blinked a few times to dispel her dizziness. Maybe, she should stop for several minutes? No, she might lose her nerve, altogether. Amanda breathed deeply and kept driving.

* * * *

Petah Tikva was old. Street after street, similar white three –to five-story houses proudly flapped their laundry on every balcony. Trees and bushes grew in the backyards. Children ran from school, carrying backpacks. Housewives hurried home with their grocery bags. In the town center, all the shops sported sidewalk sales beneath the awnings.

Amanda checked her map, again and turned onto a side street. She stopped in front of a four-story, white house that stood perpendicular to the street. In flat number six of this house lived a Dina Goldberg. Maybe even the right one—Gloria's birth mother.

Amanda's breathing became fast and sporadic as she glared at the house from the sanctuary of her car. The scraggly bushes stood like grim guardians between the pavement and the yard. A few local, hardy flowers survived the heat, manifesting their yellow heads above the burnt, brown grass. Like in every other house, laundry hung limply in the hot, windless air.

Amanda hugged herself. She was cold. Maybe she should turn down the air-conditioner. She definitely should get out of the car and walk the few steps to the house, but she didn't. She sat inside and watched a produce store across the street. Huge, red tomatoes and a pile of yellow bananas outside its doors contrasted merrily with something green.

The nearby bakery presented a mouth-watering window display. A young, freckled girl of about ten came out of the bakery, munching on a pastry. The girl's red hair, arranged into two curly ponytails, swung gaily. She nodded enthusiastically, skipping along the sidewalk to the tune from her earphones.

A red-haired girl. Amanda's eyes watered. Unable to tear her gaze away from the girl, she tapped a melody from *The Sound of Music* on the wheel. Maybe, this girl in her denim shorts and pink T-shirt was listening to the same melody. Maybe, she was her granddaughter. Only when the girl vanished into the lane behind the bakery did Amanda finally drag herself out of the car and toward the house. She felt dizzy, again.

The stairway was dim and blessedly cool. It was much cleaner than the similar stairways she had seen in Russia. No steel guarded any of the doors. As in many old houses, there was no elevator. The door with the large number six was on the second floor. Amanda shivered. Before she could chicken out and run away, she inhaled sharply once, twice, and pressed the buzzer.

"Who is it?" a melodic, female voice asked in Russian.

All Amanda's carefully pre-planned openings deserted her. "Are you Dina Goldberg?" she croaked. "Do you have a daughter named Sofia?"

The door swung open. "What happened to Sofia?" The woman was short and plump, pale with fear.

"Nothing," Amanda said. Her head began spinning, and she grabbed the door frame. "My daughter Gloria was born on April thirtieth in Vladimir, thirty-four years ago. In the maternity ward number one. I'm Canadian. Did you give birth to Sofia there?"

"Oh, the Canadian. Another redheaded girl." Dina visibly relaxed. Her skin resumed its dusky tint, and even her short, fuzzy curls seemed to perk up." She smiled. "I remember you. You called her Gloria?"

"Yes," Amanda said. She couldn't get enough air into her lungs despite breathing as fast as she could, and she had trouble keeping upright. Her knees wobbled, and her fingers clutching Dina's door frame hurt from the effort.

"You're dehydrated," Dina said abruptly. She frowned. "Come in." She yanked Amanda into the kitchen, pushed her onto a corner stool, and shoved a glass of water into Amanda's hands. "Drink!"

"I—" Amanda started to protest. She wasn't thirsty. She just needed to sit down and rest for a while.

"Drink!" Dina repeated sternly. "How long have you been in Israel?" She bustled about, putting a kettle on the stove.

Amanda sipped her water.

"You have to drink a lot. Two to three liters a day. How much did you drink, today?"

Amanda glanced at her glass in surprise. It was empty. "A cup of tea in the morning," she said faintly.

Dina shook her head. "Many visitors make this mistake. You dehydrate quickly in the heat. The kettle will be ready in a minute. Meanwhile, do you want Fanta or more water?"

"Water." Amanda quaffed the second glass much faster. The water had an unpleasant taste, much worse than in Vancouver, but she already felt better, and her dizziness was dispersing.

"Tea or coffee?" Dina pulled a large, brown mug painted with white lambs out of her cupboard.

"Coffee, please."

Dina put a teaspoonful of instant coffee into the mug, poured boiling water over it, and brought the mug to the table in front of Amanda. Reaching into her fridge, she took out a small half-liter milk jug and pushed it, together with a sugar bowl, toward Amanda. Then, she opened a tin painted with colorful flowers. It was half-full with homemade cookies. "Eat and drink," she ordered.

"Thanks." Amanda eyed the mug with misgivings. It was huge. After two large glasses of water, she wasn't sure she could hold that much liquid. To her surprise, she drained the mug in no time. "I didn't realize I was so thirsty," she mumbled.

Dina sat down on a stool on the other side of her small kitchen table. She regarded Amanda with curiosity. "Did you come all the way here just to find me?"

"I think they switched our girls in the hospital, by mistake," Amanda blurted.

Dina's eyebrows shot up. Her full lips opened slightly.

"I'm not crazy," Amanda said sulkily. "Gloria had an accident last fall. Her blood type is 'O' negative. Both my blood and my late husband's blood were 'O' positive. She can't be our daughter."

Dina stared without answering. She blinked slowly.

"Look." Amanda pushed away the empty mug. "I didn't call first, because I couldn't explain it all on the phone. I was chasing you in Russia. I went to Vladimir and then to Moscow. I love Gloria dearly." She began hyperventilating but tamped down on her own agitation. She wasn't explaining it too well. She obviously couldn't get through to Dina, who kept her stony silence.

"Dina, please. I have another daughter somewhere here. I think Sofia is my daughter. Maybe she needs my help. I'm not taking her away from you. I have so much. I've been so lucky. I want to share everything with her. Canada is a great country. Maybe we could do something for you, too. Gloria is fascinated with you. She wants to come down here and meet you. Don't you wish to meet your blood daughter? She started taking Russian lessons. She went to a synagogue. She is great, my Gloria." Amanda reevaluated her last words, and amended hastily, "Your Gloria." No, that didn't sound right, either. "Our Gloria." She winced.

Dina chuckled unhappily. "I think I'm in shock," she said huskily. "Could you... keep quiet for a few seconds?" Her large brown eyes lost some of their bleakness. She seemed to shrink, suddenly.

"Are you home alone?" Amanda looked around. The kitchen was small and very clean. The cabinets and the plastic working surfaces were old, shabby, and scrubbed spotless. Through the open doorway, she could see a corner of an old TV, turned on to some Russian program. The anchor talked animatedly, and the background glittered, contrasting with the threadbare upholstery of the armchair in front of the TV.

Amanda returned her attention to Dina. The woman looked tired and worn. "Maybe you should call your daughters? I'm sorry to stress you out like that, but there is no way to say what I had to say without some...emotional upheaval. It took me a while to absorb that Gloria is not really mine. I mean, she is my daughter, but she is yours, too. So is Sofia. Don't you see?"

"You seem to know a lot about me," Dina said finally.

"Yes. I've been asking questions. I talked to that woman in Vladimir, Lyubov Kasatkina. She told me that your younger daughter is called Lilia. She said that Sofia is a dancer. Is she?"

Dina laughed, although there wasn't much mirth in that laughter. "I think I need a drink."

"Good idea," Amanda agreed. "I can go buy something. Is there a liquor store nearby?"

"Just shut up! Get a bottle from the fridge." Dina pointed. She hadn't moved from her stool.

Amanda opened the fridge. A large bottle of red raspberry liquor, shaped like a huge raspberry, took up lots of the shelf's space. Retrieving it from the fridge, Amanda glanced expectantly at her hostess.

Dina stared back. The audience on the TV laughed uproariously.

"Ummm, we need glasses," Amanda prompted.

"Right. They are in the buffet in the living room."

Amanda went to the living room. It was spotlessly clean and steeped in twilight behind the tightly closed shutters. An air-conditioner buzzed quietly in the corner opposite the TV, which was the only source of light in the room. The sofa and the armchair looked cheap and faded. Behind the glass doors of the buffet stood six large, Bohemian crystal goblets. Decorated with colored enamel, they sparkled with the reflected TV light. Beside their baroque splendor, a set of four smaller, cut-crystal wineglasses looked tastefully elegant. Taking two smaller glasses, Amanda turned off the TV and returned to the kitchen.

Dina sat in the same pose, hands folded on her knees. "I thought big goblets," she said, her face expressionless.

"Do you want me to call someone for you?" Amanda poured the liquor into both glasses and offered one to Dina. She sipped from the other one. The liquor was smooth and sweet. "Where is your husband? I should talk to him, too."

Dina didn't pick up her glass. She stared at Amanda.

Amanda put her glass back on the table with a bang. The red liquid sloshed inside. "Snap out of it, Dina!" she yelled. "Please! Talk to me. For both our daughters' sakes."

"My husband is dead," Dina said. "He died in January. Which daughter's sake? You're telling me that Sofia is not my daughter." She sounded forlorn, like a lost child.

Amanda's heart ached. "She is, but she is also mine." She circled the small table and embraced the smaller woman. "I'm so sorry about your husband, Dina. My husband died, too. Five years ago. I have Gloria's photos. Do you want to see them?"

"Yes!"

"Drink!" Amanda nudged Dina's glass closer to her hand.

"Right!" Dina emptied the glass into her mouth and coughed from the strong spirit.

Amanda pulled out her wallet. "Look." She flipped it open. "This is Gloria."

"Who is the guy?" Dina asked in a quivering voice.

"My late husband, Donald."

Dina's small, plump finger moved along the plastic cover between the two photographs. "Gloria," she said. "Wait." She jumped up and disappeared into the living room, returning momentarily with a large photo album. Opening it, she hastily turned a few pages before rotating it toward Amanda. "Here is my late husband Gregory and Sofia, right before we emigrated."

Now, it was Amanda's turn to stare. On the large photo, father and daughter laughed together on a wooden bench in a park. Both were redheaded. Gregory's hair shined like coppery wire enmeshed with silver above his large-boned, freckled face. Beside him, dainty Sofia in a white blouse looked delicate and beautiful like a porcelain statuette. Like many dancers, she wore her auburn hair in a tight bun at the back of her neck. "Gosh, she looks like Donald," Amanda breathed. "Only much lovelier. And Gloria..." She couldn't continue. If she did, she would cry.

"A copy of Gregory, isn't she?" Dina's eyes devoured Gloria's small photo in Amanda's wallet. "Green-eyed, too."

"So pretty," Amanda said wistfully, studying her daughter's graceful features. She turned the page. There was Sofia again, holding a little girl in her arms and kissing the girl's glowing cheek. The girl's laughter was so infectious that Amanda had to smile back.

"Much good her pretty face did her!" Dina said vehemently. "Married that thieving, Russian leech." Her tone softened. "Is Gloria married? Any children?"

"No. Is it Sofia's daughter?"

"Ksenya, yes."

"Neat!" Amanda breathed. "I'm a grandmother! She is so sweet!"

Dina snorted. "She was sweet. Now, the little parasite is in league with her bloodsucking father. Both are robbing Sonechka, sucking her dry. The Russian swine and his little piglet." She grimaced. "Sorry. Ksyushka is really a good girl, just confused."

"How old is Ksenya, now?"

"Fourteen. Sonechka had her early, when she was twenty."

"Let's drink for them."

"Yeah.

They drank.

"Could you tell me more?" Amanda settled on her stool, again. "Do they live in Petah Tikva, too? Can I see them?" She turned another page in the photo album. There was Sofia again with another young woman. This one was bigger and had some facial similarity with Gloria, just like Dina's late husband. "Is this your other daughter?"

"Yes, Lilechka." Dina's voice shook. "Where in Canada do you live?"

Alarmed that Dina might be crying, Amanda glanced up.

Dina was laughing, a bit hysterically.

"In Vancouver," Amanda said uncertainly.

"Oh, no!" Dina laughed so hard, she had to bend down. "Oh, God! Oh, God," she muttered breathlessly. Tears glistened in her eyes.

"What?" Amanda watched warily. "Are you crying?"

"Sonechka doesn't live here." Dina could hardly push the words out through the paroxysms of laughter. "She immigrated to Canada two years ago. She lives in Vancouver." Still laughing, she sobbed suddenly.

Speechless, Amanda stared. "In Vancouver?" she mouthed. "I flew around the globe to find her?" Her voice came out as an indignant squeak. "And she lives in the same city?"

Dina moaned, all her body shaking. "In Marpole."

"Fifteen minutes drive from me? That's so unfair!" Amanda wailed. She poured more liquor in both glasses.

Dina's hysterical howling began to subside, and she took a long, heaving breath. "Let's drink another one."

"Yes!" Amanda guzzled this one up without tasting it. Then, she started giggling. "In Vancouver! Maybe it's destiny." She pushed her empty glass toward Dina. "One more!"

"Right." Dina poured. "You should've gotten the bigger goblets."

"I should've," Amanda agreed.

After they polished off half the bottle, their chat became much less stilted. They swapped story for story. Amanda talked about Gloria. Dina talked about Sofia.

Chapter Twenty-One
Amanda

A couple of hours later, they were still at the kitchen table.

"I'm not giving up Sonechka," Dina said firmly. "She is my daughter. Well, she is yours too, but she is really mine." She fell into a quiet retrospective.

"I want to help her," Amanda insisted. She popped a tiny cookie from the jar into her mouth. Sugar crunched under her teeth.

"She doesn't need your help. Anyone's help. We don't need it," Dina said and hiccupped.

Amanda picked up her glass. To her chagrin, it was empty, again. "I love my daughter." She twirled the glass in her hand, watching light sparkling like a rainbow off the multiple facets of the cut crystal. A few remaining crimson drops of liquor inside tinted the rainbow in rose color.

"Which one?"

"Pardon me? Oh, daughters? Both of them. I'm not giving Gloria up, as well. We'll both be their mothers, right?"

"Right," Dina said. "What about Lilechka? You're not her mother?"

Amanda thought about the question. She turned the glass sideways. It didn't supply the answer. "No," she said uncertainly. She grabbed another cookie. "I think I'm drunk."

Dina picked up the raspberry bottle and upended it. A couple of red drops plopped onto the gray, plastic surface of the table. "Drunk?" She studied the empty bottle with regret. "We need to eat." Standing up, she shambled toward the fridge, swaying a little.

"Yes," Amanda said. She didn't dare stand up. She didn't think her legs would carry her. Even her stool seemed to have trouble holding her weight. She kept sliding off it. She put her head on the table, on top of her hands. That seemed to stabilize her position. Reassured she would stay on the stool, she drifted off.

When she came to, she was still sitting on the stool. The kitchen was dark. Her back cramped from her bent, unnatural pose. Behind a narrow window, the night lights were springing up. Dina wasn't in the kitchen, but a bowl of Russian salad stood on the table beside the open cookie tin. Cookie crumbs littered the table surface.

Amanda stood up, stretched, and gulped in a scream. All her muscles and joints clamored viciously. She stood still for a few seconds, adjusting to the vertical mode. Then, she swiped the crumbs off the table into her palm and shook them into the miniature sink. Swallowing the goo in her mouth, she grimaced from the vile taste. She hadn't been so inebriated since her student days, if even then. Such a shame, to do it in front of Dina—the mother of her daughter. Amanda shook her head. No, that was wrong. Dina was the mother of her own daughter, and Amanda was...she couldn't at the moment formulate the correct relationships.

"Dina!" she called.

"Yeah." Wincing, Dina appeared in the doorway of her living room. "We're good, aren't we? Two old cows, slurping up the liquor like old, stinking mops."

Amanda snickered. "I probably should go," she said. "I'll return tomorrow."

"No. You should stay the night. You're not fit to drive. Go wash up, and I'll warm some turkey." She ambled into the kitchen and turned on the overhead light. "Don't tell Sonya. I don't think I've ever been so drunk."

"Never!" Amanda vowed. "You don't tell Gloria."

"How? I couldn't even if I wanted to. I speak very limited English." Dina sniffed at the salad, nodded in satisfaction, and squatted in front of her fridge.

Amanda sniffed at the salad, too. It smelled delicious. "Gloria is going to come here soon," she said. "She wants to meet you."

"When?" Dina's curly head popped up from behind the fridge's door. Her eyes rounded with terror.

"Not yet." Amanda reassured her. "As soon as she can speak Russian. I told you she is taking lessons, didn't I? She is a very fast learner. She might come for Christmas."

"When did you tell me?"

Amanda shrugged. "Maybe I didn't. Maybe I imagined it."

"Maybe," Dina agreed. "Maybe you did tell me, but I don't remember. Anyway, she's welcome. We don't celebrate Christmas here, but she's welcome to come any time. We have Chanukah." She put a small, green casserole on the stove, turned on the heat, and reached into her top cupboard. "Here is a new toothbrush for you."

"Thank you." Amanda grabbed the toothbrush in its plastic package and hurried into the washroom. It was tiny, shabby, and immaculately clean, like everything in Dina's home. She felt much better after a thorough wash up.

They finished off the salad and the casserole of turkey and rice, talking all the while, remembering good times and bad.

"I feel so old," Dina complained. "Sonechka was born thirty-four years ago. Can you comprehend the numbers?"

"I try not to." Amanda grinned. "You're a terrific cook!" She licked her fork.

"I know," Dina said. "I enjoy cooking, but Sonya always grumbled. As a dancer, she couldn't eat much."

Amanda nodded. "Is she still dancing?"

"No."

"What is she doing?"

"She works at a burger place and cares for an invalid. She's slaving like a donkey, day and night. She was saving money to enroll in an art institute next fall. I don't remember the name of it—some Canadian painter. She can't now, anyway. All her money went to pay the rent for her alcoholic ex."

"Emily Carr Institute?"

"That's the one." Dina withdrew into dark brooding.

"I can help," Amanda said.

"Don't wave your money in front of me like a red flag!" Dina snapped.

"I'm not. Please, don't be upset. I really want to help. She doesn't have to fry burgers, anymore. I can pay for her lessons. Is she good at her art? Is she an artist?"

"Sorry." Dina looked up, her brown eyes glinting. "She is very gifted, makes beautiful tapestries. I guess it might be good for them both, to have you around. Ksyushka needs someone too, but I'm here. Sonya is working all the time, and her father is always drunk. "

"I'll be there for them," Amanda promised. "Donald was gifted, too. He painted. Do you have any other relatives here?"

"My younger daughter and about a hundred cousins, aunts, and nephews. Why?"

"Gloria is the only child, and so were Donald and myself. Gloria always wanted more relatives. You know, noisy celebrations and birthdays."

"Let her come here. She would get tired of noisy celebrations. *Bar mitzvahs* every month. Everyone would be dying to meet her."

Dina pushed her empty plate away. "Such an outrageous story. Of course, first I'll have to tell Lilia. Oh, Amanda." She sniffed loudly, put her head on her hands, and began crying."

"Mother-daughter minuet," Amanda said softly. "That's what Gloria called it. Don't cry, Dina. We'll both gain another daughter."

"Gregory would never see Gloria." Dina hiccupped. Her cheeks glistened with tears. "Gosh, I can't get over it. I started singing in our community choir, but it doesn't help. I tried a craft club, but I can't. I think about him all the time." Her eyes were dull with pain.

"I know," Amanda said. "The first year was tough." She knelt beside Dina, putting her hand on Dina's plump thigh in a printed, *chintz* skirt. "Why don't you come to Vancouver with me?"

"I can't. I just came back. To receive my pension, I can't stay outside of Israel for more than three months in one year. I have already overstayed that when I visited Sonechka. Next year, maybe." Dina wiped her wet face with a tissue. "How did you deal with it, Amanda?"

Amanda looked up from her kneeling pose and her lips curved mischievously. She made the decision. "I slept with a younger man," she said. "Very invigorating."

Dina chortled in surprise. Her brown eyes twinkled. "How much younger?" Her tears retreated.

"Fifteen years or so."

"Did it help?"

"Oh, yes!"

"The girls would spit on me," Dina said glumly.

"Don't tell them."

They stared at each other for a few moments before bursting into simultaneous laughter.

"A younger man?" Dina wheezed. "That's a thought. How long after your husband's death?"

Amanda sobered. "Five years. Maybe your widowhood is too recent."

"Maybe." Dina's laughter dwindled to nothing. Then, her eyes sparkled again, as she did some mental calculations. "Wait a minute. You said your husband died five years ago."

"Russian men are the best for a dalliance," Amanda said primly. She climbed to her feet.

"Yuck, Russians!" Dina said. "Come, I'll make your bed on the sofa. Tell me about that Russian man of yours."

"Some Jewish men are good, too," Amanda murmured,

thinking of Michael's soft, plump body.

"Russian *and* Jewish? How many did you have?"

"Canadian state secret!" Amanda followed her hostess into the living room. "Better tell me about Sonechka and her family."

* * * *

"Gloria, I found her," Amanda reported into the phone from her hotel room the next evening. "I'm coming home, soon."

"Tell me about her and her mother. My mother. Damn it, Mom. I don't even know what to call you or her, anymore."

"Mom is good." Amanda smiled. "You won't believe it. Sofia lives in Vancouver."

"What?"

"Dina is such a wonderful person. You'll like her."

"I'd better," Gloria growled.

"We got so tanked, together. She had the best raspberry liquor I've ever tasted. You know, honey, we kind of bonded. It was so easy to talk to her, like instant camaraderie. So strange. It's never happened to me before."

"You never got sloshed before, either," Gloria said thoughtfully.

"The occasion warranted it," Amanda murmured. "She gave me Sofia's address and telephone. She lives in Marpole." Holding the receiver to her ear, Amanda kicked off her slippers and snuggled into her king-sized bed.

"Can I call her?"

"Ummm," Amanda stalled. "Maybe I should be the one to contact her first."

"You should ask her for a blood test before you proceed with any legal actions."

"Legal actions? Blood test? What are you talking about?" Suddenly, the bed wasn't so comfortable. Its down pillows felt suffocating, and Amanda straightened.

"That's how you knew I'm not yours," Gloria continued. "You must be sure. What if—"

"Wait a minute!" Amanda interrupted. She had had enough! She wouldn't allow Gloria to push her around, anymore. "I'm not going to proceed with any legal actions. You're my daughter, and she is Dina's, and that is that. I'm not going to change anything legally. It would be a nightmare to prove, especially with both my husband and hers being dead. Besides, I don't want to. You, young lady, better stop goading me. I've decided that the company would be eighty percent yours. You deserve it. As for the rest, you'll have to share. So, stop it!"

"Mom?"

For the first time since Gloria had been in the second grade, Amanda heard uncertainty in her daughter's voice. She realized she had been yelling and lowered her tone. "I'm tired of us arguing all the time. Let's not, Gloria. If it'll make you feel better, I'll ask Sonya for a blood test, but who else should she be. She looks like...your dad. And you, honey..." She sighed and leaned on the pillows once more. "I saw Dina's photo album. You look so much like her dead husband and her younger daughter. Dina said she'll call Sonya and tell her about me. Us. She didn't ask for your blood test."

Silence in the phone stretched. "Gloria?" Amanda prodded gently.

"I'm sorry, Mom," Gloria said finally. "You've changed. When are you coming home?"

"I'm flying home in a week. There is so much you should know about Sonya and Dina. Wait until I get comfortable, and I'll tell you."

Chapter Twenty-Two
Sonya

Neither Sonya nor Ksenya said a word in the taxi. As soon as Sonya locked the front door, Ksenya stripped frantically, dropped all her wet clothing beside the door, and darted, naked and barefoot, to the bathroom. She was in the shower for so long, Sonya began worrying.

"Ksyushka, are you all right?" Sonya stuck her head into the hot, steamy bathroom.

"I'm coming out," Ksenya said, invisible behind the flowery curtain.

"Okay. I need to shower, too," Sonya reminded her. She had already added her soaked clothing to Ksenya's pile at the door, but she couldn't put on anything clean. She felt so dirty, she needed a shower first, just like her daughter. She understood the girl's need to wash off everything that had happened today.

Shivering in her underwear, Sonya regarded herself critically in the hall mirror. A slender figure with long legs and arms. Plain, white bra. Plain, white panties. Pale, freckled skin awash with goosebumps. Dark stains beneath her eyes. Wet hair hanging limply down her back and dripping to the floor. She lost her hair band somewhere.

Could she start dancing, again? She lifted her hands above her head in the first position, grinned, and dropped them. Yes, she could. She only needed bright costumes and good makeup to create an image of mystery and allure. Something like a mix between a strip dance and a folk dance, exotic and sensual. Could she choreograph the entire show herself? Probably not. She had some ideas, but maybe she should start looking for collaborators.

She definitely needed better underwear. Maybe she should spend her savings on funky panties and bras? Black lace? Why was she even thinking about it, now? She had just gone through a major crisis. Her daughter had been hurt or worse, and she was thinking about panties! She was pathetic. She should cry. Instead, she grinned lopsidedly in the mirror. Black lace would definitely look good on her.

"Go. I haven't turned it off." Ksenya appeared in the doorway to the bathroom, squeaky clean, pink, and cute like a Barbie in her old, blue pajamas with little, smiling cows. If not for the big bruise covering the entire left side of her face, she would've looked like old Ksenya, like nothing had happened.

"Thanks." Sonya rushed into the shower. Should she berate Ksenya? Explain...what? Her mind was blank, except for the various models of dancing costumes and panties. She could think about nothing but panties and how cute Ksenya was in her pajamas. She still shivered, unable to get warm.

Her feet and hands felt like icicles despite the heat in the bathroom. The shower water running down her face suddenly became salty. She was crying, after all. She turned the water hotter, sat down in the bathtub, hugged herself, and indulged in a fit of self-pity, wailing and swaying under the scalding torrent of the shower.

When she came out, she was finally warm. The skin of her fingers was crimped with pink wrinkles. Ksenya perched on Sonya's bed. The girl's eyes were filled with uncertainty.

Sonya smiled sadly and climbed into bed beside her daughter. "Doesn't wash off, does it, kitten? Not right away."

"No. Can I stay here, tonight?" Ksenya's alto quivered.

"Sure. Come inside." Sonya gestured.

Ksenya hurriedly crawled to Sonya's side under the blanket, snuggling as close as she could. She grabbed Sonya's nightie with both hands, hugging Sonya tightly. In the dim glow of the miniature nightlight, her bruise seemed huge and ugly. Sonya caressed the girl's silky hair, damp from the shower.

"Are you hurt? Anywhere?"

"No." Ksenya was silent for a few minutes, clinging to Sonya, rubbing her good cheek on Sonya's nightgown. "A little bit. You cried in the shower." She winced. Her hand crept out of the blanket, touched the torn edge of her mouth, and quickly resumed her grip on Sonya's gown.

"I worried." Abruptly, Sonya sat upright. "Gosh, I have to call the police!"

"Why?" Ksenya's body tensed under Sonya's hands.

"I called them and told them you were missing. Now, I have to call and say that you're home and everything is okay." Sonya clicked off the nightlight and lay down again, burrowing back under the blanket. "Tomorrow morning."

"You worried?"

Sonya opened her mouth to deliver some scathing retort about parents' love but thought better of it. "I worried," she repeated softly. "I called all the hospitals in the Lower Mainland and the morgues."

"You did?" Ksenya's grip on Sonya's nightie tightened. "The morgues?"

"Didn't you know I would be worried? Silly kitten. Of course I was. You should at least have called me."

"I'm sorry," Ksenya whispered.

They huddled together, warm and comfortable. "Kitten," Sonya said after awhile. "You're not pregnant, are you?"

"No. I have my period. That's why Felix got mad. He wanted..."

"He doesn't have AIDS, does he?"

"No. Anyway, Mom, I'm not stupid." Old spunk enlivened Ksenya's previously dull responses. "We used condoms."

"He didn't do anything terrible to you?"

"No. Just hit me a couple of times." Ksenya let go of Sonya's gown and sat up. "Mom, you don't think Felix might come after me?" In the predawn milky air, her eyes seemed black and bottomless.

"No, I think your dad taught him a good lesson. The little worm wouldn't dare come close to you, again. Did you like him?"

Ksenya sighed. "Not really," she said. "Dad was scary. Did he beat you...sometimes?"

"No!" Sonya pushed herself higher too, glaring indignantly. "Never!"

Ksenya nodded. "If you want to see that man, Yuri, you can. I won't mind," she said.

"I don't want to. Not anymore. Now, tell me something. You smoked marijuana?"

"Yeah. A couple of times." Ksenya looked away.

Sonya regarded the number of times as inconsequential. "Have you ever taken stronger drugs?"

"Once. I took E," Ksenya murmured.

Sonya had hoped for a "No". She wasn't prepared for a "Yes". What should she say? All the possible objections she could've raised, Ksenya had already heard from her teachers at school. Besides, what was E?

"What's E?" she asked. Was it something terrible? She didn't know anything about drugs. She should ask Jane.

"Ecstasy." Ksenya's mouth curved. "I won't do it, again. I swear. I didn't like it, anyway." She brightened, grinning impishly. "Do you know what they make it from? Rat poison."

Sonya gulped. "Rat poison? You put that in your mouth? Gosh, Ksen'ka. You're crazy. Did you think that something fatal for a rat could be good for you?"

Ksenya giggled. "Mom, you're such a baby. You don't know anything."

"In this case, I'm proud of my ignorance," Sonya said primly. Her resolve to pump Jane for drug information hardened. "Do you want some tea?" she asked to change the subject. She hated the idea of Ksenya and drugs. Together. Even talking about it was painful.

"Yes. I'm not sleepy." Ksenya skidded closer, kissing Sonya lightly on the cheek. "I'll make tea," she offered and jumped out of bed.

* * * *

The next morning, Sonya called in sick and luxuriated in bed until almost eleven. Then, they both got up and made pancakes for breakfast. Sonya ate two of them with the fresh strawberry jam she had made only three days ago. Ksenya devoured the pancakes with maple syrup. After she loaded the sixth big one on her plate, Sonya shook her head.

"Didn't you eat anything, yesterday?" she demanded.

"Felix only had potato chips."

"The guy was starving you? I'm glad your dad beat him up," Sonya said. The *pogrom* of the last night had already receded into surrealism of the impossible. She could joke about it, now. It hadn't really happened the way she remembered. It couldn't have. "I wish Alexei came home with us yesterday," she said wistfully.

Ksenya pushed away her half-eaten pancake and stood up. "Thank you," she said stiffly. "It's better that he didn't. He was drunk."

"No, actually he wasn't," Sonya said. She suddenly realized that the terror of the last night was still real for the girl. Alexei's brutality in dealing with Felix had shaken Ksenya. To see her soft-spoken, gentle musician father turn into a destructive, almost feral monster, meting out death for what was his, was a trauma that wouldn't heal easily. Ksenya needed an explanation. "He was worried about you," Sonya said lamely.

Ksenya turned her disbelieving eyes toward her mother. "Worried, yeah!"

Sonya rubbed her arms. They had been skimming around the

last night's events, but they would have to talk about them, eventually. The policeman she spoke with earlier was very serious, even though Sonya hadn't told him about Felix. She made up a story about Ksenya being at her father's who didn't have a phone. She would have to tell Alexei, in case the police started asking questions. All three of them should have their versions straight.

"So, can you tell me what happened?" Sonya asked. She sat down on the sofa and beckoned Ksenya to sit beside her. "Why didn't you come home?"

Instead of sitting beside Sonya, the girl settled on a floor cushion, facing her mother. She stared at the floor, while her thin finger traced the cushion's autumn pattern. "I was pissed at you," she said reluctantly. "I went to meet Felix, and he saw I was pissed. He said..." She obviously edited what she was going to say next. She still gazed at the floor. "He said we should go to his place, and I agreed. He said I shouldn't go home." Her voice turned very small. "He said I should teach you a lesson. I'm sorry, Mom, but I was so mad at you."

"Why?" Sonya whispered.

"I don't know," Ksenya mumbled. She finally looked up. "I don't know, Mom. I don't want to argue with you, but it always happens."

Sonya stood up and dropped on the cushion next to Ksenya. "I don't want to argue with you either, kitten. Let's try not to." She kissed the girl's good cheek, but Ksenya didn't return the kiss. Instead, she hid her face in Sonya's chest as she went on with her story.

"We were okay at first. Then, I thought I should go home, anyway. That I was stupid to stay the night. Someone came to see him, but I hid in the bathroom. Then, we were alone again, but he wouldn't let me go home. Then, I got hungry in the morning, and we argued."

"About what?" Sonya raked her fingers through Ksenya's loose hair. She started braiding the hair.

"Lots of stuff." Ksenya turned her head to give Sonya's fingers better access. "Then, he hit me, and I hit him. Then...you came."

Sonya wasn't sure she believed such an abbreviated explanation, but she didn't see how she could get any more details. Maybe it was better not to push right now. "Okay." She sighed. "You need a hair band. I'm glad it's nothing more sinister. Did you know he was a drug pusher, a criminal?"

"Kind of," Ksenya said softly, almost inaudibly.

"I hope you don't want to see him, again."

"No!" Ksenya pulled away and looked Sonya in the eyes. "No, Mom!" she repeated firmly. "He was a jerk."

"Good." Sonya smiled. "I applaud your taste." She climbed to her feet.

"I should've known," Ksenya said gloomily.

"What's important is that you learn from your mistakes." She wasn't sure she herself learned from hers, but she didn't voice her doubts. Anti-pedagogic.

Before Ksenya could reply, the phone rang, and Sonya grabbed it.

"The police, again?" Ksenya mouthed with a troubled expression in her eyes.

Sonya shrugged. "Hello," she said cautiously into the receiver. Perhaps it was Alexei.

"Sonechka." Dina's voice in the receiver made Sonya exhale her pent-up breath.

"Mama?" She glanced at the clock. "It's late in Israel. Why are you not in bed?"

"Grandma?" Ksenya sidled closer. "Don't tell her!" She mimicked a hand across her neck.

Sonya shook her head. "No," whispered, closing the receiver with her palm.

"I have news for you," Dina said. "Kind of unusual."

"Unusual news?" Sonya repeated for Ksenya's benefit.

The girl's eyes sparkled with curiosity. Sonya gestured to the mess on the table. "Clean up," she mouthed. Ksenya nodded and began removing the breakfast stuff.

"What news, Mama?" Sonya said into the phone. She didn't like Dina's long pauses.

Dina sighed loudly. "Do you remember I told you about a Canadian woman who gave birth to her daughter the same day you were born?"

"Yes." Sonya's brows climbed up. This was old news. The story was a family legend by now. She had heard it at least 100 times. "The other redheaded baby girl. I remember."

"That woman visited me a few of days ago." Another long pause followed. Then, Dina started talking rapidly.

Sonya listened in a daze, producing some strangled sounds now and again. She had another birth mother?

"She should be in Vancouver, already. I promised I would warn you," Dina rushed on, "but I couldn't gather enough courage.

She is going to call, maybe visit you. I gave her your address and telephone."

"Visit me?" Sonya squeaked in alarm. "In this hovel? When? I have to at least empty the rain bucket. I have to vacuum!" She glanced quickly toward the door. The pile of her and Ksenya's clothing from yesterday, wet and filthy, still heaped there. She didn't want to touch it.

"Sonechka." Sonya heard her mother crying. "She's bought a house for you. In Kitsilano."

"Oh?" Sonya couldn't find words. She felt like a fish out of her element. She opened her mouth, closed it again, and stared at the opposite wall in confusion. She should be celebrating, but she just felt bewildered. A house in Kitsilano—one of the best areas in Vancouver—would cost around a million dollars, maybe more. Yet, she was worrying about a rain bucket? It all seemed as surreal as yesterday's carnage at Felix's.

"Mom?" Ksenya shook Sonya's shoulder, a wrinkle of concern between her dark blonde brows. "Are you okay? What happened?"

"Mama—" Sonya started, but Dina interrupted her.

"Meet with her." The phone receiver sniffed. "She is rich. She can help you with those classes you want to take. She thinks she owes you. She wants to help."

"Mama," Sonya said firmly. "Whatever happened in that hospital thirty-four years ago, you are my mother. I can't just switch a mother, because she is rich."

Ksenya's eyes widened and her mouth dropped open at these words. She planted herself firmly in front of Sonya.

"She wants to take Ksenya on a cruise around the world. I can't, you know," Dina said. "Just meet with her. Let her be...your rich aunt." Dina's voice struck apologetic notes. "I agreed to meet her daughter Gloria. I mean, *my* daughter Gloria, although I would never call a girl Gloria. She wants to meet me. She would be kind of your sister. No. She is Lilechka's sister, really. It seems you don't have a sister. I love you, Sonechka. You'll always be my daughter, but she has rights. She went around the globe searching for you. She went to Vladimir."

"Vladimir? Gosh! Lil'ka must be thrilled."

"Lilia doesn't know, yet. You're the first to know." Dina giggled. "You must be."

"Right. Mama, are you drunk?"

"No. I'm still dazzled, though. I got drunk with Amanda. The evening she told me. Her name is Amanda Barnett. Have I told you? Sonechka? She is a nice woman, really nice."

"I'll meet with her," Sonya said grimly. "If she calls. Good night, Mama."

"Yes. Tell me how it goes. Uhhh...how are you and Ksyushka?" Dina asked belatedly.

"We're fine. Kiss you." Sonya put down the receiver and looked at Ksenya.

"Tell!" the girl demanded.

Sonya told her.

"Mom, it's great! A house in Kitsilano! A trip around the world!" Ksenya clapped her hands in exuberance. "We'll go to Paris!" She whirled, dancing in place, her arms fully extended. "Paris!" she sang happily.

"Yes, great," Sonya agreed with a faint smile. "What if she wasn't rich? What if she was dirt poor and an invalid like Jane? Would we still want to adopt her?"

Ksenya's jubilation abated. "She *is* rich," she said uncertainly.

"That's why I will agree that she is my mother, right? What about my real mother, the one in Israel? Do I just forget her, because she is poor? Sounds like selling myself...for a house in Kitsilano."

"You could enroll in Emily Carr, then," Ksenya argued. "You don't have to forget Grandma. You'll just get another one. Like I'll have three grandmothers, you'll have two mothers." She perked up at finding the right arguments, hugging Sonya from behind. "Mom," she whispered. "Maybe you could help Dad? Maybe he could go to some clinic to stop drinking."

"Maybe," Sonya said. "You want to go on a trip around the world, do you?"

"Yes! Don't you?" Ksenya's whisper turned seductive.

"I want to dance," Sonya said.

"It's not selling," Ksenya pushed. "It's...a Canadian way. A Canadian fairytale. They will show us on TV."

"Like a soap opera," Sonya suggested with a smirk. She started laughing. "I'll have multiple mothers, one for every country." She sputtered, unable to stop. She leaned down on her gleaming sofa cushions, shuddering from laughter. "Lots of money. A house in Kitsilano. No rain bucket."

"Mom? Please, stop."

At last, Sonya quit laughing, spearing her daughter with an intense gaze. "Do you want another mother, Ksenya? A rich one?"

The girl's lips began trembling. "No," she breathed.

"Smart girl," Sonya approved with a sad snicker. "Thinking right and speaking right."

"Mom! Please stop," Ksenya repeated miserably.

"I'm sorry." Sonya stood up and strode to the window. Her rain bucket was only one-third full. Outside, a sunny day was in full swing. Having swept away the clouds, the hot summer sun ruled its clean, blue kingdom. Sonya stared at the azure sky and the green tops of the trees, swaying in a breeze. There was a woman out there who loved her so much, she went around the world in search of her. There was another one who was willing to give her up out of love. The least she could do for both of them was to accept their offerings and make life better for her daughter and herself. Maybe for Alexei, too. She blinked the tears away.

"What do you think, Ksyushka? When will she call?" Sonya asked without turning.

"I don't know," Ksenya said in a tiny voice.

"Ksenya, if someone came to me with the same tale about you, I would've thrown such a woman away, money or no money," Sonya said. Her vehemence surprised even herself. "I wouldn't have shared you. I guess my mother is a better person than I am. Maybe she loves me better."

"Which mother?" Ksenya asked softly.

Sonya grinned. "That's the question, isn't it?" She thought for several minutes. "That will always be the question," she said and turned.

Ksenya was watching her—her expression hopeful, hovering on the brink of a smile.

"I have to name them." Sonya smiled back. "I'll call one 'Mama Dina' and the other 'Mama Amanda', if that 'Mama Amanda' ever calls."

"She will." Ksenya's voice held absolute conviction. "She went to Russia and Israel to find you, *and* she lives in Vancouver, like us. It's destiny."

"You watch too many sitcoms," Sonya said sternly, although she wondered. Maybe it *was* destiny? "We're going shopping tomorrow," she announced triumphantly. "I'm getting new underwear. Black lace."

"Yahoo! Me, too!" Ksenya thrust her small fist into the air in a jubilant salute. "Black lace! Hooray!"

Chapter Twenty-Three
Sonya

Sonya opened the door to the sound of a vacuum cleaner.

"They are coming!" Ksenya turned off the vacuum. Her wide smile lit up the small hall of their apartment. "Hurry, Mom. You're late. I'll finish up."

"I went to the dance shop," Sonya said guiltily. She tossed her bag on the dresser beside the door and darted into the bathroom.

Ksenya put her head in. "How was the shop?"

"Poor," Sonya said. Stripping off her sweaty work clothes, she turned on the shower and climbed in. Today was the big day. Amanda was coming to meet her for the first time, but Sonya had wanted to have her own private celebration first, so she detoured to the dance shop on Broadway. All these years, she had sturdily avoided the shop. Now, having decided to go back to dancing, she had to check it out. "They have some shoes, although not very good. No costumes to speak of. I'll have to make my own costumes."

"Why did you go today, of all days? You're almost late."

"I had the time," Sonya mumbled behind the shower curtain. "I got into a traffic jam later. Get my new underwear, Ksen'ka."

Ksenya snickered and withdrew her disheveled head.

When Sonya came out, wearing only her new black lace bra and panties, Ksenya had already put away the vacuum cleaner. The apartment looked spotless, flooded with the late afternoon sunlight from the window. Ksenya stood ready with a hairdryer and a brush.

"I'll dry your hair," she said firmly. "Don't you dare put it up. It should be down." She pointed to the mirror. She was impervious, like a princess, if one disregarded the yellow, healing bruise marring the left side of her face.

"Yes, ma'am," Sonya said meekly, submitting to her daughter's ministrations.

"You're going to a restaurant Downtown," Ksenya announced, vibrating with excitement. The hairdryer blew warm air all over Sonya's back, as the girl carefully pulled the brush through Sonya's long, auburn tresses. “With Amanda and Gloria.”

“Me? What about you? Why are you not dressed?” Sonya frowned, watching her daughter’s old denim shorts in the mirror. “You’re not going to a posh restaurant in this get up!”

The wattage of Ksenya’s smile dimmed. “I can’t,” she said gloomily, pointing to her left cheek.

Sonya regarded the bruise critically. It had shrunk and paled, but it was still apparent. “Don’t worry. Most of the restaurants in Vancouver have darkened interiors, especially the expensive ones. Nobody will notice. I’ll do your makeup. We can make it hardly visible.”

“You think?” Ksenya’s hip pushed Sonya away from the mirror. The hairdryer, still on, blew warm air into the empty space. Ksenya stared at herself in the mirror—her black tank top, naked midriff, tiny frayed shorts, and the long legs in the polka dot blue socks.

“Hey.” Sonya appropriated the hairdryer and the brush, shouldering Ksenya away from the mirror. She glanced at the clock. “They will be here in half an hour. Go get dressed!” she commanded.

Ksenya shook her head. “Everyone will notice,” she said in a voice of the doomed.

“Ksenya. She’s your Grandma. The third one. She wants to meet you. You have to be with us.” Sonya’s eyes wandered to the window and widened in horror. “Ksen’ka, the bucket!” she exclaimed.

“Yikes!” Ksenya skipped to the window, grabbed the bucket, pushed it under the kitchen sink, and half-turned, gazing at Sonya. “Are you sure, Mom?”

“Of course! Go make yourself presentable.”

“Okay.” Ksenya disappeared into her bedroom.

Sonya made several more passes with the dryer and turned it off. What should she wear for this meeting, her first meeting with Amanda? Her heart fluttered in her chest, as if it was the most important premier in her life. Maybe it was. She rummaged in her closet, discarding one item after another. She had lots of beautiful things, most of them old or made by herself. She hadn’t bought anything new since she came to Vancouver. Sonya signed. If Amanda gave her some money, she and Ksenya would embark on a shopping spree.

She smiled happily, and then winced. She was such a mercenary. No matter. She would still go shopping! She set her jaw stubbornly and settled on a black crepe dress with very short sleeves, a deep, U-shaped neckline, and a flowing skirt, falling in soft folds to her ankles.

Bought more than ten years ago in Finland and decorated with black silk embroidery, it was the most expensive and glorious item in her wardrobe. It looked so ceremonial that she didn't wear it often. Today was the occasion, though. Sonya put it on and opened her meager jewelry box. Oh, yes!

A smile played with her lips, as she took out a thin, golden chain with the golden Magen David encrusted with diamonds—her parents' gift for Ksenya's birth. Thankfully, Ksenya didn't give this one to Alexei to pay his debts. Wincing at the memory, Sonya put the golden trinket on. It fit the black dress perfectly, besides being a statement. No matter how many new mothers she would acquire in the future, her first and prime mother was a Jew, and so was she.

"Wow!" Ksenya said when Sonya emerged from her room. "Cool!" Her eyes sparkled.

Sonya examined Ksenya's jeans, riding low on her slim hips, and a teal T-shirt with the pattern of silver skulls and bones. The result was festive. If one didn't look closely, one could mistake the skulls for an abstract, silver design. "Not bad," she said. "Sit down. I'll put some base on your bruise." She pulled out her makeup kit.

"It's still visible," Ksenya protested a few minutes later, studying her face in the mirror.

"Just a bit," Sonya said dismissively. "Goes well with your skulls. Move off." She shoved Ksenya away from the mirror, planting herself in her daughter's place.

Ksenya giggled and shoved back.

Sonya stood firm. "Have I put on too much mascara?" They stood side-by-side in front of the narrow mirror, pushing at each other's hips, competing for a better view.

"You're perfect, Mom. Do you think we should go downstairs and wait there?" Ksenya asked. Suddenly, her cavalier attitude vanished. She stepped away from the mirror. "Do you think she'll like me?"

Before Sonya could answer, the door buzzer rang twice. Sonya exchanged a quick glance with her daughter. Then, she took a deep breath and opened the door.

"Hi," said a tall woman with short, thick, ash-blonde hair dressed in gray slacks and a white, silk blouse. "You must be Sofia." A small smile flickered on and off her smooth face, as if she was unsure of the reception.

Sonya swallowed and licked her dry lips. "Hi," she said, her voice crackling slightly. "I am, and you must be Amanda." Thoughts swirled inside her head, but nothing meaningful came out. They stood on the opposite sides of the doorway, staring at each other.

"Mom?" Ksenya cleared her throat behind Sonya's back.

"Oh, sorry." Blushing, Sonya stepped aside. "Please, come in." What should she do? Should she hug the woman? Kiss her? Shake her hand? She didn't feel any blood call or anything. She felt admiration, though. Amanda wasn't exactly pretty, but she was beautiful. Brimming with good taste. Imposing. Reserved. Her gray eyes shined with intelligence.

Amanda entered. "You must be Ksenya," she said, regarding the girl with her serious, assessing gaze. "Come here."

Ksenya came closer. "Yes," she piped. Her eyes were huge and very curious.

"My granddaughter," Amanda said. "What happened to you?" She nodded at Ksenya's bruise.

"An accident," Sonya intervened quickly.

Amanda nodded. "Ksenya, Gloria is waiting downstairs with the car. Dark blue Honda. Why don't you run down and join her? I'd like a few minutes with your mom. Alone."

Ksenya glanced at Sonya. Sonya nodded and watched the girl's jeans flash in the doorway. Doubtful at what to do next, she faced Amanda.

"Sofia," Amanda said quietly. She didn't attempt to touch Sonya. She just stood there, devouring her new-found daughter with hungry eyes. A tear appeared at the edge of one eye and slid down her cheek. Amanda licked the tear and smiled again, managing to look regal and embarrassed simultaneously. "You're lovely," she said. "Better than in the photos."

"Thank you." Sonya grinned. The woman was smart enough to appeal to her vanity first, and Sonya was absurdly pleased with the praise.

"I don't presume to take your mother's place in your heart," Amanda said. "I just want to be allowed to be...your friend." She paused. "Maybe something of a rich aunt?"

"That's what my mama said. A rich aunt. This is strange, really." Sonya shivered. "Mama said you went to Russia and Israel to search for me." She grinned faintly. "Thank you."

"Well." Amanda licked her lips.

Sighing deeply, Sonya rushed in to fill their awkward silence.

"What should I call you?"

"Amanda is good," Amanda said.

"How about Mama Amanda? The other one would be simply Mama, so I wouldn't confuse you two. You wouldn't be upset, would you?"

"Oh, Sofia!" Amanda's lips trembled. "Thank you." Breathing fast, she lifted her long-fingered hand with neat nails, painted pale purple, to caress Sonya's bare arm. Her touch was cool and smooth, like a velvet glove. Sonya leaned into it.

"We can visit each other during holidays, have lunch together a couple times a month, and give each other presents." Amanda cocked her head to the side. "Like a family, you know." Then, a surprise flickered in her gaze. "You're wearing a Magen David?"

"You're wearing a cross," Sonya retorted, nodding at Amanda's small, golden pendant, studded with diamonds like hers.

"It's not what you think," Amanda murmured. "I'm not really religious."

"Neither am I." Sonya's lips twisted mischievously. "It's a kind of a cultural statement."

"Yes," Amanda said. Her smile widened. "I think we'll understand each other."

"I think we will." Sonya picked up her skirt, smiled her triumphant stage smile, and sank into a deep curtsy. When she straightened, she lifted her arms wide, inviting an embrace. "Should we... hug and kiss?"

"Oh, Sofia!" Amanda sobbed suddenly, clutching at Sonya.

Awkwardly, Sonya patted Amanda's shaking shoulders. Her mother was so much taller, it was strange to be the strong one next to her. Amanda's silk blouse felt sleek under Sonya's caressing fingers.

"We'll be friends, I'm sure," Sonya whispered.

At last, Amanda pulled away. "I'm sorry," she said. Her cheeks acquired two sharp red spots. She sniffed.

"Do you want a tissue?" Sonya tugged the older woman toward the sofa.

Sitting down, Amanda accepted a box of tissues and blotted off her tear-stained cheeks. "Have I smeared my makeup?"

"A little bit." Sonya knelt in front of her, picked up another tissue, and carefully wiped a smudge of mascara off Amanda's patrician nose. "As good as new," she reported with a proprietary pride.

Amanda cupped Sonya's cheek with her palm. "Thank you, dear. I wasn't going to liquefy on you."

"Of course," Sonya said. She liked Amanda. In fact, she liked her so much, she was surprised at herself. She wasn't usually that fast at making friends.

"You know," Amanda said. "You remind me of Donald, my late husband." She paused as if evaluating her next words.

Sonya waited.

"Your father," Amanda said. "We fell in love instantly when we met." Her voice dropped to a whisper, but her gaze never strayed from Sonya's face. "Now, it's...happening all over, again."

Sonya felt bereft of worlds. "Thank you" would be so inadequate. "I'm sorry I can't know him," she said finally.

"You're the only thing that's left of him." Amanda's eyes at last broke the connection. They roamed the living room until they halted on the tapestry with a fawn. "Dina said you make such things." She pointed. "It's marvelous!"

Sonya glanced over her shoulder at the little, freckled deer. "I like it, too," she agreed. "It came out well." She shrugged self-consciously.

"Do you want to enroll in the Emily Carr in the fall?"

"Perhaps."

"Could you help Gloria with interior decorations? You know, she runs our construction company, and she needs a designer." Amanda sighed. "Her former designer was a rat. He quit."

Sonya grinned. "I'll try to help, but I don't have any special education."

"You have impeccable taste," Amanda said.

"I'll do what I can for your company."

"It's going to be your company, too. Twenty percent of it would be yours after I die."

"Oh. Thank you." Sonya wasn't sure she wanted such a development. Anticipating a bumpy relationship with Gloria, she dreaded the possible complications.

"What about Gloria?" she asked. "Doesn't she mind?"

"Ah, Gloria." Amanda sighed. "Gloria wants to convert to Judaism."

"Why?"

"She wants to be a real Jew. Explore her heritage." Amanda stepped away from Sonya, facing the tapestry. "You're a real Jew, right? You're not religious. Can you talk some sense into her? I don't want to lose her."

"I don't think it's possible," Sonya said quietly. "Being a Jew... it's not in religion, at least not for me. It's...inside me, a mentality.

Like I can dance, express myself in movement, but the others around me can't. Gloria comes from the outside, so she needs the trappings of religion, something tangible to immerse in, but it might be a stage. She might learn to dance, too." She glided closer and put her hand on Amanda's shoulder, squeezing lightly. She wanted to reassure the older woman, to make it right for her, but she didn't know how. "I'm sure you're a wonderful mother. She must love you very much. You won't lose her, just like my mom won't lose me. Does it make sense?"

Amanda turned. "Thank you, dear." She watched Sonya with a small, elusive smile.

"I'll talk to her, but I don't know if it'd make any difference," Sonya said. "I've never been good at talking. Even with Ksenya. I'm much better at dancing." She grinned to cover her embarrassment and felt her cheeks heat. "Ummm...Mama Amanda. Actually, I want to resume dancing. If you could help me raise some money? A loan, maybe? I'm not really that old, right? Thirty-four."

"Not at all, honey. I'd like to see you dancing. I'll help." Amanda pulled away. "Let's go view your new house. You can't move in until next month, though. Gloria should be finished with the renovations by then. Should she put in a dance studio? With a big mirror. You must instruct her on the placement."

"Mama Amanda, a house is too expensive," Sonya began. "Maybe you shouldn't—"

"Rubbish! Your mother and father—how much money have they spent on you since you were born? Do you know?" Amanda asked gravely. "You've never said to them that maybe they shouldn't, have you?"

"That's different."

"How? I'm your mother. I'm just cramming all the expenses I couldn't make before into one big gift. A birthday gift." Amanda's eyes glittered militantly. "Today is our first meeting. Today is the birthday of our relationship. Mother and daughter. Don't you dare say 'No' to me, Sofia."

"I don't have a gift for you."

"You do. Ksenya is the best gift I could've asked for."

"Some gift." Sonya snorted. Magic had suddenly disappeared between them, leaving an instant, growing friendship. She felt easy with her new mother, ready to laugh and argue.

"I'm a scholar of Russian literature," Amanda said suddenly.

"I know. So?" Raising her brows, Sonya wondered what would come next. She couldn't fathom the connection between Ksenya and literature, other than they were both Russian.

Amanda switched to Russian. “There is a children’s story, written by the writer Victor Dragunsky, right? About the boy Deniska. Do you remember what Deniska said about his green, starlet firefly?”

Sonya’s throat closed. She smiled through her unexpected tears and also switched to Russian. “Of course I remember. Every kid in Russia knows that story. He said, ‘It’s alive and glowing.’”

“Ksenya is alive and glowing,” Amanda said. “My little starlet firefly. Don’t you dare say ‘No’ to me!”

“Okay,” Sonya agreed meekly. She wanted to cry and dance. She sniffed.

“Let’s go.” Amanda grabbed Sonya’s hand, tugging her toward the door. “They’re waiting.”

“You press all the right buttons,” Sonya accused, allowing Amanda to pull her along.

“I’m your mother,” Amanda said.

About the Author:

Olga is a writer from Vancouver, Canada. She's been making up stories since she was very young but only started writing professionally in the 21st century. Before that, she was a computer programmer.

Besides writing short stories and novels, she also works as a journalist for a local newspaper. She enjoys writing cultural pieces and personal profiles of the local artists. Olga's articles appear regularly in her newspaper, and her short fiction credits include multiple small magazines.

She thinks her greatest accomplishments up to date are her two wonderful children: a son and a daughter. Both have already flown the nest, so instead of children she now collects monkeys. She has over 300 monkey figurines in her collection.

Also from Eternal Press:

Fly Away Peta
by Juanita Kees

eBook ISBN: 9781615727087
Print ISBN: 9781615727094

Contemporary Romance
Short Novel of 45,556 words

The time has come to face her worst fear and the clock is ticking...

Peta Johnson will go to extreme lengths to protect her daughter Bella. When the child is kidnapped, the search for her takes Peta back to the small Western Australian country town of Williams, a place she'd vowed never to return to. The town where her dreams were shattered and her nightmare began. Back to the place she'd been destined to meet two very powerful, yet very different men. One would break her heart, the other would destroy her soul. Both would change her life forever.

Also from Eternal Press:

Mommy Blogger
by Carla Caruso

eBook ISBN: 9781615727223
Print ISBN: 9781615727230

Contemporary Romance Humor
Novel of 68,698 words

One baby, one lie–and a whole new career. Stella lands a great job as a mommy blogger. The catch is she's never had children. Plunged into a world of insanity every mother faces, she must learn to cope as her lies build upon one another. A sexy ex comes into the picture, forcing her to choose between him or the job and a handsome 'keeper' of a coworker. It can't last forever.

CPSIA information can be obtained
at www.ICGtesting.com
Printed in the USA
FSOW02n1215300914
3160FS

9 781615 728787